The Presidential Papers

NORMAN MAILER

**WITH A NEW PREFACE
BY THE AUTHOR**

A BERKLEY WINDHOVER BOOK
published by
BERKLEY PUBLISHING CORPORATION

Published by arrangement with
G. P. Putnam's Sons

G. P. Putnam's Sons
200 Madison Avenue
New York, N.Y. 10016

SBN 425-03243-4

BERKLEY WINDHOVER BOOKS are published by
Berkley Publishing Corporation
200 Madison Avenue
New York, N.Y. 10016

BERKLEY WINDHOVER BOOK ® TM

Printed in the United States of America

Berkley Windhover Edition, OCTOBER, 1976

PREFACE
TO *The Presidential Papers*

It is possible *The Presidential Papers* has the most cloying mannerisms of any of my books. That is laying a claim. Should I have a vice in writing, it is to be over-mannered when uncertain, and I was not close to large portions of this book. It was conceived out of economic necessity at a time when I was broke, and a paperback publisher succumbed to the cogent conversational skills of my agent Scott Meredith and gave me $10,000 for a collection of short pieces already written, if I would only do some connecting material in the vein of *Advertisements For Myself*. I confess I did not feel any pain as the wrist was twisted. That would come later when I had a month to put *The Presidential Papers* in shape, and came to recognize that I was lumping together some of the best and worst pieces of a four-year period from 1959 to 1963. They did not have much common denominator, not as much as I was hoping would justify the title and the premise that a new concept in politics which might be called existential was on its way.

I brooded over that idea. Of course, a month of fast writing is not a fecund season for entering the best levels of brooding. Once again I was in depression as I wrote, once again I had not let my ideas develop at their own rate. I was guilty of the same crime the premature ecologist in me was ready to condemn in others: over-stimulation of ground not ready for another crop. Of course, that could be the story of a writing life—is there any of my books over the last twelve years which was not written too quickly? It is just that one's own flaws are never so apparent as in those intercalations called First Presidential Paper, Second Presidential Paper, etc.

Nonetheless, this book has its value. It can be seen as a paradigm of the prodigious anxiety which attached to politics in the early sixties. In the fifties, every subliminal political sense was ready to tell us that the country was being run by the corporations, the FBI, the CIA and the Mafia, and they were working in an overt and covert association so well joined together that nobody could begin to point an accusation without wondering if he were irremediably paranoid. In the sixties, that cancer seal began to crack—Kennedy's election was the hairline split in the American totalitarianism of the fifties. Some of us may have sensed that through the split would come the submerged wrath of some good American minds. Such a perception hardly reduced the anxiety. The battles were still ahead, and no one alive had a glimmer of what was actually to come: assassinations, Vietnam, civil rights, and student revolutions. There was only the nightmarish sensation that a lot was going to happen, and much of it would be dreadful.

In that state, therefore, of unfocussed paranoia, trying to throttle one's own near-suffocated wrath into a reasonable, even an agreeable tone, the style came out in the only way it could. It was arch and it was phony, about as arch and just about as phony as the icing of a Gothic arch on a racketeer's wedding cake.

Still, I would not steer readers further away from this book. Its anxiety is its anxiety, and its half-satisfied ambition is very much its throttled ambition, but for anyone who would like a clue to the mood of the country in the summer of 1963 just before that autumn of assassination which would change the psychic history of America forever, the book is a document. Besides—I whisper it—*The Presidential Papers* does have a couple of the better pieces I've written. They seemed to emerge out of bad pieces. It is a thought with which to juggle. For America is the most dialectical of nations (or will be until the superhighway paves us over) and the best of our history is coupled as in no other nation with much of our worst. May there be a few lines to that clue in this book.

SPECIAL PREFACE
TO THE FIRST BERKLEY EDITION

The Presidential Papers were written while Jack Kennedy was alive, and so the book was put together with the idea that the President might come to read it. One did not mean of course that he would literally read it right away in that giant-killing stride of his (reputed to cross over more than half a thousand words of prose each minute). No, the author had the idea instead that people about the President might look at the book in pieces and parts, and conversations would ensue; over the years, who could be certain? The President might put his head into its pages for a few seconds. Thus the book was inspired by a desire to have its influence. Slow that might be and near to subterranean, but it was a book aimed nonetheless at some favorite notions of the President and the American Establishment: therefore the irreverence of the prose was as necessary as the feathers on the shaft of an arrow. In America few people will trust you unless you are irreverent; there was a message returned to us by our frontier that the outlaw is worth more than the sheriff.

One was therefore irreverent to the President. But the extent of one's irreverence was discovered to be also the measure of one's unsuspected affection: that one discovered the day he was killed; discovered that again during the weeks of depression which followed. For he was no ordinary sheriff—he was an outlaw's sheriff, he was one sheriff who could have been an outlaw himself. Such Presidents can be quickly counted: Jefferson, Andrew Jackson, Lincoln, Franklin Delano Roosevelt, John F. Kennedy. One doubts if there are any others. While this is the only kind of sheriff for whom an outlaw can feel love, one should still of course not be excessively polite, for every sheriff must labor finally on the side of all those mediocrities who made a profit from mediocrity by extinguishing (let a new Marx rise among us) the promise of others.

Still, John F. Kennedy was a remarkable man. A modern democracy is a tyranny whose borders are undefined; one discovers how far one can go only by traveling in a straight line until one is stopped; Kennedy was not in a hurry to stop us. I would not be surprised if he believed that the health of America (which is to say our vitality) depended in part on the inventiveness and passion of its outlaws.

Then, of course, he was killed by an outlaw. Which is tragic, but not startling. For heroism often gives life to a creation which is bound and determined to kill the hero. Ultimately a hero is a man who would argue with the gods, and so awakens devils to contest his vision. The more a man can achieve, the more he may be certain that the devil will inhabit a part of his creation.

These theological illuminations are of vast use to the reader, doubtless; but they lead the author astray from the point to his introduction. He was trying to say that we have here a book which was written in part for a man very much alive. This book is now homeless, for it has ceased to thrive inside its original intention. One had hoped to quicken the content of criticism, to darken the political soup with marrow. Now, like a displaced person, the book is a document. It speaks from the far cliff of a divide, from a time which is past, from history. Given these overtones, the book has an unintentional echo: it tells the story of a President and of a Presidential time which was neither conclusive nor legislatively active, but which was nonetheless a period not without a suspicion of greatness, greatness of promise at the very least, for it was a time when writers could speak across the land in intimate dialogue with their leader.

He was a good and serious man, one now suspects. Only such a man would neglect to cover himself with the pompous insulations of the state. Still, one would not retract what one has written: his faults were his faults, his lacks were his lacks, his political maneuverings were no better than the others, his dull taste was certainly his dull taste. But what one did not recognize sufficiently was the extent of his humor. That humor created an atmosphere in which one could attempt this book; now, as a document which circles mournfully about its subject, one can hear in the echoes of his absence the proportions of that humor, and thus feel the loss. Fifty years may go by before such a witty and promising atmosphere comes to life in America again. So the corridors are gloomy. "He was a great man," said a girl at a party the other night. "No, he wasn't a great man," I said. "He was a man who could have become great or could have failed, and now we'll never know. That's what's so awful." That *is* what is so awful. Tragedy is amputation: the nerves of one's memory run back to the limb which is no longer there.

NORMAN MAILER

This book is dedicated to some ladies
who have aided and impeded
the author in his composition

They are
Beverly Rentz Sugarfoot Bentley
Jeanne Louise Slugger Campbell

my daughters   Susan
                      Dandy
                      Betsy
                      Kate

my adopted daughter Jeanne H. W. The Invaluable Johnson
my secretary   Anne Morse Towel-Boy Barry
my sister   Barbara Jane Alson

         and Sadie
         and Hetty Diggs
         and Every-Mae

A TABLE OF CONTENTS

A PREFATORY PAPER—Heroes and Leaders

Since this book chooses to call itself *The Presidential Papers*, let it now be modest enough to explain its function. There are essays and interviews gathered here, a few poems, an open letter or two, some literary criticism, portions picked from magazine columns, a large section from an unpublished philosophical dialogue, there is altogether a fair part gathered of what has been written since *Advertisements for Myself* was published in 1959. What will not be found in this collection is a five-hour play which the writer has been seeking to improve for five years, as well as any of the work done on a long novel talked about in *Advertisements*. It is not wise to show this portion yet.

No, these short pieces (some of them not so brief—the three longest put together make fifty thousand words) are concerned for the most part, indeed were chosen for this collection because their subject matter is fit concern for a President. One is of course not throwing any disqualified devil's wishes into the ring for oneself, no, no, these are the Presidential papers of a court wit, an amateur advisor. They are papers written *to* the President, *for* him, they are his private sources of information. The President suffers from one intellectual malady— intellectual malnutrition. That particular anemia visits leaders surrounded by advisors who do not tell the truth. Advisors are dishonest because they are professional. By the developed habits of his craft, a professional automatically suppresses as much information as he divulges; nor is this to speak of the various kinds of information a professional is incapable of receiving because the language necessary for the inquiry does not belong to his vocational jargon. So a President suffers intellectual horrors. His information is predigested—his mind is allowed as much stimulation as the second stomach of a cow. He is given not nuances but facts; indeed he is given facts not in whole, but facts masticated, their backs broken.*

The natural work of the modern Presidency destroys a man's ability for abstract thought. He becomes able to think not of the mystery in the atom bomb but of its engineering. He sprouts a mind like a financial see-saw: on the one side percentages of overkill declared adequate for balancing Russian overkill, on the other budgetary calculations. A 25 per cent overkill will demand a disbursement of X billions which has Y probability of passing Z committee in Congress. It is all hard tough clear strategic thinking, the sort of thinking that the less literary seniors at Harvard used to do over the bridge table years ago. Now the stakes are higher and they're still doing it. One does well not to sneer at them: the sort of Harvard men who got into the bridge games in the House Common Rooms after dinner seem now to be the archetype of the kind of men who run the world: what they lack in imagination is filled with strategic estimate; what they do not know about moral depth is replaced by forthrightness and point-by-point program. I suppose the kind of man who goes to bed and worries even once a year, "My God, what if, when all is said, the Russians are right?" or even worse, "My God, what if, when all is said, the Russians are *half* right?" cannot ever become President in the twentieth century. The time he loses one night a year is enough to put him out of the race.

But let us not leave the President with his virtues and vices. He is presumably an expert on political matters which can be translated into arithmetic. He can recite government incomes and expenses, budgets, taxes, reserves; figures for the gainfully employed and the locally unemployed over the last individual ten years, and by ten-year periods; figures for armament in category, in gross; he can give you percentiles and/or profile curves on shifts in political party sentiment over twenty-five years in key political counties of America; in two minutes he can look up the figure for additional square feet of housing built in 1962 against calculated need for new housing in Plan A, Plan B, Plan G; he can tell you the number of words in a speech by glancing at the pages; he can read six hundred words a minute and count on retaining 84 per cent of what he reads; he can give you the critical numbers and index factors on foreign trade, new investment in heavy

*See Appendix A for a small demonstration of the accuracy in one of the President's typical general sources of information.

industry, rate of failure against rates of incorporation for small business; the literacy rate; the projected farm surplus surpluses; the number of Communists in the American Communist Party, the number of FBI men in the American Communist Party; the number of United States Marshals in Southern cities who can be concentrated at a trouble point when a school is integrated, the number of schools which have been integrated, the number which have not; he can give you an estimate by denomination of the number of churches in America, the number of synagogues, orthodox, conservative, and reformed, he can probably make an informed guess on the number of clergymen in each state. It must be certain he has enough facts in his head filed under enough separate departments to make a fair extempore competitor for the *World Almanac*.

Now this is not the only qualification of the President. He happens also to have a personality which is agreeable to most (in a way that Thomas E. Dewey's was not, nor Richard Nixon's) and he is also a man of personal bravery, a fact one does well not to ignore. He studied for his occupation, he had the money to find it, and the family to help him find it. He has a sense of the tradition of the Presidency and a sense of history—he wishes to be a great man. Indeed he has every qualification for a great President—a sense of politics, a sense of mass response, a nose for propaganda, the ability to acquire information, the ability to keep cool when the world is in great heat, the wit to stop the legislative and administrative parts of the government from warring on one another, the perhaps excessive ability to avoid making needless enemies—yes, he has every qualification but one. He has no imagination. He does not have the kind of mind which can see a new solution to an old problem. Rather he manipulates the best single elements in the old solutions, and applies his political craft to composing a package with new consumer interest. In effect it is the old apple pie still tasting of soggy cardboard and cheap flour, but the container is new—it has a picture on its cellophane cover which motivation research has discovered is more effective than the old cover for selling apple pie.

Now with the exception of his single large defeat in the Bay of Pigs and his single large victory after Khrushchev sent missiles to Castro, a victory and defeat which are linked umbilically to the island of Cuba, the President has done nothing new. One cannot point to any move in foreign affairs or labor or military spending or housing or education or race relations or popular culture which is radically different from the work of Truman or Eisenhower, different from the intellectual inspiration of Franklin Delano Roosevelt. One can point to the Peace Corps perhaps, but there is something unctuous about its face in public relations. The Peace Corps seems to have inherited the political timidity of the CCC without its air of a barracks democracy.

No, there's no feeling of a new political atmosphere in the country. The liberals pump up their balloons, the conservatives flush out bile and bilge, but a real issue is never found. Politics is the art of the possible, and what is always possible is to reduce the amount of real suffering in a bad time, and to enrich the quality of life in a good time. This is precisely what is not being done in America. We are in a good time in America, a prosperous time, a time of relative wealth and relative lack of poverty which was created not by Roosevelt, Truman, Eisenhower, nor Kennedy, but by the economic mathematics of finding an ever-expanding market whose ultimate consumer is the enemy soldier. We have been living in the curious but prosperous hollow of planned military obsolescence. In fact we have built so many different airplanes since the Second World War that soon there ought to be enough to give one to each high school class in the land.

But we've done nothing to approach the center of the problem which is that life in America becomes more economically prosperous and more psychically impoverished each year. The real life of America is not being enriched. It is suffering from political monotony. The President has commissions and commissars and bureaus and agents and computer machines to calculate the amount of schooling needed to keep America healthy, safe, vigorous, proof against the Russians. To keep America *up*. Virility is the unspoken salesman in American political programs today: the politician slaps his facts and figures on the table like a shillelagh: curious are the vitamins implicit in a massive collection of facts and figures—it is as if a man who can keep that much information in his head might be able to maintain that much erection in his will.

The President has programs. They keep America *up*. His educational programs calculate floor space and cubic feet of breathing space. They pick pastel colors for toilets and study rooms, they pipe public address systems from auditoriums to classrooms, they have aerials for classroom television, side rooms for PTA functions, they do everything, they have everything. Everything but a good book.

There is a total and depressing lack of attention for that vast heart of political matter which is utterly resistant to categorization, calculation, or statistic. Politics is arithmetic, but politics is also rhetoric, passion, and an occasional idea to fire the imagination of millions. For his arithmetic the President gets a mark of 98 per cent. For his imagination: zero. For his passion: 40 per cent. For his rhetoric: 50 per cent. So this book has been put together for him. It is imperfect, incomplete, and somewhat deficient in its arithmetic. Its statistical studies are absent. Its grasp of the machinery of government is comparable at best to the sort of talented amateur mechanic who knows how to change a tire. But still there is something in this book, something useful to the President. This book has an existential grasp of the nature of reality, and it is the unspoken thesis of these pages that no President can save America from a descent into totalitarianism without shifting the mind of the American politician to existential styles of political thought.

If the question is now asked what can possibly be meant by "an existential grasp of the nature of reality" or "existential styles of political thought" the answer which is not without facetiousness can nonetheless only be that one must read this book. In the run of its pages exists the possible seed of the idea.

But can one at least give a clue? I suppose it would rest in the notion that the disease of the state is intensified when large historic ideas come to power without men to personify them or dramatize their qualities. It has long been the thesis of this self-appointed Presidential advisor that the FBI has done more damage to America than the American Communist Party. It has done it for a variety of reasons, some well-intentioned, some delivered from pits of foul intention, but the FBI has chilled the potentiality of America to enrich the private lives of its people. It has put a sense of inhibition into the popular arts and the popular mind. It has been an evil force. What has made it even more deadening has been the personality of its director, which is to say, the *lack* of personality in its director. The FBI has been a political idea; its essence could be stated: America is in need of a secret police whose devotion, dedication, untiring effort, professional competence and political purity entitle it to scrutinize every aspect of American life it deems worthy to scrutinize. The idea is fearful enough, but when no personality embodies it, no other personality may contest it. The cause of secret police-ness advances like a plague. So an existential President would look for a man with a salient personality to put as head of the FBI. Under such a man, the fortunes of the FBI would prosper or falter, but its activities would be dramatized, its victories would come from open struggle, and its success would cease to resemble the certainty of the house percentage in a gambling casino. The FBI would be forced to exist rather than proliferate. If its leader was not heroic as a man, the FBI would proceed to exist less, it would lose existence because it would be in open competition for existence with other organs of the government. But with an heroic leader it would prosper, it would *deserve* to prosper. Existential politics is rooted in the concept of the hero, it would argue that the hero is the one kind of man who *never* develops by accident, that a hero is a consecutive set of brave and witty self-creations. All heroes are leaders—even if, like Don Quixote, they have but one man to follow them—but not all leaders are heroes. An unheroic leader is a man who embodies his time but is not superior to it—he is historically faceless. Roosevelt was a hero, Calvin Coolidge or Herbert Hoover were leaders, nominal leaders. So was Eisenhower. The FBI has at present a leader, but not a hero. So it is faceless in history. And because it is faceless it is insidious, plague-like, an evil force. Power without a face is the disease of the state. But if the FBI had a hero for a leader and its fortunes prospered on open political market, then even if its ideas seemed odious, one would have to accept its prosperity as an historic event, a force with precise features. McCarthy was such an embodiment. He was a hero, a most distressing kind of hero, but because he was a hero he encountered opponents as well as attracted followers, and he was finally defeated. With his fall went the threat that his ideas would dominate America. How fortunate for the Left that a hero arose on the Right at that moment. For if not, the leaders of the Right might have strangled the liberties of America somewhat further by remaining a faceless force.

Politics is like a body of organs. When the body is sick, it is usually because one or another organ has become too weak or too powerful in its function. If the disproportion is acute, a war goes on in the body, an inflammatory sickness, a fever, a crisis. The war decided, the organ subsides, different in size, stronger or weaker, it returns to its part of the body's function. Acute disease is cure. It is the war which initiates a restoration of balance. It has features, symptoms, results. Acute diseases are like political forces personified by heroes. And slack diseases, featureless, symptomless diseases like virus and colds and the ubiquitous cancer are the appropriate metaphor of all those political forces like the FBI, or like the liberalism of the Democratic Party, which are historically faceless.

It is true that we have a President with a face. And it is the face of a potential hero. But he embodies nothing, he personifies nothing, he is power, rather a quizzical power, without light or principle. His liberalism is acquired at second hand; he came to it the way a general comes to an army of mercenaries—he cannot win his war without them. He is neither religious nor irreligious, he is not provocative nor predictably dull, he is not entertaining, he is always potentially of interest.

He learned too much and too early that victory goes to the discreet, that one does not speak one's opinion, that ideally one does not even develop one's opinion. For a man with opinion is less free to move with the turn of power. So we have a President who is brave but politically neuter, adept at obtaining power and a miser at spending it, an intellectual with a mind like a newspaper's yearbook, and a blank somewhat stricken expression about the eyes, a numbed mind seems to speak behind them. It is narcotized away from the true problems of a President's task. A President is supposed to enrich the real life of his people—the mind which looks out from this President's eyes has lost the way. The expression lives in all the dull avenues of precedent.

So here is a book of Presidential papers about all the topics a President ought to consider and rarely does, and some of the topics he considers every day, but rarely in a fashion which is fresh. There will be little of oceanic profundity here, but a few streams of possibility. One has hopes the advisors to the President can read, can read well enough to pass this book along. Here are some of its topics:

Capital Punishment
Censorship
Drug Addiction
Juvenile Delinquency
America's Need for a Hero
Political Conventions
The CIA
Castro
The Black Bourgeoisie
The Negro Emergence
Fallout Shelters

The First Lady as a Television Entertainer
The First Lady as a Hostage
The Nature of the Jews
The Nature of Dread
The Dialectic of God and the Devil
The Press
The Mafia
The Magic of Large Events
The Negro as Churchgoer and Magician
The Logic of Death Versus the Establishment's Defense of
    Life
Scatology
Witchcraft
Revolution
The State Conservatism of Senator Goldwater
The End of the Cold War
The War Between the Conservative and the Rebel
Cannibalism
Digestion and the Unconscious
Being and Soul
Courage, Cowardice, and Food
Sex of Upper Classes and Lower Classes
Architecture
Totalitarianism
        and there is also an Appendix in three parts.

Ambitious young men, ready to become President in twenty or
thirty years, will do worse than to read my book, for its studies are
appropriate to the education of a Commander-in-Chief. So submits
this devil.

THE FIRST PRESIDENTIAL PAPER

—Existential Legislation

A Program for the Nation*

If one were a Freshman Congressman as was the President once, it might be an existential duty to introduce a bill for A New Capital Punishment. It would never pass, but a new idea might be alive. Nothing is more exceptional than to introduce a new idea into America.

Yet this paper, written at the very beginning of 1960, is now dated. Proposal 3 and Proposal 5 no longer seem exceptional. Proposal 4 will be taken up sooner or later by the Kennedy team. Only Proposal 1 and Proposal 2 are still at liberty—they are of course the integral part of the program.

Last August I received a letter from *Esquire* magazine. Its first two paragraphs read:

Looking ahead to the 1960 presidential election, this magazine feels that it would be an interesting and useful undertaking to present the opinions of outstanding men of ideas regarding the candidates proposed and the issues involved. For the political parties and the electorate, there is the decision of which candidate, among the several already prominent, is to be given presidential authority and responsibility. Yet, during the campaign there may be such concentration on the personalities of the candidates that issues

*For date of publication and other details see Appendix B.

13

to be debated and decided become neglected. We believe that the publication of the opinions of leaders in fields other than politics will be a contribution to intelligent public discussion.

Accordingly, we should be grateful if you will consider, and answer, these two questions:
1. Among those mentioned as possible presidential candidates, whom do you prefer for president in 1960?
2. What, to your mind, should be the most important issues in the election?

Attached is a list of those who, like yourself, are being asked to participate. There has been a fair attempt to select persons whose individual opinions are valued within their fields, and whose collective opinions will present a wide spectrum of response.

I went no further with the letter, but took a look at who had been invited. There were 150 names. About ten of us in the literary garden, and a wide range of other minds, frauds, generals, stuffed shirts, bureaucrats, after-dinner speakers, and figures in the news: Bernard Baruch, Dr. Ralph Bunche, Gen. Lucius Clay, Henry Ford II, Gen. James M. Gavin, William Randolph Hearst, Jr., Ernest Hemingway, Dr. Sidney Hook, Rev. Martin Luther King, Jr., Henry R. Luce, Gen. Douglas MacArthur, George Meany, Edward R. Murrow, Dr. Reinhold Niebuhr, Walter Reuther, Rear Adm. Hyman G. Rickover, Dr. Jonas Salk, Gen. David Sarnoff, Francis Cardinal Spellman, Dr. Frank Stanton, Bishop Fulton J. Sheen, Dr. Wernher von Braun, DeWitt Wallace, Hon. John Hay Whitney.

Over breakfast, I decided the hell with it, I was not going to answer, and went through the rest of the day without thinking any more about the letter. Late that night, after a party, I tried to go to sleep half-drunk, and instead found myself awake with that particular clarity alcohol can give in the last thirty minutes before it starts to wear away. I was thinking about the letter from *Esquire*, and at three in the morning it seemed right to answer it. So I went downstairs, and worked at fever speed for an hour or less, not altogether innocent of manic glee at the thought of how this long answer to question 2 should look in the pages of a mass-media magazine. The draft written, I went to bed and enjoyed a self-satisfied sleep.

In the morning I thought to take another look at the letter from *Esquire*. In its third paragraph was the following sentence:

Answers to Question 2 will be collated, with a discussion of the issues cited by the author of the article, Walter Friedenberg, a scholar-journalist and Fellow of the Institute of Current World Affairs.

As an afterthought, the letter remarked:

Esquire holds no political position and will advance none.

So I did not mail in my suggestions; it occurred to me they might roil the processes of collation.

What follows is the first draft as I wrote it, touched here and cut there:

I think I would be in favor of legislation whose inner tendency would be to weaken the bonds of legislation. An example:

1. I would like to see a law passed which would abolish capital punishment, except for those states which insisted on keeping it. Such states would then be allowed to kill criminals provided that the killing is not impersonal but personal and a public spectacle: to wit that the executioner be more or less the same size and weight as the criminal (the law could here specify the limits) and that they fight to death using no weapons, or weapons not capable of killing at a distance. Thus, knives or broken bottles would be acceptable. Guns would not.

The benefit of this law is that it might return us to moral responsibility. The killer would carry the other man's death in his psyche. The audience, in turn, would experience a sense of tragedy, since the executioners, highly trained for this, would almost always win. In the flabby American spirit there is a buried sadist who finds the bullfight contemptible—what he really desires are gladiators. Since nothing is worse for a country than repressed sadism, this method of execution would offer ventilation for the more cancerous emotions of the American public.

2. Cancer is going to become the first political problem of America in twenty years. The man who finds a cure could run successfully for President. But I doubt if a cure will be found until all serious cancer

researchers, and most especially the heads of department are put under sentence of mortal combat (with a professional executioner) if they have failed to make progress in their part of the program after two years. This would keep committeemen out of the project—it would also help in the search for a cure, since one may suspect that only a brave man living in the illumination of approaching death could brood sufficiently over the nature of disease to come up with a cure which was not worse than the illness.

3. Pass a bill making legal the sale of drugs. I happen to think that people who take drugs burn up the best part of their minds and gut their sex, but the same is true for those who drink too much, and alcohol is in a favored legal position because the liquor industries are so rich. While it would not necessarily be attractive to see a larger proportion of people destroy themselves with drugs, it must be recognized that the right to destroy oneself is also one of the inalienable rights, because others cannot know the reason for the self-destruction. It is possible that many people take heroin because they sense unconsciously that if they did not, they would be likely to commit murder, get cancer, or turn homosexual.

4. Since the Russians seem to have more vigor than we do at the moment, I would make every effort to pass them our diseases. I would encourage the long-term loan to them of countless committees of the best minds we have on Madison Ave. If our hucksters have been able in fifteen years to leech from us the best blood of the American spirit, they should be able to debilitate the Russians equally in an equivalent period; if not, my admiration for the soporific power of Madison Ave. is misplaced.

5. I would pass a bill abolishing all forms of censorship. Censorship is an insult to democracy because it makes men unequal—it assumes that some have more sexual wisdom than others, and it imprisons everyone in excessive guilt. Besides, pornography is debilitating to sex—the majority of people would stay away from it once they discovered how wan it left them. Given the force of the hangover, most people do not get drunk every night, and the same, I believe, would apply here. It is possible I am indulging a shallow liberal optimism, and America would become a cesspool of all-night pornographic drive-in movies, the majority of the population becoming night people who meet for cocktails at one in the morning. But this

could also serve as the salvation of the Republic, for America would then become so wicked a land that Russia would never dare to occupy us, nor even to exterminate us by the atom bomb, their scientists having by then discovered that people who are atomized disseminate their spirit into the conqueror.

THE SECOND PRESIDENTIAL PAPER

—Juvenile Delinquency

"She Thought the Russians Was Coming"

This is an account of a few visits with a gang in Brooklyn. I think it has the virtue of being true to the mood of what happened. The photographer, Bruce Davidson, was kind enough to say that I had caught the sound. But I was not very proud of the piece: I had thought to do a major essay, but decided I did not know enough and did not have time enough: I was working on a staged reading of The Deer Park *at Actors' Studio, and only had a few days to do the piece.*

The existential message of the paper is that juvenile delinquents have a need of danger. This thought is caught up in a postscript.

I first went down to Brooklyn to see the gang on a bone-cold February afternoon this year. They were waiting for Bruce Davidson and me in a candy store about a half mile from their turf, a parlor they had begun to use lately because their own was too small. The new place had a juke box, and three booths to the rear, and when we entered five or six girls and a dozen boys were milling around in the back.

For the first minute, a bit of tension: nothing all-out hostile, more an air of stony curiosity, studied on their part, studied on mine. One cannot get around it—there are situations which belong more to the movies than to life, and all of us were obeying an archetypal scene in a gangster movie or a Western—a stranger had come to visit. This mood shifted quickly enough. Bruce had already told the

21

Royal Dealers, which is the fictitious name we might as well use, that *Esquire* magazine had bought his pictures. (For a year he had been friendly with these kids and the sight of him with the Leica up to his face had come to seem as natural as lighting a cigarette.) Now a few of them had been let in on the new information that a writer was here today to write them up, and this explanation for my presence passed around quickly. They were picked up by it. Conversation began to go, and before fifteen minutes we had found a common ground; we were passing back and forth our prescriptions for odd kicks.

Had I ever heard of ground aspirin being mixed with tobacco and rolled in a cigarette?

No; that one I hadn't heard of.

"That's the most, man—I was out of my skull for two hours."

"You creep, you're a fag," said one of the kids to the kid who had been out of his skull.

"No, man, that aspirin is a boss kick."

Laughter. General derision. It seems somebody had offered marijuana to the kid with the aspirin and he had punked out.

So the stories went. Whitey had taken fifteen saccharine tablets once. "Man, that's a drag. I was throwing up all afternoon," said Whitey.

We discussed dried leaves, and nutmeg, and Sterno; one of them had even heard of a way to find some juice in lighter fluid.

Then talk shifted to the Dealers' account of a rumble they had been in last summer, a big rumble which made the newspapers. Ten of them had been brought to court for beating up a kid in the park, and they were now on probation. Since none of them were going to school any more, they were using up a good part of the money they had made at work to pay off their various lawyers. One of the kids was talking now about his case. Not a member of the Royal Dealers, he had gotten into trouble for something else.

"What's your lawyer charging you?" Whitey asked. Although he was the smallest of the Juniors, a thin, brooding kid of sixteen with clean, proud features, he seemed the natural leader.

"Two and a half," said the other.

"Two and a half bucks?"

A sneer. "Two and a half cents."

"What'll you get?"

"I don't know."

"A year, you bastard. You deserve a year."

I never found out what the act had been. Conversation turned back to the rumble. The Dealers had been cutting through the park last summer when they saw a Puerto Rican gang which had eyes for them. One of the Seniors was with them, Terry, a big kid about twenty who had done some boxing in the Army and had natural military ability. He collected the Dealers in a nest of bushes at the peak of a small hill, and sent four of the Juniors down to serve as decoys on the paved path in the draw below, a run of thirty or forty yards down the hill. It had seemed close enough, but when the Puerto Rican gang attacked, they struck so suddenly that the decoys were dropped hard. One of them got a baseball bat on the side of his skull, and bled badly. He was unconscious by the time Terry led the charge. But the Dealers' cavalry took the day. The Juniors, beefed by Terry the Senior, beat up on the Puerto Ricans. After forty seconds the other gang was in flight. Terry picked up the decoy with the bleeding head, and carried him under his arm all the way out of the park. Whitey, who has heart in a rumble, was the last to leave—he gave a final clout to the casualty he had been fighting, and said, "This is from the Dealers."

Back to their turf by separate ways, they had all collected in the candy store. I could hear how their voices must have sounded, because in combat, after a fire-fight, we would all be a little hysterical, and would all be laughing and singing out at once about what had happened to us and how, and where we had been. Those were some of the few good moments in the war. So the Dealers had been staking out their claims in the candy store for star roles in the gang legend of the battle. They were home from the war, and full of charge. They would have new cartel with the chicks.

But the police have the Greek sense of Nemesis. The siren of a squad car sounded outside the door of the candy store. "This is from the Dealer," Whitey had made the mistake of saying, and the kid who had been left by the gang which lost gave the message to the cops when they arrived on the scene at the park.

It was a dull, hot, newsless day in summer, so it made the newspapers. All too inaccurately according to the Dealers. Ten vicious juvenile delinquents beat up a cripple, went the jazz. "Hell, man, it wasn't like that at all," one of them said, "it was a fair rumble." We'll never know. Once a newspaper touches a story, the facts are lost forever, even to the protagonists.

Now it was February, a quiet scene. Since that rumble, the Dealers have been cooling it. Of necessity. But talk of the rumble had stirred them up. Not long afterward, we went out of the candy store into the iron-grey cold, and took the subway down to Coney Island. A couple of Dealers were going to get tattoos.

We had just missed a train and it was empty on the subway platform. The kids began to put on a production for me. Ricky, a short, heavy Italian kid went out to the very end of the station, and urinated on the tracks. There were jokes about hitting the third rail, and when they got to the point of saying what Ricky would lose, and how little he would lose, he turned to the others, about five of them, and pulled out a Japanese knife, one of those small, sharp, steak knives which are inserted into a wooden scabbard and cost about a dollar, and he waved it at us, and ran up the platform stairs about ten steps. "You guy think I'm not tough. Come up here and I'll kill you. I'll kill the first one. I'm Al Capone—you watch out for me." And a good imitation it was, of Rod Steiger as Al Capone.

I had a water pistol in my pocket, a small model of a short-barreled forty-five which I had taken on impulse earlier in the day from Bruce Davidson who had been about to drop it in a trash barrel. I flipped it up the subway stairs to Ricky, shouting, "Quick, man, here's a gun." In the air, it looked real, and Ricky had a natural look of dismay, not knowing whether to catch it or to drop it, and if it were loaded would it go off? Or was it a gag? That much went over his face, and then he dropped it, and the gun made a tinny, clanking little sound, the inimitable sound of a toy, and the other Dealers roared in mockery. But Ricky had talent and for a young actor he can use a prop with the best. The gun went into his right hand, the knife into his left, and the brown scabbard for the steak knife went into his mouth like a cigar. "All right," he said, lining us up with the gun, waving it like a movie murderer, "this is the St. Valentine's Day massacre. You're all dead. In one minute you're all gonna get it. Bop. Bop. Bop. Bop"— mowing us down. Johnny, one of the best fighters in the Dealers, about eighteen, good-looking, a little taller than the rest, rushed him, and they scuffled on the stairs, Ricky at a disadvantage because he had to put down the knife. Just then a train came in. It was going in the wrong direction, but it was the right kind of diversion. Ricky broke loose from Johnny, ran down the stairs back to the platform, and approached the open door of the train. A ten-year-old kid was sitting across the aisle, and Ricky waved the gun at him through the open door. The kid took it well, half-scared, half-grinning, and then the door closed, and Ricky began to walk along the platform, rapping on windows in order to study the expression of the people who turned around to see a gun about three feet from their mouth. If street robbery were a trade, this could serve as apprenticeship, for one might learn quickly which types will freeze and which will not when an adolescent is pointing a gun at them. Ricky had time for four or five close, quick studies before the train picked up too much speed. Then one of the other Dealers pushed him from behind and scared him royally because he was only two feet from the side of the moving train, and the distance was halved before he recovered. Then Whitey, Johnny, and the first Dealer took hold of Ricky and made a play of pushing him into the train, but Ricky broke loose—six inches from contact with the moving side wall of the subway car—and started to shoot again at us. "Bop, bop, bop. Bee-owww—" offering us ricochets as well. Johnny went over and whispered something to him. As Ricky bent over to listen, Johnny backhanded him in the belly, and then ducked back as Ricky tried to slug him on the arm.

Our train came in. We had a car almost to ourselves, and all the way to Coney Island they asked me questions about combat. How many grenades had I carried? How many would they let you carry? Had I ever killed anybody? Did I carry a gun now? And vague talk of pot. Johnny had a dream. He would collect two pounds of pot, and then he would go away for a couple of years and travel around the country— there were a lot of things he wanted to do once he got on the road. It turned out he was the reader in the Dealers. He was reading *The Beat Generation and the Angry Young Men* now, and he liked Kerouac. He had been trying to read my piece, *The White Negro*, in that anthology, but it was too hard. "It's deep. Like I know, man, you got to think," he told me with a grin.

That day, Davidson and I stayed with them at the tattoo parlor while Whitey and another bought new tattoos. Medical science has come to the tattoo parlor, and the inner sanctum was in surgical white with sterilizers and antiseptic procedure. But love of the tattoo is a subject in itself, and I don't know that I am the one to write about it. Leave it that the kids covet and worry every choice of a tattoo the way a bride picks each piece of furniture for her bedroom. The fear of making a mistake is heavy, because a coiled serpent on the arm demands that you develop the strength of a serpent or else you're a phony, and a Betty Boop on the calf—well, you might end up marrying Betty Boop.

A couple of nights later in a bar Ricky said, "I'm going to put a naked dame on my arm."

"What'll your wife say when you get married?"

He didn't hesitate a minute. "I'll put her name under it."

But then some of the Dealers have a gone wit when they're drunk. I met Terry that night, a big one, twenty as I mentioned, with a black leather jacket, good features, blank face, and a string of bon mots. The longer we drank, the faster they came. "You know who I'd like to make," he told me; "one of those jazz singers. I'd like to make her right on the floor while she's singing. I'd like to drill her." Talking of the past and past happiness he said, "She had a set of knockers on her would choke a mule—she was boss, man." But the best I remember was the tale of his evening with a society girl: "When I came up to her door in my hopped-up '50 Mercury, va va, hoo hoo, hmmm, she thought the Russians was coming." Much later that night, at three in the morning, we took a race through the park in my no-longer-hopped-up '53 Studebaker, Bruce Davidson, Terry, Johnny and myself, and Terry led me to the historic ground where the Dealers had their apocalyptic rumble and he went over the terrain with me, the two of us reconsidering the problem like old Civil War generals warm with nostalgia. It was a good night.

Altogether I saw the Dealers three times. The last trip I took my wife, and a friend and his girl, to one of their dances, but the evening never came off right, because the air of decorum was heavy. I had been promised in advance that a fight would start that night, but it never did. The dance was given by another club in a veterans' hall, and the Dealers were only one of four or five gangs present so everybody had to be on best behavior, and the evening ended early—a couple of kids pulled out the rubber plugs in the tanks on the water closets in the men's room. That flooded the floor, and in disgust the bartenders closed the dance down early. We took Terry, Johnny and Whitey back to the Village to hear some jazz, but they were off their turf and subdued that night.

It occurs to me, as I read over what I have written, that this piece is anti-climactic. I wonder if that is not right. Because I sometimes think the drama of the rumbler, the would-be rumbler, and the adolescent along for the ride is not too far away from the sweat of any artist, any salesman, any adventurer, any operator. Their imagination is too vivid, and so they spend the days and nights of their adolescent years waiting for the apocalyptic test which almost never comes off. It is common in any editorial about juvenile delinquents to speak of wasted lives and growing blight, but what junk these editorials are, for there is not one root to juvenile delinquency, but two. For all the talk of broken homes, submarginal housing, overcrowding in the schools and cultural starvation, the other root is more alive, and one kills it at one's peril. It is the root for which our tongues once found the older words of courage, loyalty, honor and the urge for adventure. It may be that when one gets to know them well, some of the Dealers are bad pieces of work, but I would gamble that most of them are rather good pieces of work, bright, sensitive to what is true and what is not true in what you say to them, loyal if they like you, and in congress together they are as alive as a pack of monkeys. They suffer from only one disease, the national disease—it is boredom. If their conversation runs the predictable riverbed of sex, gang war, drugs, weapons, movies and crazy drunks, well, at least they live out a part of their conversational obsession, which is more than one can say for the quiet, inhibited, middle-aged desperadoes of the corporation and the suburb. If we are to speak of shadows which haunt America today, the great shadow is that there is a place for everybody in our country who is willing to live the way others want him to, and talk the way others want him to, with our big, new, thick, leaden vocabulary of political, psychological, and sociological verbiage. Yes, there is a place for everybody now in the American scene except for those who want to find the limits of their growth by a life which is ready to welcome a little danger as part of the Divine cocktail.

POSTSCRIPT TO THE SECOND PRESIDENTIAL PAPER

A long time ago, back in 1960, when I had the practical idea to run for Mayor of New York and proceeded to destroy it with the same diabolical care one often reserves for the best of one's ambitions, I advanced the idea on a television show that the best way to combat juvenile delinquency was to give artistic outlet to the violence, creativity, and sense of pageantry which drives the average wild adolescent into disaster. Why not have medieval jousting tournaments in Central Park, I suggested. Some of the children of Harlem might move up out of junk and the lust to rumble long enough to spend a winter grooming their horses, designing their livery, learning how to ride, how to use the lance, how to oil the armor.

It was only one of a set of suggestions. Why couldn't there be horse races through the downtown streets of Little Italy similar to the great horse race in Siena, or a municipal circus which would train young acrobats, trapeze artists, lion tamers, and high-wire acts? Once a year there might be drag races down Broadway from 205th Street to the Battery and back. Mountaineers could even be trained in New York. They would learn to make the ascent of difficult skyscrapers. One could build a pool one hundred feet deep and train juveniles in skin diving, one could erect a great ski jump in Central Park. And one might also have boxing and judo and karate and free-style fighting societies. But separated from the Police Department. The kind of juvenile who becomes a law-abiding citizen through the agency of the police sometimes goes so far as to become a policeman himself, and reformed juveniles always make the worst sort of cops.

Existential politics is simple. It has a basic argument: if there is a strong ineradicable strain in human nature, one must not try to suppress it or anomaly, cancer, and plague will follow. Instead one must find an art into which it can grow. So a word to the ear of the President: a Peace Corps is not enough. Start an Adventurer's Corps as well. Let the louts who inhabit the crossroads and pharmacy doorways of every small town in America know that there is an amateur army they can join, a free men's club, an outfit where they may discover if they are potentially brave or fearfully lazy. Even the soul of a lout has anguish—it is the dull urgent apathy that there is something in his heart which is too large to be a bum and yet he does not know if he is of sufficient stature to claim he is a man. So give him the Adventurer's Corps where he can go to the Everglades and fight alligators with a knife or sit on the side of the swamp and watch, where he can learn to fly a glider or spit tobacco in the hangar, where he can ski the snow fields of mountains or go to sleep in the warming hut.

It is the mark of gentlemen that they are economically and spiritually free to go off on a season of expedition or adventure whenever *their soul is stale or their spirit dead. Why should we leave that exceptional privilege to the rich in a democracy? The poor have as much right to novelty, to danger, to exploration and surprise. Let Congress commission two hundred yachts for the Adventurer Corps —they will cost no more than two hundred jet bombers and will not become obsolete for fifty years. Which must be twenty times the life of the airplanes. Let the louts at the crossroads sail the seven seas and climb the mast in the middle of a storm. The President, loving his yacht, would not wish to keep such joy from others.*

THE THIRD PRESIDENTIAL PAPER

—The Existential Hero

Superman Comes to the Supermarket

Not too much need be said for this piece; it is possible it can stand by itself. But perhaps its title should have been "Filling the Holes in No Man's Land."

American politics is rarely interesting for its men, its ideas, or the style of its movements. It is usually more fascinating in its gaps, its absences, its uninvaded territories. We have used up our frontier, but the psychological frontier talked about in this piece is still alive with untouched possibilities and dire unhappy all-but-lost opportunities. In European politics the spaces are filled—the average politician, like the average European, knows what is possible and what is impossible for him. Their politics is like close trench warfare. But in America, one knows such close combat only for the more banal political activities. The play of political ideas is flaccid here in America because opposing armies never meet. The Right, the Center, and what there is of the Left have set up encampments on separate hills, they face one another across valleys, they send out small patrols to their front and vast communiqués to their rear. No Man's Land predominates. It is a situation which calls for guerrilla raiders. Any army which would dare to enter the valley in force might not only determine a few new political formations, but indeed could create more politics itself, even as the guerrilla raids of the Negro Left and Negro Right, the Freedom Riders and the Black Muslims, have discovered much of the secret nature of the American reality for us.

I wonder if I make myself clear. Conventional politics has had so little to do with the real subterranean life of America that none of us

33

know much about the real—which is to say the potential*—historic nature of America. That lies buried under apathy, platitudes, Rightist encomiums for the FBI, programmatic welfare from the liberal Center, and furious pips of protest from the Peace Movement's Left. The mass of Americans are not felt as a political reality. No one has any idea of how they would react to radically new sense. It is only when their heart-land, their no man's land, their valley is invaded, that one discovers the reality. In Birmingham during the days of this writing, the jails are filled with Negro children, 2000 of them. The militancy of the Negroes in Birmingham is startling, so too is the stubbornness of the Southern white, so too and unbelievable is the procrastination of the Kennedy administration. Three new realities have been discovered. The potential Left and potential Right of America are more vigorous than one would have expected and the Center is more irresolute. An existential political act, the drive by Southern Negroes, led by Martin Luther King, to end segregation in restaurants in Birmingham, an act which is existential precisely because its end is unknown, has succeeded en route in discovering more of the American reality to us.*

If a public speaker in a small Midwestern town were to say, "J. Edgar Hoover has done more harm to the freedoms of America than Joseph Stalin," the act would be existential. Depending on the occasion and the town, he would be manhandled physically or secretly applauded. But he would create a new reality which would displace the old psychological reality that such a remark could not be made, even as for example the old Southern psychological reality that you couldn't get two Negroes to do anything together, let alone two thousand has now been destroyed by a new and more accurate psychological reality: you can get two thousand Negroes to work in cooperation. The new psychological realities are closer to history and so closer to sanity and they exist because, and only because, the event has taken place.

It was Kennedy's potentiality to excite such activity which interested me most; that he was young, that he was physically handsome, and that his wife was attractive were not trifling accidental details but, rather, new major political facts. I knew if he became President, it would be an existential event: he would touch depths in American life which were uncharted. Regardless of his politics, and even then one could expect his politics would be as conventional as his personality was unconventional, indeed one could expect his politics to be pushed toward conventionality precisely to counteract his essential unconventionality, one knew nonetheless that regardless of his overt politics, America's tortured psychotic search for security would finally be torn loose from the feverish ghosts of its old generals, its MacArthurs and Eisenhowers—ghosts which Nixon could cling to— and we as a nation would finally be loose again in the historic seas of a national psyche which was willy-nilly and at last, again, adventurous. And that, I thought, that was the hope for America. So I swallowed my doubts, my disquiets, and my certain distastes for Kennedy's dullness of mind and prefabricated politics, and did my best to write a piece which would help him to get elected.

For once let us try to think about a political convention without losing ourselves in housing projects of fact and issue. Politics has its virtues, all too many of them—it would not rank with baseball as a topic of conversation if it did not satisfy a great many things—but one can suspect that its secret appeal is close to nicotine. Smoking cigarettes insulates one from one's life, one does not feel as much, often happily so, and politics quarantines one from history; most of the people who nourish themselves in the political life are in the game not to make history but to be diverted from the history which is being made.

If that Democratic Convention which has now receded behind the brow of the Summer of 1960 is only half-remembered in the excitements of moving toward the election, it may be exactly the time to consider it again, because the mountain of facts which concealed its features last July has been blown away in the winds of High Television, and the man-in-the-street (that peculiar political term which refers to the quixotic voter who will pull the lever for some reason so salient as: "I had a brown-nose lieutenant once with Nixon's looks," or "that Kennedy must have false teeth"), the not so easily estimated man-in-the-street has forgotten most of what happened and could no more tell you who Kennedy was fighting against than you or I could place a bet on who was leading the American League in batting during the month of June.

So to try to talk about what happened is easier now than in the days of the convention, one does not have to put everything in—an act of writing which calls for a bulldozer rather than a pen—one can try to make one's little point and dress it with a ribbon or two of metaphor. All to the good. Because mysteries are irritated by facts, and the 1960 Democratic Convention began as one mystery and ended as another.

Since mystery is an emotion which is repugnant to a political animal (why else lead a life of bad banquet dinners, cigar smoke, camp chairs, foul breath, and excruciatingly dull jargon if not to avoid the echoes of what is not known), the psychic separation between what was happening on the floor, in the caucus rooms, in the headquarters, and what was happening in parallel to the history of the nation was mystery enough to drown the proceedings in gloom. It was on the one hand a dull convention, one of the less interesting by general agreement, relieved by local bits of color, given two half hours of excitement by two demonstrations for Stevenson, buoyed up by the class of the Kennedy machine, turned by the surprise of Johnson's nomination as vice-president, but, all the same, dull, depressed in its over-all tone, the big fiestas subdued, the gossip flat, no real air of excitement, just moments—or as they say in bullfighting—details. Yet it was also, one could argue—and one may argue this yet—it was also one of the most important conventions in America's history, it could prove conceivably to be the most important. The man it nominated was unlike any politician who had ever run for President in the history of the land, and if elected he would come to power in a year when America was in danger of drifting into a profound decline.

A Descriptive of the Delegates: Sons and Daughters of the Republic in a Legitimate Panic; Small-time Practitioners of Small-town Political Judo in the Big Town and the Big Time

Depression obviously has its several roots: it is the doubtful protection which comes from not recognizing failure, it is the psychic burden of exhaustion, and it is also, and very often, that discipline of the will or the ego which enables one to continue working when one's unadmitted emotion is panic. And panic it was I think which sat as the largest single sentiment in the breast of the collective delegates as they came to convene in Los Angeles. Delegates are not the noblest sons and daughters of the Republic; a man of taste, arrived from Mars, would take one look at a convention floor and leave forever, convinced he had seen one of the drearier squats of Hell. If one still smells the faint living echo of a carnival wine, the pepper of a bullfight, the rag, drag, and panoply of a jousting tourney, it is all swallowed and regurgitated by the senses into the fouler cud of a death gas one must rid oneself of—a cigar-smoking, stale-aired, slack-jawed, butt-littered, foul, bleak, hard-working, bureaucratic death gas of language and faces ("Yes, those *faces*," says the man from Mars: lawyers, judges, ward heelers, *mafiosos*, Southern goons and grandees, grand old ladies, trade unionists and finks), of pompous words and long pauses which lay like a leaden pain over fever, the fever that one is in, over, or is it that one is just behind history? A legitimate panic for a delegate. America is a nation of experts without roots; we are always creating tacticians who are blind to strategy and strategists who cannot take a step, and when the culture has finished its work the institutions handcuff the infirmity. A delegate is a man who picks a candidate for the largest office in the land, a President who must live with problems whose borders are in ethics, metaphysics, and now ontology; the delegate is prepared for this office of selection by emptying wastebaskets, toting garbage and saying yes at the right time for twenty years in the small political machine of some small or large town; his reward, one of them anyway, is that he arrives at an invitation to the convention. An expert on local catch-as-catch-can, a small-time, often mediocre practitioner of small-town political judo, he comes to the big city with nine-tenths of his mind made up, he will follow the orders of the boss who brought him. Yet of course it is not altogether so mean as that: his opinion is listened to—the boss will consider what he has to say as one interesting factor among five hundred, and what is most important to the delegate, he has the illusion of partial freedom. He can, unless he is severely honest with himself—and if he is, why sweat out the low levels of a political machine?—he can have the illusion that he has helped to choose the candidate, he can even worry most sincerely about his choice, flirt with defection from the boss, work out his own small political gains by the road of loyalty or the way of hard bargain. But even if he is there for no more than the ride, his vote a certainty in the mind of the political boss, able to be thrown here or switched there as the boss decides, still in some peculiar sense he is reality to the boss, the delegate is the great American public, the bar he owns or the law practice, the piece of the union he represents, or the real-estate office, is a part of the political landscape which the boss uses as his own image of how the votes will go, and if the people will like the candidate. And if the boss is depressed by what he sees, if the candidate does not feel right to him, if he has a dull intimation that the candidate is not his sort (as, let us say, Harry Truman was his sort, or Symington might be his sort, or Lyndon Johnson), then vote for him the boss will if he must; he cannot be caught on the wrong side, but he does not feel the pleasure of a personal choice. Which is the center of the panic. Because if the boss is depressed, the delegate is doubly depressed, and the emotional fact is that Kennedy is not in focus, not in the old political focus, he is not comfortable; in fact it is a mystery to the boss how Kennedy got to where he is, not a mystery in its structures; Kennedy is rolling in money, Kennedy got the votes in primaries, and, most of all, Kennedy has a jewel of a political machine. It is as good as a crack Notre Dame team, all discipline and savvy and go-go-go, sound, drilled, never dull, quick as a knife, full of the salt of hipper-dipper, a beautiful machine; the boss could adore it if only a sensible candidate were driving it, a Truman, even a Stevenson, please God a Northern Lyndon Johnson, but it is run by a man who looks young enough to be coach of the Freshman team, and that is not comfortable at all. The boss knows political machines, he knows issues, farm parity, Forand health bill, Landrum-Griffin, but this is not all so adequate after all to revolutionaries in Cuba who look like beatniks, competitions in missiles, Negroes looting whites in the Congo, intricacies of nuclear fallout, and NAACP men one does well to call Sir. It is all out of hand, everything important is off the center, foreign affairs is now the lick of the heat, and senators are candidates instead of governors, a disaster to the old family style of political measure where a political boss knows his governor and knows who his governor knows. So the boss is depressed, profoundly depressed. He comes to this convention resigned to nominating a man he does not understand, or let us say that, so far as he understands the candidate who is to be nominated, he is not happy about the secrets of his appeal, not so far as he divines these secrets; they seem to have too little to do with politics and all too much to do with the private madnesses of the nation which had thousands—or was it hundreds of thousands—of people demonstrating in the long night before Chessman was killed, and a movie star, the greatest, Marlon the Brando out in the night with them. Yes, this candidate for all his record, his good, sound, conventional liberal record has a patina of that other life, the second American life, the long electric night with the fires of neon leading down the highway to the murmur of jazz.

An Apparent Digression: A Vivid View of the
"City of Lost Angels"; The Democrats Defined;
A Pentagon of Traveling Salesmen;
Some Pointed Portraits of the Politicians

"I was seeing Pershing Square, Los Angeles, now for the first time . . . the nervous fruithustlers darting in and out of the shadows, fugitives from Times Square, Market Street SF, the French Quarter— masculine hustlers looking for lonely fruits to score from, anything from the legendary $20 to a pad at night and breakfast in the morning and whatever you can clinch or clip; and the heat in their holy cop uniforms, holy because of the Almighty Stick and the Almightier Vagrancy Law; the scattered junkies, the small-time pushers, the queens, the sad panhandlers, the lonely, exiled nymphs haunting the entrance to the men's head, the fruits with the hungry eyes and the jingling coins; the tough teen-age chicks—'dittybops'—making it with the lost hustlers . . . all amid the incongruous piped music and the flowers—twin fountains gushing rainbow colored: the world of Lonely America squeezed into Pershing Square, of the Cities of Terrible Night, downtown now trapped in the City of lost Angels . . . and the trees hang over it all like some type of apathetic fate."
—JOHN RECHY: *Big Table 3*

Seeing Los Angeles after ten years away, one realizes all over again that America is an unhappy contract between the East (that Faustian thrust of a most determined human will which reaches up and out above the eye into the skyscrapers of New York) and those flat lands of compromise and mediocre self-expression, those endless half-pretty repetitive small towns of the Middle and the West, whose spirit is forever horizontal and whose marrow comes to rendezvous in the pastel monotonies of Los Angeles architecture.

So far as America has a history, one can see it in the severe heights of New York City, in the glare from the Pittsburgh mills, by the color in the brick of Louisburg Square, along the knotted greedy façades of the small mansions on Chicago's North Side, in Natchez' antebellum homes, the wrought-iron balconies off Bourbon Street, a captain's house in Nantucket, by the curve of Commercial Street in Provincetown. One can make a list; it is probably finite. What culture we have made and what history has collected to it can be found in those few hard examples of an architecture which came to its artistic term, was born, lived and so collected some history about it. Not all the roots of American life are uprooted, but almost all, and the spirit of the supermarket, that homogenous extension of stainless surfaces and psychoanalyzed people, packaged commodities and ranch homes, interchangeable, geographically unrecognizable, that essence of the new postwar SuperAmerica is found nowhere so perfectly as in Los Angeles' ubiquitous acres. One gets the impression that people come to Los Angeles in order to divorce themselves from the past, here to live or try to live in the rootless pleasure world of an adult child. One knows that if the cities of the world were destroyed by a new war, the architecture of the rebuilding would create a landscape which looked, subject to specifications of climate, exactly and entirely like the San Fernando Valley.

It is not that Los Angeles is altogether hideous, it is even by degrees pleasant, but for an Easterner there is never any salt in the wind; it is like Mexican cooking without chile, or Chinese egg rolls missing their mustard; as one travels through the endless repetitions of that city which is the capital of suburbia with its milky pinks, its washed-out oranges, its tainted lime-yellows of pastel on one pretty little architectural monstrosity after another, the colors not intense enough, the styles never pure, and never sufficiently impure to collide on the eye, one conceives the people who live here—they have come out to express themselves, Los Angeles is the home of self-expression, but the artists are middle-class and middling-minded; no passions will calcify here for years in the gloom to be revealed a decade later as the tessellations of a hard and fertile work, no, it is all open, promiscuous, borrowed, half bought, a city without iron, eschewing wood, a kingdom of stucco, the playground for mass men—one has the feeling it was built by television sets giving orders to men. And in this land of the pretty-pretty, the virility is in the barbarisms, the vulgarities, it is in the huge billboards, the screamers of the neon lighting, the shouting farm-utensil colors of the gas stations and the monster drugstores, it is in the swing of the sports cars, hot rods, convertibles, Los Angeles is a city to drive in, the boulevards are wide, the traffic is nervous and fast, the radio stations play bouncing, blooping, rippling tunes, one digs the pop in a pop tune, no one of character would make love by it but the sound is good for swinging a car, electronic guitars and Hawaiian harps.

So this is the town the Democrats came to, and with their unerring instinct (after being with them a week, one thinks of this party as a crazy, half-rich family, loaded with poor cousins, traveling always in caravans with Cadillacs and Okie Fords, Lincolns and quarter-horse mules, putting up every night in tents to hear the chamber quartet of Great Cousin Eleanor invaded by the Texas-twanging ,steel-stringing geetarists of Bubber Lyndon, carrying its own mean high-school principal, Doc Symington, chided for its manners by good Uncle Adlai, told the route of march by Navigator Jack, cut off every six months from the rich will of Uncle Jim Farley, never listening to the mechanic of the caravan, Bald Sam Rayburn, who assures them they'll all break down unless Cousin Bubber gets the concession on the garage; it's the Snopes family married to Henry James, with the labor unions thrown in like a Yankee dollar, and yet it's true, in tranquility one recollects them with affection, their instinct is good, crazy family good) and this instinct now led the caravan to pick the Biltmore Hotel in downtown Los Angeles for their family get-together and reunion.

The Biltmore is one of the ugliest hotels in the world. Patterned after the flat roofs of an Italian Renaissance palace, it is eighty-eight times as large, and one-millionth as valuable to the continuation of man, and it would be intolerable if it were not for the presence of Pershing Square, that square block of park with cactus and palm trees, the three-hundred-and-sixty-five-day-a-year convention of every junkie, pot-head, pusher, queen (but you have read that good writing already). For years Pershing Square has been one of the three or four places in America famous to homosexuals, famous not for its posh, the chic is round-heeled here, but because it is one of the avatars of the good old masturbatory sex, dirty with the crusted sugars of smut, dirty rooming houses around the corner where the score is made, dirty book and photograph stores down the street, old-fashioned out-of-the-Thirties burlesque houses, cruising bars, jukeboxes, movie houses; Pershing Square is the town plaza for all those lonely, respectable, small-town homosexuals who lead a family life, make children, and have the Philbrick psychology (How I Joined the Communist Party and Led Three Lives). Yes, it is the open-air convention hall for the small-town inverts who live like spies, and it sits in the center of Los Angeles, facing the Biltmore, that hotel which is a mausoleum, that Pentagon of traveling salesmen the Party chose to house the headquarters of the Convention.

So here came that family, cursed before it began by the thundering absence of Great-Uncle Truman, the delegates dispersed over a run of thirty miles and twenty-seven hotels: the Olympian Motor Hotel, the Ambassador, the Beverly Wilshire, the Santa Ynez Inn (where rumor has it the delegates from Louisiana had some midnight swim), the Mayan, the Commodore, the Mayfair, the Sheraton-West, the Huntington-Sheraton, the Green, the Hayward, the Gates, the Figueroa, the Statler Hilton, the Hollywood Knickerbocker—does one have to be a collector to list such names?—beauties all, with that up-from-the-farm Los Angeles décor, plate-glass windows, patio and terrace, foam-rubber mattress, pastel paints, all of them pretty as an ad in full-page color, all but the Biltmore where everybody gathered every day—the newsmen, the TV, radio, magazine, and foreign newspapermen, the delegates, the politicos, the tourists, the campaign managers, the runners, the flunkies, the cousins and aunts, the wives, the grandfathers, the eight-year-old girls, and the twenty-eight-year-old girls in the Kennedy costumes, red and white and blue, the Symingteeners, the Johnson Ladies, the Stevenson Ladies, everybody—and for three days before the convention and four days into it, everybody collected at the Biltmore, in the lobby, in the grill, in the Biltmore Bowl, in the elevators, along the corridors, three hundred deep always outside the Kennedy suite, milling everywhere, every dark-carpeted grey-brown hall of the hotel, but it was in the Gallery of the Biltmore where one first felt the mood which pervaded all proceedings until the convention was almost over, that heavy, thick, witless depression which was to dominate every move as the delegates wandered and gawked and paraded and set for a spell, there in the Gallery of the

Biltmore, that huge depressing alley with its inimitable hotel color, that faded depth of chiaroscuro which unhappily has no depth, that brown which is not a brown, that grey which has no pearl in it, that color which can be described only as hotel-color because the beiges, the tans, the walnuts, the mahoganies, the dull blood rugs, the moaning yellows, the sick greens, the greys and all those dumb browns merge into that lack of color which is an over-large hotel at convention time, with all the small-towners wearing their set, starched faces, that look they get at carnival, all fever and suspicion, and proud to be there, eddying slowly back and forth in that high block-long tunnel of a room with its arched ceiling and square recesses filling every rib of the arch with art work, escutcheons and blazons and other art, pictures I think, I cannot even remember, there was such a hill of cigar smoke the eye had to travel on its way to the ceiling, and at one end there was galvanized-pipe scaffolding and workmen repairing some part of the ceiling, one of them touching up one of the endless squares of painted plaster in the arch, and another worker, passing by, yelled up to the one who was working on the ceiling: "Hey, Michelangelo!"

Later, of course, it began to emerge and there were portraits one could keep, Symington, dogged at a press conference, declaring with no conviction that he knew he had a good chance to win, the disappointment eating at his good looks so that he came off hard-faced, mean, and yet slack—a desperate dullness came off the best of his intentions. There was Johnson who had compromised too many contradictions and now the contradictions were in his face: when he smiled the corners of his mouth squeezed gloom; when he was pious, his eyes twinkled irony; when he spoke in a righteous tone, he looked corrupt; when he jested, the ham in his jowls looked to quiver. He was not convincing. He was a Southern politician, a Texas Democrat, a liberal Eisenhower; he would do no harm, he would do no good, he would react to the machine, good fellow, nice friend—the Russians would understand him better than his own.

Stevenson had the patina. He came into the room and the room was different, not stronger perhaps (which is why ultimately he did not win), but warmer. One knew why some adored him; he did not look like other people, not with press lights on his flesh; he looked like a lover, the simple truth, he had the sweet happiness of an adolescent who has just been given his first major kiss. And so he glowed, and one was reminded of Chaplin, not because they were the least alike in features, but because Charlie Chaplin was luminous when one met him and Stevenson had something of that light.

There was Eleanor Roosevelt, fine, precise, hand-worked like ivory. Her voice was almost attractive as she explained in the firm, sad tones of the first lady in this small town why she could not admit Mr. Kennedy, who was no doubt a gentleman, into her political house. One had the impression of a lady who was finally becoming a woman, which is to say that she was just a little bitchy about it all; nice bitchy, charming, it had a touch of art to it, but it made one wonder if she were not now satisfying the last passion of them all, which was to become physically attractive, for she was better-looking than she had ever been as she spurned the possibilities of a young suitor.

Jim Farley. Huge. Cold as a bishop. The hell he would consign you to was cold as ice.

Bobby Kennedy, that archetype Bobby Kennedy, looked like a West Point cadet, or, better, one of those unreconstructed Irishmen from Kirkland House one always used to have to face in the line in Harvard house football games. "Hello," you would say to the ones who looked like him as you lined up for the scrimmage after the kickoff, and his type would nod and look away, one rock glint of recognition your due for living across the hall from one another all through Freshman year, and then bang, as the ball was passed back, you'd get a bony king-hell knee in the crotch. He was the kind of man never to put on the gloves with if you wanted to do some social boxing, because after two minutes it would be a war, and ego-bastards last long in a war.

Carmine DeSapio and Kenneth Galbraith on the same part of the convention floor. DeSapio is bigger than one expects, keen and florid, great big smoked glasses, a suntan like Mantan—he is the kind of heavyweight Italian who could get by with a name like Romeo—and Galbraith is tall-tall, as actors say, six foot six it could be, terribly thin, enormously attentive, exquisitely polite, birdlike, he is sensitive to the stirring of reeds in a wind over the next hill. "Our grey eminence," whispered the intelligent observer next to me.

Bob Wagner, the mayor of New York, a little man, plump, groomed, blank. He had the blank, pomaded, slightly worried look of the first barber in a good barbership, the kind who would go to the track on his day off and wear a green transparent stone in a gold ring.

And then there was Kennedy, the edge of the mystery. But a sketch will no longer suffice.

*Perspective from the Biltmore Balcony: The
Colorful Arrival of the Hero with the Orange-
brown Suntan and Amazingly White Teeth;
Revelation of the Two Rivers Political Theory*

"... it can be said with a fair amount of certainty that the essence of his political attractiveness is his extraordinary political intelligence. He has a mind quite unlike that of any other Democrat of this century. It is not literary, metaphysical and moral, as Adlai Stevenson's is. Kennedy is articulate and often witty, but he does not seek verbal polish. No one can doubt the seriousness of his concern with the most serious political matters, but one feels that whereas Mr. Stevenson's political views derive from a view of life that holds politics to be a mere fraction of existence, Senator Kennedy's primary interest is in politics. The easy way in which he disposes of the question of Church and State—as if he felt that any reasonable man could quite easily resolve any possible conflict of loyalties—suggests that the organization of society is the one thing that really engages his interest." —RICHARD ROVERE: *The New Yorker*, July 23, 1960

The afternoon he arrived at the convention from the airport, there was of course a large crowd on the street outside the Biltmore, and the best way to get a view was to get up on an outdoor balcony of the Biltmore, two flights above the street, and look down on the event. One waited thirty minutes, and then a honking of horns as wild as the getaway after an Italian wedding sounded around the corner, and the Kennedy cortege came into sight, circled Pershing Square, the men in the open and leading convertibles sitting backwards to look at their leader, and finally came to a halt in a space cleared for them by the police in the crowd. The television cameras were out, and a Kennedy band was playing some circus music. One saw him immediately. He had the deep orange-brown suntan of a ski instructor, and when he smiled at the crowd his teeth were amazingly white and clearly visible at a distance of fifty yards. For one moment he saluted Pershing Square, and Pershing Square saluted him back, the prince and the beggars of glamour staring at one another across a city street, one of those very special moments in the underground history of the world, and then with a quick move he was out of the car and by choice headed into the crowd instead of the lane cleared for him into the hotel by the police, so that he made his way inside surrounded by a mob, and one expected at any moment to see him lifted to its shoulders like a matador being carried back to the city after a triumph in the plaza. All the while the band kept playing the campaign tunes, sashaying circus music, and one had a moment of clarity, intense as a *déjà vu*, for the scene which had taken place had been glimpsed before in a dozen musical comedies; it was the scene where the hero, the matinee idol, the movie star comes to the palace to claim the princess, or what is the same, and more to our soil, the football hero, the campus king, arrives at the dean's home surrounded by a court of open-singing students to plead with the dean for his daughter's kiss and permission to put on the big musical that night. And suddenly I saw the convention, it came into focus for me, and I understood the mood of depression which had lain over the convention, because finally it was simple: the Democrats were going to nominate a man who, no matter how serious his political dedication might be, was indisputably and willy-nilly going to be seen as a great box-office actor, and the consequences of that were staggering and not at all easy to calculate.

Since the First World War Americans have been leading a double life, and our history has moved on two rivers, one visible, the other underground; there has been the history of politics which is concrete, factual, practical and unbelievably dull if not for the consequences of the actions of some of these men; and there is a subterranean river of untrapped, ferocious, lonely and romantic desires, that concentration of ecstasy and violence which is the dream life of the nation.

The twentieth century may yet be seen as that era when civilized man and underprivileged man were melted together into mass man, the iron and steel of the nineteenth century giving way to electronic circles which communicated their messages into men, the unmistakable tendency of the new century seeming to be the creation of men as interchangeable as commodities, their extremes of personality singed out of existence by the psychic fields of force the communicators would impose. This loss of personality was a catastrophe to the future of the imagination, but billions of people might first benefit from it by having enough to eat—one did not know—and there remained citadels of resistance in Europe where the culture was deep and roots were visible in the architecture of the past.

Nowhere, as in America, however, was this fall from individual man to mass man felt so acutely, for America was at once the first and most prolific creator of mass communications, and the most rootless of countries, since almost no American could lay claim to the line of a family which had not once at least severed its roots by migrating here. But, if rootless, it was then the most vulnerable of countries to its own homogenization. Yet America was also the country in which the dynamic myth of the Renaissance—that every man was potentially extraordinary—knew its most passionate persistence. Simply, America was the land where people still believed in heroes: George Washington; Billy the Kid; Lincoln, Jefferson; Mark Twain, Jack London, Hemingway; Joe Louis, Dempsey, Gentleman Jim; America believed in athletes, rum-runners, aviators; even lovers, by the time Valentino died. It was a country which had grown by the leap of one hero past another—is there a county in all of our ground which does not have its legendary figure? And when the West was filled, the expansion turned inward, became part of an agitated, overexcited, superheated dream life. The film studios threw up their searchlights as the frontier was finally sealed, and the romantic possibilities of the old conquest of land turned into a vertical myth, trapped within the skull, of a new kind of heroic life, each choosing his own archetype of a neo-renaissance man, be it Barrymore, Cagney, Flynn, Bogart, Brando or Sinatra, but it was almost as if there were no peace unless one could fight well, kill well (if always with honor), love well and love many, be cool, be daring, be dashing, be wild, be wily, be resourceful, be a brave gun. And this myth, that each of us was born to be free, to wander, to have adventure and to grow on the waves of the violent, the perfumed, and the unexpected, had a force which could not be tamed no matter how the nation's regulators—politicians, medicos, policemen, professors, priests, rabbis, ministers, *idéologues*, psychoanalysts, builders, executives and endless communicators—would brick-in the modern life with hygiene upon sanity, and middle-brow homily over platitude; the myth would not die. Indeed a quarter of the nation's business must have depended upon its existence. But it stayed alive for more than that—it was as if the message in the labyrinth of the genes would insist that violence was locked with creativity, and adventure was the secret of love.

Once, in the Second World War and in the year or two which followed, the underground river returned to earth, and the life of the nation was intense, of the present, electric; as a lady said, "That was the time when we gave parties which changed people's lives." The Forties was a decade when the speed with which one's own events occurred seemed as rapid as the history of the battlefields, and for the mass of people in America a forced march into a new jungle of emotion was the result. The surprises, the failures, and the dangers of that life must have terrified some nerve of awareness in the power and the mass, for, as if stricken by the orgiastic vistas the myth had carried up from underground, the retreat to a more conservative existence was disorderly, the fear of communism spread like an irrational hail of boils. To anyone who could see, the excessive hysteria of the Red wave was no preparation to face an enemy, but rather a terror of the national self: free-loving, lust-looting, atheistic, implacable—absurdity beyond absurdity to label communism so, for the moral products of Stalinism had been Victorian sex and a ponderous machine of material theology.

Forced underground again, deep beneath all *Reader's Digest* hospital dressings of Mental Health in Your Community, the myth continued to flow, fed by television and the film. The fissure in the national psyche widened to the danger point. The last large appearance of the myth was the vote which tricked the polls and gave Harry Truman his victory in '48. That was the last. Came the Korean War, the shadow of the H-bomb, and we were ready for the General. Uncle Harry gave way to Father, and security, regularity, order, and the life of no imagination were the command of the day. If one had any doubt of this, there was Joe McCarthy with his built-in treason detector, furnished by God, and the damage was done. In the totalitarian wind of those days, anyone who worked in Government formed the habit of being not too original, and many a mind atrophied from disuse and private shame. At the summit there was benevolence without leadership, regularity without vision, security without safety, rhetoric without life. The ship drifted on, that enormous warship of the United States, led by a Secretary of State whose cells were seceding to cancer, and as the world became more fantastic—Africa turning itself upside down, while some new kind of machine man was being made in China—two events occurred which stunned the confidence of America into a new night: the Russians put up their Sputnik, and Civil Rights—that reluctant gift to the American Negro, granted for its effect on foreign affairs—spewed into real life at Little Rock. The national Ego was in shock: the Russians were now in some ways our technological superiors, and we had an internal problem of subject populations equal conceivably in its difficulty to the Soviet and its satellites. The fatherly calm of the General began to seem like the uxorious mellifluences of the undertaker.

Underneath it all was a larger problem. The life of politics and the life of myth had diverged too far, and the energies of the people one knew everywhere had slowed down. Twenty years ago a post-Depression generation had gone to war and formed a lively, grousing, by times inefficient, carousing, pleasure-seeking, not altogether inadequate army. It did part of what it was supposed to do, and many, out of combat, picked up a kind of private life on the fly, and had their good time despite the yaws of the military system. But today in America the generation which respected the code of the myth was Beat, a horde of half-begotten Christs with scraggly beards, heroes none, saints all, weak before the strong, empty conformisms of the authority. The sanction for finding one's growth was no longer one's flag, one's career, one's sex, one's adventure, not even one's booze. Among the best in this newest of the generations, the myth had found its voice in marijuana, and the joke of the underground was that when the Russians came over they could never dare to occupy us for long because America was too Hip. Gallows humor. The poorer truth might be that America was too Beat, the instinct of the nation so separated from its public mind that apathy, schizophrenia, and private beatitudes might be the pride of the welcoming committee any underground could offer.

Yes, the life of politics and the life of the myth had diverged too far. There was nothing to return them to one another, no common danger, no cause, no desire, and, most essentially, no hero. It was a hero America needed, a hero central to his time, a man whose personality might suggest contradictions and mysteries which could reach into the alienated circuits of the underground, because only a hero can capture the secret imagination of a people, and so be good for the vitality of his nation; a hero embodies the fantasy and so allows each private mind the liberty to consider its fantasy and find a way to grow. Each mind can become more conscious of its desire and waste less strength in hiding from itself. Roosevelt was such a hero, and Churchill, Lenin and De Gaulle; even Hitler, to take the most odious example of this thesis, was a hero, the hero-as-monster, embodying what had become the monstrous fantasy of a people, but the horror upon which the radical mind and liberal temperament foundered was that he gave outlet to the energies of the Germans and so presented the twentieth century with an index of how horrible had become the secret heart of its desire. Roosevelt is of course a happier example of the hero; from his paralytic leg to the royal elegance of his geniality he seemed to contain the country within himself; everyone from the meanest starving cripple to an ambitious young man could expand into the optimism of an improving future because the man offered an unspoken promise of a future which would be rich. The sexual and the sex-starved, the poor, the hard-working and the imaginative well-to-do could see themselves in the President, could believe him to be like themselves. So a large part of the country was able to discover its energies because not as much was wasted in feeling that the country was a poisonous nutrient which stifled the day.

Too simple? No doubt. One tries to construct a simple model. The thesis is after all not so mysterious; it would merely nudge the notion that a hero embodies his time and is not so very much better than his time, but he is larger than life and so is capable of giving direction to the time, able to encourage a nation to discover the deepest colors of its character. At bottom the concept of the hero is antagonistic to impersonal social progress, to the belief that social ills can be solved by social legislating, for it sees a country as all-but-trapped in its character until it has a hero who reveals the character of the country to itself. The implication is that without such a hero the nation turns sluggish. Truman for example was not such a hero, he was not sufficiently larger than life, he inspired familiarity without excitement, he was a character but his proportions came from soap opera: Uncle Harry, full of salty common-sense and small-minded certainty, a storekeeping uncle.

Whereas Eisenhower has been the anti-Hero, the regulator. Nations do not necessarily and inevitably seek for heroes. In periods of dull anxiety, one is more likely to look for security than a dramatic confrontation, and Eisenhower could stand as a hero only for that large number of Americans who were most proud of their lack of imagination. In American life, the unspoken war of the century has taken place between the city and the small town: the city which is dynamic, orgiastic, unsettling, explosive and accelerating to the psyche; the small town which is rooted, narrow, cautious and planted in the life-logic of the family. The need of the city is to accelerate growth; the pride of the small town is to retard it. But since America has been passing through a period of enormous expansion since the war, the double-four years of Dwight Eisenhower could not retard the expansion, it could only denude it of color, character, and the development of novelty. The small-town mind is rooted—it is rooted in the small town—and when it attempts to direct history the results are disastrously colorless because the instrument of world power which is used by the small-town mind is the committee. Committees do not create, they merely proliferate, and the incredible dullness wreaked upon the American landscape in Eisenhower's eight years has been the triumph of the corporation. A tasteless, sexless, odorless sanctity in architecture, manners, modes, styles has been the result. Eisenhower embodied half the needs of the nation, the needs of the timid, the petrified, the sanctimonious, and the sluggish. What was even worse, he did not divide the nation as a hero might (with a dramatic dialogue as the result); he merely excluded one part of the nation from the other. The result was an alienation of the best minds and bravest impulses from the faltering history which was made. America's need in those years was to take an existential turn, to walk into the nightmare, to face into that terrible logic of history which demanded that the country and its people must become more extraordinary and more adventurous, or else perish, since the only alternative was to offer a false security in the power and the panacea of organized religion, family, and the FBI, a totalitarianization of the psyche by the stultifying techniques of the mass media which would seep into everyone's most private associations and so leave the country powerless against the Russians even if the denouement were to take fifty years, for in a competition between totalitarianisms the first maxim of the prizefight manager would doubtless apply: "Hungry fighters win fights."

*The Hipster as Presidential Candidate: Thoughts
on a Public Man's Eighteenth-Century Wife;
Face-to-Face with the Hero; Significance of a
Personal Note, or the Meaning of His Having
Read an Author's Novel*

Some part of these thoughts must have been in one's mind at the moment there was that first glimpse of Kennedy entering the Biltmore Hotel; and in the days which followed, the first mystery—the profound air of depression which hung over the convention—gave way to a second mystery which can be answered only by history. The depression of the delegates was understandable: no one had too much doubt that Kennedy would be nominated, but if elected he would be not only the youngest President ever to be chosen by voters, he would be the most conventionally attractive young man ever to sit in the White House, and his wife—some would claim it—might be the most beautiful first lady in our history. Of necessity the myth would emerge once more, because America's politics would now be also America's favorite movie, America's first soap opera, America's best-seller. One thinks of the talents of writers like Taylor Caldwell or Frank Yerby, or is it rather *The Fountainhead* which would contain such a fleshing of the romantic prescription? Or is it indeed one's own work which is called into question? "Well, there's your first hipster," says a writer one knows at the convention, "Sergius O'Shaugnessy born rich," and the temptation is to nod, for it could be true, a war hero, and the heroism is bona-fide, even exceptional, a man who has lived with death, who, crippled in the back, took on an operation which would kill him or restore him to power, who chose to marry a lady whose face might be too imaginative for the taste of a democracy which likes its first ladies to be executives of home-management, a man who courts political suicide by choosing to go all out for a nomination four, eight, or twelve years before his political elders think he is ready, a man who announces a week prior to the convention that the young are better fitted to direct history than the old. Yes, it captures the attention. This is no routine candidate calling every shot by safety's routine book ("Yes," Nixon said, naturally but terribly tired an hour after his nomination, the TV cameras and lights and microphones bringing out a sweat of fatigue on his face, the words coming very slowly from the tired brain, somber, modest, sober, slow, slow enough so that one could touch emphatically the cautions behind each word, "Yes, I want to say," said Nixon, "that whatever abilities I have, I got from my mother." A tired pause . . . dull moment of warning, ". . . and my father." The connection now made, the rest comes easy, ". . . and my school and my church." Such men are capable of anything.)

One had the opportunity to study Kennedy a bit in the days that followed. His style in the press conferences was interesting. Not terribly popular with the reporters (too much a contemporary, and yet too difficult to understand, he received nothing like the rounds of applause given to Eleanor Roosevelt, Stevenson, Humphrey, or even Johnson), he carried himself nonetheless with a cool grace which seemed indifferent to applause, his manner somehow similar to the poise of a fine boxer, quick with his hands, neat in his timing, and two feet away from his corner when the bell ended the round. There was a good lithe wit to his responses, a dry Harvard wit, a keen sense of proportion in disposing of difficult questions—invariably he gave enough of an answer to be formally satisfactory without ever opening himself to a new question which might go further than the first. Asked by a reporter, "Are you for Adlai as vice-president?" the grin came forth and the voice turned very dry, "No, I cannot say we have considered *Adlai* as a vice-president." Yet there was an elusive detachment to everything he did. One did not have the feeling of a man present in the room with all his weight and all his mind. Johnson gave you all of himself, he was a political animal, he breathed like an animal, sweated like one, you knew his mind was entirely absorbed with the compendium of political fact and maneuver; Kennedy seemed at times like a young professor whose manner was adequate for the classroom, but whose mind was off in some intricacy of the Ph.D. thesis he was writing. Perhaps one can give a sense of the discrepancy by saying that he was like an actor who had been cast as the candidate, a good actor, but not a great one—you were aware all the time that the role was one thing and the man another—they did not coincide, the actor seemed a touch too aloof (as, let us say, Gregory Peck is usually too aloof) to become the part. Yet one had little sense of whether to value this elusiveness, or to beware of it. One could be witnessing the fortitude of a superior sensitivity or the detachment of a man who was not quite real to himself. And his voice gave no clue. When Johnson spoke, one could separate what was fraudulent from what was felt, he would have been satisfying as an actor the way

Broderick Crawford or Paul Douglas are satisfying; one saw into his emotions, or at least had the illusion that one did. Kennedy's voice, however, was only a fair voice, too reedy, near to strident, it had the metallic snap of a cricket in it somewhere, it was more impersonal than the man, and so became the least-impressive quality in a face, a body, a selection of language, and a style of movement which made up a better-than-decent presentation, better than one had expected.

With all of that, it would not do to pass over the quality in Kennedy which is most difficult to describe. And in fact some touches should be added to this hint of a portrait, for later (after the convention), one had a short session alone with him, and the next day, another. As one had suspected in advance the interviews were not altogether satisfactory, they hardly could have been. A man running for President is altogether different from a man elected President: the hazards of the campaign make it impossible for a candidate to be as interesting as he might like to be (assuming he has such a desire). One kept advancing the argument that this campaign would be a contest of personalities, and Kennedy kept returning the discussion to politics. After a while one recognized this was an inevitable caution for him. So there would be not too much point to reconstructing the dialogue since Kennedy is hardly inarticulate about his political attitudes and there will be a library vault of text devoted to it in the newspapers. What struck me most about the interview was a passing remark whose importance was invisible on the scale of politics, but was altogether meaningful to my particular competence. As we sat down for the first time, Kennedy smiled nicely and said that he had read my books. One muttered one's pleasure. "Yes," he said, "I've read . . ." and then there was a short pause which did not last long enough to be embarrassing in which it was yet obvious no title came instantly to his mind, an omission one was not ready to mind altogether since a man in such a position must be obliged to carry a hundred thousand facts and names in his head, but the hesitation lasted no longer than three seconds or four, and then he said, "I've read *The Deer Park* and . . . the others," which startled me for it was the first time in a hundred similar situations, talking to someone whose knowledge of my work was casual, that the sentence did not come out, "I've read *The Naked and the Dead* . . . and the others." If one is to take the worst and assume that Kennedy was briefed for this interview (which is most doubtful), it still speaks well for the striking instincts of his advisers.

What was retained later is an impression of Kennedy's manners which were excellent, even artful, better than the formal good manners of Choate and Harvard, almost as if what was creative in the man had been given to the manners. In a room with one or two people, his voice improved, became low-pitched, even pleasant—it seemed obvious that in all these years he had never become a natural public speaker and so his voice was constricted in public, the symptom of all orators who are ambitious, throttled, and determined.

His personal quality had a subtle, not quite describable intensity, a suggestion of dry pent heat perhaps, his eyes large, the pupils grey, the whites prominent, almost shocking, his most forceful feature: he had the eyes of a mountaineer. His appearance changed with his mood, strikingly so, and this made him always more interesting than what he was saying. He would seem at one moment older than his age, forty-eight or fifty, a tall, slim, sunburned professor with a pleasant weathered face, not even particularly handsome; five minutes later, talking to a press conference on his lawn, three microphones before him, a television camera turning, his appearance would have gone through a metamorphosis, he would look again like a movie star, his coloring vivid, his manner rich, his gestures strong and quick, alive with that concentration of vitality a successful actor always seems to radiate. Kennedy had a dozen faces. Although they were not at all similar as people, the quality was reminiscent of someone like Brando whose expression rarely changes, but whose appearance seems to shift from one person into another as the minutes go by, and one bothers with this comparison because, like Brando, Kennedy's most characteristic quality is the remote and private air of a man who has traversed some lonely terrain of experience, of loss and gain, of nearness to death, which leaves him isolated from the mass of others.

The next day while they waited in vain for rescuers, the wrecked half of the boat turned over in the water and they saw that it would soon sink. The group decided to swim to a small island three miles away. There were other islands bigger and nearer, but the Navy officers knew that they were occupied by the Japanese. On one island, only one mile to the south, they could see a Japanese camp. McMahon, the engineer whose legs were disabled by burns, was unable to swim. Despite his own painfully crippled back, Kennedy swam the three miles with a breast stroke, towing behind him by a life-belt strap that he held between his teeth the helpless McMahon . . . it took Kennedy and the suffering engineer five hours to reach the island.

The quotation is from a book which has for its dedicated unilateral title, *The Remarkable Kennedys*, but the prose is by one of the best of the war reporters, the former *Yank* editor, Joe McCarthy, and so presumably may be trusted in such details as this. Physical bravery does not of course guarantee a man's abilities in the White House—all too often men with physical courage are disappointing in their moral imagination—but the heroism here is remarkable for its tenacity. The above is merely one episode in a continuing saga which went on for five days in and out of the water, and left Kennedy at one point "miraculously saved from drowning (in a storm) by a group of Solomon Island natives who suddenly came up beside him in a large dugout canoe." Afterward, his back still injured (that precise back injury which was to put him on crutches eleven years later, and have him search for "spinal-fusion surgery" despite a warning that his chances of living through the operation were "extremely limited") afterward, he asked to go back on duty and became so bold in the attacks he made with his PT boat "that the crew didn't like to go out with him because he took so many chances."

It is the wisdom of a man who senses death within him and gambles that he can cure it by risking his life. It is the therapy of the instinct, and who is so wise as to call it irrational? Before he went into the Navy, Kennedy had been ailing. Washed out of Freshman year at Princeton by a prolonged trough of yellow jaundice, sick for a year at Harvard, weak already in the back from an injury at football, his trials suggest the self-hatred of a man whose resentment and ambition are too large for his body. Not everyone can discharge their furies on an analyst's couch, for some angers can be relaxed only by winning power, some rages are sufficiently monumental to demand that one try to become a hero or else fall back into that death which is already within the cells. But if one succeeds, the energy aroused can be exceptional. Talking to a man who had been with Kennedy in Hyannis Port the week before the convention, I heard that he was in a state of deep fatigue.

"Well, he didn't look tired at the convention," one commented.

"Oh, he had three days of rest. Three days of rest for him is like six months for us."

One thinks of that three-mile swim with the belt in his mouth and McMahon holding it behind him. There are pestilences which sit in the mouth and rot the teeth—in those five hours how much of the psyche must have been remade, for to give vent to the bite in one's jaws and yet use that rage to save a life: it is not so very many men who have the apocalyptic sense that heroism is the First Doctor.

If one had a profound criticism of Kennedy it was that his public mind was too conventional, but that seemed to matter less than the fact of such a man in office because the law of political life had become so dreary that only a conventional mind could win an election. Indeed there could be no politics which gave warmth to one's body until the country had recovered its imagination, its pioneer lust for the unexpected and incalculable. It was the changes that might come afterward on which one could put one's hope. With such a man in office the myth of the nation would again be engaged, and the fact that he was Catholic would shiver a first existential vibration of consciousness into the mind of the White Protestant. For the first time in our history, the Protestant would have the pain and creative luxury of feeling himself in some tiny degree part of a minority, and that was an experience which might be incommensurable in its value to the best of them.

A Vignette of Adlai Stevenson; The Speeches:
What Happened When the Teleprompter
Jammed: How U.S. Senator Eugene McCarthy
Played the Matador. An Observation
on the Name Fitzgerald

As yet we have said hardly a word about Stevenson. And his actions must remain a puzzle unless one dares a speculation about his motive, or was it his need?

So far as the people at the convention had affection for anyone, it was Stevenson, so far as they were able to generate any spontaneous enthusiasm, their cheers were again for Stevenson. Yet it was obvious he never had much chance because so soon as a chance would present itself he seemed quick to dissipate the opportunity. The day before the nominations, he entered the Sports Arena to take his seat as a delegate—the demonstration was spontaneous, noisy and prolonged; it was quieted only by Governor Collins' invitation for Stevenson to speak to the delegates. In obedience perhaps to the scruple that a candidate must not appear before the convention until nominations are done, Stevenson said no more than: "I am grateful for this tumultuous and moving welcome. After getting in and out of the Biltmore Hotel and this hall, I have decided I know whom you are going to nominate. It will be the last survivor." This dry reminder of the ruthlessness of politics broke the roar of excitement for his presence. The applause as he left the platform was like the dying fall-and-moan of a baseball crowd when a home run curves foul. The next day, a New York columnist talking about it said bitterly, "If he'd only gone through the motions, if he had just said that now he wanted to run, that he would work hard, and he hoped the delegates would vote for him. Instead he made that lame joke." One wonders. It seems almost as if he did not wish to win unless victory came despite himself, and then was overwhelming. There are men who are not heroes because they are too good for their time, and it is natural that defeats leave them bitter, tired, and doubtful of their right to make new history. If Stevenson had campaigned for a year before the convention, it is possible that he could have stopped Kennedy. At the least, the convention would have been enormously more exciting, and the nominations might have gone through half-a-dozen ballots before a winner was hammered into shape. But then Stevenson might also have shortened his life. One had the impression of a tired man who (for a politician) was sickened unduly by compromise. A year of maneuvering, broken promises, and detestable partners might have gutted him for the election campaign. If elected, it might have ruined him as a President. There is the possibility that he sensed his situation exactly this way, and knew that if he were to run for president, win and make a good one, he would first have to be restored, as one can indeed be restored, by an exceptional demonstration of love—love, in this case, meaning that the Party had a profound desire to keep him as their leader. The emotional truth of a last-minute victory for Stevenson over the Kennedy machine might have given him new energy; it would certainly have given him new faith in a country and a party whose good motives he was possibly beginning to doubt. Perhaps the fault he saw with his candidacy was that he attracted only the nicest people to himself and there were not enough of them. (One of the private amusements of the convention was to divine some of the qualities of the candidates by the style of the young women who put on hats and clothing and politicked in the colors of one presidential gent or another. Of course, half of them must have been hired models, but someone did the hiring and so it was fair to look for a common denominator. The Johnson girls tended to be plump, pie-faced, dumb sexy Southern; the Symingteeners seemed a touch mulish, stubborn, good-looking pluggers; the Kennedy ladies were the handsomest; healthy, attractive, tough, a little spoiled—they looked like the kind of girls who had gotten all the dances in high school and/or worked for a year as an airline hostess before marrying well. But the Stevenson girls looked to be doing it for no money; they were good sorts, slightly horsy-faced, one had the impression they played field hockey in college.) It was indeed the pure, the saintly, the clean-living, the pacifistic, the vegetarian who seemed most for Stevenson, and the less humorous in the Kennedy camp were heard to remark bitterly that Stevenson had nothing going for him but a bunch of Goddamn Beatniks. This might even have had its sour truth. The demonstrations outside the Sports Arena for Stevenson seemed to have more than a fair proportion of tall, emaciated young men with thin, wry beards and three-string guitars accompanied (again in undue proportion) by a contingent of ascetic, face-washed young Beat ladies in sweaters and dungarees. Not to mention all the Holden Caulfields one could see from here to the horizon. But of course it is unfair to limit it so, for the Democratic gentry were also committed half en masse for Stevenson, as well as a considerable number of movie stars, Shelley Winters for one: after the convention she remarked sweetly, "Tell me something nice about Kennedy so I can get excited about him."

What was properly astonishing was the way this horde of political half-breeds and amateurs came within distance of turning the convention from its preconceived purpose, and managed at the least to bring the only hour of thorough-going excitement the convention could offer.

But then nominating day was the best day of the week and enough happened to suggest that a convention out of control would be a spectacle as extraordinary in the American scale of spectator values as a close seventh game in the World Series or a tied fourth quarter in a professional-football championship. A political convention is after all not a meeting of a corporation's board of directors; it is a fiesta, a carnival, a pig-rooting, horse-snorting, band-playing, voice-screaming medieval get-together of greed, practical lust, compromised idealism, career-advancement, meeting, feud, vendetta, conciliation, of rabble-rousers, fist fights (as it used to be), embraces, drunks (again as it used to be) and collective rivers of animal sweat. It is a reminder that no matter how the country might pretend it has grown up and become tidy in its manners, bodiless in its legislative language, hygienic in its separation of high politics from private life, that the roots still come grubby from the soil, and that politics in America is still different from politics anywhere else because the politics has arisen out of the immediate needs, ambitions, and cupidities of the people, that our politics still smell of the bedroom and the kitchen, rather than having descended to us from the chill punctilio of aristocratic negotiation.

So. The Sports Arena was new, too pretty of course, tasteless in its design—it was somehow pleasing that the acoustics were so bad for one did not wish the architects well; there had been so little imagination in their design, and this arena would have none of the harsh grandeur of Madison Square Garden when it was aged by spectators' phlegm and feet over the next twenty years. Still it had some atmosphere; seen from the streets, with the spectators moving to the ticket gates, the bands playing, the green hot-shot special editions of the Los Angeles newspapers being hawked by the newsboys, there was a touch of the air of promise that precedes a bullfight, not something so good as the approach to the Plaza Mexico, but good, let us say, like the entrance into El Toreo of Mexico City, another architectural monstrosity, also with seats painted, as I remember, in rose-pink, and dark, milky sky-blue.

Inside, it was also different this nominating day. On Monday and Tuesday the air had been desultory, no one listened to the speakers, and everybody milled from one easy chatting conversation to another—it had been like a tepid Kaffeeklatsch for fifteen thousand people. But today there was a whip of anticipation in the air, the seats on the floor were filled, the press section was working, and in the gallery people were sitting in the aisles.

Sam Rayburn had just finished nominating Johnson as one came in, and the rebel yells went up, delegates started filing out of their seats and climbing over seats, and a pullulating dance of bodies and bands began to snake through the aisles, the posters jogging and whirling in time to the music. The dun color of the floor (faces, suits, seats and floor boards), so monotonous the first two days, now lit up with life as if an iridescent caterpillar had emerged from a fold of wet leaves. It was more vivid than one had expected, it was right, it felt finally like a convention, and from up close when one got down to the floor (where your presence was illegal and so consummated by sneaking in one time as demonstrators were going out, and again by slipping a five-dollar bill to a guard) the nearness to the demonstrators took on high color, that electric vividness one feels on the side lines of a football game when it is necessary to duck back as the ballcarrier goes by, his face tortured in the concentration of the moment, the thwomp of his tackle as acute as if one had been hit oneself.

That was the way the demonstrators looked on the floor. Nearly all had the rapt, private look of a passion or a tension which would finally be worked off by one's limbs, three hundred football players, everything from seedy delegates with jowl-sweating shivers to livid models, paid for their work that day, but stomping out their beat on the floor with the hypnotic adulatory grimaces of ladies who had lived for Lyndon these last ten years.

Then from the funereal rostrum, whose color was not so rich as mahogany nor so dead as a cigar, came the last of the requests for the delegates to take their seats. The seconding speeches began, one minute each; they ran for three and four, the minor-league speakers running on the longest as if the electric antenna of television was the lure of the Sirens, leading them out. Bored cheers applauded their concluding Götterdämmerungen and the nominations were open again. A favorite son, a modest demonstration, five seconding speeches, tedium.

Next was Kennedy's occasion. Governor Freeman of Minnesota made the speech. On the second or third sentence his television prompter jammed, an accident. Few could be aware of it at the moment; the speech seemed merely flat and surprisingly void of bravura. He was obviously no giant of extempore. Then the demonstration. Well-run, bigger than Johnson's, jazzier, the caliber of the costumes and decorations better chosen: the placards were broad enough, "Let's Back Jack," the floats were garish, particularly a papier-mâché or plastic balloon of Kennedy's head, six feet in diameter, which had nonetheless the slightly shrunken, over-red, rubbery look of a toy for practical jokers in one of those sleazy off-Time Square magic-and-gimmick stores; the band was suitably corny; and yet one had the impression this demonstration had been designed by some hands-to-hip interior decorator who said, "Oh, joy, let's have fun, let's make this *true* beer hall."

Besides, the personnel had something of the Kennedy *élan*, those paper hats designed to look like straw boaters with Kennedy's face on the crown, and small photographs of him on the ribbon, those hats which had come to symbolize the crack speed of the Kennedy team, that Madison Avenue cachet which one finds in bars like P. J. Clarke's, the elegance always giving its subtle echo of the Twenties so that the raccoon coats seem more numerous than their real count, and the colored waistcoats are measured by the charm they would have drawn from Scott Fitzgerald's eye. But there, it occurred to one for the first time that Kennedy's middle name was just that, Fitzgerald, and the tone of his crack lieutenants, the unstated style, was true to Scott. The legend of Fitzgerald had an army at last, formed around the self-image in the mind of every superior Madison Avenue opportunist that he was hard, he was young, he was In, his conversation was lean as wit, and if the work was not always scrupulous, well the style could aspire. If there came a good day . . . he could meet the occasion.

The Kennedy snake dance ran its thirty lively minutes, cheered its seconding speeches, and sat back. They were so sure of winning, there had been so many victories before this one, and this one had been scouted and managed so well, that hysteria could hardly be the mood. Besides, everyone was waiting for the Stevenson barrage which should be at least diverting. But now came a long tedium. Favorite sons were nominated, fat mayors shook their hips, seconders told the word to constituents back in Ponderwaygot County, treacly demonstrations tried to hold the floor, and the afternoon went by; Symington's hour came and went, a good demonstration, good as Johnson's (for good cause—they had pooled their demonstrators). More favorite sons, Governor Docking of Kansas declared "a genius" by one of his lady speakers in a tense go-back-to-religion voice. The hours went by, two, three, four hours, it seemed forever before they would get to Stevenson. It was evening when Senator Eugene McCarthy of Minnesota got up to nominate him.

The gallery was ready, the floor was responsive, the demonstrators were milling like bulls in their pen waiting for the *toril* to fly open—it would have been hard not to wake the crowd up, not to make a good speech. McCarthy made a great one. Great it was by the measure of convention oratory, and he held the crowd like a matador, timing their *oles!*, building them up, easing them back, correcting any sag in attention, gathering their emotion, discharging it, creating new emotion on the wave of the last, driving his passes tighter and tighter as he readied for the kill. "Do not reject this man who made us all proud to be called Democrats, do not leave this prophet without honor in his own party." One had not heard a speech like this since 1948 when Vito Marcantonio's voice, his harsh, shrill, bitter, street urchin's voice screeched through the loud-speakers at Yankee Stadium and lashed seventy thousand people into an uproar.

"There was only one man who said let's talk sense to the American people," McCarthy went on, his muleta furled for the *naturales*. "There was only one man who said let's talk sense to the American people," he repeated. "He said the promise of America is the promise of greatness. This was his call to greatness. . . . Do not forget this man. . . . Ladies and Gentlemen, I present to you not the favorite son of one state, but the favorite son of the fifty states, the favorite son of every country he has visited, the favorite son of every country which has not seen him but is secretly thrilled by his name." Bedlam. The kill. "Ladies and Gentlemen, I present to you Adlai Stevenson of Illinois." Ears and tail. Hooves and bull. A roar went up like the roar one heard the day Bobby Thomson hit his home run at the Polo Grounds and the Giants won the pennant from the Dodgers in the third playoff game of the 1951 season. The demonstration cascaded onto the floor, the gallery came to its feet, the Sports Arena sounded like the inside of a marching drum. A tidal pulse of hysteria, exaltation, defiance, exhilaration, anger and roaring desire flooded over the floor. The cry which had gone up on McCarthy's last sentence had not paused for breath in five minutes, and troop after troop of demonstrators jammed the floor (the Stevenson people to be scolded the next day for having collected floor passes and sent them out to bring in new demonstrators) and still the sound mounted. One felt the convention coming apart. There was a Kennedy girl in the seat in front of me, the Kennedy hat on her head, a dimpled healthy brunette; she had sat silently through McCarthy's speech, but now, like a woman paying her respects to the power of natural thrust, she took off her hat and began to clap herself. I saw a writer I knew in the next aisle; he had spent a year studying the Kennedy machine in order to write a book on how a nomination is won. If Stevenson stampeded the convention, his work was lost. Like a reporter at a mine cave-in I inquired the present view of the widow. "Who can think," was the answer, half frantic, half elated, "just watch it, that's all." I found a cool one, a New York reporter, who smiled in rueful respect. "It's the biggest demonstration I've seen since Wendell Willkie's in 1940," he said, and added, "God, if Stevenson takes it, I can wire my wife and move the family on to Hawaii."

"I don't get it."

"Well, every story I wrote said it was locked up for Kennedy."

Still it went on, twenty minutes, thirty minutes, the chairman could hardly be heard, the demonstrators refused to leave. The lights were turned out, giving a sudden theatrical shift to the sense of a crowded church at midnight, and a new roar went up, louder, more passionate than anything heard before. It was the voice, it was the passion, if one insisted to call it that, of everything in America which was defeated, idealistic, innocent, alienated, outside and Beat, it was the potential voice of a new third of the nation whose psyche was ill from cultural malnutrition, it was powerful, it was extraordinary, it was larger than the decent, humorous, finicky, half-noble man who had called it forth, it was a cry from the Thirties when Time was simple, it was a resentment of the slick technique, the oiled gears, and the superior generals of Fitzgerald's Army; but it was also—and for this reason one could not admire it altogether, except with one's excitement—it was also the plea of the bewildered who hunger for simplicity again, it was the adolescent counterpart of the boss's depression before the unpredictable dynamic of Kennedy as President, it was the return to the sentimental dream of Roosevelt rather than the approaching nightmare of history's oncoming night, and it was inspired by a terror of the future as much as a revulsion of the present.

Fitz's Army held; after the demonstration was finally down, the convention languished for ninety minutes while Meyner and others were nominated, a fatal lapse of time because Stevenson had perhaps a chance to stop Kennedy if the voting had begun on the echo of the last cry for him, but in an hour and a half depression crept in again and emotions spent, the delegates who had wavered were rounded into line. When the vote was taken, Stevenson had made no gains. The brunette who had taken off her hat was wearing it again, and she clapped and squealed when Wyoming delivered the duke and Kennedy was in. The air was sheepish, like the mood of a suburban couple who forgive each other for cutting in and out of somebody else's automobile while the country club dance is on. Again, tonight, no miracle would occur. In the morning the papers would be moderate in their description of Stevenson's last charge.

*A Sketch of the Republicans Gathered
in Convention: The Choice Between the
Venturesome and the Safe; What May
Happen at Three O'clock in the Morning
on a Long Dark Night*

One did not go to the other convention. It was seen on television, and so too much cannot be said of that. It did however confirm one's earlier bias that the Republican Party was still a party of church ushers, undertakers, choirboys, prison wardens, bank presidents, small-town police chiefs, state troopers, psychiatrists, beauty-parlor operators, corporation executives, Boy-Scout leaders, fraternity presidents, tax-board assessors, community leaders, surgeons, Pullman porters, head nurses and the fat sons of rich fathers. Its candidate would be given the manufactured image of an ordinary man, and his campaign, so far as it was a psychological campaign (and this would be far indeed), would present him as a simple, honest, dependable, hard-working, ready-to-learn, modest, humble, decent, sober young man whose greatest qualification for president was his profound abasement before the glories of the Republic, the stability of the mediocre, and his own unworthiness. The apocalyptic hour of Uriah Heep.

It would then be a campaign unlike the ones which had preceded it. Counting by the full spectrum of complete Right to absolute Left, the political differences would be minor, but what would be not at all minor was the power of each man to radiate his appeal into some fundamental depths of the American character. One would have an inkling at last if the desire of America was for drama or stability, for adventure or monotony. And this, this appeal to the psychic direction America would now choose for itself was the element most promising about this election, for it gave the possibility that the country might be able finally to rise above the deadening verbiage of its issues, its politics, its jargon, and live again by an image of itself. For in some part of themselves the people might know (since these candidates were not old enough to be revered) that they had chosen one young man for his mystery, for his promise that the country would grow or disintegrate by the unwilling charge he gave to the intensity of the myth, or had chosen another young man for his unstated oath that he would do all in his power to keep the myth buried and so convert the remains of Renaissance man as rapidly as possible into mass man. One might expect them to choose the enigma in preference to the deadening certainty. Yet one must doubt America's bravery. This lurching, unhappy, pompous and most corrupt nation—could it have the courage finally to take on a new image for itself, was it brave enough to put into office not only one of its ablest men, its most efficient, its most conquistadorial (for Kennedy's capture of the Democratic Party deserves the word), but also one of its more mysterious men (the national psyche must shiver in its sleep at the image of Mickey Mantle-cum-Lindbergh in office, and a First Lady with an eighteenth-century face). Yes, America was at last engaging the fate of its myth, its consciousness about to be accelerated or cruelly depressed in its choice between two young men in their forties who, no matter how close, dull, or indifferent their stated politics might be, were radical poles apart, for one was sober, the apotheosis of opportunistic lead, all radium spent, the other handsome as a prince in the unstated aristocracy of the American dream. So, finally, would come a choice which history had never presented to a nation before—one could vote for glamour or for ugliness, a staggering and most stunning choice—would the nation be brave enough to enlist the romantic dream of itself, would it vote for the image in the mirror of its unconscious, were the people indeed brave enough to hope for an acceleration of Time, for that new life of drama which would come from choosing a son to lead them who was heir apparent to the psychic loins? One could pause: it might be more difficult to be a President than it ever had before. Nothing less than greatness would do.

Yet if the nation voted to improve its face, what an impetus might come to the arts, to the practices, to the lives and to the imagination of the American. If the nation so voted. But one knew the unadmitted specter in the minds of the Democratic delegates: that America would go to sleep on election eve with the polls promising Kennedy a victory on the day to come, yet in its sleep some millions of Democrats and

Independents would suffer a nightmare before the mystery of uncharted possibilities their man would suggest, and in a terror of all the creativities (and some violences) that mass man might now have to dare again, the undetermined would go out in the morning to vote for the psychic security of Nixon the way a middle-aged man past adventure holds to the stale bread of his marriage. Yes, this election might be fearful enough to betray the polls and no one in America could plan the new direction until the last vote was counted by the last heeler in the last ambivalent ward, no one indeed could know until then what had happened the night before, what had happened at three o'clock in the morning on that long dark night of America's search for a security cheaper than her soul.

POSTSCRIPT TO THE THIRD PRESIDENTIAL PAPER

This piece had more effect than any other single work of mine, and I think this is due as much to its meretriciousness as to its merits. I was forcing a reality, I was bending reality like a field of space to curve the time I wished to create. I was not writing with the hope that perchance I could find reality by being sufficiently honest to perceive it, but on the contrary was distorting reality in the hope that thereby I could affect it. I was engaging in an act of propaganda.

During the period after Kennedy was nominated, there was great indifference to him among the Democrats I knew; disaffection was general; outright aversion was felt by most of the liberal Left—the white collar SANE sort of professional who had been for Stevenson. The Kennedy machine worked well to overcome apathy and inertia; so did the debates with Nixon. Through the early Fall, before the election, people who had been going along with the Democratic Party for years began somewhat resignedly to accept their fate: they would go out after all and vote for John F. Kennedy. But there was no real enthusiasm, no drive. My piece came at the right time for him—three weeks before the election. It added the one ingredient Kennedy had not been able to find for the stew—it made him seem exciting, it made the election appear important. Around New York there was a turn in sentiment; one could feel it; Kennedy now had glamour.

As will be seen in the essay on Jackie Kennedy, I took to myself some of the critical credit for his victory. Whether I was right or wrong in fact may not be so important as its psychological reality in my own mind. I had invaded No Man's Land, I had created an archetype of Jack Kennedy in the public mind which might or might not be true, but which would induce people to vote for him, and so would tend to move him into the direction I had created. Naturally there would be forces thrusting him back out of No Man's Land, back to conventional politics, but so far as I had an effect, it was a Faustian one, much as if I had made a pact with Mephisto to give me an amulet, an art-work, which might arouse a djinn in history.

The night Kennedy was elected, I felt a sense of woe, as if I had made a terrible error, as if somehow I had betrayed the Left and myself. It was a spooky emotion. In the wake of the election, one note was clear—the strength the Left had been gaining in the last years of Eisenhower's administration would now be diluted, preempted, adulterated, converted and dissolved by the compromises and hypoc-risies of a new Democratic administration. And so I began to follow Kennedy's career with obsession, as if I were responsible and guilty for all which was bad, dangerous, or potentially totalitarian within it. And the papers which follow are written under the shadow of this private fact, this conviction that I was now among the guilty, another genteel traitor in the land.

THE FOURTH PRESIDENTIAL PAPER

—Foreign Affairs

An Open Letter to
John Fitzgerald Kennedy and Fidel Castro

The letter to Fidel Castro was written in short sessions of manic work over several weeks, writing usually when drunk and late at night. But it was gone over in the mornings when sober, and it was put together and taken apart many times. It was made finally as good as I could make it, which may not be that good, * *for I was in a state of huge excitement at the time, I was running for Mayor of New York, I had just begun my campaign, the Presidential election was upon us and then over, and I was going to announce my campaign two days before Thanksgiving with a press conference. There I would read the Open Letter to Fidel Castro. That was to be on Tuesday, and on the preceding Saturday night I threw a big night at my apartment. It was a combination of a birthday party for my friend Roger Donoghue, and an unofficial kickoff for the Mayoralty campaign. The evening ended in fights on the street, debacle, disaster, a stabbing—my wife. What my friends were later so kind as to call The Trouble. The "Open Letter to Fidel Castro" with its prepared one hundred mimeographed copies in Spanish (Eugenio Villacuña had done an exquisite translation which allowed the letter to read as if it had been written originally in Spanish) never went to any newspapers at all. It stayed in the*

---

*In fact, rereading the letter to Castro, one cannot avoid the glum conviction that much of the prose is sentimental and bad. A few paragraphs seem better than ever, however, and so I took the liberty to put them in italics for this edition. The reader in a hurry may skip the rest.

71

drawer for months. One got out of Bellevue, one did a little work
again. The marriage broke up. The man wasn't good enough. The
woman wasn't good enough. A set of psychic stabbings took place.

In Deaths for the Ladies *there is a fragment written about a week
before the marriage was finally lost. It is a companion piece to the
letter to Fidel Castro, and can be found by those who are curious in
Appendix C which ends this book.*

*A month later, in April, came the Bay of Pigs. There is no vast need
to dwell on the outrage, fury, sense of betrayal, so forth, so forth, that
one was feeling. Indeed it is talked about in the piece on Jacqueline
Kennedy. No, these emotions will be found evident in the writings of
the open letters as will also be evident how furious I was at myself. The
jeering but all sophomoric tone adopted for addressing the President
is proof enough.*

*But of course Kennedy had committed one of the blunders of the
century. We can only be grateful he did not compound the blunder by
sending in a force massive enough to conquer Castro. We would still
be occupying Cuba; every day bodies of American soldiers and
Marines would be found ambushed by guerrillas in the hills. All of
Latin America and South America would be moving silently and
steadily toward the Communists. This way the road was left open for
Khrushchev to commit a blunder as large as Kennedy's; when the
atomic missiles were sent to Cuba, Khrushchev was returning back to
America the fifty years of political advantage Kennedy had given him.
There may even be a political principle here that one large blunder
disturbs the balance sufficiently to create another.*

*The Bay of Pigs remains a mystery. One can doubt if it will ever be
found out how it came to pass, or who in fact was the real force behind
it. But there is a tool of investigation for political mysteries. It is
Lenin's formula: "Whom?" Whom does this benefit? Who prospers
from a particular act?*

*Well, whom? Kennedy and the liberal center did not gain honor
from the Bay of Pigs. Castro most certainly did not gain an advantage
for he was forced now finally to commit his hand altogether to Russia.
The Left in America, that fine new Left of Pacifists and beatniks and
Negro militants and college students who just knew something was
bad—this Left certainly did not benefit from the Bay of Pigs because
they were now divided about Castro even as an earlier generation of
Leftists had been divided by the Moscow Trials.*

No, the people who benefited from the Bay of Pigs were the people who wanted a serious Communist threat to exist within ninety miles of America's shore. They were the people who had taken the small and often absurd American Communist Party and had tried to exaggerate its menace to the point where the country could be pistol-whipped into silence at the mention of its name. They had infiltrated this party until even the Saturday Evening Post *offered hints that a large part of the American Communist Party was by now made up of FBI men. These were indeed the people, these secret policemen, who would face an excruciating dilemma if the Communist threat disappeared altogether in America. Because then what would they do? If there were no Communists, the FBI would be required by the logic of their virility to take on the next greatest danger to American life, the Mafia, and how were they ever to do that, how were they to investigate the Mafia without ripping the Republican and Democratic parties up from top to bottom? Because the Republican Party was supported by the Mafia, and the Democratic Party was supported by the Mafia. Through and through. Down at the low level where the little heelers and the small cops got their bite at the local bar, and up at the high level where the monster housing projects were contracted out, and the superhighways, and the real estate grafts. No, it was safer by far that Cuba go Communist. That would be good for the FBI, and it would be good for the Chinese Communists who wished to increase the pressure on Khrushchev's back. Whom? asked Lenin, who benefits? And the answer is clear. All the totalitarians of the world were benefited by the Bay of Pigs and the missiles which followed.*

Dear Jack:

Back in a certain nice Summer before a long Fall, I wrote an essay for one of our large garish national magazines about the Democratic Convention, the city of Los Angeles, and John Fitzgerald Kennedy. In that piece, I may have made the error of sailing against the stereotype that you were a calculating untried over-ambitious and probably undeserving young stud who came from a very wealthy and much unloved family.

I took a hard skimming tack against the wind of that probability and ventured instead into the notion that you gave promise of becoming the first major American hero in more than a decade. I also upheld the private hope that you were—dare I use the word, it has become so abused—that you were Hip, that your sense of history was subtle because it extracted as much from flesh as fact. Finally, I suggested that America's mutilated vision of a renaissance might find new and necessary life in that inevitably romantic and rather royal image you and your wife would furnish all us minor-league soap operas with our malnourished electronic psyches.

Obviously, I hoped you would get in. I did my best to help you. I wrote 13,000 words of rich chocolate prose to balm the flaccid hearts of all those sick little Democrats I know, and I think I even made the club. I may be one of the 5000 charter members who can boast that: Jack would not have gotten in without me. Of course Jim Farley, Jake Arvey, Lyn Johnson, J. Edgar, and even old Dick Nix (America can't stand pat) also figure they made the real difference in your 100,000 votes. But blow it. I don't know that my Narcissism is kept tasty any longer by being part of the club. I don't get much pleasure in saying this, but I think you are beginning to act a little like all bad hippies—responsibility is turning you to plumber's lead.

I mean: Wasn't there anyone around to give you the lecture on Cuba? Don't you sense the enormity of your mistake—you invade a country without understanding its music.

You listen to intelligence agents and fail to interpret the style of the prose in which they submit their reports. You, with your shrewd sense of character, neglect to see that none of your boys and men can tell you the truth about Cuba because it would flagellate them too psychically to consider the existential (that is, indescribable) quality of what they report. So they turn nuances into facts, and lose other nuances, and mangle facts into falsities. It keeps you perhaps from recognizing what all the world knows, that we have driven Cuba inch by inch to alliance with the Soviet, as deliberately and insanely as a man setting out to cuckold himself.

But allow me to offer you an unsolicited guide. Six months ago I intended to run for Mayor of New York. I planned to publish an open letter to Fidel Castro as the first rocket in the campaign. Through October and the beginning of November, I worked at the letter, polished it here, cut it there. Then a rocket went off in a direction I had not anticipated and I smashed a thousand pieces in people around me.

That letter is one of the broken pieces. It made no sense to publish it any longer since I had lost the right to use my name in any happy way.

Now, however, you come to my aid. It occurs to me that that prose, now half a year old, will help you to understand Cuba no less well than you have managed to do so far on the basis of those marvelous reports which come in from your Mr. Allen Dulles. I mean: think of all the studs and girlygoos in CIA who held hands and toes and told each other the invasion was bound to succeed. Success, America!

The Letter to Castro

Dear Fidel Castro:

I have said nothing in public about you and your country since I signed a statement last year in company with Baldwin, Capote, Sartre, and Tynan that we believe in "Fair Play for Cuba." But now I am old enough to believe that one must be ready to be faithful to one's truth. So, Fidel Castro, I announce to the City of New York that you gave all of us who are alone in this country, and usually not speaking to one another, some sense that there were heroes left in the world. One felt life in one's cold overargued blood as one picked up in our newspapers the details of your voyage.

But I go too fast. Since this is an open letter, and thus meant for the people of New York as much as for you, I suppose I must write first of events with which you are more than familiar.

Back in December, 1956, you landed near Niquero in the Oriente of Cuba with 82 men and a few arms. Your plan was to ignite an insurrection which would rid Cuba of Batista in a few weeks. Instead, you were to lose all but 12 of these men in the first few days, you were to wander through fields and forests in the dark, without real food or water, living on sugar-cane for five days and five nights. In the depth of this disaster, you were to announce to the few men still with you: "The days of the dictatorship are numbered."

"This man is crazy," one of them admits he said to himself.

It took you more than 20 days to reach the summit of the Pico Turquino, the high peak in Cuba, high in the Sierra Maestra. You reached it on Christmas Eve. There you stayed for two years. For much of that time you were no more than a symbol.

Through Cuba passed the word that 12 men lived on a mountain top,

12 men who had sworn to destroy the tyranny. It was incredible. What that token of resistance came to signify! Day after day, month by month, grew a spirit of rebellion in Cuba.

As the underground developed, so developed Batista's methods of torture, his excesses, his murders, his unrecountable atrocities, at last so open and so foul that he ended by alienating some of the wealthy, the well-born, the best of his own support.

For those two years your army discovered itself; your skill as a military leader developed art, your diplomatic talents untied the complexities of an underground choking with factions and old feuds.

You survived skirmishes, negotiations, and battles; you suffered a major defeat, and recovered quickly enough to hold off 14 battalions of Batista's army with no more than 300 of your own men, you came at last out of the hills to defeat an army of 30,000 professional soldiers. Two years and a month after the disaster of your landing, you were able to enter Havana in triumph.

It was not unheroic. Truth, it was worthy of Cortes.

It was as if the ghost of Cortes had appeared in our century riding Zapata's white horse. You were the first and greatest hero to appear in the world since the Second War.

Better than that, you had a face. One had friends with faces like yours. In silence, many of us gave you our support. In silence. We did not have an organization to address you, we talked very little about you, we said: "Castro, good guy," and let it go, but all the while you were giving us the idea that everything was not hopeless. There has been a new spirit in America since you entered Havana. I think you must be given credit for some part of a new and better mood which has been coming to America.

Now, you did not feel friendly to my country when you had won your war. There was the bitter memory of our Ambassadors, Mr. Gardner and Mr. Smith, and the photographs they took all too often with Batista and his friends; there was the recollection of the American rockets which had been sold to the Cuban government at a time when Batista's Air Force was burning the huts of peasants in your hills; there were the headlines in Cuban newspapers: DULLES TOASTS BATISTA which appeared the day before Batista held his last false election. You must have wondered why Dulles had chosen that particular day to visit Ambassador Arroyo at the Cuban Embassy in Washington. You may even have wondered why our newspapers chose to print so many of Batista's stories that you were Communist.

Still the situation was not very bad. Much of our press gave you good treatment here, and some of our largest newspapers and magazines welcomed your victory. A general wave of congratulation passed through our mass-media. For a few days, you were popular in America.

Then you had your public executions. I suppose tragedy cannot exist without irony. If Batista's people had just been shot, all 500 of them, shot in their homes, their bars, the automobiles in which they were fleeing, our newspapers would have complained a bit, but it would have been attributed to the excesses of a victorious army, a retaliation in kind upon Batista's assassins.

You, however, were interested in justice, in proclamation, in propaganda—you were saying to the people of Cuba: "I am not a bandit like the ones who come before me, I am the leader of a revolution—I execute the torturers of the past before the eyes of the present."

Our newspapers erupted against you. They used the executions to condemn everything in your regime. One would have thought you were almost a successor to Adolf Hitler the way they excoriated you because 500 Batistas were condemned to death in trials of public spectacle, 500 cut-throats who had maimed the heads, crushed the hearts, and disfigured the genitalia of your men and your women. The worst of our newspapers screamed with rage and terror. As if you were killing them.

And you were. Like Bolivar, you were sending the wind of new rebellion to our lungs. You were making it possible for us to breathe again. You were aiding our war.

But then, I do not know if you can understand our war here.

In Cuba, hatred runs over into the love of blood; in America all too few blows are struck into flesh. We kill the spirit here, we are experts at that. We use psychic bullets and kill each other cell by cell.

We live in a country very different from Cuba. We have had a tyranny here, but it did not have the features of Batista; it was a tyranny one breathed but could not define; it was felt as no more than a slow deadening of the best of our possibilities, a tension we could not name which was the sum of our frustrations. We all knew that the best of us used up our memories in long nights of drinking, exhausted our vision in secret journeys of the mind; our more stable men and women of some little good will watched the years go by—their idealism sank into apathy. By law we had a free press; almost no one spoke his thoughts. By custom we had a free ballot; was there ever a choice? We were a league of silent defeated men who could not even assent on which were the true battles we lost. In silence we gave you our support. You were aiding us, you were giving us psychic ammunition, you were aiding us in that desperate silent struggle we have been fighting with sick dead hearts against the cold insidious cancer of the power that governs us, you were giving us new blood to fight our mass communications, our police, our secret police, our corporations, our empty politicians, our clergymen, our editors, our cold frightened bewildered bullies who govern a machine made out of people they no longer understand, you were giving us hope they would not always win.

That is why America persecuted you. That is why our newspapers made their subtle distortions, lied about your accomplishments, put dirt on your name, wrote in a prose of cheap glow that you were sick and would certainly die in a few months, and were even more furious when somehow you did not die, and no power agreeable to America arose in Cuba to steal your power. That is why they mocked your speech at the U.N.

They had reported you were very ill: it did not vouch well for their reliability that now you spoke for four and a half hours. How can anyone talk that long they say now and giggle nervously. He must be a compulsive, they say. They do not admit to themselves that no one here in this country dares to talk for more than four and a half minutes they are so afraid they will give themselves away.

Now, at the moment, revolted by the cheap muck of the most cess-filled brains in our land, disheartened by the impossibility of receiving a fair report from us, you are obviously getting ready to commit your political fortune to Khrushchev. I do not know the complexities of the situation. Maybe no one does. We hear everything here. We hear that you are committed completely to the Russians, we hear that you are still your own man. The combinations offered are endless. What worries us is that the facts are too many to be able to know what one reads.

I would guess you were not ever a Communist, that you are not now—you have always had too much of a private vision to be Communist—I would speculate of you, sir, that you came to power ready to make a revolution which could give more of what is noble to the people. You were simply bewildered when the American press turned on you. Then it was I would guess that you began to give the Communists your ear. What an argument they had now. "Look," they must have said, "why believe America's lies about the Communists, why believe them when you see how they lie about you?"

Well, we lie about the Communists. They lie as well. We deaden the life of millions by hypocrisy and go on to claim we are the hope of civilization; they liquidate the life of millions and argue they are the imagination of the future.

Of course it may not be agreeable to listen to this now. You have a new friend. He was good to you at a time when my country promulgated its disgrace. You are Latin. Your honor is to be loyal. Still, I must say that as one of your sympathizers I do not trust your new friend. He is a wise peasant bully. Yet an intellectual should not forget that he came to power because of one exceptional ability: he was able to live as a flea in the stumpy tail of a wild old bear named Josef Stalin; this old bear was notorious for eating his tail. At the end Khrushchev was the only flea left who had strength. Perhaps he was the flea closest to the root. Since then he has grown big as a man.

Of course you may not like these words about Khrushchev. At a time when our large newspapers were writing like small-town gossips about the condition in which you left your rooms in one of our New York hotels (what do the same rooms look like after a convention of American salesmen have left, you must have wondered), at a time when you could not make a move in our city without being able to read the next day in the newspapers about it as an act sinister or foolish, Khrushchev had the genius to kiss you on the cheek for our photographers, and so restore your honor.

He has good manners, that man—I suppose a part of you will like him forever because of his embrace that day. But revolutionaries are different from Commissars, and a kiss from one is not the same as a kiss from the other. Khrushchev kissed many before you, and he has signed the papers which removed them forever. He is a Commissar—they like to kiss. But Commissars never made a revolution.

So Khrushchev will never be able to understand that you are serious. He will think he is a realist, and you are an actor. Realists endure, goes the logic of Khrushchev, actors can be replaced. Khrushchev will never understand that when no personal authority

exists in a leader, a country sinks into the authority of public relations—it has a vacuum at its center. Khrushchev will never understand
that Cuba does not have its strength because the Communists give you
arms but because so many of the people still believe in you, they cry
out for you to cover yourself when you speak in the rain.

Look! Plain words. I hear from the source of a source that the
situation is bad in your country now. I hear Communists control Cuba
and shut you into the psychic prison of their encirclement, I hear they
manipulate you to say the things which will most irritate our press into
striking back in the way which will most irritate you. By every step of
this logic you distrust your new friends less, hate America more, and
thus begin to prepare yourself for a war you may even begin to desire
as a sedative to personal madness, so great is your rage at the
monuments of *mierda* laid upon the cross of your expedition down
from the peak into the city, so great is your anguish at the filth you
must breathe to keep alive the simple idea of the mountain air: one
must free the people and give them life. This is what I hear. I do not
want to believe it, but I can no longer ignore what I hear, because my
private sources are people still sympathetic to Cuba and to you. They
go on to declare that the Communists want America to attack. Their
hope—so goes the argument of my source—is that America will be
incited by you to invade Cuba, create a new Korea, and alienate the
people of Latin and South America forever. As a Communist strategy
it is excellent. Of course Cuba will lose another 58 years. But the
Communists are used to considering small nations expendable—it is
part of their pride that they will sacrifice their followers.

It is not so difficult for them. In the other country they do not kill
people—they liquidate. Certain people become fascinating, they are
too rich in their private time—the State does not care to afford them.
They disappear. Friends do not even know if they are dead—one
cannot hold a funeral in their memory. One knows just that it is better
not to talk about the missing friend. A new shame chases the other.
Remembrance of the past turns to fog.

Fidel, is this what you wish for Cuba, for your Cuba which is so
alive? I cannot believe it. Your people went through a little too much.
They are not statistics. You cannot want them to talk like machines of
the state in the new Cuba. You cannot. You must play for power, not
commit yourself to it. So do not give up on my country too quickly.

I know it is a bad place, I know well how bad it is, I know millions will be squeezed out of existence here in the center of prosperity, stricken by the deadness of a life which can find no love. Yet one thing will be said for my country. They allow me to speak my mind in a way I never could in the other country. You who are a poet will know this is a freedom some of us do not want to live without.

Besides, in my country, it is possible the people are better than their government: they could come to understand you if you would think of how to speak to us.

I do not expect the way is to listen to your present advisers. You would do better to hire a public-relations man from our Madison Ave. They are corrupt, our men of Madison, so corrupt they will work as well for you as for the corporation. Fact, they will work better. By now, they hate our country more than you could, they know it better.

Bad humor. Forgive it. I have a proposal. Address an open letter in your name to Ernest Hemingway. Many would say—I am one of them—that he has been our greatest writer. It is certain he created my generation—he told us to be brave in a bad world and to be ready to die alone.

Actually he is afraid of our country. He is a very brave old man, I believe, but he does not have a cancer-detector, so he stays away from us, from our smog-ridden, atom-haunted city. He prefers Cuba, as doubtless you know. He has lived there off and on for 20 years. He no longer writes to us. Maybe a letter once in a while. We do not talk about him any longer. Some of us are bitter about him. We feel he has deserted us and produced no work good enough to justify his silence.

There are many of us who will curse his memory if he dies in silence.

So do the old man a favor. Send him an invitation to come back to Cuba, at his own expense or at yours. He may not want to come. He has his work to do, he has a big book on which he has been working for 15 years. If this work is going well it would be an excessive sacrifice for him to interrupt it. But, then, he may not mind an interruption. In the past 15 years he has interrupted his work many times to write about other things. He may come to see that it would not be so very bad to write about you. If he agrees, it is your duty to those of us who care about your fate to let him tell the world whether he likes what is happening with you or not.

Show the world that you will let a Nobel Prize writer who speaks the language of the country travel anywhere in your territory, unmolested, unobstructed, unindoctrinated. Let him come, let him get to know you if he wishes, hope that he will write something about Cuba, a paragraph, a line, a poem, a statement—whatever he says cannot be ignored in my country. The world will read what Hemingway has to say, the world will read it critically, because he will be making a history, he may even be preparing a ground on which you and our new President can meet.

Whether our new President is a good man, I do not know. I had no sense of his moral being the two brief times I talked to him. One had the impression he is a brave man and a complicated man, and he has intelligence. But I thought he had a taint I could not name. It is not an interesting taint, evil, decadent, or extraordinary, it was more a sense that he was dead and dull in little places where some of us are still alive. It is possible he does not understand or is lacking some of the necessary and vital emotions of most people.

I think it is not impossible he will become a great President, but I also think he could lead us into dictatorship. It is not only up to him, but to many of us, whether he becomes a good leader or a bad one. The question is whether he has a mind deep enough to comprehend the size of the disaster he has inherited here.

If America had a mind and one could stare into it, the landscape of our psyche might be bleak, gutted, scorched by 15 years of mindless government, all nerves withered by the management of men who were moral poltroons. Many of us have hope that Kennedy will help our national mind to see again, but of course one does not know. One does not want to hope too soon. I think Kennedy's statements on Cuba during the election campaign were ugly. They took away the enthusiasm one felt in voting for him. Still, one voted. It was the first time one voted in 12 years. It seemed self-evident he was superior to the other. You could not talk to the other. I think you could talk to our new President, I think he might come to recognize that if a man of Hemingway's age was willing to give up some important moment of his time to write new words about your country, that the culture of the world—that culture existing in every cultivated mind—would be judging Kennedy if he did not respond or react to Hemingway's view (whatever it might be) of your country. And Kennedy wishes to be considered a great man in the cultivated verdicts of history.

So respond to this letter, Fidel. There is value in it for you. If we get no word, it will come to mean that you care no longer about those who want to believe in you, it will come to mean that you have lost interest in all but your hatred of America. So you will then given strength to our enemies here; they will delight in your silence and your hatred.

But I do not know that you will give them such pleasure. You may still believe in that larger part of the world which endures in the possibility that neither the United States nor Russia will triumph, that there is a third way, that futures are not built nor civilizations kept alive by super-states, but that it is rather people who make history, people more brave, more talented, or more generous than there was any reason to be. You belong not to the United States nor to the Russians but to We of the Third Force. So long as you exist and belong neither to America nor to Russia, you give a bit of life to the best and most passionate men and women all over the earth, you are the answer to the argument of Commissars and Statesmen that revolutions cannot last, that they turn corrupt or total or eat their own. You are the one who can show the world that a revolutionary belongs to no one, that his actions cannot be predicted because he is possessed by a vision: he knows the world must grow better at a breathless rate or there will be no mankind. Just super-states, endless machines, and empty men who flee the night in all terror of eternity.

Still your brother,
Norman Mailer

Mr. President, I could say that letter to Fidel Castro makes me sad, because it might have accomplished a little, and did not have its chance. But, indeed, what chance? While the letter was being written we were training invasion armies in Florida and Texas and Guatemala and the Keys and other points and holes of the Caribbean. In the *Herald Tribune* of Tuesday, April 25, 1961, we read that:

> New information was revealed about Mr. Nixon's role in urging the Eisenhower Administration to act against Cuba. After Castro visited Washington in 1959, Mr. Nixon proposed in a memorandum that the United States help anti-Castro Cubans overthrow the regime. The State Department was divided and within the Administration Mr. Nixon was in a minority for a year. By March 1960, however, his view prevailed and the program for training anti-Castro forces was begun.

What a pity Nixon was not elected. If he had invaded Cuba, half of America would have cheered at our defeat. Yes, you are a danger,

Jack. You occupy the center like no Republican ever could.

No letter, no argument could have turned this issue. When one holds an invasion army whose roots are in United Fruit and the Commissars of Decency, one must use that army, or there is no peace for the authority.

So the test was made. The authority used its army. What America claimed was the truth of Cuba would now be observable as a working hypothesis: if Cuba was a miserable land seething with hatred of its leaders, such invasion would fire its own success.

Now, as gentlemen, we ought to obey the logic of our failure, face into the mirror of our tragedy and our comedy. Do we now see that we bent over and beseeched the Soviet Union to drive a spike into our bottom? Do we agree it may now be said by history that the Kennedy invasion of Cuba in 1961 put Communism permanently on the shores of Latin and South America? Their flag was planted in the Bahia de Cochinos, that Bay of Pigs our Intelligence chose for a landing.

Sad. A nation as large as ours, blinded by the lies of the men who feed us our news. With the best intention in the world, our reporters and our secret agents cannot tell the truth any longer, their habits for lying have grown so profound the lie shines with the clarity of a truth.

It may be that now there is only one answer left for us in Cuba. It is to begin again. Begin again. Take our hat in our hands and say we were wrong. We have been wrong for 58 years.

We do not expect you, Cuba, to trust us in a hurry, but we ask you to consider the possibility of forgiving us. We will no longer try to destroy your revolution. We recognize that we cannot win this way, we will merely have a war between Soviet tanks and planes and American tanks and planes, and Cuba will be destroyed, and our name will be loathed throughout the Western Hemisphere.

No, we will admit that we were wrong, that maybe we were criminally wrong to try to win Cuba by invasion. So now we ask you to believe that we can see our error, and that we want, yes, you will not believe us, but humbly we wish to fight with Russia in Cuba.

Not with guns, not even with ideas (because the ideas of democracies are too subtle and existential to war polemically with the clanking jargons of the total mind) but as styles. As liberties. We do it because we cannot leave you alone with Russia, lost to what we can offer. There is one way in which we are a greater nation than Russia. Our creative artists are greater. Our writers, our poets, our painters, our jazz musicians. We have a life in all our private arts which they do not possess.

Cuba, you can flourish more with the arts of our best styles than with theirs. So we will help you with your economy and pay the price of having tried first to injure it, and we will play the long slow stubborn painful game of winning your neutrality back from the Russians. Yes, we accept your revolution with all the political cess we will have to pay at home to those cess-filled centers where our Commissars of Decency prevail. We know that is the price we have to pay for the brutally stupid errors we have made and the fear we have had of Cuba's tropic air. But we do it, because we still wish to become a great nation. Only a nation so dedicated would dare to admit its mistake.

Will we say that, Jack?

In the pig's hole we will. You've cut the shape of your plan for history, and it smells. It smells rich and smug and scared of the power of the worst, dullest, and most oppressive men of our land. You will use brains but fear minds, seek for experts and eschew spirit, look for force and sap courage, promise sex and dull beauty. You will increase the power of this country and use up its marrow.

You are a virtuoso in political management but you will never understand the revolutionary passion which comes to those who were one way or another too poor to learn how good they might have been; the greediness of the rich had already crippled their youth.

Without this understanding you will never know what to do about Castro and Cuba. You will never understand that the man is the country, revolutionary, tyrannical, brilliant, extraordinary, hysterical, violent, passionate, brave as the best of animals, doomed perhaps to end in tragedy, but one of the great figures of the twentieth century, at the present moment a far greater figure than yourself.

Jack, if all your soldiers were saints you could not take Cuba, because your soldiers would arrive in the name of our land, and to the peasant of Cuba, Castro is now God and we in America are the Devil. Do you propose to get around that by putting higher I.Q.s into the seersuckers of the Central Intelligence Agency?

No, commander. You are in trouble. Your best troops now fear you are not deep enough to direct the destinies of our lives. And if you are not, the country will deaden a little more, even as it increases in its fevers, and the imagination of the best will begin to harden into the separate undergrounds of a new Left and a new Right, ready to war against the oppressive, flatulent, and totalitarian center of our beleaguered land.

Do not hold to that center, Jack, it is a pusillanimous sludge of liberal and conservative bankruptcies, a pus of old jargons which will whip into no militant history, but may be analyzed eventually by the chemists as the ingredient which smudges the ink on such mothers of the center as the *N. Y. Post*.

Your near-contemporary,

N. M.

P.S. I was in a demonstration the other day of five literary magazines (so help me) which marched in a small circle of protest against your intervention in Cuba. One of the pickets was a very tall poetess with black hair which reached near to her waist. She was dressed like a medieval varlet, and she carried a sign addressed to your wife:

JACQUELINE, VOUS AVEZ
PERDU VOS ARTISTES

Tin soldier, you are depriving us of the Muse.

Postscript to the Fourth Presidential Paper

There is a last irony in the Letter to Castro. Hemingway is gone; the missiles have replaced him. Yet Cuba has come near to full circle. Having gone all the way over to the Communists, there is a possibility they have now come some part of the way back. We could still do worse than to send good writers to Cuba, Castro could do worse than invite them. For of one thing we may be certain—the average American reporter writing for the average American paper is as well-equipped to discuss the complexities of Cuba and the nuances of Castro's personality as a horse is equipped to teach syntax.

I can think of a few writers to send: John Steinbeck, John Dos Passos, James T. Farrell, and Dwight Macdonald who always tells the truth as he sees it. James Baldwin, Saul Bellow perhaps, Truman

Capote. J. D. Salinger—let him try something interesting for once. Or James Jones—let him do something worthy for once. Ralph Ellison—who may contain the essence of the observer. Lionel Trilling, Alfred Kazin, Norman Podhoretz, Robert Lowell, Bernard Malamud, Vance Bourjaily, Tennessee Williams, Edward Albee, Arthur Miller. There are enough writers. I would like to be one of them but I am disqualified on too many counts. I have a vested interest in the health of the Cuban Revolution.

But it would be right if Castro has the wit to invite these writers, and let them move around. It would drive a wedge into the totalitarian certainties of the mass media's attitude to Cuba. The mass media knows their reports are worth nothing compared to the eye and voice of a serious writer. Like bad cowardly bulls, people in the mass media paw the ground when one comes near.

THE FIFTH PRESIDENTIAL PAPER

—The Existential Heroine

An Evening with Jackie Kennedy, or,
The Wild West of the East

Existential politics reveals itself with Jackie Kennedy. It is as if one stains a microscope slide with a well-chosen dye. Once inserted into politics, a lady betrays the difference between a person and their project. A man, particularly a political man, is often a project, and no more than a project—all of his person goes to the project. One need only think of Bobby Kennedy or Barry Goldwater; can one conceive of them as people separate from their purpose? But Jackie Kennedy is first a lady, and is a political force only after. That her power as a political force may be sizably more enormous than her real power as a woman is less to the point than that she produces a cross-fertilization of the categories of project and person. If one writes about her as a woman, one arouses political reactions; if one criticizes her political effect, the words read as an attack upon her. At a certain point in "An Evening with Jackie Kennedy" there is a reference to the First Lady's legs—this was seen by many conservative readers as an attack upon the flag. Toward the end of the piece, a somewhat formal assault on the value of her political contribution to her television show was treated in letters to Esquire *as an onslaught on her person.*

A lady of beauty caught willy-nilly in political life reveals the insubstantial existential nature of political acts. She shows that a political act is as fragile as a personal act: it may create a new reality or equally it may spoil one. And this disturbs the American need to believe that political life is as concrete and reasonable as the kind of

91

engineering which produces bridges. In fact, the recognition that political life is fragile arouses huge anxiety in many people. Small wonder if the press prefers to treat the President and his First Lady as impregnable institutions.

The reactions to my piece were therefore extreme. My friend Roger Donoghue, the former prizefighter, was sufficiently irritated when he read the manuscript to be unable to speak. We had been to the Griffith-Paret fight a short time before, we had witnessed the death of Benny Paret, and Donoghue finally said, "You're like Benny. You think you can go around taking punches to the head in order to give punches to the head, and you're going to get killed one of these days." Others were dubious that Esquire *would print the piece.*

They did without hesitation, or at least they never voiced an objection. Which may offer the appropriate opportunity to say something nice of Esquire—*they have been a good magazine to work for, and the freedom they offer must be twice the liberty one can find in other mass magazines.*

A few of you may remember that on February 14, last winter, our First Lady gave us a tour of the White House on television. For reasons to be explained in a while, I was in no charitable mood that night and gave Mrs. Kennedy a close scrutiny. Like anybody else, I have a bit of tolerance for my vices, at least those which do not get into the newspapers, but I take no pride in giving a hard look at a lady when she is on television. Ladies are created for an encounter face-to-face. No man can decide a lady is trivial until he has spent some minutes alone with her. Now while I have been in the same room with Jackie Kennedy twice, for a few minutes each time, it was never very much alone, and for that matter I do not think anyone's heart was particularly calm. The weather was too hectic. It was the Summer of 1960, after the Democratic Convention, before the presidential campaign had formally begun, at Hyannis Port, site of the Summer White House—those of you who know Hyannis ("High-anus," as the natives say) will know how funny is the title—all those motels and a Summer White House too: the Kennedy compound, an enclosure of three summer homes belonging to Joe Kennedy, Sr., RFK, and JFK, with a modest amount of lawn and beach to share among them. In those historic days the lawn was overrun with journalists, cameramen, magazine writers, politicians, delegations, friends and neighboring gentry, government intellectuals, family, a prince, some Massachusetts state troopers, and red-necked hard-nosed tourists patrolling outside the fence for a glimpse of the boy. He was much in evidence, a bit of everywhere that morning, including the lawn, and particularly handsome at times as one has described elsewhere (*Esquire*, November, 1960), looking like a good version of Charles Lindbergh at noon on a hot August day. Well, Jackie Kennedy was inside in her living room sitting around talking with a few of us, Arthur Schlesinger, Jr. and his wife Marian, Prince Radziwill, Peter Maas the writer, Jacques Lowe the photographer, and Pierre Salinger. We were a curious assortment indeed, as oddly assembled in our way as some of the do-gooders and real baddies on the lawn outside. It would have taken a hostess of broad and perhaps dubious gifts, Perle Mesta, no doubt, or Ethel Merman, or Elsa Maxwell, to have woven some mood into this occasion, because pop! were going the flashbulbs out in the crazy August sun on the sun-drenched terrace just beyond the bay window at our back, a politician—a stocky machine type sweating in a dark suit with a white shirt and white silk tie—was having his son, seventeen perhaps, short, chunky, dressed the same way, take a picture of him and his wife, a Mediterranean dish around sixty with a bright, happy, flowered dress. The boy took a picture of father and mother, father took a picture of mother and son—another heeler came along to take a picture of all three—it was a little like a rite surrounding *droit du seigneur*, as if afterward the family could press a locket in your hand and say, "Here, here are contained three hairs from the youth of the Count, discovered by me on my wife next morning." There was something low and greedy about this picture-taking, perhaps the popping of the flashbulbs in the sunlight, as if everything monstrous and overreaching in our insane public land were tamped together in the foolproof act of taking a sun-drenched picture at noon with no shadows and a flashbulb—do we sell insurance to protect our cadavers against the corrosion of the grave?

And I had the impression that Jackie Kennedy was almost suffering in the flesh from their invasion of her house, her terrace, her share of the lands, that if the popping of the flashbulbs went on until midnight on the terrace outside she would have a tic forever in the corner of her eye. Because that was the second impression of her, of a lady with delicate and exacerbated nerves. She was no broad hostess, not at all; broad hostesses are monumental animals turned mellow: hippopotami, rhinoceri, plump lion, sweet gorilla, warm bear. Jackie Kennedy was a cat, narrow and wild, and her fur was being rubbed every which way. This was the second impression. The first had been simpler. It had been merely of a college girl who was nice. Nice and clean and very merry. I had entered her house perspiring—talk of the politician, I was wearing a black suit myself, a washable, the only one in my closet not completely unpressed that morning, and I had been forced to pick a white shirt with button-down collar: all the white summer shirts were in the laundry. What a set-to I had had with Adele Mailer at breakfast. Food half-digested in anger, sweating like a goat, tense at the pit of my stomach for I would be interviewing Kennedy in a half hour, I was feeling not a little jangled when we were introduced, and we stumbled mutually over a few polite remarks, which was my fault I'm sure more than hers for I must have had a look in my eyes—I remember I felt like a drunk marine who knows in all clarity that if he doesn't have a fight soon it'll be good for his character but terrible for his constitution.

She offered me a cool drink—iced verbena tea with sprig of mint no doubt—but the expression in my face must have been rich because she added, still standing by the screen in the doorway, "We do have something harder of course," and something droll and hard came into her eyes as if she were a very naughty eight-year-old indeed. More than one photograph of Jackie Kennedy had put forward just this saucy regard—it was obviously the life t ner charm. But I had not been prepared for another quality, of shyness conceivably. There was something quite remote in her. Not willed, not chilly, not directed at anyone in particular, but distant, detached as the psychologists say, moody and abstracted the novelists used to say. As we sat around the coffee table on summer couches, summer chairs, a pleasant living room in light colors, lemon, white and gold seeming to predominate, the sort of living room one might expect to find in Cleveland, may it be, at the home of a fairly important young executive whose wife had taste, sitting there, watching people go by, the group I mentioned earlier kept a kind of conversation going. Its center, if it had one, was obviously Jackie Kennedy. There was a natural tendency to look at her and see if she were amused. She did not sit there like a movie star with a ripe olive in each eye for the brain, but in fact gave conversation back, made some of it, laughed often. We had one short conversation about Provincetown, which was pleasant. She remarked that she had been staying no more than fifty miles away for all these summers but had never seen it. She must, I assured her. It was one of the few fishing villages in America which still had beauty. Besides it was the Wild West of the East. The local police were the Indians and the beatniks were the poor hard-working settlers. Her eyes turned merry. "Oh, I'd love to see it," she said. But how did one go? In three black limousines and fifty police for escort, or in a sports car at four a.m. with dark glasses? "I suppose now I'll never get to see it," she said wistfully.

She had a keen sense of laughter, but it revolved around the absurdities of the world. She was probably not altogether unlike a soldier who has been up at the front for two weeks. There was a hint of gone laughter. Soldiers who have had it bad enough can laugh at the fact some trooper got killed crossing an open area because he wanted to change his socks from khaki to green. The front lawn of this house must have been, I suppose, a kind of no-man's-land for a lady. The story I remember her telling was about Stash, Prince Radziwill, her brother-in-law, who had gone into the second-story bathroom that morning to take a shave and discovered, to his lack of complete pleasure, that a crush of tourists was watching him from across the road. Yes, the house had been besieged, and one knew she thought of the sightseers as a mob, a motley of gargoyles, like the horde who riot through the last pages in *The Day of the Locust*.

Since there was an air of self-indulgence about her, subtle but precise, one was certain she liked time to compose herself. While we sat there she must have gotten up a half-dozen times, to go away for two minutes, come back for three. She had the exasperated impatience of a college girl. One expected her to swear mildly. "Oh, Christ!" or "Sugar!" or "Fudge!" And each time she got up, there was a glimpse of her calves, surprisingly thin, not unfeverish. I was reminded of the legs on those adolescent Southern girls who used to go out together and walk up and down the streets of Fayetteville, North Carolina, in the Summer of 1944 at Fort Bragg. In the petulant Southern air of their boredom many of us had found something luminous that summer, a mixture of languor, heat, innocence and stupidity which was our cocktail vis-à-vis the knowledge we were going soon to Europe or the other war. One mentions this to underline the determinedly romantic aura in which one had chosen to behold Jackie Kennedy. There was a charm this other short Summer of 1960 in the thought a young man with a young attractive wife might soon become President. It offered possibilities and vistas; it brought a touch of life to the monotonies of politics, those monotonies so profoundly entrenched into the hinges and mortar of the Eisenhower administration. It was thus more interesting to look at Jackie Kennedy as a woman than as a probable First Lady. Perhaps it was out of some such motive, such a desire for the clean air and tang of unexpected montage, that I spoke about her in just the way I did later that afternoon.

"Do you think she's happy?" asked a lady, an old friend, on the beach at Wellfleet.

"I guess she would rather spend her life on the Riviera."

"What would she do there?"

"End up as the mystery woman, maybe, in a good murder case."

"Wow," said the lady, giving me my reward.

It had been my way of saying I liked Jackie Kennedy, that she was not at all stuffy, that she had perhaps a touch of that artful madness which suggests future drama.

My interview the first day had been a little short, and I was invited back for another one the following day. Rather nicely, Senator Kennedy invited me to bring anyone I wanted. About a week later I realized this was part of his acumen. You can tell a lot about a man by whom he invites in such a circumstance. Will it be a political expert or the wife? I invited my wife. The presence of this second lady is not unimportant, because this time she had the conversation with Jackie Kennedy. While I was busy somewhere or other, they were introduced. Down by the Kennedy family wharf. The Senator was about to take Jackie for a sail. The two women had a certain small general resemblance. They were something like the same height, they both had dark hair, and they had each been wearing it in a similar style for many years. Perhaps this was enough to create a quick political intimacy. "I wish," said Jackie Kennedy, "that I didn't have to go on this corny sail, because I would like very much to talk to you, Mrs.

Mailer.'' A stroke. Mrs. M. did not like many people quickly, but Jackie now had a champion. It must have been a pleasant sight. Two attractive witches by the water's edge.

II

Jimmy Baldwin once entertained the readers of *Esquire* with a sweet and generously written piece called *The Black Boy Looks at the White Boy* in which he talked a great deal about himself and a little bit about me, a proportion I thought well-taken since he is on the best of terms with Baldwin and digs next to nothing about this white boy. As a method, I think it has its merits.

After I saw the Kennedys I added a few paragraphs to my piece about the convention, secretly relieved to have liked them, for my piece was most favorable to the Senator, and how would I have rewritten it if I had not liked him? With several mishaps it was printed three weeks before the election. Several days later, I received a letter from Jackie Kennedy. It was a nice letter, generous in its praise, accurate in its details. She remembered, for example, the color of the sweater my wife had been wearing, and mentioned she had one like it in the same purple. I answered with a letter which was out of measure. I was in a Napoleonic mood, I had decided to run for Mayor of New York; in a few weeks, I was to zoom and crash—my sense of reality was extravagant. So in response to a modestly voiced notion by Mrs. Kennedy that she wondered if the ''impressionistic'' way in which I had treated the convention could be applied to the history of the past, I replied in the cadence of a Goethe that while I was now engaged in certain difficulties of writing about the present, I hoped one day when work was done to do a biography of the Marquis de Sade and the ''odd strange honor of the man.''

I suppose this is as close to the edge as I have ever come. At the time, it seemed reasonable that Mrs. Kennedy, with her publicized interest in France and the eighteenth century, might be fascinated by de Sade. The style of his thought was, after all, a fair climax to the Age of Reason.

Now sociology has few virtues, but one of them is sanity. In writing

such a letter to Mrs. Kennedy I was losing my sociology. The Catholic
wife of a Catholic candidate for President was not likely to find de
Sade as familiar as a tea cozy. I received no reply. I had smashed the
limits of such letter-writing. In politics a break in sociology is as clean
as a break in etiquette.

At the time I saw it somewhat differently. The odds were against a
reply, I decided, three-to-one against, or eight-to-one against. I did
not glean they were eight-hundred-to-one against. It is the small
inability to handicap odds which is family to the romantic, the desperate and the insane. ''That man is going to kill me,'' someone thinks
with fear, sensing a stranger. At this moment, they put the odds at
even money, they may even be ready to die for their bet, when, if the
fact could be measured, there is one chance in a thousand the danger is
true. Exceptional leverage upon the unconscious life in other people is
the strength of the artist and the torment of the madman.

Now if I have bothered to show my absence of proportion, it is
because I want to put forward a notion which will seem criminal to
some of you, but was believed in by me, is still believed in by me, and
so affects what I write about the Kennedys.

Jack Kennedy won the election by one hundred thousand votes. A
lot of people could claim therefore to be the mind behind his victory.
Jake Arvey could say the photo-finish would have gone the other way
if not for the track near his Chicago machine. J. Edgar Hoover might
say he saved the victory because he did not investigate the track.
Lyndon Johnson could point to LBJ Ranch, and the vote in Texas.
Time Magazine could tell you that the abstract intrepidity of their
support for Nixon gave the duke to Kennedy. Sinatra would not be
surprised if the late ones who glommed onto Kennedy were not more
numerous than the early-risers he scattered. And one does not even
need to speak of the Corporations, the Mob, the money they delivered
by messenger, the credit they would use later. So if I came to the cool
conclusion I had won the election for Kennedy with my piece in
Esquire, the thought might be high presumption, but it was not
unique. I had done something curious but indispensable for the campaign—succeeded in making it dramatic. I had not shifted one
hundred thousand votes directly, I had not. But a million people might
have read my piece and some of them talked to other people. The
cadres of Stevenson Democrats whose morale was low might now

revive with an argument that Kennedy was different in substance from Nixon. Dramatically different. The piece titled *Superman Comes to the Supermarket* affected volunteer work for Kennedy, enough to make a clean critical difference through the country. But such counting is a quibble. At bottom I had the feeling that if there were a power which made presidents, a power which might be termed Wall Street or Capitalism or The Establishment, a Mind or Collective Mind of some Spirit, some Master, or indeed *the* Master, no less, that then perhaps my article had turned that intelligence a fine hair in its circuits. This was what I thought. Right or wrong, I thought it, still do, and tell it now not to convince others (the act of stating such a claim is not happy), but to underline the proprietary tone I took when Kennedy invaded Cuba.

"You've cut . . ." I wrote in *The Village Voice*, April 27, 1961: ". . . the shape of your plan for history, and it smells . . . rich and smug and scared of the power of the worst, dullest and most oppressive men of our land."

There was more. A good deal more. I want to quote more. Nothing could ever convince me the invasion of Cuba was not one of the meanest blunders in our history:

You are a virtuoso in political management but you will never understand the revolutionary passion which comes to those who were one way or another too poor to learn how good they might have been; the greediness of the rich had already crippled their youth.

Without this understanding you will never know what to do about Castro and Cuba. You will never understand that the man is the country, revolutionary, tyrannical . . . hysterical . . . brave as the best of animals, doomed perhaps to end in tragedy, but one of the great figures of the twentieth century, at the present moment a far greater figure than yourself.

Later, through the grapevine which runs from Washington to New York, it could be heard that Jackie Kennedy was indignant at this piece, and one had the opportunity to speculate if her annoyance came from the postscript:

I was in a demonstration the other day . . . five literary magazines (so help me) which marched in a small circle of protest against our intervention in Cuba. One of the pickets was a very tall poetess with black hair which reached near to her waist. She was dressed like a medieval varlet, and she carried a sign addressed to your wife:

JACQUELINE, VOUS AVEZ
PERDU VOS ARTISTES

Tin soldier, you are depriving us of the Muse.

Months later, when the anger cooled, one could ask oneself what one did make of Washington now, for it was not an easy place to understand. It was intelligent, yes, but it was not original; there was wit in the detail and ponderousness in the program; vivacity, and dullness to equal it; tactical brilliance, political timidity; facts were still superior to the depths, criticism was less to be admired than the ability to be amusing—or so said the losers; equality and justice meandered; bureaucratic canals and locks; slums were replaced with buildings which looked like prisons; success was to be admired again, self-awareness dubious; television was attacked, but for its violence, not its mendacity, for its lack of educational programs, not its dearth of grace. There seemed no art, no real art in the new administration, and all the while the new administration proclaimed its eagerness to mother the arts. Or as Mr. Collingwood said to Mrs. Kennedy, "This Administration has shown a particular affinity for artists, musicians, writers, poets. Is this because you and your husband just feel that way or do you think that there's a relationship between the Government and the arts?"

"That's so complicated," answered Mrs. Kennedy with good sense. "I don't know. I just think that everything in the White House should be the best."

Stravinsky had been invited of course and Robert Frost. Pablo Casals, Leonard Bernstein, Arthur Miller, Tennessee.

"But what about us?" growled the apes. Why did one know that Richard Wilbur would walk through the door before Allen Ginsberg; or Saul Bellow and J. D. Salinger long before William Burroughs or Norman Mailer. What special good would it do to found an Establishment if the few who gave intimations of high talent were instinctively excluded? I wanted a chance to preach to the President and to the First Lady. "Speak to the people a little more," I would have liked to say, "talk on television about the things you do not understand. Use your popularity to be difficult and intellectually dangerous. There is more to greatness than liberal legislation.'' And to her I would have liked to go on about what the real meaning of an artist might be, of how the marrow of a nation was contained in his art, and one deadened artists at one's peril, because artists were not so much gifted as endowed; they had been given what was secret and best in their parents and in all the other people about them who had been generous or influenced them or made them, and so artists embodied the essence of what was best in the nation, embodied it in their talent rather than in their character, which could be small, but their talent—this fruit of all that was rich and nourishing in their lives—was related directly to the dreams and the ambitions of the most imaginative part of the nation. So the destiny of a nation was not separate at all from the fate of its artists. I would have liked to tell her that every time an artist failed to complete the full mansion, jungle, garden, armory, or city of his work the nation was subtly but permanently poorer, which is why we return so obsessively to the death of Tom Wolfe, the broken air of Scott Fitzgerald, and the gloomy smell of the vault which collects already about the horror of Hemingway's departure. I would have liked to say to her that a war for the right to express oneself had been going on in this country for fifty years, and that there were counterattacks massing because there were many who hated the artist now, that as the world dipped into the totalitarian trough of the twentieth century there was a mania of abhorrence for whatever was unpredictable. For all too many, security was the only bulwark against emptiness, eternity and death. The void was what America feared. Communism was one name they gave this void. The unknown was Communist. The girls who wore dungarees were Communist, and the boys who grew beards, the people who walked their dog off the leash. It was comic, but it was virulent, and there was a fanatic rage in much too much of the population. Detestation of the beatnik seethed like rabies on the mouths of small-town police officers.

Oh, there was much I wanted to tell her, even—exit sociology, enter insanity—that the obscene had a right to exist in the novel. For every fifteen-year-old who would be hurt by premature exposure, somewhere another, or two or three, would emerge from sexual experience which had been too full of moral funk onto the harder terrain of sex made alive by culture, that it was the purpose of culture finally to enrich all of the psyche, not just part of us, and damage to particular people in passing was a price we must pay. Thirty thousand Americans were killed each year by automobile crashes. No one talked of giving up the automobile: it was necessary to civilization. As necessary, I wanted to say, was art. Art in all its manifestations. Including the rude, the obscene, and the unsayable. Art was as essential to the nation as technology. I would tell her these things out of romantic abundance, because I liked her and thought she would understand what one was talking about, because as First Lady she was queen of the arts, she was our Muse if she chose to be. Perhaps it would not be altogether a disaster if America had a Muse.

Now it is not of much interest to most of you who read this that a small but distinct feud between the editors of *Esquire* and the writer was made up around the New Year. What is not as much off the matter was the suggestion, made at the time by one of these editors, that a story be done about Jackie Kennedy.

One liked the idea. What has been written already is curious prose if it is not obvious how much one liked the idea. Pierre Salinger was approached by the Magazine, and agreed to present the same idea to Mrs. Kennedy. I saw Salinger in his office for a few minutes. He told me: not yet a chance to talk to the Lady, but might that evening. I was leaving Washington. A few days later, one of the editors spoke to him. Mrs. Kennedy's answer: negative.

One didn't know. One didn't know how the idea had been presented, one didn't know just when it had been presented. It did not matter all that much. Whatever the details, the answer had come from the core. One's presence was not required. Which irritated the vanity. The vanity was no doubt outsize, but one thought of oneself as one of the few writers in the country. There was a right to interview Mrs. Kennedy. She was not only a woman looking for privacy, but an institution being put together before our eyes. If the people of America were to have a symbol, one had the right to read more about the creation. The country would stay alive by becoming more extraordinary, not more predictable.

III

Not with a kind eye then did I watch Mrs. Kennedy give the nation a tour. One would be fair. Fair to her and fair to the truth of one's reactions. There was now an advantage in not having had the interview.

I turned on the program a minute after the hour. The image on the screen was not of Mrs. Kennedy, but the White House. For some minutes she talked, reading from a prepared script while the camera was turned upon old prints, old plans, and present views of the building. Since Jackie Kennedy was not visible during this time, there was an opportunity to listen to her voice. It produced a small continuing shock. At first, before the picture emerged from the set, I thought I was turned to the wrong station, because the voice was a quiet parody of the sort of voice one hears on the radio late at night, dropped softly into the ear by girls who sell soft mattresses, depilatories, or creams to brighten the skin.

Now I had heard the First Lady occasionally on newsreels and in brief interviews on television, and thought she showed an odd public voice, but never paid attention, because the first time to hear her was in the living room at Hyannis Port and there she had been clear, merry and near excellent. So I discounted the public voice, concluded it was muffled by shyness perhaps or was too urgent in its desire to sound like other voices, to sound, let us say, like an attractive small-town salesgirl, or like Jackie Kennedy's version of one: the gentry in America have a dim ear for the nuances of accent in the rough, the poor, and the ready. I had decided it was probably some mockery of her husband's political ambitions, a sport upon whatever advisers had been trying for years to guide her to erase whatever was too patrician or cultivated in her speech. But the voice I was hearing now, the public voice, the voice after a year in the White House had grown undeniably worse, had nourished itself on its faults. Do some of you remember the girl with the magnificent sweater who used to give the weather reports on television in a swarmy sing-song tone? It was a self-conscious parody, very funny for a little while: "Temperature—forty-eight. Humidity—twenty-eight. Prevailing winds." It had the style of the pinup magazine, it caught their prose: "Sandra Sharilee is 37-25-37, and likes to stay in at night." The girl who gave the weather report captured the voice of those pinup magazines, dreamy, narcissistic, visions of sex on the moon. And Jackie Kennedy's voice, her public voice, might as well have been influenced by the weather girl. What madness is loose in our public communication. And what self-ridicule that consciously or unconsciously, wittingly, willy-nilly, by the aid of speech teachers or all on her stubborn own, this was the manufactured voice Jackie Kennedy chose to arrive at. One had heard better ones at Christmastime in Macy's selling gadgets to the grim.

The introduction having ended, the camera moved onto Jackie Kennedy. We were shown the broad planes of the First Lady's most agreeable face. Out of the deep woods now. One could return to them by closing one's eyes and listening to the voice again, but the image was reasonable, reassuringly stiff. As the eye followed Mrs. Kennedy and her interlocutor, Charles Collingwood, through the halls, galleries and rooms of the White House, through the Blue Room, the Green Room, the East Room, the State Dining Room, the Red Room; as the listeners were offered a reference to Dolly Madison's favorite sofa, or President Monroe's Minerva clock, Nellie Custis' sofa, Mrs. Lincoln's later poverty, Daniel Webster's sofa, Julia Grant's desk, Andrew Jackson's broken mirror, the chest President Van Buren gave to his grandson; as the paintings were shown to us, paintings entitled Niagara Falls, Grapes and Apples, Naval Battle of 1812, Indian Guides, A Mountain Glimpse, Mouth of the Delaware; as one contemplated the life of this offering, the presentation began to take on the undernourished, overdone air of a charity show, a telethon for a new disease. It was not Mrs. Kennedy's fault—she strove honorably. What an agony it must have been to establish the sequence of all these names, all these objects. Probably she knew them well, perhaps she was interested in her subject—although the detached quality of her presence on this program made it not easy to believe—but whether or not she had taken a day-to-day interest in the booty now within the White House, still she had had a script partially written for her, by a television writer with black horn-rimmed glasses no doubt, she had been obliged to memorize portions of this script, she had trained for the part. Somehow it was sympathetic that she walked through it like a starlet who is utterly without talent. Mrs. Kennedy moved like a wooden horse. A marvelous horse, perhaps even a live horse, its feet hobbled, its head unready to turn for fear of a flick from the crop. She had that intense wooden lack of rest, that lack of comprehension for each word offered up which one finds only in a few of those curious movie stars who are huge box office. Jane Russell comes to mind, and Rita Hayworth when she was sadly cast, Jayne Mansfield in deep water, Brigitte Bardot before she learned to act. Marilyn Monroe. But one may be too kind. Jackie Kennedy was more like a starlet who will never learn to act because the extraordinary livid unreality of her life away from the camera has so beclouded her brain and seduced her attention that she is incapable of the simplest and most essential demand, which is to live and breathe easily with the meaning of the words one speaks.

This program was the sort of thing Eleanor Roosevelt could have done, and done well. She had grown up among objects like this— these stuffed armchairs, these candelabra—no doubt they lived for her with some charm of the past. But Jackie Kennedy was unconvincing. One did not feel she particularly loved the past of America—not all of us do for that matter, it may not even be a crime—but one never had the impression for a moment that the White House fitted her style. As one watched this tame, lackluster and halting show, one wanted to take the actress by the near shoulder. Because names, dates and objects were boring down into the very secrets of her being—or so one would lay the bet—and this encouraged a fraud which could only sicken her. By extension it would deaden us. What we needed and what she could offer us was much more complex than this public image of a pompadour, a tea-dance dress, and a Colonial window welded together in committee. Would the Kennedys be no more intelligent than the near past, had they not learned America was not to be saved by Madison Avenue, that no method could work which induced nausea faster than the pills we push to carry it away.

Afterward one could ask what it was one wanted of her, and the answer was that she show herself to us as she is. Because what we suffer from in America, in that rootless moral wilderness of our expanding life, is the unadmitted terror in each of us that bit by bit, year by year, we are going mad. Very few of us know really where we have come from and to where we are going, why we do it, and if it is ever worthwhile. For better or for worse we have lost our past, we live in that airless no-man's-land of the perpetual present, and so suffer doubly as we strike into the future because we have no roots by which to project ourselves forward, or judge our trip.

And this tour of the White House gave us precisely no sense of the past. To the contrary, it inflicted the past upon us, pummeled us with it, depressed us with facts. I counted the names, the proper names, and the dates in the transcript. More than two hundred items were dumped upon us during that hour. If one counts repetitions, the number is closer to four hundred. One was not being offered education, but anxiety.

We are in the Green Room—I quote from the transcript:

> Mr. Collingwood: What other objects of special interest are there in the room now?
>
> Mrs. Kennedy: Well, there's this sofa which belonged to Daniel Webster and is really one of the finest pieces here in this room. And then there's this mirror. It was George Washington's and he had it in the Executive Mansion in Philadelphia, then he gave it to a friend and it was bought for Mount Vernon in 1891. And it was there until Mount Vernon lent it to us this fall. And I must say I appreciate that more than I can say, because when Mount Vernon, which is probably the most revered house in this country, lends something to the White House, you know they have confidence it will be taken care of.

A neurotic may suffer agonies returning to his past; so may a nation which is not well. The neurotic recites endless lists of his activities and offers no reaction to any of it. So do we teach with empty content and by rigid manner where there is anxiety in the lore. American history disgorges this anxiety. Where, in the pleasant versions of it we are furnished, can we find an explanation for the disease which encourages us to scourge our countryside, stifle our cities, kill the physical sense of our past, and throw up excruciatingly totalitarian new office buildings everywhere to burden the vista of our land? This disease, is it hidden in the evasions, the injustices, and the prevarications of the past, or does it come to us from a terror of what is yet to come? Whatever, however, we do not create a better nation by teaching schoolchildren the catalogues of the White House. Nor do we use the First Lady decently if she is flattered in this, for catalogues are imprisonment to the delicate, muted sensitivity one feels passing across Jackie Kennedy from time to time like a small summer wind on a good garden.

Yes, before the tour was over, one had to feel compassion. Because silly, ill-advised, pointless, empty, dull, and obsequious to the most slavish tastes in American life, as was this show, still she was trying so hard, she wanted to please, she had given herself to this work, and it was hopeless, there was no one about to tell her how very hopeless it was, how utterly without offering to the tormented adventurous spirit of American life. At times, in her eyes, there was a blank, full look which one could recognize. One had seen this look on a nineteen-year-old who was sweet and on the town and pushed too far. She slashed her wrists one night and tried to scar her cheeks and her breast. I had visited the girl in the hospital. She had blank eyes, a wide warm smile, a deadness in her voice. It did not matter about what she spoke—only her mouth followed the words, never her eyes. So I did not care to see that look in Jackie Kennedy's face, and I hoped by half—for more would be untrue—that the sense one got of her in newspaper photographs, of a ladygirl healthy and on the bounce, might come into her presence before our deadening sets. America needed a lady's humor to leaven the solemnities of our toneless power: finally we will send a man to Mars and the Martians will say, "God, he is dull."

Yes, it is to be hoped that Jackie Kennedy will come alive. Because I think finally she is one of us. By which I mean that she has not one face but many, not a true voice but accents, not a past so much as memories which cannot speak to one another. She attracts compassion. Somewhere in her mute vitality is a wash of our fatigue, of existential fatigue, of the great fatigue which comes from being adventurous in a world where most of the bets are covered cold and statisticians prosper. I liked her, I liked her still, but she was a phony—it was the cruelest thing one could say, she was a royal phony. There was something very difficult and very dangerous she was trying from deep within herself to do, dangerous not to her safety but to her soul. She was trying, I suppose, to be a proper First Lady and it was her mistake. Because there was no need to copy the Ladies who had come before her. Suppose America had not yet had a First Lady who was even remotely warm enough for our needs? Or sufficiently imaginative? But who could there be to advise her in all that company of organized men, weaned on the handbook of past precedent? If she would be any use to the nation she must first regain the freedom to look us in the eye. And offer the hard drink. For then three times three hurrah, and hats, our hats, in the air. If she were really interested in her White House, we would grant it to her, we would not begrudge her the tour, not if we could believe she was beginning to learn the difference between the arts and the safe old crafts. And indeed there was a way she could show us she was beginning to learn, it was the way of the hostess: one would offer her one's sword when Henry Miller was asked to the White House as often as Robert Frost and beat poetry's own Andy Hardy—good Gregory Corso—could do an Indian dance in the East Room with Archibald MacLeish. America would be as great as the royal rajah of her arts when the Academy ceased to be happy as a cherrystone clam, and the weakest of the beat returned to form. Because our tragedy is that we diverge as countrymen further and further away from one another, like a space ship broken apart in flight which now drifts mournfully in isolated orbits, satellites to each other, planets none, communication faint.

THE SIXTH PRESIDENTIAL PAPER

—A Kennedy Miscellany

- **The Esquire Columns**
- **Another Open Letter**
- **Presidential Poems**
- **An Impolite Interview**

This miscellany is composed of writing taken from columns, some slight but possibly amusing poems, another open letter to JFK, and the larger portion of a long interview with Paul Krassner of The Realist. *A little bit is said about many subjects, superficiality is the order of this paper, but one can offer a passing defense for the superficial. A President needs diversion now and again, his mind must sometimes be offered possibilities which are neither formal nor altogether serious, as well as some serious notions which are not in the least developed. The happiest evolvement of ideas often comes from an act of appropriation. More than one philosophy has been built from a joke which excited laughter in everyone but the philosopher who was on the spot stricken by the intellectual bacteria concealed in the humor. The President, doubtless finding attack as tonic as praise may enjoy the following as a bouquet, a spray, or a whiff of grapeshot.*

The Big Bite—November and December, 1962; January and March, 1963

These first short pieces are taken in excerpt from Esquire *columns. They talk about varied matters: styles of burial (a first requisite for a politician since he must be able to end old possibilities as well as create new ones), a few remarks about Hemingway and Marilyn Monroe (names which become legend in America are proper study for a President), a brief consideration of taped television and its relation to totalitarianism (it is characteristic of the Kennedy administration that they would seek to limit the more interesting vices of mass entertainment such as horse opera, murder, and violence while tacitly encouraging the endemic illness of television—its tendency to discourage the spontaneous), and finally a column about Adlai Stevenson's adventures with the Press, the President, and the bridge between—a Certified Leak.*

THE BIG BITE—November, 1962

The worst story I ever heard about Jack Kennedy was that he sat on his boat one day eating chicken and threw the half-chewed bones into the sea.

So few people understand what I mean it forces me to explain that you don't give the carcass of an animal to the water. It was meant to seep back into the earth.

Of course we pump our sewage out to sea, a sewage which was meant to return to the land, but then in a thousand years we may discover that the worst plagues of man, the cancer and the concentration camps, the housing projects and the fallout, the mass media and the mass nausea come from a few social vices, from the manufacture of the mirror, from the introduction of tobacco to Europe, from the advance of sanitation. Science may have been born the day a man came to hate nature so profoundly that he swore he would devote himself to comprehending her, and secretly to stifling her.

There is nothing wrong with hating nature. It is less bad than being the sort of columnist who admonishes his readers to love nature. What is bad is to fear death so completely that one loses the nerve to contemplate it. Throwing a chicken bone into the sea is bad because it shows no feeling for the root of death, which is burial. Of course Kennedy might have muttered, "Sorry, old man," as he tossed the bone. That is the difficulty with anecdotes. One cannot determine the nuance. I have the conceit that if I had been there I might have sensed whether Kennedy was genuinely rueful, oblivious to the fact, or acting like a dick, a house dick.

Some will now mutter: Can't the man be left alone? Is he entitled to no private life? The answer is: none. He is a young man who has chosen to be President. He is now paying part of the price. I suspect he is ready to pay it.

Rare was the czar or king who did not have a witness in his chamber to sniff the passing of the state. Arthur Schlesinger?

The root of death is burial. I was never particularly fond of Joe DiMaggio. His legend left me cold. But I have respect for the way he chose to give Marilyn Monroe a small funeral. If she had never been a movie star, if she had been one of those small, attractive blondes who floats like spray over the Hollywood rocks, a little drink here, bit of a call girl there, bing, bam, bad marriage, nice pot, easy head, girl friend, headshrinker, fuzz, dope, miscarriage and lowering night, if she had been no more than that, just a misty little blonde who hurt no one too much and went down inch by inch, inevitably, like a cocker spaniel in a quickbog, well then she would have ended in some small Hollywood parlor with fifteen friends invited.

Probably she was like that by the end. Sleeping pills are the great leveler. If everyone in America took four capsules of Nembutal a night for two thousand nights we would all be the same when we were done. We would all be idiots.

Any writer who takes the pills year after year ought to be able to write the tale of a club fighter whose brain turns slowly drunk with punishment. But that is the book which is never written. We learn the truth by giving away pieces of our tongue. When we know it all, there is no tongue left. Is it then one rises at dawn for the black flirtation, slips downstairs, slips the muzzle into the mouth, cool gunmetal to balm the void of a lost tongue, and goes blasting off like a rocket. Here come I, eternity, cries Ernest, I trust you no longer. You must try to find me now, eternity. I am in little pieces.

Hemingway and Monroe. Pass lightly over their names. They were two of the people in America most beautiful to us.

I think Ernest hated us by the end. He deprived us of his head. It does not matter so much whether it was suicide or an accident—one does not put a gun barrel in one's mouth, tickle the edge of an accident and fail to see that people will say it's suicide. Ernest, so proud of his reputation. So fierce about it. His death was awful. Say it. It was the most difficult death in America since Roosevelt. One has still not recovered from Hemingway's death. One may never.

But Monroe was different. She slipped away from us. She had been slipping away from us for years. Now it is easy to say that her actions became more vague every year. I thought she was bad in *The Misfits*, she was finally too vague, and when emotion showed, it was unattractive and small. But she was gone from us a long time ago.

If she had done Grushenka in *The Brothers Karamazov* the way she announced she would all those years ago, and if she had done it well, then she might have gone on. She might have come all the way back into the vault of herself where the salts of a clean death and the rot of a foul death were locked together. We take the sleeping pills when the sense of a foul and rotten death has become too certain, we look for the salt in the Seconal. Probably to stay alive Monroe had to become the greatest actress who ever lived. To stay alive Hemingway would have had to write a better book than *War and Peace*.

From *The Deer Park*: "There was that law of life, so cruel and so just, which demanded that one must grow or else pay more for remaining the same." I think that line is true. I think it is biologically true. And I think its application is more ferocious in America than anywhere I know. Because we set ourselves out around the knoll and get ready to play King of the Hill. Soon one of us is brave enough to take the center and insist it belongs to us. Then there is no rest until the new king is killed. Our good America. We are the nation of amateur kings and queens.

THE BIG BITE—December, 1962

I wonder if it is possible Ernest Hemingway was not a suicide. It may be said he took his life, but I wonder if the deed were not more like a reconnaissance from which he did not come back.

How likely that he had a death of the most awful proportions within him. He was exactly the one to know that cure for such disease is to risk dying many a time. Somewhere in the deep coma of mortal illness or the transfixed womb of danger, death speaks to us. If we make our way back to life, we are armed with a new secret.

I wonder if, morning after morning, Hemingway did not go downstairs secretly in the dawn, set the base of his loaded shotgun on the floor, put the muzzle to his mouth, and press his thumb into the trigger. There is a no-man's-land in each trigger. For the dull hand it is a quarter of an inch. A professional hunter can feel to the division of a millimeter the point where the gun can go off. He can move the trigger up to that point and yet not fire the gun. Hemingway was not too old to test this skill. Perhaps he was trying the deed a first time, perhaps he had tried just such a reconnaissance one hundred times before, and felt the touch of health return ninety times, ninety respectable times when he dared to press the trigger far into the zone where the shot could go. If he did it well, he could come close to death without dying. On that particular morning in July, it is not impossible he said (because the curiosity could be that indeed he talked to himself the way he talked in his books), Look, we can go in further. It's going to be tricky and we may not get out, but it will be good for us if we go in just a little further, so we have to try, and now we will, it is the answer to the brothers Mayo, ergo now we go in, damn the critics and this Fiedler fellow, all will be denied if papa gets good again, write about Monroe, and Jimmy Durante, God bless, umbriago, hose down the deck, do it clean, no sweat, no sweat in the palm, let's do it clean, gung ho, a little more, let's go in a little gung ho more ho. No! Oh no! Goddamn it to Hell.

There will be some who say: Nice, but it still is suicide.

Not if it went that way. When we do not wish to live, we execute ourselves. If we are ill and yet want to go on, we must put up the ante. If we lose, it does not mean we wished to die.

The sentence this month will be light. In New York and parts of the East, we have a contest every year. It is for Miss Rheingold. We fill out ballots in bars. Twenty million ballots. It is the second largest election in the country. This year, as always, six ladies are contenders. I studied their faces on a Rheingold ballot box last night. "You see the one named Loretta Rissell?" asked a friend. "Well, she's way ahead. She'll walk away with it." One of the prides of my friend is that he knows what the smart money knows.

I nod. I am in agreement for once. I also think Loretta Rissell will win. The reason is simple. She looks like Jack Kennedy.

THE BIG BITE—January, 1963

Citizens, I have something serious to present to you. Virtually all television shows without a prepared script are filmed in advance, and put on tape. That means nothing unforeseen can now appear on television. In fact, knowing this, anyone invited to a television show censors himself. Because if one is talking to a microphone which will not be open to an audience until three hours later, or three weeks later, one will not try to be too candid.

I remember in the old days, five, six years ago, we used to go out into the fine jungle of live television. It was an exquisite sensation—a little like making love, a little like being in the electric chair—to know that one million people were listening to you at that instant. It gave a certain life to the performer which presumably he passed on to the audience. Now, it's more like cold coffee. One appears on a show which will be seen at midnight, but it is only two in the afternoon. A nap is in order. Instead one breathes back a yawn for the show. What can this do to the psyche of Americans still awake in the very early morning? They think you are there before them, sober, bored, mild, with the night half gone. Whereas in fact you're watching yourself. What good can it do the country to mistake midnight for two in the afternoon?

Actually, the real danger is that the totalitarians have taken one of the gates to the city. Conceive of a situation where America, on the edge of an apocalyptic shift in its destiny, is held for a few days in some subtle concealed *coup d'état* by totalitarian leaders. Could Jack Paar then have his finest hour? Could he tell the people who listen to him and trust his voice that America had lost its liberty that day? Yes. He could do it on tape in the afternoon. By evening, six hours later, the show would not be seen. The network regrets to inform you that Mr. Paar was taken ill tonight. In private you would get the news that he offended a minority group. Some such jazz.

It's New Year's. So I tell you, John Birch Society, go into that excellent activity of yours which can drop one thousand letters on any target in the world, and drop them on Newton Minow, Federal Communications Commission, Washington 25, D.C. Tell him that the freedom of America is endangered by taped television.

And you, dear friends of the Center and the Left. Don't write any letters to Minow. Let the Right Wing write the letters. Let them tell

Minow that art and the war of the intellect feed the marrow of a nation. Let them be the ones to give reasons why a nation is cheated of its best future when the present is born in the past.

THE BIG BITE—March, 1963

The newspapers are rich in self-examination these last two mornings. Like beatniks or poets they are studying themselves, their digestion, their elimination, their neuroses, their arts. They are examining the secrets of their own formula for making history. They are trying to decide whether Adlai Stevenson is in serious disfavor with President Kennedy or is not. As in a laboratory experiment, they have a specimen to examine, tests to make.

The specimen is an article in *The Saturday Evening Post* by Stewart Alsop and Charles Bartlett. The article finds Stevenson guilty of expressing a *soft* policy toward Cuba during several *secret* conferences, those talks of the Executive Committee in which Kennedy discussed what to do about Soviet missiles in Cuba. Since Charles Bartlett is known to the newspaper business as a *leak* for the President, one basic theme proposes itself immediately: the President, or somebody very close to the President, gave Bartlett the idea that an attack upon Stevenson was not impermissible. It is an administrative way of seizing Stevenson by the throat and slamming him against a wall.

What? Soft on Cuba you son of a bitch?

Newspapers and politics are married. One cannot have a theme without its development. So a contrary and second hypothesis emerges from the first; it goes: Bartlett is not merely a leak for the President, but indeed has a set of spigots for a dozen different members of the administration. The President knew nothing in advance of Alsop and Bartlett's article, goes the second interpretation. On the contrary it is a plot by the Right Wing of the administration to eat up the Left Wing. Since this second conception is Liberal, it concludes that the President will not destroy Adlai Stevenson but rescue him.

Then there is a full theory in the center. It is created out of the othe two theories. It supposes that Kennedy gave the secret of the conversa tions to Bartlett in order to rescue Adlai Stevenson later. By thi supposition, John F. Kennedy must be much like Madame de Staël. I was remarked of this heroine that she liked to throw her friends into th pool in order to have the pleasure of fishing them out again.

I do not think the President throws his assistants into the pool fo such a ladylike reason. Doubtless, he acts more like the pure moo man and good scientist he is. He knows that polls are not enough to tes the pulse of the public. One needs a small explosion here, a bit of blas there. Hot ore to examine. Hot ants. One way to test the ferment of the extreme Right is to tie Adlai Stevenson to their anthill, put a splash o gasoline at his feet, and strike a match. Will he be burned? will he be bitten to death by ants? will he recover? If this last option show vitality and Stevenson survives, one may assume the Right Wing i growing weak. On the other hand, if by the time you read thi Stevenson is no longer our Ambassador to the U.N., then the Righ Wing has more strength now than it did before Cuba became the cente of the world.

I make a prediction. I think Stevenson will still be Ambassador to the U.N. Once the President proved he was ready for an atomic war, the National Ticket was finally created. John F. Kennedy for Presi- dent, Barry Goldwater for Vice-President. Adlai Stevenson and Wil- liam F. Buckley, Jr. to stand on the platform beside them.

The only people who will vote against the National Ticket will be a few hundred unreconstructed Birchites, a few followers of George Lincoln Rockwell, fifty very old socialists loyal to Daniel De Leon, five or six junkies, eighty-two beatniks brave enough to keep wearing beards, a covey of vegetarians, a flying squad of pacifists, the three remaining bona-fide Communists of America, and the ten thousand members of the FBI who have infiltrated the Communist Party and will be afraid to vote for fear that one of the three bona-fide live Communists might see them and expose them to the wrath of the Party.

After the National Ticket is elected, we could have the Jack and

Barry show. Edward Murrow might see his way clear to give us a tour of the Vice-President's electronic shack in Arizona.

Write me a letter. Tell me that what I do in this column is no more than nightclub smut and patter. Remind me that I am trying to deface the sanctity of America's institutions.

For fact, the only institutions which remain alive in American life are those which afford a press representative. The newspaper does not report history any longer. It must make it. The press representative helps them to make it. So the newspapers help to create institutions (that is to say: instrumentalities) which will supply them with news.

For the most part, newspapers tell nothing but lies. They prefer therefore to accept news from institutions which tell lies. Everyone knows that. The reason we still believe what we read in the papers is that we like to spend five cents, seven cents, or a dime, and relax for a while. We cannot relax if we admit to ourselves that a lie is entering the nervous system. Somewhere in the censor of the mind, one decides it is less debilitating to accept a ration of lies as a squad of facts.

It used to be, not very many years ago, that politicians could use the Washington Press Corps as a series of Certified Leaks. They could play the body politic like the strings of a harp. A piece of news was rarely what it presented itself to be—it was rather a lie which, put next to other lies, gave the intimation of a clue. At its best, a news story was the key to a cryptogram.

One offers a mythical example. The New York *Times* on a given day some ten or twelve years ago has a story with byline on page three. It is trivial and it is dull. But it is on page three. So its importance is underlined. The story states that an "undisclosed reliable source" has said today that sentiment among the West Germans to end the Nuremberg Trials is increasing. One knows the "source" is the Secretary of State because the reporter is his Certified Leak. Now of course this story has no sociological bottom. The Secretary of State did not conduct a private poll of West Germans. Nor is he interested to serve the public with the latest information available to him. On the contrary he has no information: he is simply announcing to various experts in

America, Europe, and West Germany that America is getting ready to end its de-Nazification program. Since the Secretary of State does not speak in his own name but through his Certified Leak, the experts are also advised to advise their particular institutions that the announcement of this new policy is several weeks to several months away. Objections by the separate institutions may be considered. Democratic process.

Those were the good old days of the Truman or Eisenhower Administration. With a code-breaking machine at hand, it was a high navigational pleasure to read a paper. Supplied with a handbook of Certified Leaks, one could explore the news tributaries of the world. A genius could have put out a great newspaper without ever leaving his room. He just had to be a plumber with a plumber's snake.

But the Serpent entered Paradise. The Certified Leaks began to make news independently. Sometimes they were even known to betray their officials. The strings of the Goat's harp began to move in new ways. An official would try to play the harp, and a string would call, it would say, "Come here, index finger, touch me. If you don't, I'll start to vibrate without you." The Twist had entered History.

Who knows? Playing touch football, Kennedy gives the ball to Bartlett on an end around. "Don't give Adlai the ax," whispers the quarterback. "Oh, Jeez, dad," says Charley B. after his touchdown is called back, "I thought you said, *give* Adlai the ax." In such a game, which playmaker can know if his tongue is thickening or son is hip to Dad.

A Second Open Letter to JFK

This piece appeared in The Village Voice. *The comment in New York went as follows: Why wouldn't Jack Kennedy want to send his wife to New York? He probably doesn't love her.*

I was shocked. Not love Jackie Kennedy? Impossible.

With love or without love, the President could never offer his wife as a hostage to New York. It would dramatize the fact that everyone in New York is doomed if there is an atomic attack. And Left Existentialists in politics might realize that there is more political explosive in starting a campaign to make Jackie Kennedy our hostage than fifty membership drives to Ban-the-Bomb.

Dear Mr. President:

For a few days I thought I might be going to the conference you will have in Nassau with Prime Minister Macmillan on December 19 and December 20 [1962]. Then a personal matter interfered and I knew I couldn't leave. It did not matter too much. There was only one question I wanted to ask, and it is doubtful if I could have posed it to you at a press conference. I would have had to clear the question first. That might not have been possible. And the question once asked would not have been picked up by the newspapers.

Of course, Mr. President, one does not even know whether it pleases you that America is to a degree totalitarian, or whether like us, in some half-hearted bewildered way you too are wresting with the

Leviathan of our communications, our regimented communications
Yes, it is difficult to know. Your personality has nuances, almost too
many nuances. Will you be the one to save us or to blow us up?

Now, of course, this would not have been my question. It would
have been unprofessional. It would also have been impossible to
answer. Like any complex man of our time, you know that the final
intent of your heart is inscrutable even to yourself. You could answer
with the fiercest sincerity that you trusted yourself, that you believed
your motive was good, and yet one nerve might tingle in your
fingertip. That nerve might be the only indication of a demon buried
within yourself.

During that historic week in the fall of 1962 when America and
Russia were on a collision course, and it was possible the death of all
we had known could come at one minute or another, I would try to
contemplate how iron must be your nerve, and I came to the conclusion that your nerve was either very great or that you were nerveless
which is another matter. If Russia has been the villain of these years
and we the relative heroes, if we—all guilt acknowledged—have been
relatively more innocent than Russia, and our secret aim has been to
avoid war if possible, then your action was noble, your nerve worthy
of the great generals of history. But if the existence of our being is not
really essential to you or to your associates, if in depth beneath depth
of your mind there is not fear but a high calm joy at the thought of
atomic war, then what you were showing us that week was not fine
nerve but nervelessness, for then you were like a poker player with a
royal flush, a revolver in his hand, unlimited money to raise each bet
and a string of carefully graded insults calculated to tip the table and let
the shooting begin.

One does not know the answer. But the sensation is uneasy. There
was an article in *Look*, December 18. Its title was "Washington in
Crisis—154 Hours that shook the world: the untold story of our plan to
invade Cuba." Let me quote from it.

> Changes were made weekly as Castro's Cuba rattled with more rifles,
> tanks, and guns from Russia. By October 16, 1962, the invasion plan—a
> series of black loose-leaf notebooks in Pentagon safes—called for the
> massing of 100,000 men to take the island, a swarm of Air Force bombers
> and fighters and hundreds of Navy warships, from aircraft-laden carriers to
> assault landingcraft. This time, the pros would take no chances.
> *As part of the invasion plan, President Kennedy, his Cabinet, and top*

military and civilian leaders would repair to secret, atom-proof shelters in the mountains of Virginia and Maryland—for once the troops jumped off, no man could foretell with certainty the Kremlin's response. (Italics mine.)

It is not your secret atom-proof shelters in the mountains of Virginia which cause the terror—one can accept the fact that by the logic of war, you would have to be protected. It's been true for almost half a century that the General with the highest rank is to be found in the deepest part of the ground. Besides, your physical bravery is not in question.

But there is panic at the thought that your own personal safety may affect the secret estimates of your mind. None of us can be certain that our own protection from death may not leave us secretly indifferent to the extinction of a million others. Which one of us can say we wept in childhood for the famine and death of ten million Chinese?

It provokes a further question. What of your family? Does your daughter, your son, your wife go down into the bomb shelter with you? Do you know yourself to be so pure that even if you lose nothing yourself, you still can feel concern for us? Or are we militarily expendable?

So I ask you this. Why not send us a hostage? Why not let us have Jacqueline Kennedy? The moment an invasion is let loose, and you as the Commander in Chief go to your deep bomb shelter, why not send us your wife and children to share our fate in this city? New York is the place where we have air raid drills every year and no way at all to save a single body from a single Russian bomb. Yes, let your wife's helicopter land on the Hotel Carlyle, and we will know it is likely you are ready to suffer as we suffer, and that the weakness we feel before war is not merely our own pathetic inability to stare into the mountain passes of Heaven, the stench of Hell, or the plastic of cancer, but is the impotence of men who would be brave, and yet must look at the children they have become powerless to protect. You see, we in New York are now like the ten million Chinese. Show us that you understand our condition, put a hostage from your flesh into our doomed city, or know that we can never trust you completely, for deep within yourself may be contained a bright mad psychic voice which leaps to give the order that presses a button.

Yours respectfully,
Norman Mailer

Presidential Poems

One of the princes in the palace guard around the Kennedys once saw fit to tell a wife of mine that I was "an intellectual adventurer." I was struck with the accuracy of the remark. Only an intellectual adventurer would write an open poem to the President. It came at a curious time in the inner life of JFK because he was contemplating the possibilities of an all-out fallout-shelter drive, which if successful (and the largest campaigns in America seem to be the easiest ones) would have left us Egyptian as a nation: a million underground one-room crypts stocked to the barrel top with canned goods, toys, and the beginnings (undertaken by children) of cave drawings. Something went wrong with the campaign; maybe the President had a bad dream. At any rate this poem was one of a hundred thousand items which might have been present to shift his mind.

Open Poem to John Fitzgerald Kennedy

fallout
   is the hormone
   of the small town mind

a fallout shelter
   is sex

126

think how warm
  at the thought
are all of U
and little Mrs. U S A
bonging the gong
            below
while bigcity flesh
all that blond hair
      and black hair
      straight and long
      short and highly curled
      floating in through
             the trees
         a dew
         of homogenized bone
         and blood mist
    atom bombs
      are not so bad
      says small-time
        in the town mind
      they disinfect
        the big city
      and jazz us to the toes
        out here in God's Country

    fingering is lovely
      on the edge of the grave.

Mr. President
  you realize of course
  that your shelter program
    for every home owner
    is sexing up the countryside
    and killing us in the
        bigcity bar.
  If this is good
    for the vitality
    of the nation

(I mean that countryside
   could stand some sex)
then Mr. President
you are a genius
and corporation executives
living in the suburbs
with the five thousand
                  dollar
                  shelters
ought to salute you.
                  I do.

A few short poems. The first was written during a week when the
President was on a campaign to help the dairy industries of America.

The President
      has asked us
      to drink a glass of milk
            each day.

I'm sure
      he doesn't ask
      us
      to do this
just because
      the milk is full
      of fallout now.

Men
who are not
      married
      and grow beards
      are insecure,
      said the CIA
before
      it went
      to Cuba.

Freedom of the Press

Let every
  writer
  tell his
      own
      lies
That's freedom
      of the
      press.

Exodus

Goodbye America
    Jesus said.
Come back, boy!
  we cried
  too late.

A. When Napoleon
    met Goethe
    it was the
    Emperor
    who wrote the poem.

B. When I met
    Kennedy . . .

C. Either:
    Jack
    is a
    greater
      man than
        me,
      Or—
        times have
          changed.

Mr.
President,
replied the matador
to the intercom,
                we
                are
                indeed hot
                        on
                        the track
                        of the
                        wonder
                        disease
                                and
                                are
                        now feeding
                        the penicillin
                        its dose.
                Expect to save
                        it
                        and all
                        group-related
                                compounds
                                if the
                        television
                                does not collapse.

        put down
                that
        penicillin
                        dad

                get me
                a dozse
                of gonorrhee

                        doing the limbo bit
                        it's good enough
                                        for me

A plague is
    coming
    named
      Virus Y S X
      still unsolved
         promises to be
     proof
     against
     antibiotics
     psychoanalysis
     research projects
     vitamins
     awards
     crash programs
     crash diets
     symposiums
     foundations
     rest
     rehabilitation
     tranquilizers
     aspirin
     surgery
     brainwashing
     lobotomies
     rises in status
     box office boffo
     perversions
        and
        even
        a
        good
        piece
        of

When that unhappy day
   comes to America
   let the Russians
   take over.

The best defense is
       infection.

To the lower classes

Noblesse
    Oblige
  has one rule
     and
  one rule only

You must be
    so nice
    so bright
    so quick and
    so well turned
      that
    no one need
      tell you
      a second time.

Tell me what?
    that the world
      is well-lost
      for love
    and the upper
      classes
      are the
      law above?

I tell you this:
    if the
    upper classes
    are kin to God
      in style—
    (which is one hypothesis
      we do not ignore:
        how else account
        for elegance?)

if the
upper classes
are kin to God
        in style
then God has no love
but guilt, nor a style
apart from fashion,
no courage but to
do in duty
                what
one does not desire
and no worth
but for His love
                at beauty

For there
        is noble's work
  their plea:
                that they
  love in truth
with all sense
            of Christian
            love
   divorced from self
the air of beauty
            and her pomp.

The poor know naught
            but death
        they do not free
        they obliterate.

Stripped of its
            distinctions
        life is a flat city
            whose isolated spurs
            cut the sky
            like housing projects.

Think of the air
      whose heart is bruised
      by touching such artifacts.
      (*Does* the cutworm forgive the plough?)

I tell you, say the rich,
            the poor are naught
            but dirty wind
            welling in air-shafts
            over the cinders
            and droppings of
            the past, their
            voices thick
            with grease
            and ordure,
            sewer-greed
            to corrode the ear
            with the horrors
            of the past
          and the voids
            of new stupidity.
          One could drown
            waiting for the poor
            to make
            one fine distinction.
Yes, destroy us
            say the rich
            and you lose
               the roots
               of God.

Destroy them
            say the poor
         we cannot breathe
         nor give
         until we etch
            on their rich nerve
            the cruel razor

and heartless club
of our past,
those sediments of
waste
which curbed
our genes
and flattened
the vision we
would give
the chromosome.

Yes, destroy them
say the poor
burn them, rob them
gorge their tears
and such half of beauty
lost to pomp
will flower
unglimpsed wonders
in the rose,
will flower
unglimpsed wonders
in the rows.

I wonder,
said the Lord
I wonder if I know the answer
any more.

Classes

When I was young
I went to the
Bowery and
slept in a flop-
house.
Next morning

my mother said
to me, "Son, don't
come in the house.
Take off your clothes
in the hall
                    and
I'll run a bath."

But my wife
has a moth-
er who would
have said on
her return,
            "Oh good.
                You're just in time.
I hope you've
caught some lice.
Don't take off
        a thing.
We're going to visit
        a woman I detest
and I want you to sit
        on all her seats."

Poem to the Book Review at *Time*

You will keep hiring
        picadors from the back row
        and pic the bull back
        far back along his spine
You will pass a wine
        poisoned on the vine
You will saw the horns off
        and murmur
The bulls are
        ah, the bulls are not
        what once they were

Before the corrida is over
    there will be Russians in the plaza
Swine some of you will say
what did we wrong?
and go forth to kiss the conqueror.

An Impolite Interview

In this dialogue, the subjects grind by like boxcars on a two-mile freight. Never do so many intellectual items seem to be handled so quickly—it would be fatal if the cargo were fragile, or the mind of the reader. Done with elegance, such an interview might be appropriate to a President. As done by Paul Krassner and myself it reads, if one may shift the metaphor, like a blow-by-blow of two strong club fighters going sixteen rounds in a gym. Here is the schedule of our rounds: Pacifism, the FBI, the sexual revolution, birth control, literary style, totalitarianism, the new revolutionary, the aesthetics of bombing, masturbation, heterosexual sex, adolescent sex, sexual selection, homosexual sex, the sex of the upper class, and Negro sex. What a fight! Considerately, the last round is devoted to mysticism.

Q. When you and I first talked about the possibility of doing an impolite interview, we kind of put it off because you said: "I find that when I discuss ideas, it spills the tension I need to write." Which seems like a very Freudian explanation. Does it still apply?

A. It does. Sure it does. I think putting out half-worked ideas in an interview is like premature ejaculation.

Q. Then why bother?

A. I got tired of saying no to you.

Q. That's all?

A. I'm beginning to get a little pessimistic about the number of ideas I never write up. Perhaps the public is better off with premature ejaculation than no intellectual sex at all. I'm just thinking of the public, not myself.

Q. All right, this is a question which I'm asking in the context of the cold war and the possibility of a hot war: Isn't there a basic dichotomy between creative artists who express themselves in their work—there's a definite excitement in their life—as opposed to the average person whose days are filled with boredom—in the factory, in the office—and who can almost find a sort of pleasure in identifying nationalistically with international tensions? And so the people who are happy in their own creative outlets are the ones who write poems about peace . . .

A. First time I've heard you talking like a totalitarian. Very few artists I know are happy. The kind of artist who writes a poem about peace is the kind of guy I flee.

There's something pompous about people who join peace movements, SANE, and so forth. They're the radical equivalent of working for the FBI. You see, nobody can criticize you. You're doing God's work, you're clean. How can anyone object to anybody who works for SANE, or is for banning the bomb?

Q. You're not questioning their motives, are you?

A. I *am* questioning their motives. I think there's something doubtful about these people. I don't trust them. I think they're totalitarian in spirit. Now of course I'm certainly not saying they're Communist, and they most obviously are not Fascists, but there are new kinds of totalitarians. A most numerous number since World War II.

I think, for example, most of the medical profession is totalitarian by now. At least those who push antibiotics are totalitarian. I think the FBI is totalitarian. I think pacifists are totalitarian. I think *Time* magazine is a Leviathan of the totalitarian. There's a totalitarian *Geist*, a spirit, which takes many forms, has many manifestations. People on your own side are just as likely to be totalitarian as people on the other side.

Q. Yes, but totalitarian to me implies force—

A. A dull, moral, abstract force. There is just such a force in the campaign for "Ban the bomb." It's too safe. That's the thing I don't like about it. You don't *lose* anything by belonging to a committee to ban the bomb. Who's going to hurt you? Is the FBI going to stick you in jail?

Q. There are certain employers who frown upon it—

A. Which employer? I think many good people are beginning to get a little complacent. The sort of good people who are militant and imaginative and active and brave, and want a world they're willing to fight for; if there were a revolution they would carry a gun; if there were an underground they would fight a guerrilla war. But there is no real action for them, and so they end up in what I think are essentially passive campaigns like "Ban the bomb."

I'm against sit-down strikes. I'm against people sitting down in Trafalgar Square, and cops having to carry them off. I think if you're not ready to fight the police, you mustn't sit down and let them carry you off. You must recognize that you're not ready to fight to the very end of your principles. I was carried off in a chair not so long ago and I'm not proud of it.

Q. Well, extending this to its logical conclusion, then, would you say that Mahatma Gandhi was a totalitarian?

A. I think so. He was a fine man, a great man, etc., etc., but many totalitarians are fine men. Sigmund Freud, for example.

For all we know—I don't know anything about Albert Schweitzer—Schweitzer might be totalitarian. How do you know? He seems too safe. The kind of people who seem to love Schweitzer are the sort who take a pill if their breasts hurt. Anybody who wants a quick solution for a permanent problem is a low grade totalitarian.

Q. At the risk of making you seem totalitarian, what would you substitute for sit-down strikes and other passive forms of protest?

A. Sketch the outline of a large argument. What I don't like about the "Ban the bomb" program, for example, is that it is precisely the sort of political program which can enlist hundreds of thousands, and then millions of people. Half or two-thirds or even three-quarters of the world could belong to such an organization, and yet you could still have an atomic war. I'm not saying the "Ban the bomb" program would *cause* an atomic war, but there's absolutely no proof it would prevent it. If you have people who are evil enough to lust for an atomic war, they are even more likely to force that war if there looks to be a real danger that they will never have a war.

Our best hope for no atomic war is that the complexities of political life at the summit remain complex. One has to assume such men as Kennedy and Khrushchev are *half-way* decent, are not *necessarily* going to blow up the world, that indeed if everything else is equal they would just as soon *not* blow up the world. So I say create complex-ities, let art deepen sophistication, let complexities be demonstrated to our leaders, let us try to make *them* more complex. That is a manly activity. It offers more hope for saving the world than a gaggle of pacifists and vegetarians. The "Ban the bomb" program is not manly. It is militant but it is not manly. So it is in danger of becoming totalitarian.

Q. Joe Heller told me that he admires you for—and may join you next time—just standing in City Hall Park and not taking shelter during the Civil Defense drill. Why is this any more manly than other activities?

A. I didn't stand there because I was a pacifist, but because I wanted to help demonstrate a complexity. It's a physical impossibility to save the people of New York in the event of atomic attack. Anyone who chooses to live in New York is doomed in such a case. That doesn't mean one should not live in New York, but I think it does mean one should know the possible price. Air raid drills delude people into believing that they're safe in New York. That's what I object to, rounding up the psyches of New Yorkers and giving them mass close order drill to the sound of an air raid siren. It's piggish. It makes cowardly pigs of people.

Q. You once referred in passing to the FBI as a religious move-ment; would you elaborate on that?

A. I think a lot of people need the FBI for their sanity. That is to say, in order to be profoundly religious, to become a saint, for example, one must dare insanity, but if one wishes instead to flee from insanity, then one method is to join an organized religion. The FBI is an organized religion.

The FBI blots out everything which could bring dread into the average mediocrity's life. Like a weak lover who rushes to immolate himself for love, since that is easier than to fight a long war for love, the mediocrity offers the FBI his complete conformity. He gives up his personal possibilities. He believes he is living for the sake of others. The trouble is that the others are just as mediocre as he is. Such people not only use themselves up, their own lives, but if there *is* a God, they use *Him* up.

Naturally these lovers of the FBI can't even think of the possibility that they've wasted themselves. Instead they believe rabidly in that force which agrees with them, that force which is rabidly for mediocrity. The only absolute organization in America, the FBI. At bottom, I mean profoundly at bottom, the FBI has nothing to do with Communism, it has nothing to do with catching criminals, it has nothing to do with the Mafia, the syndicate, it has nothing to do with trustbusting, it has nothing to do with interstate commerce, it has nothing to do with anything but serving as a church for the mediocre. A high church for the true mediocre.

Q. In terms of the mass media being a force to which one subjects oneself more voluntarily than to the FBI, isn't it possible that the mass media which you call totalitarian are a reflection rather than a cause of this condition in society?

A. A reflection of what people want? No, I don't think so. That's like saying that the United States Army was a reflection of what the soldiers wanted.

Q. But they were drafted—

A. And you're not drafted—your eye is not *drafted* when you turn on that TV set? To assume that people are getting what they want through the mass media also assumes that the men and women who direct the mass media know something about the people. But they don't know anything about the people. That's why I gave you the example of the Army. The Private exists in a world which is hermetically alienated from the larger aims of the Generals who are planning the higher strategy of the war. I mean part of the tragedy of modern war (or what used to be modern war) is that you could have a noble war which was utterly ignoble at its basic level because the people who directed the war couldn't reach the common man who was carrying the gun. As for example, Franklin Delano Roosevelt and the average infantryman.

And the reason they can't is because there *is* such a thing as classes, finally. And the upper classes don't understand the lower classes, they're incapable of it. Every little detail of their upbringing turns them away from the possibility of such understanding.

The mass media is made up of a group of people who are looking for money and for power. The reason is not because they have any moral sense, any inner sense of a goal, of an ideal that's worth fighting for, dying for, if one is brave enough. No, the reason they want power is because power is the only thing which will relieve the profound illness which has seized them. Which has seized all of us. The illness of the twentieth century. There isn't psychic room for all of us. Malthus's law has moved from the excessive procreation of bodies to the excessive mediocritization of psyches. The deaths don't occur on the battlefield any longer, or through malnutrition; they occur within the brain, within the psyche itself.

Q. There's a certain indirect irony there. I'm under the impression that you have almost a Catholic attitude toward birth control.

A. I do. In a funny way I do. But I've come a long way to get there. After all, if my generation of writers represents anything, if there's anything we've fought for, it's for a sexual revolution.

We've gotten things printed here that twenty years ago would've seemed impossible for a century or forever. I can name them. Not only *Lady Chatterley's Lover* and *Tropic of Cancer*, but little things like "The Time of Her Time"; extraordinary works like *Naked Lunch*.

We've won this war, or at least we're in the act of winning it. You might say that the church and the reactionaries are in long retreat on sex.

It's altogether their fault, as far as that goes. They flirted with sex. They used sex in order to make money or gain power. It was the Church, after all, who dominated Hollywood. They thought they could tolerate sex up to a point in Hollywood, because there was obviously a fast buck if you used sex in the movies, and they didn't want to alienate the producers of movies. So the Church compromised its principles.

What happened was that they set something going they couldn't stop. And then people came along who were sincere about sex, and idealistic, naive no doubt like a good many of us, innocent sexual totalitarians, we felt sex is good, sex has to be defended, sex has to be fought for, sex has to be liberated. We were looking for a good war. So we liberated sex.

The liberation goes on now. It's going to keep going on. But the liberation's gotten into the hands of a lot of people who aren't necessarily first-rate. A crew of sexual bullies may be taking over the world. Sexual epigones. Corporation executives who dabble.

The fact of the matter is that the prime responsibility of a woman probably is to be on earth long enough to find the best mate possible for herself, and conceive children who will improve the species.

If you get too far away from that, if people start using themselves as flesh laboratories, if they start looking for pills which prevent conception, then what they're doing, what really at bottom they're doing, is acting like the sort of people who take out a new automobile and put sand in the crank case in order to see if the sound that the motor gives off is a new sound.

Q. You're forcing me to the point of personalizing this. Do you use contraception? Do you put sand in your crank case?

A. I hate contraception.

Q. I'm not asking you what your attitude toward it is.

A. It's none of your business. Let me just say I try to practice what I preach. I *try* to.

Q. Then you believe in unplanned parenthood?

A. There's nothing I abhor more than planned parenthood. Planned parenthood is an abomination. I'd rather have those fucking Communists over here. Will you print fucking?

Q. You said it, didn't you? Just tell me if you want it spelled with two g's or a c-k.

A. Those fucking Communists.

Q. You want a 'g' on the end of it, or just an apostrophe?

A. No, I want a 'g' on the end of it.

Q. In "The Time of Her Time," the protagonist calls his penis The Avenger. Doesn't this imply a certain hostility toward women?

A. Of course it does. Is that news?

Q. All right, why is the narrator of your story—or why are you— hostile toward women?

A. If you're assuming there was an identification with the character, I can only say I *enjoyed* him. He was not altogether different from me. But he certainly wasn't me. I thought The Avenger was a good term to use. I think people walk around with terms like that in their unconscious mind. There're a great many men who think of their cock as The Avenger.

But O'Shaugnessy happened to be enormously civilized. So he was able to open his unconscious and find the word, find the concept, and use it, humorously, to himself.

Q. If there was any hostility beneath the humor, would you say it was justified?

A.   I would guess that most men who understand women at all feel hostility toward them. At their worst, women are low sloppy beasts.

Q. Do you find that men and women have reacted differently to "The Time of Her Time"?

A. I've found that most women like "The Time of Her Time" for some reason. Men tend to get touchy about it. They feel—is Mailer saying this is the way he makes love? Is he this good or is he this bad? Is he a phony? Is he advertising himself? Does he make love better than me? To which I say they're asses.

Q. Oh, so you're hostile toward men!

A. I'm hostile to men, I'm hostile to women, I'm hostile to cats, to poor cockroaches, I'm afraid of horses. You know.

Q. Several months ago I mentioned, in order to make a very definite point, a Cuban prostitute—this was the first prostitute I'd ever gone to, and I had been asking her all these questions about the Revolution—and she stopped later in the middle of fellatio to ask me if I was a Communist.

A. You were in Cuba at the time?

Q. Yes. And she was anti-Castro.

A. Because he was cleaning them out of the whorehouses?

Q. Well, there were no more tourists coming to Cuba, and it was ruining their business. Anyway, I described this incident in the Realist, *and was accused of exhibitionism by some friends of mine. And I'm secure enough in my life that I had no need to boast about this; but it was a funny, significant thing which I wanted to share with the readers.*

A. Oh, I remember that, I remember reading your piece now. I was a little shocked by it.

Q. You're kidding.

A. No, I was shocked. I wasn't profoundly shocked. It threw me slightly. I had a feeling, "That's not good writing." And the next thought was, "Mailer, you're getting old." And the next thought was, "If you're not really getting old, but there is something indeed bad about this writing, what is it that's bad about it?"

Q. And?

A. A whore practicing fellatio looks up and says, "Are you a Communist?"—that's what the modern world is all about in a way. Saying it head-on like that probably gave the atmosphere honesty. But, in some funny way, it didn't belong. I don't want to start talking like a literary buff, because I dislike most literary language, Hemingway's perhaps most of all (it was so arch), but still in a way a good writer is like a pitcher, and a reader is happy when he feels like a good batter facing a good pitcher. When the ball comes in, he gets that lift.

But writing it the way you did, Krassner, you were in effect hitting fungoes. You were making the reader field it, which is less agreeable than batting. If the reader had been able to guess that this was what was going on with the whore—I don't know how you could have done it; that would have been the art of it—to phrase the language in such a way that the reader thinks, "Oh, Jesus, she's sucking his cock, and she asks him if he's a Communist." If it had happened that way, it might have been overpowering. What a montage.

Maybe it was the use of "fellatio," maybe you just should have said, "I was having my cock sucked and she said, 'Are you a Communist?'" If you're getting into the brutality of it, get into the brutality of it. Throw a beanball. Don't use the Latinism. Maybe it was the Latinism that threw me. All I know is that there was something bad about it, the effect was *shock*.

Q. So you were shocked by a euphemism . . .

A. Shock is like banging your head or taking a dull fall; your wits are deadened.

Q. That's what I wanted to do in the writing, because that's what happened to me in the act.

A. Then you're not interested in art, you're interested in therapy. That's the trouble—there are too many people writing nowadays who give no art to the world, but draw in therapy to themselves.

Q. No, not in my case. It didn't change me one way or the other, writing it. I just wanted to put it into the consciousness of the reader. That's not therapy for me.

A. Well, then you should've said, "She was sucking my cock." I mean that's my professional opinion.

Q. It wasn't in Roget's Thesaurus. . . . Would you agree that you have an essentially biological approach to history?

A. I think I do, but I could never talk about it. I don't know enough history.

Q. To narrow it down to the present, if you were a future historian of sex, how would you look upon the Kennedy administration?

A. I'd say there's more acceptance of sexuality in America today than there was before he came in. Whether that's good or bad, I don't know. It may be a promiscuous acceptance of sexuality.

Q. Are you saying it's because of . . . ?

A. Because of Kennedy—*absolutely*. I mean, just think of going to a party given by Eisenhower as opposed to a party thrown by Kennedy. Do you have to wonder at which party you'd have a better time?

The average man daydreams about his leader. He thinks of being invited to his leader's home. If he thinks of being invited to Eisenhower's home, he thinks of how proper he's going to be. If he thinks of going to the Kennedys for a party, he thinks of having a dance with Jackie. Things liven up.

Why do you think people loved Hitler in Germany? Because they all secretly wished to get hysterical and *stomp* on things and scream and shout and rip things up and *kill*—tear people apart. Hitler pretended to offer them that. In some subtle way, he communicated it. That's why they wanted him. That's why he was good for Germany— they wanted such horror. Of course, by the end he didn't tear people apart, he gassed them.

If America gets as sick as Germany was before Hitler came in, we'll have our Hitler. One way or another, we'll have our Hitler.

But the point is, you see, the political fight right now is not to deal with the ends of the disease, but the means right here and now. To try to foil the sickness and root it out rather than calculate political programs for the future. One can have fascism come in any form at all, through the church, through sex, through social welfare, through state conservatism, through organized medicine, the FBI, the Pentagon. Fascism is not a way of life but a murderous mode of deadening reality by smothering it with lies.*

Every time one sees a bad television show, one is watching the nation get ready for the day when a Hitler will come. Not because the ideology of the show is Fascistic; on the contrary its manifest ideology is invariably liberal, but the show still prepares Fascism because it is meretricious art and so sickens people a little further. Whenever people get collectively sick, the remedy becomes progressively more violent and hideous. An insidious, insipid sickness demands a violent far-reaching purgative.

Q. When I interviewed Jean Shepherd he made the point— sarcastically—how come it's always the Bad Guys who become leaders?

*See Appendix A.

A. Lenin wasn't a Bad Guy. Trotsky wasn't a Bad Guy. I don't think Napoleon was such a Bad Guy. I don't think Alexander the Great was such a Bad Guy. Bad Guys become leaders in a bad time.

One can conceive of a man who's half-good and half-bad who comes to power in a time of great crisis and great change, a time when awful things are going on. He's going to reflect some of the awfulness of his time. He may become awful himself, which is a tragedy.

A man like Danton begins as a great man, and deteriorates. Castro may end badly, but that will be a tragedy. No one's ever going to tell me he wasn't a great man when he started.

Q. Then you're saying it's bad times which result in bad leaders.

A. Well, if a time is bad enough, a good man can't possibly succeed. In a bad time, the desires of the multitude are bad, they're low, they're ugly, they're greedy, they're cowardly, they're piggish, shitty.

Q. Let's get into this, then. How do you sap the energy of bad leaders who are caught up in their own bad time?

A. In a bad time, a leader is responsible to his own services of propaganda. He doesn't control them. In a modern state, the forces of propaganda control leaders as well as citizens, because the forces of propaganda are more complex than the leader. In a bad time, the war to be fought is in the mass media.

If anyone is a leftist, or a radical, if a man becomes an anarchist, a hipster, some kind of proto-Communist, a rebel, a wild reactionary, I don't care what—if he's somebody who's got a sense that the world is wrong and he's more-or-less right, that there are certain lives he feels are true and good and worth something, worth more than the oppressive compromises he sees before him every day, then he feels that the world has got to be changed or it is going to sink into one disaster or another. He may even feel as I do that we are on the edge of being plague-ridden forever.

Well, if he feels all these things, the thing to do, if he wants political action, is not to look for organizations which he can join, nor to look for long walks he can go on with other picketeers, although that's obviously far better than joining passive organizations, but rather it is to devote his life to working subtly, silently, steelfully, against the state.

And there's one best way he can do that. He can *join* the mass media. He can bore from within. He shouldn't look to form a sect or a cell—he should do it alone. The moment he starts to form sects and cells, he's beginning to create dissension and counter-espionage agents.

The history of revolutionary movements is that they form cells, then they defeat themselves. The worst and most paranoid kind of secret police—those split personalities who are half secret policemen and half revolutionaries (I'm talking of psychological types rather than of literal police agents)—enter these organizations and begin to manufacture them over again from within.

It's better to work alone, trusting no one, just working, working, working not to sabotage so much as to shift and to turn and to confuse the mass media and hold the mirror to its guilt, keep the light in its eye, never, never, never oneself beginning to believe that the legitimate work one is doing in the mass media has some prior value to it; always knowing that the work no matter how well intended is likely to be subtly hideous work. The mass media does diabolically subtle things to the morale and life of the people who do their work; few of us are strong enough to live alone in enemy territory. But it's work which must be done.

So long as the mass media are controlled completely by one's enemies, the living tender sensuous and sensual life of all of us is in danger. And the way to fight back is not to look to start a group or a cell or to write a program, but instead it is to look for a job in the heart of the enemy.

Q. In The Naked and the Dead, *there was a theme about the futility of violence on a grand scale; and yet, in "The White Negro," there's almost a justification of violence, at least on a personal level. How do you reconcile this apparent inconsistency?*

A. The ideas I had about violence changed 180 degrees over those years. Beneath the ideology in *The Naked and The Dead* was an obsession with violence. The characters for whom I had the most secret admiration, like Croft, were violent people.

Ideologically, intellectually, I did disapprove of violence, though I didn't at the time of "The White Negro."

But what I still disapprove of is *inhuman* violence—violence which is on a large scale and abstract. I disapprove of bombing a city. I disapprove of the kind of man who will derive aesthetic satisfaction from the fact that an Ethiopian village looks like a red rose at the moment the bombs are exploding. I won't disapprove of the act of perception which witnesses that: I think that act of perception is—I'm going to use the word again—noble.

What I'm getting at is: a native village is bombed, and the bombs happen to be beautiful when they land; in fact it would be odd if all that sudden destruction did not liberate some beauty. The form a bomb takes in its explosion may be in part a picture of the potentialities it destroyed. So let us accept the idea that the bomb is beautiful.

If so, any liberal who decries the act of bombing is totalitarian if he doesn't admit as well that the bombs were indeed beautiful.

Because the moment we tell something that's untrue, it does not matter how pure our motives may be—the moment we start mothering mankind and decide that one truth is good for them to hear and another is not so good, because while *we* can understand, those poor ignorant unfortunates cannot—then what are we doing, we're depriving the minds of others of knowledge which may be essential.

Think of a young pilot who comes along later, some young pilot who goes out on a mission and isn't prepared for the fact that a bombing might be beautiful; he could conceivably be an idealist, there were some in the war against Fascism. If the pilot is totally unprepared he might never get over the fact that he was particularly thrilled by the beauty of that bomb.

But if our culture had been large enough to say that Ciano's son-in-law not only found that bomb beautiful, but that indeed this act of perception was *not* what was wrong; the evil was to think that this beauty was worth the lot of living helpless people who were wiped out broadside. Obviously, whenever there's destruction, there's going to be beauty implicit in it.

Q. *Aren't you implying that this beauty is an absolute? Which, beauty is never . . .*

A. Well, you don't know. How do you know beauty is not an absolute? Listen, you guys on the *Realist*—I read you because I think you represent a point of view, and you carry that point of view very, very far, you're true to that point of view—but I think you're getting a touch sloppy because you get no opposition whatsoever from your own people; you'll get your head taken off at its base some day by a reactionary. He'll go right through you, because there are so many things you haven't thought out.

One of them is: How do you know beauty isn't absolute?

Q. *Recently I referred in the* Realist *to Sonny Nunez, a dead* prizefighter, and Sherri Finkbone, a pregnant woman, and I suggested that if she really wanted to get a legal abortion, she should just sign up for a boxing match—to point out the irony that it's legal to kill a man in the ring, but it's illegal to remove a fetus from a woman. Would you like to attack that comparison?

A. Ah, yes. Atrocious. I think that's taking a cheap advantage. In one case a man is killed who is able to defend himself. In the other, an embryo who may have voyaged through eternity to be born again is snuffed out because of his mother's cultural propensity for socially accepted drugs like the limb-killer thalidomide.

Q. Both incidents took place in Arizona, and I just felt it was a dramatic way—

A. If somebody takes a handful of shit and throws it against the wall at a party, that's dramatic, but it's distasteful. Your example is distasteful. You were appealing to the low emotions in your readers. You have a terrible responsibility in the *Realist*, because *your* readers have low emotions too. Just because nobody could find the sort of stuff that's printed in the *Realist* except in the *Realist*, there is a danger that the people who read the sheet are going to begin to think there's something superior about them, just from the sheer fact they're reading the *Realist*.

Q. Do you think you're something of a puritan when it comes to masturbation?

A. I think masturbation is bad.

Q. In relation to heterosexual fulfillment?

A. In relation to everything—orgasm, heterosexuality, to style, to stance, to be able to fight the good fight. I think masturbation cripples people. It doesn't cripple them altogether, but it turns them askew, it sets up a bad and often enduring tension. I mean has anyone ever studied the correlation between cigarette smoking and masturbation? Anybody who spends his adolescence masturbating, generally enters his young manhood with no sense of being a man. The answer—I don't know what the answer is—sex for adolescents may be the answer, it may not. I really don't know.

Q. But can't one kid start young with heterosexual relations and yet develop all the wrong kinds of attitudes—while another kid will go through his adolescence masturbating and yet see the humor of it, see the absurdity of it, know it's temporary?

A. I wouldn't dream of laying down a law with no variation. But let me say it another way. At the time I was growing up, there was much more sexual repression than there is today. One knew sex was good and everything was in the way of it. And so one did think of it as one of the wars to fight, if not *the* war to fight—the war for greater sexual liberty.

Masturbation was one expression of that deprivation. No adolescent would ever masturbate, presumably, if he could have sex with a girl. A lot of adolescents masturbate because they don't want to take part in homosexuality.

Q. There are certain societies where masturbation—

A. All I'm talking about is the one society I *know*. I'll be damned if I'm going to be led around with a ring in my nose by anthropologists. mean the few I've known personally have always struck me as slightly absurd. They're like eccentrics in a comic English novel. I won't take any anthropologists as a god. I'm sure they don't know A-hole from appetite about "certain societies."

But we were talking about masturbation as the result of sexual repression. I don't see any reason to defend it. If you have more sexual liberty, why the hell still defend masturbation?

One has to keep coming back to one notion: How do you make life? How do you *not* make life? You have to assume, just as a working stance, that life is probably good—if it isn't good, then our existence is such an absurdity that *any* action immediately becomes absurd—but if you assume that life is good, then you have to assume that those things which keep life from happening—which tend to make life more complex without becoming more useful, more stimulating—are bad.

Anything that tends to make a man a machine without giving him the power to increase the real life in himself is bad.

Q. Is it possible that you have a totalitarian attitude against masturbation?

A. I wouldn't say all people who masturbate are evil, probably I would even say that some of the best people in the world masturbate. But I am saying it's a miserable activity.

Q. Well, we're getting right back now to this notion of absolutes. You know—to somebody, masturbation can be a thing of beauty—

A. To what end? To what end? Who is going to benefit from it?

Q. It's a better end than the beauty of a bombing.

A. Masturbation is bombing. It's bombing oneself.

Q. I see nothing wrong if the only person hurt from masturbation is

the one who practices it. But it can also benefit—look, Stekel wrote a
book on autoeroticsm, and one of the points he made was that at least
it saved some people who might otherwise go out and commit rape. He
was talking about extremes, but—

A. It's better to commit rape than masturbate. Maybe, maybe. The
whole thing becomes very difficult.

Q. But rape involves somebody else. The minute you—

A. Just talking about it on the basis of violence: one is violence
toward oneself; one is violence toward others. And you don't recognize—let's follow your argument and be speculative for a moment—if
everyone becomes violent toward themselves, then past a certain
point the entire race commits suicide. But if everyone becomes violent
toward everyone else, you would probably have one wounded hero-
monster left.

Q. And he'd have to masturbate.

A. That's true . . . But—you use that to point out how tragic was
my solution, which is that he wins and still has to masturbate. I reply
that at least it was more valuable than masturbating in the first place.
Besides he might have no desire to masturbate. He might lie down and
send his thoughts back to the root of his being.

Q. I think there's a basic flaw in your argument. Why are you
assuming that masturbation is violence unto oneself? Why is it not
pleasure unto oneself? And I'm not defending masturbation—well,
I'm defending masturbation, yes, as a substitute if and when—

A. All right, look. When you make love, whatever is good in you
or bad in you, goes out into someone else. I mean this literally. I'm not
interested in the biochemistry of it, the electromagnetism of it, nor in
how the psychic waves are passed back and forth, and what psychic
waves are. All I know is that when one makes love, one changes a
woman slightly and a woman changes you slightly.

Q. Certain circumstances can change one for the worse.

A. But at least you have gone through a process which is part of
life.

One can be better for the experience, or worse. But one has
experience to absorb, to think about, one has literally to digest the new
spirit which has entered the flesh. The body has been galvanized for an
experience of flesh, a declaration of the flesh.

If one has the courage to think about every aspect of the act—I don't
mean think mechanically about it, but if one is able to brood over the

act, to dwell on it—then one is *changed* by the act. Even if one has been *jangled* by the act. Because in the act of restoring one's harmony, one has to encounter all the reasons one was jangled.

So finally one has had an experience which is nourishing. Nourishing because one's able to *feel* one's way into more difficult or more precious insights as a result of it. One's able to live a tougher, more heroic life if one can digest and absorb the experience.

But, if one masturbates, all that happens is, everything that's beautiful and good in one, goes up the hand, goes into the air, is *lost*. Now what the hell is there to *absorb*? One hasn't tested himself. You see, in a way, the heterosexual act lays questions to rest, and makes one able to build upon a few answers. Whereas if one masturbates, the ability to contemplate one's experience is disturbed. Instead, fantasies of power take over and disturb all sleep.

If one has, for example, the image of a beautiful sexy babe in masturbation, one still doesn't know whether one can make love to her in the flesh. All you know is that you can violate her in your *brain*. Well, a lot of good that is.

But if one has fought the good fight or the evil fight and ended with the beautiful sexy dame, then if the experience is good, your life is changed by it; if the experience is not good, one's life is also changed by it, in a less happy way. But at least one knows something of what happened. One has something real to build on.

The ultimate direction of masturbation always has to be insanity.

Q. But you're not man enough to take the other position, which is sex for the young. Except for petting, what else is there between those two alternatives?

A. I'd say, between masturbation and sex for the young, I prefer sex for the young. Of course. But I think there may be still a third alternative: At the time I grew up, sex had enormous fascination for everyone, but it had no dignity, it had no place. It was not a value. It had nothing to do with procreation, it had to do with the bathroom—it was burning, it was feverish, it was dirty, cute, giggly.

The thought of waiting for sex never occurred—when I was young my parents did not speak about sex, and no one else I knew ever discussed the possibility of holding onto one's sex as the single most important thing one has. To keep one's sex until one got what one deserved for it—that was never suggested to me when I was young.

The possibilities were to go out and have sex with a girl, have homosexual sex, or masturbate. Those were the choices. The fourth alternative—chastity, if you will—was ridiculous and absurd. It's probably more absurd today. If you talked to kids of chastity today, they would not stop laughing, I'm certain.

But the fact of the matter is, if you get marvelous sex when you're young, all right; but if you're not ready to make a baby with that marvelous sex, then you may also be putting something down the drain forever, which is the ability that you had to make a baby; the most marvelous thing that was in you may have been shot into a diaphragm, or wasted on a pill. One might be losing one's future.

The point is that, so long as one has a determinedly atheistic and rational approach to life, then the only thing that makes sense is the most comprehensive promiscuous sex you can find.

Q. Well, since I do have an essentially atheistic and more-or-less rational approach to life, I think I can speak with at least my individual authority. As a matter of fact, the more rational I become, the more selective—

A. You know, "selective" is a word that sounds like a refugee from a group therapy session.

Q. I've never been in any kind of therapy—

A. No, I know, but there's a *plague* coming out of all these centers—they go around *infecting* all of us. The words sit in one's vocabulary like bedbugs under glass.

Q. But I can't think of a better word. "Selective" is a word that means what I want to communicate to you.

A. *Selective.* It's arrogant—how do you know who's doing the selecting? I mean you are a modest man with a good sense of yourself, but suddenly it comes to sex and you're selective. Like you won't pick *this* girl, you'll pick *that* one . . .

Q. Exactly. It's arrogant, but—

A. Yeah, yeah, yeah—but the fact that one girl wants you and the other girl *doesn't*—I mean, that has nothing to do with it?

Q. Well, they have a right to be selective, too.

A. Then it's mutually selective. Which means you fall in together or go in together. Now, those are better words than "selective." They have more to do with the body and much less to do with the machine. Electronic machines *select.*

Q. Well, what I'm saying is you make a choice. A human choice. It has nothing to do with a machine . . . I'll tell you what's bugging me—it's your mystical approach. You'll use an expression like "You may be sending the best baby that's in you out into your hand"—but even when you're having intercourse, how many unused spermatozoa will there be in one ejaculation of semen?

A. Look, America is dominated by a bunch of half-maniacal scientists, men who don't know anything about the act of creation. If science comes along and says there are one million spermatozoa in a discharge, you reason on that basis. That may not be a real basis.

We just don't know what the *real* is. We just don't know. Of the million spermatozoa, there may be only two or three with any real chance of reaching the ovum; the others are there like a supporting army, or if we're talking of planned parenthood, as a body of the electorate. These sperm go out with no sense at all of being real spermatozoa under the microscope, but after all, a man from Mars who's looking at us through a telescope might think that Communist bureaucrats and FBI men look exactly the same.

Q. Well, they are.

A. Krassner's jab piles up more points. The point is that the scientists don't know what's going on. That meeting of the ovum and the sperm is too mysterious for the laboratory. Even the electron microscope can't measure the striations of passion in a spermatozoon. Or the force of its will.

But we can trust our emotion. Our emotions are a better guide to what goes on in these matters than scientists.

Q. But in the act of pleasure—go back to your instincts, as you say—in the act of sex you're not thinking in terms of procreation, you're thinking in terms of pleasure.

A. You are when you're young. As you get older, you begin to grow more and more obsessed with procreation. You begin to feel used up. Another part of oneself is fast diminishing. There isn't that much of oneself left. I'm not talking now in any crude sense of how much semen is left in the barrel. I'm saying that one's very *being* is being used up.

Every man has a different point where he gets close to his being. Sooner or later everything that stands between him and his being— what the psychoanalysts call defenses—is used up, because men have to work through their lives; just being a man they have to stand up in all the situations where a woman can lie down. Just on the simplest level . . . where a woman can cry, a man has to stand. And for that reason, men are often used more completely than woman. They have more rights and more powers, and also they are used more.

Sooner or later, every man comes close to his being and realizes that even though he's using the act, the act is using him too. He becomes, as you say, more selective. The reason he becomes more selective is that you can get killed, you literally *can* fuck your head off, you can lose your brains, you can wreck your body, you can use yourself up badly, eternally—I know a little bit of what I'm talking about.

I think one of the reasons that homosexuals go through such agony when they're around 40 or 50 is that their lives had nothing to do with procreation. They realize with great horror that all that wonderful sex they had in the past is gone—where is it now? They've used up their being.

Q. Is it possible that you're—pardon the expression—projecting your own attitude onto homosexuals?

A. You can see it in their literature, you can see it in the way they get drunk, you can see it in the sadness, the gentleness, that comes over a middle-aged homosexual. They could've been horribly malicious in the past—bitchy, cruel, nasty—but they become very, very compassionate. There comes a point where they lose their arrogance; they're sorry for themselves and compassionate for others. Not one-half their lives are behind them, but nine-tenths.

Q. Isn't it something of a paradox that your philosophy embraces both a belief in a personal God on one hand and a kind of existential nihilism on the other hand?

A. I've never said seriously that I'm an existential nihilist. I think I've said it facetiously. I am guilty of having said I'm a constitutional nihilist, which is another matter. I believe all legal structures are bad, but they've got to be dissolved with art. I certainly wouldn't want to do away with all the laws overnight.

The authorities, the oppressors, have had power for so many centuries, and particularly have had such vicious and complete power for the last fifty years, that if you did away with all the laws tomorrow, mankind would flounder in *Angst*. Nobody could think their way through to deal with a world in which there were no laws.

We've got hung up upon law the way a drug addict depends on his heroin.

Q. There's a certain irony in this thing about laws. Do you think that if you weren't a famous writer—if one weren't a famous writer and one had stabbed one's wife, would one have gotten a sentence which you escaped?

A. I have no desire to comment on that. It's a private part of my life. I don't want to talk about it. I'll just say this. As far as sentencing goes I think it would have made little difference, legally. If I had been an anonymous man, the result, for altogether different social reasons, would have been about the same.

Q. How can you say that incident I just referred to is "a private part" of your life when you seem to refer to it yourself in Deaths for The Ladies—*in a poem called "Rainy Afternoon with the Wife," you have the lines:*

> So long
>   as
>   you
>   use
>   a knife,
> there's
>   some
>   love
>   left.

A. One can talk about anything in art. I wasn't trying to reveal my private life in that poem. I was trying to crystallize a paradox.

Q. Do you think that creativity—art in general—is an effective force in society, or is it in the end, you know, a sop to the individual artist's ego, and maybe entertainment for—

A. Art is a force. Maybe it's the last force to stand against urban renewal, mental hygiene, the wave of the waveless future.

Q. In his book, Nobody Knows My Name, *James Baldwin—referring to your essay, "The White Negro"—complained about "the myth of the sexuality of Negroes which Norman Mailer, like so many others, refuses to give up." Are you still denying it's a myth?*

A. Negroes are closer to sex than we are. By that I don't mean that every Negro's a great stud, that every Negro woman is capable of giving great sex, that those black people just got rhythm.

I'm willing to bet that if you pushed Jimmy hard enough, he'd finally admit that he thought that the Negroes had more to do with sexuality than the white—but whether he really believes that or not,

Baldwin's buried point is that I shouldn't talk this way because it's bad for the Negro people, it's going to slow them up, going to hurt them; talk about Negro sexuality hurts their progress because it makes the white man nervous and unhappy and miserable.

But the white man is nervous and unhappy and miserable anyway. It's not I who think the Negro has such profound sexuality, it's the average white man all through the country. Why deny their insight? Why do you think they react so violently in the South to having their little girls and boys go to school with Negro kids if it isn't that they're afraid of sexuality in the Negro?

That's the real problem. What's the use of avoiding it?

Q. Are you saying that, whether it's a myth or not, in effect—

A. First of all, I don't believe it's a myth at all, for any number of reasons. I think that *any* submerged class is going to be more accustomed to sexuality than a leisure class. A leisure class may be more *preoccupied* with sexuality; but a submerged class is going to be more drenched in it.

You see, the upper classes are obsessed with sex, but they contain very little of it themselves. They use up much too much sex in their manipulations of power. In effect, they exchange sex for power. So they restrict themselves in their sexuality—whereas the submerged classes have to take their desires for power and plow them back into sex.

So, to begin with, there's just that much more sexual vitality at the bottom than there is at the top. Second of all, the Negroes come from Africa, which is more or less a tropical land. Now I don't care to hear how many variations there are in Africa, how complex is its geography, how there's not only jungle but pasture land, mountains, snow, and so forth—everybody knows that. Finally, Africa is, at bottom, the Congo. Now tropical people are usually more sexual. It's easier to cohabit, it's easier to stay alive. If there's more time, more leisure, more warmth, more—we'll use one of those machine words—more support-from-the-environment than there is in a Northern country, then sex will tend to be more luxuriant.

Northern countries try to build civilizations and tropical countries seek to proliferate *being*.

Besides the Negro has been all but forbidden any sort of intellectual occupation here for a couple of centuries. So he has had to learn other ways of comprehending modern life. There are two ways one can get along in the world. One can get along by studying books, or one can get along by knowing a great deal about one's fellow man, and one's fellow man's woman.

Sexuality is the armature of Negro life. Without sexuality they would've perished. The Jews stayed alive by having a culture to which they could refer, in which, more or less, they could believe. The Negroes stayed alive by having sexuality which could nourish them, keep them warm.

You know, I don't think "The White Negro" is not vulnerable; I think it can be attacked from every angle—there's hardly a paragraph that can't be attacked. I would love to see some first-rate assaults in detail upon it. Occasionally I'd like to be forced to say, "This argument is more incisive than mine."

I honestly don't believe I mind an attack on "The White Negro," but I think an attack at a low level is dim. Jimmy knows enough to know that "The White Negro" is not going to be dismissed. When he stands there and in effect says, "I as a Negro know damn well that Norman Mailer doesn't know what he's talking about when he talks about Negroes"—well, he's being totalitarian. Even Jimmy Baldwin can be totalitarian.

Q. Would you say that your conception of life is mystical as opposed to rationalistic?

A. I would assume mystics don't feel mystical. It's comfortable to them. When the savage was paddling his canoe, and a breeze entered his nose from the East, the savage said to himself, "The God of the East Wind is stirring"—he *felt* that god stirring. He could picture that god in his mind.

Now, for all we know, that god may well have existed. We don't know that he didn't exist any more than we know that beauty is not absolute.

The savage didn't say to himself, "I'm a mystic who is now thinking that the God of the East Wind is stirring. Therefore I'm engaged in a mystical transaction." He was just having a simple, animal experience.

Any mystic who's worth a damn is animal. You can't trust a mystic who gets there on drugs. I had mystical experiences on drugs, and great was my horror when I discovered I couldn't have them without the drugs.

What it meant to me was that the experiences were there to be had, but that I wasn't sufficiently animal to have them, not without having a chemical produced by a machine to break down the machine in me.

But I don't like to call myself a mystic. On the other hand, I certainly wouldn't classify myself as a rationalist. I'm not altogether unhappy living in some no-man's-land between the two.

Q. Okay, final question: You beat me two out of three times in thumb-wrestling matches; would you care to expound briefly on Zen in the art of thumb-wrestling?

A. They are the same.

A PREFACE TO
THE SEVENTH, EIGHTH, NINTH, AND TENTH
PRESIDENTIAL PAPERS

It is likely that the intellectual core of this book is found to a considerable extent in the next four papers. They are not simple papers, although I hope they are far this side of unreadability, but a warning may be in order, for there is no formal exposition of those ideas which center about Dread, the Right Wing (here termed Red Dread), Totalitarianism, and Minorities. Indeed many of the ideas overlap from piece to piece. One considered the idea of removing some repetitions, but then a few of the notions are sufficiently strange to justify their presence more than once. Indeed there is talk of God and the Devil much more than once, and some thorough condemnations of modern architecture show up in "The Real Meaning of the Right Wing" only to be developed even further in the two columns on Totalitarianism.

THE SEVENTH PRESIDENTIAL PAPER

—On Dread

- A Column from Commentary:
                              "Responses and Reactions II"
- An Esquire Column: "The Big Bite"—April, 1963

It would not be worth saying Freud had an umbilical respect for the meanings of anxiety and dread, if it were not that his epigones have reduced these concepts to little more than alarm bells and rattles of malfunction in a psychic machine. Anxiety and dread are treated by them as facts, as the clashing of gears in a neurotic act. The primitive understanding of dread—that one was caught in a dialogue with gods, devils, and spirits, and so was naturally consumed with awe, shame, and terror has been all but forgotten. We are taught that we feel anxiety because we are driven by unconscious impulses which are socially unacceptable; dread we are told is a repetition of infantile experiences of helplessness. It is induced in us by situations which remind our unconscious of weaning and other early deprivations. What is never discussed: the possibility that we feel anxiety because we are in danger of losing some part or quality of our soul unless we act, and act dangerously; or the likelihood that we feel dread when intimations of our death inspire us with disproportionate terror, a horror not merely because we are going to die, but to the contrary because we are going to die badly and suffer some unendurable stricture of eternity. These explanations are altogether outside the close focus of the psychological sciences in the Twentieth Century. Our century, at least our American Century, is a convalescent home for the shell-shocked veterans of a two-thousand-year-war—that huge struggle within Christianity to liberate or to destroy the vision of man.

Faced with our failure (for it would seem the war has gone against us) the investigators of the intellect have taken to intellectual tranquilizers. It is logical positivism, logicians, and language analysts who dominate Anglo-American philosophy rather than existentialists; it is Freudians instead of Reichians or Jungians who rule psychoanalysis; and it is journalism rather than art which forges the apathetic conscience of our time. But then politics, like journalism, is intended to hide from us the existential abyss of dread, the terror which lies beneath our sedation. Today, a successful politician is not a man who wrestles with the art of the possible in order to enrich life, alleviate hardship, or correct injustice—he is, on the contrary, a doctor of mass communications who may measure his success by the practice of a political ritual and vocabulary which diverts us temporarily from dread, from anxiety, from the mirror of the dream. Here follow two specimens of those particular emotional states which politics is designed to conceal.

Responses and Reactions II

On p. 293 of *The Early Masters** is a short story.

The Test

It is told:
When Prince Adam Czartoryski, the friend and counsellor of Czar Alexander, had been married for many years and still had no children, he went to the maggid of Koznitz and asked him to pray for him and because of his prayer the princess bore a son. At the baptism, the father told of the maggid's intercession with God. His brother who, with his young son, was

*From Martin Buber's *Tales of the Hasidim*. Published by Schocken Books. Volume I: *The Early Masters*, Volume II: *The Later Masters*.

among the guests, made fun of what he called the prince's superstition. "Let us go to your wonderworker together," he said, "and I shall show you that he can't tell the difference between left and right."

Together they journeyed to Koznitz, which was close to where they lived. "I beg of you," Adam's brother said to the maggid, "to pray for my sick son."

The maggid bowed his head in silence. "Will you do this for me?" the other urged.

The maggid raised his head. "Go," he said, and Adam saw that he only managed to speak with a great effort. "Go quickly, and perhaps you will still see him alive."

"Well, what did I tell you?" Adam's brother said laughingly as they got into their carriage. Adam was silent during the ride. When they drove into the court of his house, they found the boy dead.

What is suggested by the story is an underworld of real events whose connection is never absurd. Consider, in parallel, this Haiku:*

> So soon to die
> and no sign of it is showing—
> locust cry.

The sense of stillness and approaching death is occupied by the cry of the locust. Its metallic note becomes the exact equal of an oncoming death. Much of Haiku can best be understood as a set of equations in mood. Man inserting himself into a mood extracts an answer from nature which is not only the reaction of the man upon the mood, but is a supernatural equivalent to the quality of the experience, almost as if a key is given up from the underworld to unlock the surface of reality.

Here for example is an intimation of the architecture concealed beneath:

Upsetting the Bowl †

It is told:
Once Rabbi Elimelekh was eating the Sabbath meal with his disciples. The servant set the soup bowl down before him. Rabbi Elimelekh raised it

---

An Introduction to Haiku by Harold G. Henderson, p. 43. The poem is by Matsuo Basho, translated by Henderson.

> *Yagate shinu*
> *keshiki wa mei-zo*
> *semi-no koe*

† *The Early Masters*, p. 259.

and upset it, so that the soup poured over the table. All at once young Mendel, later the rabbi of Rymanov, cried out: "Rabbi what are you doing? They will put us all in jail!" The other disciples smiled at these foolish words. They would have laughed out loud, had not the presence of their teacher restrained them. He, however, did not smile. He nodded to young Mendel and said: "Do not be afraid, my son!"

Some time after this, it became known that on that day an edict directed against the Jews of the whole country had been presented to the emperor for his signature. Time after time he took up his pen, but something always happened to interrupt him. Finally he signed the paper. Then he reached for the sand-container but took the inkwell instead and upset it on the document. Hereupon he tore it up and forbade them to put the edict before him again.

A magical action in one part of the world creates its historical action in another—we are dealing with no less than totem and taboo. Psychoanalysis intrudes itself. One of the last, may it be one of the best approaches to modern neurosis is by way of the phenomenological apparatus of anxiety. As we sink into the apathetic bog of our possible extinction, so a breath of the Satanic seems to rise from the swamp. The magic of materials lifts into consciousness, proceeds to dominate us, is even enthroned into a usurpation of consciousness The protagonists of *Last Year at Marienbad* are not so much people as halls and chandeliers, gaming tables, cigarettes in their pyramid of 1, 3, 5, and 7. The human characters are ghosts, disembodied servants, attendants who cast their shadows on the material. It is no longer significant that a man carries a silver cigarette case; rather it is the cigarette case which is significant. The man becomes an instrument to transport the case from the breast pocket of a suit into the air; like a building crane, a hand conducts the cigarette case to an angle with the light, fingers open the catch and thus elicit a muted sound of boredom, a silver groan from the throat of the case, which nows offers up a cigarette, snaps its satisfaction at being shut, and seems to guide the hand back to the breast pocket. The man, on leave until he is called again, goes through a pantomime of small empty activities—without the illumination of his case he is like all dull servants who cannot use their liberty.

That, one may suppose, is a proper portrait of Hell. It is certainly the air of the phenomenological novel. It is as well the neurotic in slavery to the material objects which make up the locks and keys of his compulsion.

But allow me a quick portrait of a neurotic. He is a sociologist, let us say, working for a progressive foundation, a disenchanted atheist ("Who knows—God may exist as some kind of thwarted benevolence"), a liberal, a social planner, a member of SANE, logical positivist, a collector of jokes about fags and beatniks, a lover of that large suburban land between art and the documentary. He smokes two packs of cigarettes a day: he drinks—*when* he drinks—eight or ten tots of blended whiskey in a night. He does not get drunk, merely cerebral, amusing, and happy. Once when he came home thus drunk, he bowed to his door and then touched his doorknob three times. After this, he went to bed and slept like a thief.

Two years later he is in slavery to the doorknob. He must wipe it with his fingertips three times each morning before he goes out. If he forgets to do this and only remembers later at work, his day is shattered. Anxiety bursts his concentration. His psyche has the air of a bombed city. In an extreme case, he may even have to return to his home. His first question to himself is whether someone has touched the knob since he left. He makes inquiries. To his horror he discovers the servant has gone out shopping already. She has therefore touched the knob and it has lost its magical property. Stratagems are now necessary. He must devote the rest of the day to encouraging the servant to go out in such a manner that he can open the door for her, and thus remove the prior touch of her hand.

Is he mad? the man asks himself. Later he will ask his analyst the same question. But he is too aware of the absurdity of his activities. He suffers at the thought of the work he is not accomplishing, he hates himself for being attached to the doorknob, he tries to extirpate its dominance. One morning he makes an effort to move out briskly. He does not touch the brass a second and third time. But his feet come to a halt, his body turns around as if a gyroscope were revolving him, his arm turns to the knob and pats it twice. He no longer feels his psyche is to be torn in two. Consummate relief.

Of course his analysis discloses wonders. He has been an only son. His mother, his father, and himself make three. He and his wife (a naturally not very happy marriage) have one child. The value of the trinities is considered dubious by the analyst but is insisted upon by the patient. He has found that he need touch the doorknob only once if he repeats to himself, "I was born, I live, and I die." After a time he finds that he does not have to touch the knob at all, or upon occasion, can use his left hand for the purpose. There is a penalty, however. He is obliged to be concerned with the number nine for the rest of the day. Nine sips of water from a glass. A porterhouse steak consumed in nine bites. His wife to be kissed nine times between supper and bed. "I've kicked over an ant hill," he confesses to his analyst. "I'm going bugs."

They work in his cause. Two testes and one penis makes three. Two eyes and one nose; two nostrils and one mouth; the throat, the tongue, and the teeth. His job, his family, and himself. The door, the doorknob, and the act of opening it.

Then he has a revelation. He wakes up one morning and does not reach for a cigarette. There is a tension in him to wait. He suffers agonies—the brightest and most impatient of his cells seem to be expiring without nicotine—still he has intimations of later morning bliss, he hangs on. Like an infantryman coming up alive from a forty-eight hour shelling, he gets to his hat, his attaché case, and the doorknob. As he touches it, a current flows into his hand. "Stick with me, pal," says the message. "One and two keep you from three."

Traveling to the office in the last half hour of the subway rush, he is happy for the first time in years. As he holds to the baked enamel loop of the subway strap, his fingers curl up a little higher and touch the green painted metal above the loop. A current returns to him again. Through his fingertips he feels a psychic topography which has dimensions, avenues, signals, buildings. From the metal of the subway strap through the metal of the subway car, down along the rails, into the tunnels of the city, back to the sewer pipes and electric cables which surround the subway station from which he left, back to his house, and up the plumbing, up the steam pipe, up the hall, a leap through the air, and he has come back to the doorknob again. He pats the subway strap three times. The ship of his body will sink no further. "Today," thinks the sociologist, "I signed my armistice. The flag of Faust has been planted here."

But in his office he has palpitations. He believes he will have a heart attack. He needs air. He opens the window, leans out from the waist. By God, he almost jumped!

The force which drew him to touch the knob now seems to want to pull his chest through the window. Or is it a force opposed to the force which made him touch the doorknob? He does not know. He thinks God may be telling him to jump. That thwarted benevolent God.

"You are swearing allegiance to materials," says a voice. "Come back, son. It is better to be dead."

Poor man. He is not bold enough to be Faust. He calls his analyst.

"Now, for God's sake, don't do anything," says the analyst. "This is not uncommon. Blocked material is rising to the surface. It's premature, but since we've gotten into it, repetition compulsions have to do with omnipotence fantasies which of course always involve Almighty figures and totemic Satanistic contracts. The urge to suicide is not bona fide in your case—it's merely a symbolic contraction of the anxiety."

"But I tell you I almost went through the window. I felt my feet start to leave the floor."

"Well, come by my office then. I can't see you right now—trust me on this—I've got a girl who will feel I've denied her her real chance to bear children if I cut into her hour, she's had too many abortions. You know, she's touchy"—rare is the analyst who won't gossip a *little* about his patients, it seems to calm the other patients—"but I'll leave an envelope of tranquilizers for you on the desk. They're a new formula. They're good. Take two right away. Then two more this afternoon. Forget the nausea if it comes. Just side-effect. We'll get together this evening."

"Mind if I touch your doorknob three times?"

"Great. You've got your sense of humor back. Yes, by all means, touch it."

> So soon to die
> and no sign of it is showing—
>   locust cry.

The Big Bite—April, 1963

The rite of spring is in the odor of the air. The nerve of winter which enters one's nose comes a long far way like a scythe from the peak of mountains. To the aged it can feel like a miasma up from the midnight corridors of a summer hotel, empty and out of season. Winter breath has the light of snow when the sun is on it, or the bone chill of a vault. But spring air comes up from the earth—at worst it can be the smell of new roots in bad slimy ground, at best the wine of late autumn frost is released from the old ice. Intoxication to the nostril, as if a filbert of fine sherbet had melted a sweet way into the tongue back of the throat down from the teeth. Spring is the season which marks the end of dread—so it is the season of profound dread for those who do not lose their fear.

Looking back on the winter and fall, one thinks of a long season of dread. There was that week toward the end of October when the world stood like a playing card on edge, and those of us who lived in New York wondered if the threat of war was like an exceptional dream which would end in a happy denouement (as indeed it did) or whether the events of each day would move, ante raised on ante, from boats on a collision course to invasions of Cuba, from threats of nuclear reprisal to the act itself, the Götterdämmerung of New York. Or would the end come instantly without prevision or warning, we would wonder as well, were we now heroes in a movie by Chaplin, was our house at the edge of the cliff, would we open the door and step into an abyss? There was dread that week. One looked at the buildings one passed and wondered if one was to see them again. For a week everyone in New York was like a patient with an incurable disease—would they be dead tomorrow or was it life for yet another year?

We sat that week in New York thinking of little. When movies are made of the last week on earth, the streets thrive with jazz, the juveniles are unrestrained, the adults pillage stores, there is rape, dancing, caterwauling laughter, sound of sirens and breaking glass, the roller coaster of a brave trumpet going out on its last ride. But we sat around. All too many watched television. Very few of us went out at night. The bars were half empty. The talk was quiet. One did not have the feeling great lovers were meeting that week, not for the first time nor for the last. An apathy came over our city. A muted and rather empty hour which lasted for a week. If it all blew up, if it all came to so little, if our efforts, our loves, our crimes added up to no more than a sudden extinction in a minute, in a moment, if we had not even time before the bomb (as civilians did once) to throw one quick look at some face, some trinket, some child for which one had love, well, one could not complain. That was our fate. That was what we deserved. We did not march in the street or shake our fists at the sky. We waited in our burrow like drunks in the bullpen pacing the floor of our existence, waiting for court in the morning while the floor was littered with the bile that came up in our spit and the dead butts of our dying lung's breath. Facing eternity we were convicts hanging on the dawn. There was no lust in the streets nor any defiance with which to roar at eternity. We were guilty.

We gave our freedom away a long time ago. We gave it away in all the revolutions we did not make, all the acts of courage we found a way to avoid, all the roots we destroyed in fury at that past which still would haunt our deeds. We divorced ourselves from the materials of the earth, the rock, the wood, the iron ore; we looked to new materials which were cooked in vats, long complex derivatives of urine which we called plastic. They had no odor of the living or of what once had lived, their touch was alien to nature. They spoke of the compromise of incompatibles. The plastic which had invaded our bathrooms, our kitchens, our clothing, our toys for children, our tools, our containers, our floor coverings, our cars, our sports, the world of our surfaces was the simple embodiment of social cowardice. We had tried to create a world in which all could live even if none could breathe. There had been a vast collective social effort in the twentieth century—each of us had tried to take back a critical bit more from existence than we had given to it.

There was a terror to contemplate in the logic of our apathy. Because if there was a God and we had come from Him, was it not the first possibility that each of us had a mission, one of us to create, another to be brave, a third to love, a fourth to work, a fifth to be bold, a sixth to be all of these. Was it not possible that we were sent out of eternity to become more than we had been?

What then if we had become less? There was a terror in the logic. Because if there was a God, there was also in first likelihood a Devil. If the God who sent us out demanded our courage, what would be most of interest to the other but our cowardice?

Which of us could say that nowhere in the secret debates of our dreams or the nightmare of open action, in those stricken instants when the legs are not as brave as the mind or the guts turn to water, which of us could say that never nor nowhere had we struck a pact with the Devil and whispered, Yes, let us deaden God, let Him die within me, it is too frightening to keep Him alive, I cannot bear the dread.

That is why we did not roar into the street and shout that it was unnatural for mankind to base its final hope on the concealed character of two men, that it was unnatural to pray that Kennedy and Khrushchev taken together were more good than evil. What an ignoble suppliant hope for civilization to rest its security on two men, no more, two men. What had happened to the dream of the world's wealth guarded by the world's talent, the world's resource?

We sat in apathy because most of us, in the private treacherous dialogues of our sleep, had turned our faith away from what was most vital in our mind, and had awakened in depression. We had drawn back in fright from ourselves, as if in our brilliance lay madness, and beyond the horizon dictated by others was death. We had been afraid of death. We had been afraid of death as no generation in the history of mankind has been afraid. None of us would need to scream as eternity recaptured our breath—we would be too deep in hospital drugs. We would die with deadened minds and twilight sleep. We had turned our back on the essential terror of life. We believed in the Devil, we hated nature.

So we watched the end approach with apathy. Because if it was God we had betrayed and the vision with which He had sent us forth, if our true terror now was not of life but of what might be waiting for us in death, then how much easier we might find it to be blasted into eternity deep in the ruin of ten million others, how much better indeed if the world went with us, and death was destroyed as completely as life. Yes, how many of the millions in New York had a secret prayer: that whomever we thought of as God be exploded with us, and Judgment cease.

THE EIGHTH PRESIDENTIAL PAPER

—Red Dread

The Debate with William Buckley—The Real Meaning of the Right Wing in America

It could be argued that the impetus to America's cold war with communism has come from a collective psychosis, from a monster which has borne almost no relation to the objective cold war going on in these years, a particular real cold war which has been concrete, limited, ugly, detailed, and shrewd in its encounters. The Russians have shown a tough tenacious sly somewhat dishonorable and never-tiring regard for local victory in each of their episodes with us. We have dealt with this international opposition in terms which were schizophrenic. On the working diplomatic level any adjectives applied to the Russians could have applied to us. We also have been tough tenacious sly somewhat dishonorable and have hardly ever slackened in our regard for local victory; but at the level of domestic political consumption we have presented the Russians to the American public as implacable, insane, and corrupting. We could have been talking equally of the plague or some exotic variety of sex. Obviously we were afraid of something more than the Communists. Dread has been loose in the twentieth century, and America has shivered in its horror since the Depression and the Second War.

The speech written for the debate with Buckley is an attempt to explore into this dread. It is also an attempt to explode Senator Goldwater's intellectual pretensions which are sheer mountebank.

Would you care to hear a story Robert Welch likes to tell?

"The minister has preached a superb sermon. It has moved his congregation to lead nobler and more righteous lives. Then the minister says, 'That, of course, was the Lord's side. For the next half hour, to be fair, I'll give equal time to the Devil.' "

Well, ladies and gentlemen, upon me has fallen the unhappy task of following Mr. Buckley. Mr. Buckley was so convincing in his speech that if I had not been forewarned that the Devil cannot know how far he has fallen from Paradise, I would most certainly have decided Mr. Buckley was an angel. A dishonest angel, perhaps, but then which noble speaker is not?

I did not come here, however, to give Mr. Buckley compliments. I appear, presumably, to discuss the real meaning of the Right Wing in America, a phenomenon which is not necessarily real in its meaning, for the Right Wing covers a spectrum of opinion as wide as the peculiarities one encounters on the Left. If we of the Left are a family of anarchists and Communists, socialists, pacifists, nihilists, beatniks, international spies, terrorists, hipsters and Bowery bums, secret agents, dope addicts, sex maniacs and scholarly professors, what indeed is one to make of the Right, which includes the president of a corporation or the Anglican headmaster of a preparatory school, intellectually attired in the fine ideas of Edmund Burke, down the road to the Eisenhower-is-a-Communist set of arguments, all the way down the road to an American Nazi like George Lincoln Rockwell, or to the sort of conservatives who attack property with bombs in California. On a vastly more modest and civilized scale, Mr. Buckley may commit a mild mayhem on the American sense of reality when he says McCarthy inaugurated no reign of terror. Perhaps, I say, it was someone else.

But it is easy to mock the Right Wing. I would rather put the best face one can on it. I think there are any number of interesting adolescents and young men and women going to school now who find themselves drawn to the Right. Secretly drawn. Some are drawn to conservatism today much as they might have been attracted to the Left 30 years ago. They are the ones who are curious for freedom, the freedom not only to make money but the freedom to discover their own nature, to discover good and to discover—dare I say it?—evil. At bottom they are ready to go to war with a ready-made world which they feel is stifling them.

I hope it is evident that I do not see the people in the Right Wing as a simple group of fanatics, but rather as a contradictory stew of reactionaries and individualists, of fascists and libertarians, libertarians like John Dos Passos for example. It could be said that most Right Wingers don't really know what they want. I would not include Mr. Buckley in this category, but I think it can be said the politics of the Right in America reflects an emotion more than an insight.

I think of a story told me by a Southerner about his aunt. She lived in a small town in South Carolina. She was a spinster. She came from one of the better families in town. Not surprisingly, the house where she lived had been in the family for a long time. She loved the trees on the walk which bordered each side of the street which ran by her house. They were very old trees.

The City Council passed a bill to cut down those trees. The street had to be widened. A bypass from the highway was being constructed around the old bypass of the business district. The reason for the new bypass was to create a new business district: a supermarket, a super-pharmacy, a superservice station, a chromium-plated diner, a new cemetery with plastic tombstones, a new armory for the Army Reserve, an auto supply store, a farm implements shop, a store for Venetian blinds, a laundromat and an information booth for tourists who would miss the town on the new bypass but could read about it in the Chamber of Commerce's literature as they drove on to Florida.

Well, the old lady fought the bypass. To her, it was sacrilege that these trees be cut down. She felt that if there were any value to some older notions of grace and courtesy, courage under duress, and gallantry to ladies, of faith in God and the structure of His ways, that if there were any value at all to chivalry, tradition and manners, the children of the new generations could come to find it more naturally by walking down an avenue of old homes and trees than by reading the *National Review* in front of the picture window under the metal awning of the brand-new town library.

Secretly the old lady had some radical notions. She seemed to think that the old street and the trees on this old street were the property of everyone in the town, because everyone in the town could have the pleasure of walking down that street. At her gloomiest she even used to think that a new generation of Negroes growing up in the town, strong, hostile, too smart, and just loaded with Northern ideas, would hate the South forever and never forgive the past once the past was destroyed. If they grew up on the edge of brand-new bypasses in cement-brick homes with asbestos roofs and squatty hothouse bushes in the artificial fertilizer of the front yard, why then, how could they ever come to understand that not everyone in the old South was altogether evil and that there had been many whites who learned much from the Negro and loved him, that it was Negro slaves who had first planted these trees, and that it was Negro love of all that grew well which had set the trunks of these trees growing in so straight a route right into the air.

So the old lady fought the execution of these old trees. She went to see the Mayor, she talked to everyone on the City Council, she circulated a petition among her neighbors, she proceeded to be so active in the defense of these trees that many people in town began to think she was just naturally showing her age. Finally, her nephew took her aside. It was impossible to stop the bypass, he explained to her, because there was a man in town who had his heart set on it, and no one in town was powerful enough to stop this man. Not on a matter so special as these trees.

Who was this powerful and villainous man? she wanted to know. Was it a Communist? No. Was it the leader for the National Association for the Advancement of Colored People? No. Was it perhaps a Freedom Rider? No. Was it a beatnik or a drug addict? No. Wasn't it one of those New York agitators? No, no, it wasn't even a Cuban. The sad fact of the matter was that the powerful and villainous man was married to the richest woman in the county, came himself from an excellently good family, owned half the real estate around, and was president of the biggest local corporation, which was a large company for making plastic luncheon plates. He was a man who had been received often in the old lady's house. He had even talked to her about joining his organization. He was the leader of the local council of the John Birch Society.

Mr. Buckley may say I am being unfair. The man who puts the new bypass through does not have to be the local leader of the John Birch Society. He can also be a liberal Republican, or a Democratic mayor, a white liberal Southerner, or—and here Mr. Buckley might tell my story with pleasure—he could be a Federal man. The bypass might be part of a national superhighway. The villain might even be a Federal man who is under scrutiny by the Senate Investigating Committee, the House Un-American Affairs Committee, the FBI, and the CIA. It seems not to matter—a man can be a fellow-traveler or a reactionary—either way those trees get chopped down, and the past is unreasonably destroyed.

The moral well may be that certain distinctions have begun to disappear. The average experience today is to meet few people who are authentic. Our minds belong to one cause, our hands manipulate a machine which works against our cause. We are not our own masters. We work against ourselves. We suffer from a disease. It is a disease which afflicts almost all of us by now, so prevalent, insidious and indefinable that I choose to call it a plague.

I think somewhere, at some debatable point in history, it is possible man caught some unspeakable illness of the psyche, that he betrayed some secret of his being and so betrayed the future of his species. I could not begin to trace the beginning of this plague, but whether it began early or late, I think it is accelerating now at the most incredible speed, and I would go so far as to think that many of the men and women who belong to the Right Wing are more sensitive to this disease than virtually any other people in this country. I think it is precisely this sensitivity which gives power to the Right Wing's passions.

Now this plague appears to us as a sickening of our substance, an electrification of our nerves, a deterioration of desire, an apathy about the future, a detestation of the present, an amnesia of the past. Its forms are many, its flavor is unforgettable: It is the disease which destroys flavor. Its symptoms appear everywhere: in architecture, medicine, in the deteriorated quality of labor, the insubstantiality of money, the ravishment of nature, the impoverishment of food, the manipulation of emotion, the emptiness of faith, the displacement of sex, the deterioration of language, the reduction of philosophy, and the alienation of man from the product of his work and the results of his acts.

What a modest list! What a happy century. One could speak for hours on each of the categories of this plague. I will try to do no more than list the symptoms of this plague.

Even 25 years ago architecture, for example, still told one something about a building and what went on within it. Today, who can tell the difference between a modern school and a modern hospital, between a modern hospital and a modern prison, or a prison and a housing project? The airports look like luxury hotels, the luxury hotels are indistinguishable from a modern corporation's home office, and the home office looks like an air-conditioned underground city on the moon.

In medicine, not so long ago, just before the war, there still used to be diseases. Diphtheria, smallpox, German measles, scarlet fever. Today there are allergies, viruses, neuroses, incurable diseases. Surgery may have made some mechanical advances, but sickness is more mysterious than ever. No one knows quite what a virus is, nor an allergy, nor how to begin to comprehend an incurable disease. We have had an avalanche of antibiotics, and now we have a rampage of small epidemics with no name and no distinctive set of symptoms.

Nature is wounded in her fisheries, her forests. Airplanes spray insecticides. Species of insects are removed from the chain of life. Crops are poisoned just slightly. We grow enormous tomatoes which have no taste. Food is raised in artificial circumstances, with artificial nutrients, full of alien chemicals and foreign bodies.

Our emotions are turned like television dials by men in motivational research. Goods are not advertised to speak to our needs but to our secret itch. Our secondary schools have a curriculum as interesting as the wax paper on breakfast food. Our educational system teaches us not to think, but to know the answer. Faith is half-empty. Until the churches can offer an explanation for Buchenwald, or Siberia or Hiroshima, they are only giving solace to the unimaginative. They are neglecting the modern crisis. For all of us live today as divided men. Our hope for the future must be shared with the terror that we may go exploding into the heavens at the same instant 10,000,000 other souls are being exploded beside us. Not surprising, then, if many people no longer look to sex as an act whose final purpose is to continue the race.

Language is drowning in jargons of mud. Philosophy is in danger of becoming obsolescent. Metaphysics disappears, logical positivism arises. The mass of men begin to have respect not for those simple ideas which are mysteries, but on the contrary for those simple ideas which are certitudes. Soon a discussion of death will be considered a betrayal of philosophy.

Finally, there is a vast alienation of man from responsibility. One hundred years ago Marx was writing about the alienation of man from his tools and the product of his work. Today that alienation has gone deeper. Today we are alienated from our acts. A writer I know interviewed Dr. Teller, "the father of the hydrogen bomb." There was going to be a new test of that bomb soon. "Are you going to see it?" asked the reporter.

"Who is interested in that?" asked Teller. "That is just a big bang."

Face to face with a danger they cannot name, there are still many people on the Right Wing who sense that there seems to be some almost palpable conspiracy to tear life away from its roots. There is a biological rage at the heart of much Right Wing polemic. They feel as if somebody, or some group—in New York no doubt—are trying to poison the very earth, air and water of their existence. In their mind, this plague is associated with collectivism, and I am not so certain they are wrong. The essence of biology seems to be challenge and response, risk and survival, war and the lessons of war. It may be biologically true that life cannot have beauty without its companion—danger. Collectivism promises security. It spreads security the way a knife spreads margarine. Collectivism may well choke the pores of life.

But there is a contradiction here. Not all of the Right Wing, after all, is individual and strong. Far from it. The Right Wing knows better than I would know how many of them are collectivists in their own hearts, how many detest questions and want answers, loathe paradox, and live with a void inside themselves, a void of fear, a void of fear for the future and for what is unexpected, which fastens upon Communists as equal, one to one, with the Devil. The Right Wing often speaks of freedom when what it desires is iron law, when what it really desires is collectivism managed by itself. If the Right Wing is reacting to the plague, all too many of the powerful people on the Right—the presidents of more than a few corporations in California, for example—are helping to disseminate the plague. I do not know if this applies to Senator Goldwater who may be an honorable and upright man, but I think it can do no harm to take a little time to study the application of his ideas.

As a thoroughgoing conservative, the Senator believes in increasing personal liberty by enlarging economic liberty. He is well known for his views. He would reduce the cost of public welfare and diminish the present power of the unions, he would lower the income tax, dispense with subsidies to the farmer, decentralize the Federal Government and give states' rights back to the states, he would limit the Government's spending, and he would discourage any interference by

Washington in the education of the young. It is a complete, comprehensive program. One may agree with it or disagree. But no doubt it is a working program. The reasonableness of this program is attractive. It might even reduce the depredations of the plague. There is just one trouble with it. It does not stop here. Senator Goldwater takes one further step. He would carry the cold war to the Soviet Union, he would withdraw diplomatic recognition, he would recognize, I quote, that:

> . . . If our objective is victory over communism, we must achieve superiority in all of the weapons—military, as well as political and economic—that may be useful in reaching that goal. Such a program costs money, but so long as the money is spent wisely and efficiently, I would spend it. I am not in favor of economizing on the nation's safety.

It is the sort of statement which inspires a novelist's imagination long enough to wonder what might happen to the Senator's program if he were elected President. For we may be certain he is sincere in his desire to achieve superiority in all the weapons, including such ideological weapons as arriving first on the moon. But what of the cost? There is one simple and unforgettable figure. More than 60 cents out of every dollar spent by the Government is spent on military security already. Near to two thirds of every dollar. And our national budget in 1963 will be in the neighborhood of $90,000,000,000. If we add what will be spent on foreign aid, the figure will come to more than 75 cents in every dollar.

Yet these expenditures have not given us a clear superiority to the Soviet Union. On the contrary, Senator Goldwater points out that we must still *achieve* superiority. Presumably, he would increase the amount of money spent on defense. This, I suppose, would not hinder him from reducing the income tax, nor would it force him to borrow further funds. He could regain any moneys lost in this reduction by taking the money from welfare and education, that is he could if he didn't increase our defense efforts by more than 10 percent, for if he did that, we would be spending more already than the money we now spend on welfare. And of course that part of the population which would be most affected by the cessation of welfare, that is, so to speak, the impoverished part of the population, might not be happy. And it is not considered wise to have a portion of the populace unhappy when one is expanding one's ability to go to war, unless one wishes to put them in uniform. Perhaps Goldwater might not reduce the expenditures on welfare during this period. He might conceivably increase them a little in order to show that over the short period, during the crisis, during the arms buildup while we achieve superiority over the Russians, a conservative can take just as good care of the masses as a liberal. Especially since we may assume the Russians would be trying to achieve superiority over us at the same time we are trying to achieve superiority over them, so that an arms and munitions competition would be taking place and there would be enough money spent for everyone.

But let me move on to education where the problem is more simple. To achieve superiority over the Russians there, we simply need more technicians, engineers and scientists. We also have to build the laboratories in which to teach them. Perhaps, most reluctantly, just for the duration of the crisis, which is to say for the duration of his period in office, President Goldwater might have to increase the Federal budget for education. That would be contrary to his principles. But perhaps he could recover some of those expenditures by asking the farmer to dispense with subsidies. The farmer would not mind if additional Government funds were allocated to education and welfare, and he was not included. The farmer would not mind if the larger corporations of America, General Dynamics and General Motors, General Electric, United States Steel and A.T.&T. were engaged in rather large new defense contracts. No, the farmer would not mind relinquishing his subsidy. Not at all. Still, to keep him as happy as everyone else Goldwater might increase his subsidy. Just for the duration of the crisis. Just for the duration of enlightened conservatism in office. It would not matter about the higher income tax, the increased farm subsidies, the enlarged appropriation for welfare, the new magnified role of the Federal Government in education, President Goldwater could still give the states back their rights. He would not have to integrate the schools down South. He could drive the Russians out of the Congo, while the White Councils were closing the white colleges in order not to let a black man in. Yes, he could. For the length of a 20-minute speech in Phoenix, Arizona, he could. But you know and I know and he knows what he would do—he would do what President Eisenhower did. He would do that if he wanted to keep the Russians out of the Congo.

Poor President Goldwater. At least he could cut down on the power of the unions. He could pass a Right-to-Work act. Indeed he could. He could carry the war to the Russians, he could achieve superiority, while the unions of America were giving up their power and agreeing not to strike. Yes. Yes. Of course he could. Poor President Goldwater. He might have to end by passing a law which would make it illegal ever to pass a Right-to-Work law. Under Goldwater, the American people would never have to be afraid of creeping socialism. They would just have state conservatism, creeping state conservatism. Yes, there are conservatives like the old lady who wished to save the trees and there are conservatives who talk of saving trees in order to get the power to cut down the trees.

So long as there is a cold war, there cannot be a conservative administration in America. There cannot for the simplest reason. Conservatism depends upon a huge reduction in the power and the budget of the central Government. Indeed, so long as there is a cold war, there are no politics of consequence in America. It matters less each year which party holds the power. Before the enormity of defense expenditures, there is no alternative to an ever-increasing welfare state. It can be an interesting welfare state like the present one, or a dull welfare state like President Eisenhower's. It can even be a totally repressive welfare state like President Goldwater's well might be. But the conservatives might recognize that greater economic liberty is not possible so long as one is building a greater war machine. To pretend that both can be real is hypocritical beyond belief. The conservatives are then merely mouthing impractical ideas which they presume may bring them power. They are sufficiently experienced to know that only liberalism can lead America into total war without popular violence, or an active underground.

There is an alternative. Perhaps it is ill-founded. Perhaps it is impractical. I do not know enough to say. I fear there is no one in this country who knows enough to say. Yet I think the time may be approaching for a great debate on this alternative. I say that at least this alternative is no more evil and no more visionary than Barry Goldwater's promise of a conservative America with superiority in all the weapons. So I say—in modesty and in doubt, I say—the alternative may be to end the cold war. The cold war has been an instrument of megalomaniacal delusion to this country. It is the poison of the Right Wing. It is the poison they feed themselves and it is the poison they feed the nation. Communism may be evil incarnate, but it is a most complex evil which seems less intolerable today than it did under Stalin. I for one do not understand an absolute evil which is able to ameliorate its own evil. I say an evil which has captured the elements of the good is complex. To insist communism is a simple phenomenon can only brutalize the minds of the American people. Already, it has given this country over to the power of every huge corporation and organization in America. It has helped to create an America run by committees. It has stricken us with secret waste and hatred. It has held back the emergence of an America more alive and more fantastic than any America yet created.

So I say: End the cold war. Pull back our boundaries to what we can defend and to what wishes to be defended. There is one dread advantage to atomic war. It enables one powerful nation to be the equal of many nations. We do not have to hold every loose piece of real estate on earth to have security. Let communism come to those countries it will come to. Let us not use up our substance trying to hold onto nations which are poor, underdeveloped, and bound to us only by the depths of their hatred for us. We cannot equal the effort the Communists make in such places. We are not dedicated in that direction. We were not born to do that. We have had our frontier already. We cannot be excited to our core, our historic core, by the efforts of new underdeveloped nations to expand their frontiers. No, we are better engaged in another place, we are engaged in making the destiny of Western man, a destiny which seeks now to explore out beyond the moon and in back into the depths of the soul. With some small fraction of the money we spend now on defense we can truly defend ourselves and Western Europe, we can develop, we can become extraordinary, we can go a little further toward completing the heroic vision of Western man. Let the Communists flounder in the countries they acquire. The more countries they hold, the less supportable will become the contradictions of their ideology, the more bitter will grow the divisions in their internal interest, and the more enormous their desire to avoid a war which could only destroy the economies they will have developed at such vast labor and such vast waste. Let it be their waste, not ours. Our mission may be not to raise the level of minimum subsistence in the world so much as it may be to show the first features and promise of that incalculable renaissance men may someday enter. So let the true war begin. It is not a war between West and East, between capitalism and communism, or democracy and totalitarianism; it is rather the deep war which has gone on for six centuries in the nature of Western man, it is the war between the conservative and the rebel, between authority and instinct, between the two views of God which collide in the mind of the West, the ceremonious conservative view which believes that if God allows one man to be born wealthy and another poor, we must not tamper unduly with this conception of place, this form of society created by God, for it is possible the poor man is more fortunate than the rich, since he may be judged less severely on his return to eternity. That is the conservative view and it is not a mean nor easy view to deny.

The rebel or the revolutionary might argue, however, that the form of society is not God's creation, but a result of the war between God and the Devil, that this form is no more than the line of the battlefield upon which the Devil distributes wealth against God's best intention. So man must serve as God's agent, seeking to shift the wealth of our universe in such a way that the talent, creativity and strength of the future, dying now by dim dull deaths in every poor man alive, will come to take its first breath, will show us what a mighty renaissance is locked in the unconscious of the dumb. It is the argument which claims that no conservative can ever be certain those imbued with the value of tradition did not give more devotion to their garden, their stable, their kennel, the livery of their servant and the oratorical style of their clergyman than God intended. Which conservative indeed can be certain that if his class once embodied some desire of the Divine Will, that it has not also now incurred God's displeasure after all these centuries of organized Christianity and enormous Christian greed? Which conservative can swear that it was not his class who gave the world a demonstration of greed so complete, an expropriation and spoilation of backward lands and simple people so avid, so vicious, so insane, a class which finally gave such suck to the Devil, that the most backward primitive in the darkest jungle would sell the grave and soul of his dearest ancestor for a machine with which to fight back?

That is the war which has meaning, that great and mortal debate between rebel and conservative where each would argue the other is an agent of the Devil. That is the war we can welcome, the war we can expect if the cold war will end. It is the war which will take life and power from the statistical congelations of the Center and give it over to Left and to Right, it is the war which will teach us our meaning, where we will discover ourselves and whether we are good and where we are not, so it is the war which will give the West what is great within it, the war which gives birth to art and furnishes strength to fight the plague. Art, free inquiry and the liberty to speak may be the only cure against the plague.

But first, I say, first there is another debate America must have. Do we become totalitarian or do we end the cold war? Do we accept the progressive collectivization of our lives which eternal cold war must bring, or do we gamble on the chance that we have armament enough already to be secure and to be free, and do we seek therefore to discover ourselves, and Nature willing, discover the conservative or rebellious temper of these tortured times? And when we are done, will we know truly who has spoken within us, the Lord or the Fallen Prince?

POSTSCRIPT TO THE EIGHTH PRESIDENTIAL PAPER

Afterward, I claimed victory. Indeed a few details of our debate will be found in the article on Patterson and Liston, which is printed further on in this book. One could claim the victory a fortiori, *and say it was popular with the audience, but then Buckley might argue as much for himself. The crowd was high partisan that night and cheered separately for us with the kind of excitement one expects in a crowd at a high school football game.*

No, I'd argue I won the debate on formal grounds. Our topic was "The Real Meaning of the Right Wing in America," and I had used my thirty-minute speech to give an analysis of what I thought the Right Wing might be. Since Buckley had used his prior half hour to attack some figures on the Left including Kenneth Tynan, Murray Kempton, Fidel Castro, and myself, it seemed that unless his point could be fixed as precisely this: the nature of the Right Wing is to attack figures on the Left—his burden in the remaining part of the debate was to disprove my thesis that the inspiration for the Right Wing was not political but emotional and therefore psychically misplaced. It was also up to Buckley to demolish my argument that Senator Goldwater was either a conscious or unconscious hypocrite. As can be seen by any few of you who take the trouble to go back and find the debate and read it (printed in Playboy, January and February, 1963), *Buckley never made this attempt. The second half of our debate, altogether extempore, consisted of small local skirmishes on the flanks. When the debate ended, I had succeeded in pushing a salient into the intellectual territory of the Right which was not counter-attacked by Buckley. So I claimed the victory. If we ever debate again, Buckley will be hunting for mountain lion. Knowing my opponent he will doubtless use an elephant gun.*

THE NINTH PRESIDENTIAL PAPER
—Totalitarianism

- Two columns from Esquire: "The Big Bite"—
                                    May and August, 1963

Totalitarianism has been the continuing preoccupation of this book, but one aspect of the subject might be underlined again—it is that totalitarianism is better understood if it is regarded as a plague rather than examined as a style of ideology. There was a time when simple totalitarianism could be found attached to Fascism, and perhaps to Bolshevism. It seemed synonymous with dictatorship; its syndrome was characteristic. Oppression was inflicted upon a nation through its leaders; people were forced to obey a governmental authority which was not only inhumane, but invariably antagonistic to the history of the nation's immediate past. A tension was still visible between the government as the oppressor and the people as the oppressed.

The kind of modern totalitarianism which we find in America, however, is as different from classical Fascism as is a plastic bomb from a hand grenade. The hand grenade makes an imprecise weapon. Thrown into a room full of people, one cannot know who will be hurt, who will be killed, who will escape. But the aggression is still direct: a man must throw *the grenade, and so, in the French sense of the word, he must "assist" at the performance of the act. He would have some idea of whom he was throwing it at. Whereas, the* bombe plastique, *used in the streets of Paris by terrorists in the O.A.S. toward the end of the Algerian War, consisted of a kind of putty which could be left in a trashbasket or stuck onto a wall. When it went off, an hour or two after its placement, only laws of chance were operating. The bomber*

195

could not know whom he was killing for he was usually miles away. Some of his own people might even be passing the intersection when the explosion came. The actor was now wholly separated from his act.

So the crucial characteristic of modern totalitarianism is that it is a moral disease which divorces us from guilt. It came into being as a desire to escape the judgments of the past and our responsibility for past injustice—in that sense it is a defense against eternity, an attempt to destroy that part of eternity which is death, which is punishment or reward. It arose from the excesses of theology, the exploitations of theology, and the oppressions of theology, but in destroying theology, the being of man and his vision may be reduced to a thousand year apathy, or to extinction itself. The words are abstract, but the meaning by now is I hope not altogether hidden. In our flight from the consequence of our lives, in our flight from adventure, from danger, and from the natural ravages of disease, in our burial of the primitive, it is death the Twentieth Century is seeking to avoid.

Let me close this introduction with a poem taken from Deaths for the Ladies.

Death of a Lover Who Loved Death

I find
    that
    most
    of the people I
                know
        are immature
        and cannot
            cope
            with reality
        said the suicide
His death
    followed
        a slash on each wrist.
Fit
was this end
for blood
    in its flow
    reveals

what a furnace
    had burned
        in the dungeon
        of his unconscious

Burn and bleed

He coped with
    reality
    too well.

It was unreality
        which waited
        on a midnight trail
          in that fierce
            jungle of eternity
            he heard murmuring
          on the other side

Oh, night of the jungle,
    God of mercy
    wept the suicide
    do not ask me
    to reconnoiter
        this
          dark
          trail
        when I am now
          without
          hands.

The Big Bite—May, 1963

The act of traveling is never a casual act. It inspires an anxiety which no psychoanalyst can relieve in a hurry, for if travel is reminiscent of the trauma of birth, it is also suggestive of some possible migrations after death.

For most of us death may not be peace but an expedition into all the high terror and deep melancholy we sought to avoid in our lives. So the act of travel is a grave hour to some part of the unconscious, for it may be on a trip that we prepare a buried corner of ourselves to be ready for what happens once we are dead.

By this logic, the end of a trip is a critical moment of transition. Railroad stations in large cities should properly be monumental, heavy with dignity, reminiscent of the past. We learn little from travel, not nearly so much as we need to learn, if everywhere we are assaulted by the faceless plastic surfaces of everything which has been built in America since the war, that new architecture of giant weeds and giant boxes, of children's colors on billboards and jagged electric signs. Like the metastases of cancer cells, the plastic shacks, the motels, the drive-in theatres, the highway restaurants and the gas stations proliferate year by year until they are close to covering the highways of America with a new country which is laid over the old one the way a transparent sheet with new drawings is set upon the original plan. It is an architecture with no root to the past and no suggestion of the future, for one cannot conceive of a modern building growing old (does it turn dingy or will the colors stain?); there is no way to age, it can only cease to function. No doubt these buildings will live for twenty years and then crack in two. They will live like robots, or television sets which go out of order with one whistle of the wind.

In the suburbs it is worse. To live in leisure in a house much like other houses, to live in a landscape where it is meaningless to walk because each corner which is turned produces the same view, to live in comfort and be bored is a preparation for one condition: limbo.

The architectural face of the enemy has shifted. Twenty years ago Pennsylvania Station in New York City seemed a monstrosity, forbidding, old, dingy, unfunctional, wasteful of space, depressing in its passages and waiting rooms. The gloomy exploitative echoes of the industrial revolution sounded in its grey stone. And yet today the plan to demolish it is a small disaster.

Soon the planners will move in to tear down the majestic vaults of the old building in order to rear up in its place a new sports arena, a twenty-, thirty-, forty-story building. One can predict what the new building will look like. It will be made of steel, concrete and glass, it will have the appearance of a cardboard box which contains a tube of toothpaste, except that it will be literally one hundred million times larger in volume. In turn, the sports arena will have plastic seats painted in pastel colors, sky-blue, orange-pink, dead yellow. There will be a great deal of fluorescent lighting, an electronically operated scoreboard (which will break down frequently) and the acoustics will be particularly poor, as they invariably are in new auditoriums which have been designed to have good acoustics.

The new terminal will be underground. It will waste no space for high vaulted ceilings and monumental columns, it will look doubtless like the inside of a large airport. And one will feel the same subtle nausea coming into the city or waiting to depart from it that one feels now in such plastic catacombs as O'Hare's reception center in Chicago, at United or American Airlines in Idlewild, in the tunnels and ramps and blank gleaming corridors of Dallas' airport, which is probably one of the ten ugliest buildings in the world.

Now in the cities, an architectural plague is near upon us. For we have tried to settle the problem of slums by housing, and the void in education by new schools. So we have housing projects which look like prisons and prisons which look like hospitals which in turn look like schools, schools which look like luxury hotels, luxury hotels which seem to confuse themselves with airline terminals, and airline terminals which cannot be told apart from civic centers, and the civic centers look like factories. Even the new churches look like recreation centers at large ski resorts. One can no longer tell the purpose of a building by looking at its face. Modern buildings tend to look like call girls who came out of it intact except that their faces are a touch blank and the expression in their eyes is as lively as the tip on a filter cigarette.

Our modern architecture reminds me a little of cancer cells. Because the healthy cells of the lung have one appearance and those in the liver another. But if both are cancerous they tend to look a little more alike, they tend to look a little less like anything very definite.

Definition has a value. If an experience is precise, one can know a little more of what is happening to oneself. It is in those marriages and love affairs which are neither good nor bad, not quite interesting nor altogether awful that anxiety flows like a muddy river. It is in those housing projects which look like prisons that juvenile delinquency increases at a greater rate than it used to do in the slums.

Once I had the luck to have an argument with a United States Senator from New York. He was very proud of his Governor. What has Rockefeller done? I asked. What? cried the Senator. And the list came back. Education, roads, welfare, housing. But isn't it possible people can be happier living in slums than housing projects? I asked.

I might just as well have said to a devout Catholic that I thought all nuns should be violated. The Senator lost his temper. Listen, young man, went his theme, I grew up in a slum.

But then for years I too lived in a slum. I had a cold-water flat which was sixty-feet long and varied in width from eight feet to eleven feet. I bought a stove and a refrigerator, and I spent two weeks putting in a sink and a bathtub and two gas heaters. The plaster was cracked and continued to develop its character as I lived there. I was as happy in that cold-water flat as I've been anywhere else. It was mine. When I stay in a modern apartment house for a few days, I feel as if I'm getting the plague walking down those blank walls.

So I tried to argue with the Senator. What if a government were to take a fraction of the money it cost to dispossess and relocate slum tenants, demolish buildings, erect twenty stories of massed barracks, and instead give a thousand or two thousand dollars to each slum tenant to spend on materials for improving his apartment and to pay for the wages of whatever skilled labor he needed for small specific jobs like a new toilet, a new window, a fireplace, new wiring, wallpaper, or a new wall. The tenant would be loaned or rented the tools he needed, he would be expected to work along with his labor. If he took the first hundred dollars he received and drank it up, he would get no more money.

By the time such a project was done, every slum apartment in the city would be different. Some would be worse, some would be improved, a few would be beautiful. But each man would know at least whether he wished to improve his home, or truly didn't care. And that might be better than moving into a scientifically allotted living space halfway between a hospital and a prison.

For the housing projects radiate depression in two directions. The people who live in them are deadened by receiving a gift which has no beauty. The people who go past the housing projects in their automobiles are gloomy for an instant, because the future, or that part of the future we sense in our architecture, is telling us that the powers who erected these buildings expect us to become more like one another as the years go by.

The conservatives cry out that the welfare state will reduce us to a low and dull common denominator. And indeed it will unless the welfare which reaches the poor can reach them directly in such a way that they can use their own hands to change their own life. What do you say, Senator Goldwater? Do you think the government could afford the funds to give a man who lives in a slum some money for his hammer and nails and a carpenter to work along with him, or do you think the housing projects ought to continue to be built, but only by private funds (somewhat higher rents), and no government interference? Just revenue for large real-estate interests and huge architectural firms who design edifices which reveal no more than the internal structure of a ten-million-dollar bill.

The Big Bite—August, 1963

Some of you will remember that the column for the May issue talked about the approaching destruction of Pennsylvania Station and the plague of modern architecture, a plague which sits like a plastic embodiment of cancer over our suburbs, office buildings, schools, prisons, factories, churches, hotels, motels, and airline terminals. A fair number of letters came in for that column, and I would like to quote from part of one:

> I'm curious about something. Why is it that [some] people have such strong dislike for a form of architecture which [other] people are able not

only to accept, but to accept as positive values in our society—goals to try to achieve? My husband's answer is that nobody really likes the current building trend, but that few people think about it enough to define their own emotions. But I can't accept that as a full answer. [The fact remains] that some people react with . . . aversion to modern architecture, . . . others . . . value it. Do you have an answer?

I think I do. But it rests on a premise most of you may find intolerable. The best short poem of the twentieth century, I would think, is Yeats' *The Second Coming*, which goes, in part:

> Things fall apart; the centre cannot hold;
> Mere anarchy is loosed upon the world,
> The blood-dimmed tide is loosed, and everywhere
> The ceremony of innocence is drowned,
> The best lack all conviction, while the worst
> Are full of passionate intensity.
>
> . . . Somewhere in sands of the desert
> A shape with lion body and the head of a man,
> A gaze blank and pitiless as the sun,
> Is moving its slow thighs. . . .

and ends:

> . . . What rough beast, its hour come round at last,
> Slouches towards Bethlehem to be born?

That rough beast is a shapeless force, an obdurate emptiness, an annihilation of possibilities. It is totalitarianism: that totalitarianism which has haunted the twentieth century, haunted the efforts of intellectuals to define it, of politicians to withstand it, and of rebels to find a field of war where it could be given battle. Amoeboid, insidious, totalitarianism came close to conquering the world twenty years ago. In that first large upheaval the Nazis sang of blood and the deep roots of blood and then proceeded to show their respect for the roots of blood by annihilating their millions through the suffocations of the gas chamber. No wilder primitive song was ever sung by a modern power, no more cowardly way of exercising a collective will has been yet encountered in history. The Nazis came to power by suggesting they would return Germany to the primitive secrets of her barbaric age, and then proceeded to destroy the essential intuition of the primitive, the umbilical idea that death and the appropriate totems of burial are as essential to life as life itself.

That first huge wave of totalitarianism was like a tide which moved in two directions at once. It broke upon the incompatible military force of Russia and of America. But it was an ocean of plague. It contaminated whatever it touched. If Russia had been racing into totalitarianism before the war, it was pervasively totalitarian after the war, in the last half-mad years of Stalin's court. And America was altered from a nation of venture, exploitation, bigotry, initiative, strife, social justice and social injustice, into a vast central swamp of tasteless toneless authority whose dependable heroes were drawn from FBI men, doctors, television entertainers, corporation executives, and athletes who could cooperate with public-relations men. The creative mind gave way to the authoritative mind, the expert took over from the small businessman, the labor executive replaced the trade-union organizer, and that arbiter of morals, the novelist, was replaced by the psychoanalyst. Mental health had come to America. And cancer with it. The country had a collective odor which was reminiscent of a potato left to molder in a plastic box.

That period began with Truman and was continued by Eisenhower. It came to an historic fork with Kennedy's administration. America was faced with going back to its existential beginnings, its frontier psychology, where the future is unknown and one discovers the truth of the present by accepting the risks of the present; or America could continue to go on in its search for totalitarian security. It is characteristic of the President's major vice that he chose to go in both directions at once. But then his character contains a similar paradox. He is on the one hand possessed of personal bravery, some wit, some style, an aristocratic taste for variety. He is a consummate politician, and has a potentially dictatorial nose for the manipulation of newspapers and television. He is a hero. And yet he is a void. His mind seems never to have been seduced by a new idea. He is the embodiment of the American void, that great yawning empty American mind which cannot bear any question which takes longer than ten seconds to answer. Given his virtues, suffering his huge vice, his emptiness, his human emptiness, we have moved as a nation, under his regime, deeper into totalitarianism, far deeper than his predecessors could have dreamed, and have been granted (by the cavalier style of his personal life and the wistfulness of his appreciation for the arts) the possible beginnings of a Resistance to the American totalitarianism.

But first one must recognize the features of the plague. If it appeared first in Nazi Germany as a political juggernaut, and in the Soviet Union as a psychotization of ideology, totalitarianism has slipped into America with no specific political face. There are liberals who are totalitarian, and conservatives, radicals, rightists, fanatics, hordes of the well-adjusted. Totalitarianism has come to America with no concentration camps and no need for them, no political parties and no desire for new parties, no, totalitarianism has slipped into the body cells and psyche of each of us. It has been transported, modified, codified, and inserted into each of us by way of the popular arts, the social crafts, the political crafts, and the corporate techniques. It sits in the image of the commercials on television which use phallic and vaginal symbols to sell products which are otherwise useless for sex, it is heard in the jargon of educators, in the synthetic continuums of prose with which public-relations men learn to enclose the sense and smell of an event, it resides in the taste of frozen food, the pharmaceutical odor of tranquilizers, the planned obsolescence of automobiles, the lack of workmanship in the mass, it lives in the boredom of a good mind, in the sexual excess of lovers who love each other into apathy, it is the livid passion which takes us to sleeping pills, the mechanical action in every household appliance which breaks too soon, it vibrates in the sound of an air conditioner or the flicker of fluorescent lighting. And it proliferates in that new architecture which rests like an incubus upon the American landscape, that new architecture which cannot be called modern because it is not architecture but opposed to architecture. Modern architecture began with the desire to use the building materials of the twentieth century—steel, glass, reinforced concrete—and such techniques as cantilevered structure to increase the sculptural beauty of buildings while enlarging their function. It was the first art to be engulfed by the totalitarians who distorted the search of modern architecture for simplicity, and converted it to monotony. The essence of totalitarianism is that it beheads. It beheads individuality, variety, dissent, extreme possibility, romantic faith, it blinds vision, deadens instinct, it obliterates the past. Since it is also irrational, it puts up buildings with flat roofs and huge expanses of glass in northern climates and then suffocates the inhabitants with super-heating systems while the flat roof leaks under a weight of snow. Since totalitarianism is a cancer within the body of history, it obliterates distinctions. It makes factories look like college campuses or mental hospitals, where once factories had the specific beauty of revealing their huge and sometimes brutal function—beauty cannot exist without revelation, nor man maybe without beauty. It makes the new buildings on college campuses look like factories. It depresses the average American with the unconscious recognition that he is installed in a gelatin of totalitarian environment which is bound to deaden his most individual efforts. This new architecture, this totalitarian architecture, destroys the past. There is no trace of the forms which lived in the centuries before us, none of their arrogance, their privilege, their aspiration, their canniness, their creations, their vulgarities. We are left with less and less sense of the lives of men and women who came before us. So we are less able to judge the sheer psychotic values of the present: overkill, fallout shelters, and adjurations by the President to drink a glass of milk each day.

Totalitarianism came to birth at the moment man turned incapable of facing back into the accumulated wrath and horror of his historic past. We sink into cancer after we have gorged on all the medicines which cheated all the diseases we have fled in our life, we sink into cancer when the organs, deadened by chemical rescues manufactured outside the body, became too biologically muddled to dominate their cells. Departing from the function of the separate organs, cancer cells grow to look like one another. So, too, as society bogs into hypocrisies so elaborate they can no longer be traced, then do our buildings, those palpable artifacts of social cells, come to look like one another and cease to function with the art, beauty, and sometimes mysterious proportion of the past.

I can try to answer the lady who wrote the letter now: people who admire the new architecture find it of value because it obliterates the past. They are sufficiently totalitarian to wish to avoid the consequences of the past. Which of course is not to say that they see themselves as totalitarian. The totalitarian passion is an unconscious one. Which liberal fighting for bigger housing and additional cubic feet of air space in elementary schools does not see himself as a benefactor? Can he comprehend that the somewhat clammy pleasure he obtains from looking at the completion of the new school—that architectural horror!—is a reflection of a buried and ugly pleasure, a totalitarian glee that the Gothic knots and Romanesque oppressions which entered his psyche through the schoolhouses of his youth have

now been excised. But those architectural wounds, those forms from
his childhood not only shamed him and scored him, but marked upon
him as well a wound from culture itself—its buried message of the
cruelty and horror which were rooted in the majesties of the past. Now
the flat surfaces, blank ornamentation and pastel colors of the new
schoolhouses will maroon his children in an endless hallway of the
present. A school is an arena to a child. Let it look like what it should
be, mysterious, exciting, even gladiatorial, rather than a musical
comedy's notion of a reception center for war brides. The totalitarian
impulse not only washes away distinctions but looks for a style in
buildings, in clothing, and in the ornamentations of tools, appliances
and daily objects which will diminish one's sense of function, and
reduce one's sense of reality by reducing to the leaden formulations of
jargon such emotions as awe, dread, beauty, pity, terror, calm
horror, and harmony. By dislocating us from the most powerful
emotions of reality, totalitarianism leaves us further isolated in the
empty landscapes of psychosis, precisely that inner landscape of void
and dread which we flee by turning to totalitarian styles of life. The
totalitarian liberal looks for new schools and more desks; the real (if
vanishing) liberal looks for better books, more difficult books to force
upon the curriculum. A high school can survive in a converted cow
barn if the seniors are encouraged to read *Studs Lonigan* the same
week they are handed *The Cardinal* or *The Seven Storey Mountain*.

Yes, the people who admire the new architecture are unconsciously
totalitarian. They are looking to eject into their environment and
landscape the same deadness and monotony life has put into them. A
vast deadness and a huge monotony, a nausea without spasm, has been
part of the profit of American life in the last fifteen years—we will pay
in the next fifteen as this living death is disgorged into the buildings
our totalitarian managers will manage to erect for us. The landscape of
America will be stolen for half a century if a Resistance does not form.
Indeed it may be stolen forever if we are not sufficiently courageous to
enter the depression of contemplating what we have already lost and
what we have yet to lose.

THE TENTH PRESIDENTIAL PAPER

—Minorities

- **The Commentary Columns:**
                    "Responses and Reactions I, III, IV"

- **A Review of The Blacks**

The modern American politician—read: the Democratic or Republican liberal—often begins his career with a modest passion to defend the rights of minorities. By the time he is successful, his passion has been converted to platitude.

Minority groups are the artistic nerves of a republic, and like any phenomenon which has to do with art, they are profoundly divided. They are both themselves and the mirror of their culture as it reacts upon them. They are themselves and the negative truth of themselves. No white man, for example, can hate the Negro race with the same passionate hatred and detailed detestation that each Negro feels for himself and for his people; no anti-Semite can begin to comprehend the malicious analysis of his soul which every Jew indulges every day.

For decades the Jews have been militant for their rights, since the Second War the Negroes have emerged as an embattled and disciplined minority. It is thus characteristic of both races that they have a more intense awareness of their own value and their own lack of value than the awareness of the white Anglo-Saxon Protestant for himself. Unlike the Protestant of the center, minorities have a nature which is polarized. So it is natural that their buried themes, precisely those preoccupations which are never mentioned by minority action groups like the Anti-Defamation League or the NAACP, are charged with paradox, with a search for psychic extremes. To a Protestant, secure in the middle of American life, God and the Devil, magic, death and eternity, are matters outside himself. He may contemplate them but he does not habitually absorb them into the living tissue of his brain. Whereas the exceptional member of any minority group feels as if he possesses God and the Devil within himself, that the taste of his own death is already in his cells, that his purchase on eternity rises and falls with the calm or cowardice of his actions. It is a life exposed to the raw living nerve of anxiety, and rare is the average Jew or Negro who can bear it for long—so the larger tendency among minorities is to manufacture a mediocre personality which is a dull replica of the manners of the white man in power. Nothing can be more conformist, more Square, more profoundly depressing than the Jew-in-the-suburbs or the Negro as member of the Black Bourgeoisie. It is the price they pay for the fact that not all self-hatred is invalid—the critical faculty turned upon oneself can serve to create a personality which is exceptional, which mirrors the particular arts and graces of the white gentry, but this is possible only if one can live with one's existential nerve exposed. Man's personality rises to a level of higher and more delicate habits only if he is willing to engage a sequence of painful victories and cruel defeats in his expedition through the locks and ambushes of social life. One does not copy the manner of someone superior; rather one works an art upon it which makes it suitable for oneself. Direct imitation of a superior manner merely produces a synthetic manner. The collective expression of this in a minority group is nothing other than assimilation.

To the degree each American Jew and American Negro is assimilated he is colorless, a part of a collective nausea which is encysted into the future. The problem in a democracy is not to assimilate minorities but to avoid stifling them as they attain their equality. If the Jews and Negroes attain a brilliant equality with the white Anglo-Saxon Protestant and the Irish Catholic, then America will be different. Whatever it will become, it will be different from anything we can conceive. Whereas if the Negro and Jew are assimilated into the muted unimaginative level of present-day American life, then America will be very much like it is now, only worse. The problem is similar to the difficulty in dealing with juvenile delinquents—one can pacify them by any one of a number of unimaginative programs and be left with a human material which is apathetic if indeed not anchored to moronic expectations; or one can search for arts which transmute violence into heroic activity. An inflammation or rent in the body can heal in such a way that the limb or organ offers new powers of coordination which did not exist before; equally the inflammation can subside to a chronic leaden dullness of function.

So with minorities, one must look for more than the insurance of their rights—one must search to liberate the art which is trapped in the thousand acts of perception which embody their self-hatred, for self-hatred ignored must corrode the roots of one's past and leave one marooned in an alien culture. The liberal premise—that Negroes and Jews are like everybody else once they are given the same rights—can only obscure the complexity, the intensity, and the psychotic brilliance of a minority's inner life.

The pieces which follow involve certain preoccupations of the minority, but what they have to say about Jews and Negroes is special, for they deal with the extreme ends of the spectrum. The Hasidim embodied the most passionate and individual expression of Jewish life in many centuries, the Negro as actor, or to anticipate the next paper, the Negro as heavyweight champion and contender is certainly as exceptional. But the argument of existential politics might be that one never understands a people or a time by contemplating a common denominator, for the average man in a minority group is no longer a member of that minority—he is instead a social paste which has been compounded out of the grinding stone of the society which contains him. He is not his own authentic expression. By this logic, the average Negro or Jew is not so much a black man or a Semite as a mediocre ersatz Protestant. That does not mean he is altogether an inferior man of the center—in his suppressed nerve, in his buried heart, exist the themes which the exceptional man of the minority can embody. So a responsible politician, a President, let us say, professionally sensitive to minority groups, cannot begin to be of real stature to that minority until he becomes aware of what is most extraordinary in a people as well as what is most pressing and ubiquitous in their need. The Jews have staggered along for centuries wondering to their primitive horror whether they have betrayed God once in the desert or again twice with Christ: so they are obsessed in their unconscious nightmare with whether they belong to a God of righteousness or a Devil of treachery—their flight from this confrontation has rushed to produce a large part of that mechanistic jargon which now rules American life in philosophy, psychoanalysis, social action, productive process, and *the arts themselves. The Negro, secretly fixed upon magic—that elixir of nature which seems to mediate between God and Devil—has never made his peace with Christianity, or mankind. The Negro in the most protected recesses of his soul still does not know if he is a part of mankind, or a special embodiment of nature suspended between society and the gods. As the Negro enters civilization, Faust may be his archetype, even as the Jew has fled Iago* as the despised image of himself.*

Responses and Reactions I

Disraeli once made a speech in Commons to the effect that the most damaging mistake a conservative party could make was to persecute the Jews, since they were naturally conservative and turned to radical ideas only when they were deprived of an organic place in society. The statement is certainly not without interest, but may grasp no more than a part of the truth. It is more likely the instinct of the Jews to be attracted to large whole detailed views of society, to seek intellectual specifications of the social machine, and to enter precisely those occupations which subtly can offer institutional, personal, and legislative possibilities to a man of quick wit and sensible cohesive culture. The precise need of the essentialist, the authoritarian, or the progressive is to have a social machine upon which one can apply oneself. Later, having earned sufficient and satisfactory power, one may tinker with the machine. It is small wonder that the four corners of modern Protestantism are pegged on Judaistic notions, upon a set of social ideas given bulk and mass only by a most determinedly circumscribed conception of heaven, hell, divine compassion, and eter-

*Not Shylock. *Iago*.

nal punishment. For modern man, Judaeo-Christian man, the social world before him tends to become all of existence.

Yet if the Jews have a greatness, an irreducible greatness, I wonder if it is not to be found in the devil of their dialectic, which places madness next to practicality, illumination side by side with duty, and arrogance in bed with humility. The Jews first saw God in the desert—that dramatic terrain of the present tense stripped of the past, blind to the future. The desert is a land where man may feel insignificant or feel enormous. On the desert can perish the last of one's sensitivities; one's end can wither in the dwarf's law of a bleak nature. Or to the contrary, left alone and in fever, a solitary witness, no animal or vegetable close to him, man may come to feel immensely alive, more portentous in his own psychic presence than any manifest of nature. In the desert, man may flee before God, in terror of the apocalyptic voice of *His* lightning, *His* thunder; or, as dramatically, in a style that no Christian would ever attempt, man dares to speak directly to God, bargains with Him, upbraids Him, rises to scold Him, stares into God's eye like a proud furious stony-eyed child. It may be the anguish of the Jew that he lives closer to God and farther away than men of other religions; certainly it must be true that the Jewish ritual leads one closer to the family, the community, to one's duty, but does not encourage a transcendent vault into the presence of any Power or Divine. It is even possible the Orthodox ritual may have evolved out of some sense in the Community that the Jews had better not dare a rhapsodic and *personal* communion with God, not by themselves, not divorced from ritual, not alone, precisely not alone because they had such voracious instincts and such passionate desires for ecstatic union that they might burn with madness and destroy the race. Given their sober gloomy estimate of reality, they would find malaise and nausea in any communion with God which was too private. It would seem a condition somewhat obscene. This tension may even have helped to create their humor. "What of the *kinder* if I dance naked in the streets?"

Responses and Reactions III

Before the Coming of the Messiah*

The Baal Shem said:

"Before the coming of the Messiah there will be great abundance in the world. The Jews will get rich. They will become accustomed to running their houses in the grand style and moderation will be cast to the winds. Then the lean years will come; want and a meager livelihood, and the world will be full of poverty. The Jews will not be able to satisfy their needs, grown beyond rhyme or reason. And then the labor which will bring forth the Messiah, will begin."

Yet to our knowledge, no Messiah was brought forth from the concentration camps. Or were a hundred delivered to die with the victims, secret Angels of Death?

It is possible the Jews will never recover from the woe that no miracle visited the world in that time. Perhaps that is why we are now so interested in housing, in social planning, interfaith councils, and improvement of the PTA in the suburbs. Perhaps that is why half of the American Jews have fallen in love with a super delicatessen called Miami, and much of the other half have developed a subtly over-bearing and all but totalitarian passion for the particular sallow doctor who is their analyst. Perhaps that is why we have lost the root. And had the lust to build a world of plastic surfaces whose historic root is urea.

From the Look-Out of Heaven†

At a time of great anguish for Israel, Rabbi Elimelekh brooded more and more on his griefs. Then his dead master, the maggid of Mezritch, appeared to him. Rabbi Elimelekh cried out: "Why are you silent in such dreadful need?" He answered: "In Heaven we see that all that seems evil to you is a work of mercy."

To die before one's time in a gas chamber may offer the good fortune that one does not have to live beyond one's time and be kept

* *The Early Masters*, p. 82. (See footnote on page 168.)
† *The Early Masters*, p. 112.

alive by medicines which do not reach the disease but only deaden the pain. In a gas chamber one loses one's life and conceivably saves one's death. If there is eternity, and we possess a soul which can either carry through life into death, or perish in life and never reach eternity, then the real need for a Messiah would appear in that part of the world, or history, where souls are becoming dead rather than lives being lost. By this logic, there would be more unconscious demand for the Messiah in a country at peace than a city at war.

The logic is unassailable if God has no need of Time and merely studies the way we save our souls or lose them. But if there is any urgency in God's intent, if we are not actors working out a play for our salvation, but rather soldiers in an army which seeks to carry some noble conception of Being out across the stars, or back into the protoplasm of life, then a portion of God's creative power was extinguished in the camps of extermination. If God is not all-powerful but existential, discovering the possibilities and limitations of His creative powers in the form of the history which is made by His creatures, then one must postulate an existential equal to God, an antagonist, the Devil, a principle of Evil whose signature was the concentration camps, whose joy is to waste substance, whose intent is to prevent God's conception of Being from reaching its mysterious goal. If one considers the hypothesis that God is not all-powerful, indeed not the architect of Destiny, but rather, the creator of Nature, then evil becomes a record of the Devil's victories over God. It is not so comforting a postulation as the notion of God Omnipotent able to give us Eternal Rest, but it must also be seen that if God is all-powerful, the Jews cannot escape the bitter recognition that He considered one of His inscrutable purposes to be worth more than the lives of half His chosen people. Indeed this recognition may have paralyzed the organized religious spirit of the American Jews. The Catholic Church becomes more powerful every year, the American Protestants have produced several existential philosophers of importance—who have come to a consideration of the mysteries of anxiety—but the conventional Jews in America, which is to say the ones who are formally attached to the religion, build new synagogues which look like recreation centers and go to them because it would make their mothers happy. *Angst* is left to the mechanical formulations of the analyst who now leans less on Freud and more on Equanil.

The Teaching of the Soul*

Rabbi Pinhas often cited the words: " 'A man's soul will teach him,' " and emphasized them by adding: "There is no man who is not incessantly being taught by his soul."

One of his disciples asked: "If this is so, why don't men obey their souls?"

"The soul teaches incessantly," Rabbi Pinhas explained, "but it never repeats."

If God and the Devil are locked in an implacable war, it might not be excessive to assume their powers are separate, God the lord of inspiration, the Devil a monumental bureaucrat of repetition. To learn from an inner voice the first time it speaks to us is a small bold existential act, for it depends upon following one's instinct which must derive, in no matter how distorted a fashion, from God, whereas institutional knowledge is appropriated by the Devil. The soul speaks once and chooses not to repeat itself, because to repeat a message is to give the Devil in one's psyche a chance to prepare a trap. People repeat the same message over and over in order to employ a Satanic principle— the audience before them must be deadened by the monotony of making the same response, or must reveal—by the separate ways in which the question is answered—some protected corner of their nature.

For the Sake of Renewal†

Rabbi Pinhas said: "Solomon, the preacher, says: 'Vanity of vanities, all is vanity,' because he wants to destroy the world, so that it may receive new life."

Not all destruction destroys. Not all construction creates. If the world, seen through the eyes of Marx, is the palpable embodiment of a vast collective theft—the labor which was stolen from men by other men over the centuries—then one need not retire in terror from the idea that the power of the world belongs to the Devil, and God needs men to overthrow him.

The entrance of the Devil into aesthetics is visible in a new airline

*The Early Masters, p. 121.
† The Early Masters, p. 124.

terminal, a luxury hotel, a housing project, or a civic center. Their flat surfaces speak of power without vision, their plastic materials suggest flesh without the unmanageable details of blood.

The Secret of Sleep*

Rabbi Zusya's younger son said:
"The zaddikim who, in order to serve, keep going from sanctuary to sanctuary, and from world to world, must cast their life from them, time and again, so that they may receive a new spirit, that over and over, a new revelation may float above them. This is the secret of sleep."

Can it be that insomnia is the rage of the Devil determined not to let us sleep long enough to receive a new spirit and thus be curious enough to defy our pact with him again? Or can insomnia also be the anger of the Lord who knows that the new spirit he provides in sleep will be handed over to the Devil in the morning? On those occasions when we do not know if it is God or the Devil we must fear, do we not have insomnia with *Angst*, does not madness insinuate itself? There is a suggestion to go out on the street and look for the adventure One or the Other is demanding. Most of us stay home. All right then, so we die of cancer, goes the sigh in the wind of our small depleted courage.

With the Evil Urge†

Once, when Rabbi Pinhas entered the House of Study, he saw that his disciples, who had been talking busily, stopped and started at his coming. He asked them: "What were you talking about?"
"Rabbi," they said, "we were saying how afraid we are that the Evil Urge will pursue us."
"Don't worry," he replied. "You have not gotten high enough for it to pursue you. For the time being, you are still pursuing it."

* *The Early Masters*, p. 252.
† *The Early Masters*, p. 132.

Responses and Reactions IV

Through the Hat*

Once Rabbi Mikhal visited a city where he had never been before. Soon some of the prominent members of the congregation came to call on him. He fixed a long gaze on the forehead of everyone who came, and then told him the flaws in his soul and what he could do to heal them. It got around that there was a zaddik in the city who was versed in reading faces, and could tell the quality of the soul by looking at the forehead. The next visitors pulled their hats down to their noses. "You are mistaken," Rabbi Mikhal said to them. "An eye which can see through the flesh, can certainly see through the hat."

Reading faces is a frontier art. An honest face may be either honest or a masterpiece of treachery. Consider this: every inanimate form in nature is the record of a war—the shape of a stone reflects the obduracy of the material versus the attrition of the elements. Whereas the meaning of the forms in a man's face or body is more complex. An honest mouth hints of battles taken against everything dishonest in the world and in oneself, but an honest mouth cannot necessarily be trusted, for humans have the ability to displace the psychic war within themselves. A man can influence the growth of his features, the shape of his body, he may be able to transpose the revelation of his personal forms from the surface of his skin to the function of his organs. An actor can cultivate an honest mouth and suffer in exchange a bad digestive system. An honest man can let his mouth go slack in order to protect the well-being of his stomach. The art of reading faces depends on more than an instinct for the language of forms; one must also be able to sense the dialectic between a face, a temporary mood, and the formal character of the man before one. It is this instinct upon which Mikhal was obviously depending. So a hat could bother him little. Obviously, he would "see *through* the flesh."

The Story of the Cape†

A woman came to Rabbi Israel, the maggid of Koznitz, and told him, with many tears, that she had been married a dozen years and still had not borne a son. "What are you going to do about it?" he asked her. She did not know what to say.

---

* *The Early Masters*, p. 142. (See footnote on page 168.)
† *The Early Masters*, p. 286.

"My mother," so the maggid told her, "was aging and still had no child. Then she heard that the holy Baal Shem was stopping over in Apt in the course of a journey. She hurried to his inn and begged him to pray she might bear a son. 'What are you willing to do about it?' he asked. 'My husband is a poor book-binder,' she replied, 'but I do have one fine thing I shall give to the rabbi.' She went home as fast as she could and fetched her good cape, her 'Katinka,' which was carefully stowed away in a chest. But when she returned to the inn with it, she heard that the Baal Shem had already left for Mezbizh. She immediately set out after him and since she had no money to ride, she walked from town to town with her 'Katinka' until she came to Mezbizh. The Baal Shem took the cape and hung it on the wall. 'It is well,' he said. My mother walked all the way back, from town to town, until she reached Apt. A year later, I was born."

"I, too," cried the woman, "will bring you a good cape of mine so that I may get a son."

"That won't work," said the maggid. "You heard the story. My mother had no story to go by."

One could use that anecdote as an introduction to *An Intelligent Woman's Guide to Existentialism*. Death, despair, and dread, intimations of nothingness, the mystery of mood, and the logic of commitment have been the central preoccupations of the existentialists. In this country, there has been a tendency to add our American obsession with courage and sex. These concerns are the no-man's-land of philosophy. Insubstantial, novelistic, too intimate for the coiled cosmological speculations of metaphysics, irrational and alien to the classical niceties of ethics, utter anathema to the post-Logical Positivists of Oxford, existentialism remains nonetheless the one non-sterile continuation open to modern philosophy, for it is the last of the humanisms, it has not given its unconditional surrender to science.

The existential premise in "The Story of the Cape" is that we learn only from situations in which the end is unknown. As an epistemological scheme it suggests that man learns more about the nature of water by jumping into the surf than by riding a boat. Certainly he learns more about the nature of water if he comes close to drowning. Restated in a framework of Zen, one might say that the nature of experience is comprehended to the degree it is seen in purity, in the purity of no concept. A career soldier, armed with the professional necessity to be brave, can go through combat without ever entering an existential moment. His duty is simple. It is to fight until he dies or wins. It is only if he goes through enough combat to exhaust the concept of his duty and is thus reduced to a man who may either have the will to continue or the desire to quit, that he will have then entered the existential terrain where one discovers authenticity in one's desires. Such situations were at the heart of Hemingway's work until *The Old Man and the Sea*, which permits no existential moment for the fisherman: the old man is never reduced to the point of debating whether to let the big fish go.

The logic in searching for extreme situations, in searching for one's authenticity, is that one burns out the filament of old dull habit and turns the conscious mind back upon its natural subservience to the instinct. The danger of civilization is that its leisure, its power, its insulation from nature, so alienate us from instinct that our consciousness and our habits take on an autonomy which may censor even the most alienated from instinct, begins to construct its intellectual formulations over a void. The existential moment, by demanding the most extreme response in the protagonist, tends to destroy psychotic autonomies in the mind—since they are unreal, they give way first—one is returned closer to the reality of one's personal strength or weakness. The woman in search of a child goes on a pilgrimage in which her end is unknown—she may find the Baal Shem or she may not, but her commitment is complete, and the suggestion intrudes itself that on the long miles of her march, her mind, her habits, and her body were affected sufficiently to dissolve the sterilities of her belly and prepare her for a child.

Her commitment created her new condition. In giving herself to a concept outside herself, the experience she encountered was able to change her. The second woman having heard the story was trying to cheat an existential demand. She was looking not for commitment but obedience to a precedent. And precedent is the spine of all consciousness which is constructed upon a void. Precedent, it can be said, is the description of an event which occurred in the past, and has therefore altered the present in such a way that the same event could not take place again.

Knowledge*

They say that in his youth, Rabbi Israel studied eight hundred books of the Kabbalah. But the first time he saw the maggid of Mezritch face to face, he instantly knew that he knew nothing at all.

The Early Masters, p. 287.

A Review of Jean Genet's The Blacks

It was printed in two parts by The Village Voice, *May 11 and May 18, 1961, it was attacked with intermittent efficiency and some good writing by Lorraine Hansberry in the issue of June 1, and in a reply I wrote for the issue of June 8, I explained in the following way some of the indifferent writing I had done:*

It is a bitch to write a hasty and ambitious essay for a newspaper, but one cannot apologize for the pressure of time any more than a general who lost a great battle can explain how he would have carried the afternoon if only the 111th Hussars had not been fagged by a 50-mile march. Writing for a newspaper is like running a revolutionary war, you go into battle not when you are ready but when action offers itself.

Looking over the piece two years later, the bad writing tends to separate from the less bad writing. Most of what I had to say directly about the play and about acting was mannered and not very original. So I cut it from publication here. This leaves the piece top-heavy. There is much intellectual essay and very little dramatic criticism. Still, I was right to keep what I did. The remarks which are made about Jews, Negroes, cancer, totalitarianism, Genet, and surrealism still seem interesting whereas the specific criticism of the production must by now be obsolete—the play has been running for two years Off Broadway.

In the answer to Hansberry is a sentence which belongs in an essay "After the White Negro"—as yet unwritten.

The orgasm is anathema to [the liberal] mind because it is the inescapable existential moment. Every lie we have told, every fear we have indulged, every aggression we have tamed arises at that instant to constrict the turns and possibilities of our becoming. If we gain the world and our timing is dulled—as was Stalin's and Eisenhower's—then the world is deadened, and damn our revolution, we were better without it, better to be banging away like jungle bunnies in the brush. What is at stake in the twentieth century is not the economic security of man—every bureaucrat in the world lusts to give us this—it is, on the contrary, the peril that they will extinguish the animal in us.

Please note this rule of thumb, Mr. President.

THEATRE: *The Blacks*

No one who believes in the greatness of certain plays would go to any one of our houses to enjoy them. They exist as thundering productions in the mind only. We know how they might be done (*King Lear*, for example, should be played by Ernest Hemingway), but one also knows that way lies nightmare, madness, and no hurricane's spout. Our theatre is cancer gulch. Anyone who has worked in it, felt the livid hate-twisted nerves of the actresses, the fag-ridden spirit of the actors, the gulping mannerless yaws of our directors, hysterical at resistance, ponderous at exposition, and always psychoanalytical, must admit that yes, at its best, our theatre is a rich ass and/or hole, at its worst, the heavens recoil.

By way of preface to some remarks on *The Blacks*. If one is tempted to say it is a great play (with insidious, even evil veins of cowardice in its cruel bravery), one has to add immediately that such greatness exists as still another of those exquisite lonely productions off imagination's alley. The show, the literal show on the boards, ended as good theatre, shocking as a rash, bughouse with anxiety to some, nervous feverhot for all. (A lot of people left.) It is a good production, one of the doubtless best productions in New York this year, and yet it fails to find two-thirds of the play. It is a hot hothouse tense livid off-fag deep-purple voodoo Mon Doo production, thick, jungle bush, not unjazzy, never cool, but at its worst, and Gene Frankel's touch is not always directed to the fine, the gloomy accolade one must offer is that Frankel does an honest job, he clarifies the play—at a cost, but he does make it easier to see the play than to read it—he enriches the production upon occasions. The rich farty arts, that only grace our theatre can claim, are used with good force. The savory in Genet is laid on rich and that is probably right. Consider this speech as a clue to the heat of the evening. Delivered with considerable elegance and cold fire by Mr. Roscoe Lee Browne:

> ARCHIBALD (gravely): I order you to be black to your very veins. Pump black blood through them. Let Africa circulate in them. Let Negroes negrify themselves. Let them persist to the point of madness in what they're condemned to be, in their ebony, in their odor, in their yellow eyes, in their cannibal tastes. Let them not be content with eating Whites, but let them cook each other as well. Let them invent recipes for shin-bones, knee-caps, calves, thick lips, everything. Let them invent unknown sauces. Let them invent hiccoughs, belches and farts that'll give out a deleterious jazz. Let them invent a criminal painting and dancing. Negroes, if they change toward us, let it not be out of indulgence, but terror.

Contemplate the problem of a director. He is to deal with 13 actors, all Negro, in the truest and most explosive play anyone has yet written at all about the turn in the tide, and the guilt and horror in the white man's heart as he turns to face his judge.

Rehearsals inevitably must commence in a state. For the actors are not Africans. They are American Negroes, they belong some of them to the Black Bourgeoisie which any proud Negro is quick to tell you is a parody of the white bourgeoisie—the party's-getting-out-of-line kind of cramp on the jazz. They belong to the Center, to the Left Minority Center, the New York *Post*, Max Lerner, Rose Franzblau, Jackie Robinson (bruises the heart to list his name), Muscular Dystrophy, Communities-of-Cancer, synagogue-on-Sunday, put up those housing projects, welfare the works, flatten the tits, mash the best, beef the worst, and marry the slack and mediocre Negro to the slack and mediocre Jew. Whew!

But organized religion is the death of the essay. Let us leave the mediocre at this: the real horror worked on the Jews and the Negroes since the Second War is the mass-communication of nothingness into their personality. They were two of the greatest peoples in America, and half of their populations sold themselves to the suburb, the center, the secure; that diarrhea of the spirit which is embodied in the fleshless query: "Is this good for the Jews?" So went the Jew. So went the Negro. The mediocre among them rushed for the disease.

Well, the Negro at least has his boast. They are part, this black bourgeoisie, of a militant people moving toward inevitable and much-deserved victory. They cannot know because they have not seen themselves from outside (as we have seen them), that there is a genius in their race—it is possible that Africa is closer to the root of whatever life is left than any other land. The genius of that land is a cruel one, it may be even an unrelenting genius, void of forgiveness, but it is impossible that the survival, emergence, and eventual triumph of the Negro during his three centuries in America will not be considered by history as an epic equal to the twenty centuries the Jew has wandered outside. It will be judged as superior if the Negro keeps his salt.

But for now, they are going through the bends. They suffer from that same slavery of ascent the *Geist* imposes on all of us. It is Liberal Totalitarianism. Curiosity of the age! The concentration camps exist in the jargon of our souls, one's first whiff of the gas chamber is the nausea of cancer's hour, the storm troopers wear tortoise-shell glasses, and carry attache cases to the cubicles in which they work on the Avenue of the Mad. The liberal tenets of the Center are central; all people are alike if we suppress the ugliness in each of us, all sadism is evil, all masochism is sick, all spontaneity is suspect, all individuality is infantile, and the salvation of the world must come from social manipulation of human material. That is why all people must tend to become the same—a bulldozer does not work at its best in rocks or forest. Small accident that many of the Negro leaders are as colorless as our white leaders and all too many of the Negroes one knows have a dull militancy compared to the curve and art of personality their counterparts had even 10 years ago. The misapprehension on which they march is that time is on the side of the Negro. If his hatred is contained, and his individuality reduced, the logic of the age must advance him first to equality and then to power (goes the argument), because the Center makes its dull shifts through guilt and through need. Since the Negro has finally succeeded in penetrating the conscience of the best Whites, and since the worst Whites are muzzled by our need to grant the Negro his equality or sink a little faster into the icy bogs of the Cold War, the Negro knows he need merely ape the hypocrisies of the white bourgeoisie, and he will win. It is a partial misapprehension. In the act of concealing himself, the Negro does not hasten his victory so much as he deadens the taste of it.

A fine sermon. Its application to the theatre is not arcane. The Negro tends to be superior to the White as an entertainer, and inferior as an actor. No need to discuss the social background; it is obvious the

Negro has had virtually no opportunity to develop as an actor until the last few years, and the comparison is to that large extent most unfair, but it is made nonetheless because the Negro does not generally lack professional competence as an actor, he lacks relaxation. The bad Negro actor reminds one of nothing so much as a very bad White actor: he orates, declaims, stomps, screams, prates, bellows, and binds, his emotions remain private to himself, his taste is uncertain or directly offensive to the meaning of the play, he is in short a bully.

Now this is curious. Because the greatest entertainers in America have been Negro, and the best of the Whites exhibit their obvious and enormous debt every time they make a sound. The Negro entertainer brought mood and tempo, a sense of self, an ear for audience. The cadence in the shift of the moment became as sensuous as the turning of flesh in oneself or within another. Extraordinary was the richness of intimate meaning they could bring to a pop tune. It was their fruit, the fruit of Aesopian language. Used to employing the words expected of them by the White, the Negro communicated more by voice than by his word. A simple sentence promised the richest opportunities to his sense of nuance, that is it did if the simple sentence did not speak too clearly in its language. To the extent that meaning was imprecise, the voice could prosper. For meaning was ferocious in its dangers. Back of the throat, in the clear salts of language, was the sentence graven on the palate: White man, I want to kill you.

So the style of the American Negro took on its abstract manner. Where the sentence said little, the man said much; where the words were clear, the person was blank. The entertainer thrived, the actor was stunted. The Negro, steeped in the dangers of his past, would obviously be in dread of entering the cage of formal meaning; he could hardly do it with the deep relaxation of a great actor. It is one thing for Olivier to be magnificent but for a Negro it is simply too dangerous. The emotions banked to suffocation in his heart are never far from erupting. So he speaks stiff, he declaims, he denies his person. Now, you or me can point to Sidney Poitier, to Canada Lee, to the good cast of *Raisin in the Sun*, to moments in *The Cool World*, to this, to that—I know. One speaks precisely of a tendency. Only the minds of the Center will say tomorrow that I said all Negro actors are bad. But this I do insist—they tend not to be good. And in *The Blacks*, this tendency is exacerbated.

Consider the emotions of the cast when they must utter lines like the following to a white audience:

Tonight, our sole concern will be to entertain you. So we have killed this white woman. There she lies.

You forget that I'm already knocked out from the crime I had to finish off before you arrived, since you need a fresh corpse for every performance.

And you, pale and odorless race, race without animal odors, without the pestilence of our swamps.

Invent, not love, but hatred, and thereby make poetry, since that's the only domain in which we're allowed to operate.

If I were sure that Village bumped the woman off in order to heighten the fact that he's a scarred, smelly, thick-lipped, snub-nosed Negro, an eater and guzzler of Whites and all other colors . . .
[*To be continued next week*]

THEATRE: *The Blacks* (Cont.)

It's a great deal to ask of a young Negro actor that he have the sociological sophistication to understand one can get away with this in New York, that our puritanical, bully-ridden, smog-headed, dull, humorless, deadly, violence-steeped and all but totally corrupt city is so snob-ridden and so petrified of making a martyr that one can get away with near-murder. Nobody will close *The Blacks*, or there'll be demonstrations in Paris. No one will rise up from the audience to strike the actors for sacrilege. No hoodlums will paint swastikas on the marquee. If necessary 500 police would patrol the avenue to keep *The Blacks* going. Our democracy is a soporific hulk, a deadened old beast's carcass with two or three nerves alive, no more. Like a dying patient, democracy holds on to the pain of its nerves, defends them. So the actors who play the parts are not taking their lives in their hands each night they go on, and the anxiety which lay heavy the night I saw the play, an anxiety which took the long jump from phenomenon to false conclusion (That cat in the front row has eyes for me. If I talk of killing one more White, I'll be dead myself) will begin to dissolve before the reality: *The Blacks* is secure. The play is close to greatness, it will survive. It gives life to the city. There is so little real life in the dead haunted canyons of this cancer-ridden city that a writer as surgical in his cruelties as Saint Genet gives Being back to the citizens. For in 20 years the doctors may discover that it is not only the removal of the tumor which saves the patient but the entry of the knife. Cancer thrives on indecision and is arrested by any spirit of lightning present in an act. Cancer is also arrested by answers, which is why perhaps the cancerous always seek for faith and cannot bear questions. The authoritarian wave of the twentieth century may be seen a century from now, if we still exist, as the reflection of man's anxiety before the oncoming rush of this disease, a disease which is not a disease, but a loss of self, for unlike death by other causes, cancer is a rebellion of the cells. They refuse to accept the will, the dignity, the desire, in short the *project* of the person who contains them. They betray the body because they have lost faith in it. So in desperation the man who contains such illness ceases to be existential, ceases to care about a personal choice, about making a personal history and prefers instead to deliver his will to an institution or faith outside him in the hope that it will absorb the rebellious hatreds of his Being. Man turns to society to save him only when he is sick within. So long as he is alive, he looks for love. But those dying of inanition, boredom, frustration, monotony, or debilitating defeat turn to the Church, to the FBI, to the Law, to the New York *Times*, to authoritarian leaders, to movies about the Marine Corps, or to the race for Space. For centuries it has been society's boast that if it could not save a man's soul, it could at least insure him from losing it. Ever since the orgy failed in Rome and the last decadence of the Empire welcomed the barbarian, the Western World has been relatively simple, a community of souls ruled by society. First the Church, then the Reformation, then Capitalism, Communism, Fascism, and at last Medicine-Science-and-Management. But as it evolved, so Society used up its faith in itself. Today the Managers do not understand what they manage nor what is their proper goal, the Scientists are gored by Heisenberg's principle of Uncertainty, which in rough would state that ultimates by their nature are not measurable, and Medicine is beginning to flounder at the inability to comprehend its striking impotence before cancer. The modern faiths appeal to mediocrities whose minds are too dull to perceive that they are offered not answers but the suppression of questions; the more sensitive turn to the older faiths and shrink as they swallow emotional inconsistency. The cancerous who are inclined to the Fascist look to the police, the secret police, the *Krieg* against crime, corruption, and Communists.

As a drama critic, one is here obliged to take a bow. Over the past two weeks, 4000 words have been written. One has climbed his way over small essays on the Negro as actor and entertainer, the loss of spirit in minority groups, the vices of our city, the logic of cancer. But not a word to summarize the story of the play.

Since the attempt must be made to contend with the vices of Jean Genet, I will quote here, however, from a description in the New York *Herald Tribune*:

> a group of colored players enacts before a jury of white-masked Negroes—representing in caricature a missionary bishop, an island governor general, a haughty queen and her dwarf lackey—the ritualistic murder of a white of which they have been accused. When they have played out their weird and gruesome crime they turn on their judges and condemn them to death. Then—with polite adieux to the spectators—they dance with 18th-century elegance a Mozart minuet, with which the play began . . .

It is a fair job for a short paragraph. And it points the way to the worst contradiction in Genet. He is on the one hand a brave and great writer with an unrelenting sense of where the bodies are buried. He is also an unconscionable faggot, drenched in chi-chi, adoring any perfume which conceals the smell of the dead, equally as much as he admires the murder. His first love is not art but magic. He provokes and then mystifies, points to the flower and smuggles the root. A boxer who wins every round on points and never sets himself long enough to throw three good punches in combination, Genet's best perceptions are followed by his worst. A line which is a universal blow is followed by a speech too private for his latest lover to comprehend. Like Allen Ginsberg, he is maddening. In the middle of real power, a fart; in the depth of a mood comes a sneeze. The tortures and twists of his nervous system are offered as proudly as his creations; he looks not only for art but for therapy. With the best will in the world and the finest actors, no one in an audience could ever understand every single line in any one of his works, not even if one returned a dozen of times.

He is willful, perverse. He has the mind of a master, and the manners of a vicious and overpetted child. So the clear sure statements of his work can never be found, and one senses with the whole of one's critical faculty that they are not there to be found. Each delicate truth is carefully paralyzed by a lie he winds about it, each assertion of force is dropped to its knees on a surrealist wrench of the meaning.

ARCHIBALD: By stretching language we'll distort it sufficiently to wrap ourselves in it and hide, whereas the masters contract it.

As Genet gives, he takes away; as he offers, his style chokes with spite. He cannot finally make the offer, the one who receives would not deserve it. So he builds the mansion of his art and buries it, encourages the stampede of a herd of elephants, rouses our nerves for an apocalyptic moment, and leaves us with an *entrechat*. To be satisfying, a fag's art must be determinedly minor, one stone properly polished, deliciously set. Genet throws open a Spanish chest; as we prepare to gorge, we discover the coins are heated, the settings to the jewels have poison on their points.

One does not spend one's youth as a petty thief, one's manhood as a convict in one prison after another without absorbing the viciousness of a dying world. Genet's biography is his character, never was it more so. He could become the greatest writer alive if only he dared, if only he contracted language to the point instead of stretching it.

In *The Blacks*, all the actors are Negro. Five are supposed to be White, but are White only as pretexts, as masks. In the murderous dialogues between Black and White which flicker like runs of summer lightning through the play, one never has the experience as it could be had: that moment of terror when Black and White confront one another with the clear acids of their unconscious. Witness the dialogue between the White Queen and the Negro woman Felicity:

THE QUEEN (inspired): All the same, my proud beauty, I was more beautiful than you! Anyone who knows me can tell you that. No one has been more lauded than I. Or more courted, or more toasted. Or adorned. Clouds of heroes, young and old, have died for me. My retinues were famous. At the Emperor's ball, an African slave bore my train. And the Southern Cross was one of my baubles. You were still in darkness . . .

FELICITY: Beyond that shattered darkness, which was splintered into millions of Blacks who dropped to the jungle, we were Darkness in person. Not the darkness which is absence of light, but the kindly and terrible Mother who contains light and deeds.

and a little later, The Queen:

Show these barbarians that we are great because of our respect for discipline, and show the Whites who are watching that we are worthy of their tears.

It could have the grandeur of Greek tragedy. In the context of the play it does not. One watches in one of those states of transition between wakefulness and sleep. Two principles do not oppose one another; instead a dance of three, a play of shimmers. White contends against Black but is really Black-in-White-Mask against Black, and so becomes Black against Black. Much complexity is gained; much force is lost. These masks are not the enrichments and exaggerations of Greek tragedy, they are reversals of form. The emotion aroused in the audience never comes to focus, but swirls into traps.

So with the action. One has a group of Negroes who are revolutionaries. They commit a ritual murder each night. But they are also players who entertain a world of White leaders, mounted literally above them on the stage. They are in subservience to them, yet they are not. For the audience never can quite forget that the Whites are really Blacks-in-White masks. One is asked to consider a theme which may be the central moment of the twentieth century: the passage of power from the White to those he oppressed. But this theme is presented in a web of formal contradictions and formal turns sufficiently complex to be a play in itself.

Pirandello never made this mistake. His dance of mirrors was always built on pretexts which were flimsy. If one's obsession is with the contradictory nature of reality, the audience must be allowed to dispense with the superficial reality in order to explore its depths. The foreground in *The Blacks* is too oppressive. One cannot ignore it. White and Black in mortal confrontation are far more interesting than the play of shadows Genet brings to it. If he insists with avant-garde pride that he will not be bullied by the major topicalities of his theme, and instead will search out the murmurs, the shivers, the nuances, one does not necessarily have to applaud. Certain themes, simple on their face, complex in their depths, insist on returning to the surface and remaining simple. The murder of Lumumba is thus simple. It is simple and it is overbearing. It is inescapable. One cannot treat it as a pantomime for ballet without making an aesthetic misjudgment of the first rank. It would be a strategic disaster of conception. So with Genet's choice to add the minuet to Africa. One is left not with admiration for his daring, but with a dull sense of evasion. How much real emotion and complexity we could have been given if literal White had looked across the stage at literal Black. His rhodomontades and escapades leave us finally with the suspicion that Genet has not escaped the deepest vice of the French mind: its determination, no matter how, to say something new, even if it is absurd. And it is this vice which characterizes the schism in Genet as an artist, for he is on the one hand, major, moving with a bold long reach into those unexplored territories at the edge of our awareness, and with the other, he is minor, a Surrealist, destroying the possibility of awareness even as he creates it.

Surrealist art, stripped of its merits, ignoring the exquisite talents of its painters and poets, depends in its abstract essence on a destruction of communication. To look at a painting and murmur: "I see God in the yellow," is surrealist; to say "I see God in the yellow because the color reminds me of the sun," is not. The thought is no longer a montage of two unrelated semantic objects—it has become a progression. The logic leads to a cosmogony whose center is the life-giving sun. Of course, the first sentence, the montage, is more arresting, a poetic tension is left if one says no more than "I see God in the yellow." For some, the tension is attractive, for others it is not. Art obviously depends upon incomplete communication. A work which is altogether explicit is not art, the audience cannot respond with their own creative act of the imagination, that small leap of the faculties which leaves one an increment more exceptional than when one began.

In Surrealism, the leap in communication is enormous. Purple apples, we write at random, salacious horses and cockroaches who crow like transistors. The charge comes more from sound than from meaning. Opposites and irreconcilables are connected to one another like pepper sprinkled on ice cream. Only a palate close to death could extract pleasure from the taste; it is absurd in our mouth, pepper and ice cream, but at least it is new.

As cultures die, they are stricken with the mute implacable rage of that humanity strangled within them. So long as it grows, a civilization depends upon the elaboration of meaning, its health is maintained by an awareness of its state; as it dies, a civilization opens itself to the fury of those betrayed by its meaning, precisely because that meaning was finally not sufficiently true to offer a life adequately large. The aesthetic act shifts from the creation of meaning to the destruction of it.

So, one could argue, functions the therapy of the surrealist artist, of Dada, of Beat. Jaded, deadened, severed from our roots, dulled in leaden rage, inhabiting the center of the illness of the age, it becomes more excruciating each year for us to perform the civilized act of contributing to a collective meaning. The impulse to destroy moves like new air into a vacuum, and the art of the best hovers, stilled, all but paralyzed between the tension to create and that urge which is its opposite. How well Genet personifies the dilemma. Out of the tension of his flesh, he makes the pirouette of his art, offering meaning in order to adulterate it, until at the end we are in danger of being left with not much more than the Narcissism of his style. How great a writer, how hideous a cage. As a civilization dies, it loses its biology. The homosexual, alienated from the biological chain, becomes its center. The core of the city is inhabited by a ghost who senses in the unwinding of his nerves that the only road back to biology is to destroy Being in others. What a cruel fate for Genet that he still burns with a creative heat equal to his detestation of the world. The appropriate Hell he inhabits is to be a major artist and not a minor one, the body in which he sits has the chest of a giant, and the toes, unhappily, of a dancing master.

A POSTSCRIPT ON THE NOTE TO THE

TENTH PRESIDENTIAL PAPER

Miss Hansberry's long letter in answer to the review of The Blacks *was a sophisticated version of the argument that the only difference between the white man and the black is pigmentation of the skin—all else is environment. Since I obviously believed that there were qual-*

ities, essences, innate differences of being between black and white,
Lorraine Hansberry saw fit to call me one of the "New Paternalists."
It's a decent term of abuse, and I invited her to join with James
Baldwin and myself for a three-cornered debate in Carnegie Hall. I
suggested that my part of the receipts might go to raise a fund to start a
royal caper. I thought it would be good to strip The Blacks *of its*
masks, have whites play Whites and Negroes play Blacks, and take
the play down South on a tour of Southern cities. There were great
confrontations and tragic dialogues in that play. There was a moment
when the White Queen spoke of cavaliers who had been ready to die
for a dance, or a flick of her fan. You will come to power, said the
White Queen to the Black Queen, but you will never know the joys we
knew, the delights, the elegance, the exquisiteness of that life we
maintained by dancing upon your back.

"Blow out your farts," screamed the Black Queen back.
A scene for Charleston, or Atlanta, New Orleans, Savannah.
I underlined the idea by writing:

We'll bring along a private band of 100 crack Village cats to defend the
cast and the theatre. That ought to put some gray in Bobby Kennedy's hairy
Irish head. Let him be frantic rather than me.

But I never heard a word from anyone in the Village. One ran into
Baldwin at the White Horse a few nights later. He was furious.
"You're not responsible," he said to me. We had another brotherly
quarrel.
I still say, put some gray in Bobby Kennedy's hairy Irish head.
Bring a cast of blacks and whites to Birmingham. Show the South a
mirror.

THE ELEVENTH PRESIDENTIAL PAPER

—Death

Ten Thousand Words a Minute

Champions are prodigies of will—one of the elements which sepa-rates them from club fighters or contenders is an urge which carries them through crises other fighters are not willing to endure. Thus the chance is always present that a champion can be killed in the ring. This of course was the underlying theme in the first Patterson-Liston fight; its echoes appear throughout the piece.

The close relation of death to existential politics need not be forced. The formal argument is doubtless beyond one's means, but it could be said that just as matters such as conscience or moral decision make up intrinsic dilemmas for the language analysts of Anglo-American philosophy, so the reluctance of modern European existentialism to take on the logical continuation of the existential vision (that there is a life after death which can be as existential as life itself) has brought French and German existentialism to a halt on this uninhabitable terrain of the absurd—to wit, man must lead his life as if death is meaningful even when man knows *that death is meaningless. This* revealed *knowledge which Heidegger accepts as his working hypothesis and Sartre goes so far as to assume is the certainty upon which he may build a philosophy, ends the possibility that one can construct a base for the existential ethic. The German philosopher runs aground trying to demonstrate the necessity for man to discover an authentic life. Heidegger can give no deeper explanation why man should bother to be authentic than to state in effect that man should be authentic in order to be free. Sartre's advocacy of the existential*

commitment is always in danger of dwindling into the minor aristo-
cratic advocacy of leading one's life with style for the sake of style.
Existentialism is rootless unless one dares the hypothesis that death is
an existential continuation of life, that the soul may either pass
through migrations, or cease to exist in the continuum of nature
(which is the unspoken intimation of cancer). But accepting this
hypothesis, authenticity and commitment return to the center of
ethics, for man then faces no peril so huge as alienation from his own
soul, a death which is other than death, a disappearance into nothing-
ness rather than into Eternity.

This idea is taken up in "Ten Thousand Words a Minute"; it comes
to brief overt focus after the description of the Paret-Griffith fight, and
for that matter is repeated with variations through many of the papers
in this book. In the December column in Esquire there is a section not
printed here in the Miscellany, which speaks of Dr. Robert A.
Soblen's suicide. He was an elderly man convicted by America for
espionage, but let out on bail during his appeal because he was dying
of cancer. Jumping his bail, he escaped by airplane to Israel. Forbid-
den to enter that country, he tried on his enforced return to America to
commit suicide in England.

He is condemned to go to jail for life, he is doomed to die of cancer, and
yet, obviously dissatisfied with the notion that his fate is final, he makes
two curious attempts at suicide.

Obviously there is a difference to him in the way he dies. He seems to
have a mania not to die in an American jail. His instinct tells him to clear a
space, to find a private place in which to die. But he expresses his instinct
with the power of a major passion. It gives a hint of the secret. It suggests
that the way we die, the style of our death, its condition, its mood, its
witness, is not trivial. May it be that the way we die affects the direction in
which our death may turn? Soblen is deep in cancer. Can it be that one can
die profoundly deep in cancer or not nearly so deep?

We are apparently a light-year away from political preoccupations
and yet it is a distance which must be traversed. In the Middle Ages
man endured his life as a preparation for his death, and lived out this
displacement so completely that life was in danger of perishing by
famine, plague, and the untamed encroachments of nature. Modern
man, in conquest of nature, chooses to ignore death and violate its
logic. The result may be a destruction not only of life, but of Being, of
our route from the world to Eternity and back again. A politics

devoted exclusively to the immediate needs of society murders death
as absolutely as theology once massacred the possibilities of life.

Remember that old joke about three kinds of intelligence: human, animal, and military? Well, if there are three kinds of writers: novelists, poets, and *reporters*, there is certainly a gulf between the poet and the novelist; quite apart from the kind of living they make, poets invariably seem to be aristocrats, usually spoiled beyond repair; and novelists—even if they make a million, or have large talent—look to have something of the working class about them. Maybe it is the drudgery, the long, obsessive inner life, the day-to-day monotony of applying themselves to the middle of the same continuing job, or perhaps it is the business of being unappreciated at home—has anyone met a novelist who is happy with the rugged care provided by his wife?

Now, of course, I am tempted to round the image out and say reporters belong to the middle class. Only I do not know if I can push the metaphor. Taken one by one, it is true that reporters tend to be hardheaded, objective, and unimaginative. Their intelligence is sound but unexceptional and they have the middle-class penchant for collecting tales, stories, legends, accounts of practical jokes, details of negotiation, bits of memoir—all those capsules of fiction which serve the middle class as a substitute for ethics and/or culture. Reporters, like shopkeepers, tend to be worshipful of the fact which wins and so covers over the other facts. In the middle class, the remark, "He made a lot of money," ends the conversation. If you persist, if you try to point out that the money was made by digging through his grandmother's grave to look for oil, you are met with a middle-class shrug. "It's a question of taste whether one should get into the past," is the winning reply.

In his own person there is nobody more practical than a reporter. He exhibits the same avidity for news which a businessman will show for money. No bourgeois will hesitate to pick up a dollar, even if he is not fond of the man with whom he deals: so, a reporter will do a nice story about a type he dislikes, or a bad story about a figure he is fond of. It has nothing to do with his feelings. There is a logic to news—on a given day, with a certain meteorological drift to the winds in the mass media, a story can only ride along certain vectors. To expect a reporter to be true to the precise detail of an event is kin to the sentimentality which asks a fast revolving investor to be faithful to a particular stock in his portfolio when it is going down and his others are going up.

But here we come to the end of our image. When the middle class gather for a club meeting or a social function, the atmosphere is dependably dull, whereas ten reporters come together in a room for a story are slightly hysterical, and two hundred reporters and photographers congregated for a press conference are as void of dignity, even stuffed-up, stodgy, middle-class dignity, as a slew of monkeys tearing through the brush. There is reason for this, much reason; there is always urgency to get some quotation which is usable for their story, and afterward, find a telephone: the habitat of a reporter, at its worst, is identical to spending one's morning, afternoon and evening transferring from the rush hour of one subway train to the rush hour of another. In time even the best come to remind one of the rush hour. An old fight reporter is a sad sight, he looks like an old prizefight manager, which is to say, he looks like an old cigar butt.

Nor is this true only of sports reporters. They are gifted with charm compared to political reporters who give off an effluvium which is unadulterated cancer gulch. I do not think I exaggerate. There is an odor to any Press Headquarters which is unmistakable. One may begin by saying it is like the odor in small left-wing meeting halls, except it is worse, far worse, for there is no poverty to put a guilt-free iron into the nose; on the contrary, everybody is getting free drinks, free sandwiches, free news releases. Yet there is the unavoidable smell of flesh burning quietly and slowly in the service of a machine. Have any of you never been through the smoking car of an old coach early in the morning when the smokers sleep and the stale air settles into congelations of gloom? Well, that is a little like the scent of Press Headquarters. Yet the difference is vast, because Press Headquarters for any big American event is invariably a large room in a large hotel, usually the largest room in the largest hotel in town. Thus it is a commercial room in a commercial hotel. The walls must be pale green or pale pink, dirty by now, subtly dirty like the toe of a silk stocking. (Which is incidentally the smell of the plaster.) One could be meeting bureaucrats from Tashkent in the Palace of the Soviets. One enormous barefaced meeting room, a twenty-foot banner up, a proscenium arch at one end, with high Gothic windows painted within the arch—almost never does a window look out on the open air. (Hotels build banquet rooms on the *inside* of their buildings—it is the best way to fill internal space with revenue.)

This room is in fever. Two hundred, three hundred, I suppose even five hundred reporters get into some of these rooms, there to talk, there to drink, there to bang away on any one of fifty standard typewriters, provided by the people on Public Relations who have set up this Press Headquarters. It is like being at a vast party in Limbo—there is tremendous excitement, much movement and no sex at all. Just talk. Talk fed by cigarettes. One thousand to two thousand cigarettes are smoked every hour. The mind must keep functioning fast enough to offer up stories. (Reporters meet as in a marketplace to trade their stories—they barter an anecdote they cannot use about one of the people in the event in order to pick up a different piece which is usable by their paper. It does not matter if the story is true or altogether not true, it must merely be suitable and not too mechanically libelous.) So they char the inside of their bodies in order to scrape up news which can go out to the machine, that enormous machine, that intellectual leviathan which is obliged to eat each day, tidbits, gristle, gravel, garbage cans, charlotte russe, old rubber tires, T-bone steaks, wet cardboard, dry leaves, apple pie, broken bottles, dog food, shells, roach powder, dry ball-point pens, grapefruit juice. All the trash, all the garbage, all the slop and a little of the wealth go out each day and night into the belly of that old American goat, our newspapers.

So the reporters smell also of this work, they smell of the dishwasher and the pots, they are flesh burning themselves very quietly and slowly in the service of a machine which feeds goats, which feeds The Goat. One smells this collective odor on the instant one enters their meeting room. It is not a corrupt smell, it does not have enough of the meats, the savory, and the vitality of flesh to smell corrupt and fearful when it is bad, no, it is more the smell of excessive respect for power, the odor of flesh gutted by avidities which are electric and empty. I suppose it is the bleak smell one could find on the inside of one's head during a bad cold, full of fever, badly used, burned out of mood. The physical sensation of a cold often is one of power trapped corrosively inside, coils of strength being liquidated in some center of the self. The reporter hangs in a powerless-power—his voice directly, or via the rewrite desk indirectly, reaches out to millions of readers; the more readers he owns, the less he can say. He is forbidden by a hundred censors, most of them inside himself, to communicate notions, which are not conformistically simple, simple like plastic is simple, that is to say, monotonous. Therefore a reporter forms a habit equivalent to lacerating the flesh: he learns to write what he does not naturally believe. Since he did not start presumably with the desire to be a bad writer or a dishonest writer, he ends by bludgeoning his brain into believing that something which is half true is in fact—since he creates a fact each time he puts something into a newspaper—nine-tenths true. A psyche is debauched—his own; a false fact is created. For which fact, sooner or later, inevitably, inexorably, the public will pay. A nation which forms detailed opinions on the basis of detailed fact which is askew from the subtle reality becomes a nation of citizens whose psyches are skewed, item by detailed item, away from *any* reality.

So great guilt clings to reporters. They know they help to keep America slightly insane. As a result perhaps they are a shabby-looking crew. The best of them are the shabbiest, which is natural if one thinks about it—a sensitive man suffers from the prosperous life of his lies more than a dull man. In fact the few dudes one finds among reporters tend to be semi-illiterates, or hatchet men, or cynics on two or three payrolls who do restrained public relations in the form of news stories. But this is to make too much of the extremes. Reporters along the middle of the spectrum are shabby, worried, guilty, and suffer each day from the damnable anxiety that they know all sorts of powerful information a half hour to twenty-four hours before anyone else in America knows it, not to mention the time clock ticking away in the vault of all those stories which cannot be printed or will not be printed. It makes for a livid view of existence. It is like an injunction to become hysterical once a day. Then they must write at lightning speed. It may be heavy-fisted but true, it may be slick as a barnyard slide, it may be great, it may be fill—what does it matter? The matter rides out like oats in a conveyor belt, and the unconscious takes a ferocious pounding. Writing is of use to the psyche only if the writer discovers something he did not know he knew in the act itself of writing. That is why a few men will go through hell in order to keep writing—Joyce and Proust, for example. Being a writer can save one from insanity or cancer; being a bad writer can drive one smack into the center of the plague. Think of the poor reporter who does not have the leisure of the novelist or the poet to discover what he thinks. The unconscious gives up, buries itself, leaves the writer to his cliché, and saves the truth, or that part of it the reporter is yet privileged to find, for his colleagues and his friends. A good reporter is a man who must still tell you the truth privately; he has bright harsh eyes and can relate ten good stories in a row standing at a bar.

Still, they do not quit. That charge of adrenalin once a day, that hysteria, that sense of powerless-power close to the engines of history—they can do without powerless-power no more than a gentleman junkie on the main line can do without his heroin, doctor. You see, a reporter is close to the action. He is not *of* the action, but he is close to it, as close as a crab louse to the begetting of a child. One may never be President, but the photographer working for his paper has the power to cock a flashbulb and make the eyes of JFK go blink!

However, it is not just this lead-encased seat near the radiations of power which keeps the reporter hooked on a drug of new news to start new adrenalin; it is also the ride. It is the free ride. When we were children, there were those movies about reporters; they were heroes. While chasing a lead, they used to leap across empty elevator shafts, they would wrestle automatics out of mobsters' hands, and if they were Cary Grant, they would pick up a chair and stick it in the lion's face, since the lion had had the peculiar sense to walk into the editor's office. Next to being a cowboy, or a private eye, the most heroic activity in America was to be a reporter. Now it is the welfare state. Every last cigar-smoking fraud of a middle-aged reporter, pale with prison pallor, deep lines in his cheeks, writing daily pietisms for the sheet back home about free enterprise, is himself the first captive of the welfare state. It is the best free ride anyone will find since he left his family's chest. Your room is paid for by the newspaper, your trips to the particular spots attached to the event—in this case, the training camp at Elgin, Illinois, for Patterson, and the empty racetrack at Aurora Downs for Liston—are by chartered limousine. Who but a Soviet bureaucrat, a British businessman, a movie star, or an American reporter would ride in a chartered limousine? (They smell like funeral parlors.) Your typing paper is free if you want it; your seat at the fight, or your ticket to the convention is right up there, under the ropes; your meals if you get around to eating them are free, free sandwiches only but then a reporter has a stomach like a shaving mug and a throat like a hog's trough: he couldn't tell steak tartare from *guacamole*. And the drinks—if you are at a big fight—are without charge. If you are at a political convention, there is no free liquor. But you do have a choice between free Pepsi-Cola and free Coca-Cola. The principle seems to be that the reporting of mildly psychotic actions—such as those performed by politicians—should be made in sobriety; whereas a sane estimate of an athlete's chances are neatest on booze. At a fight Press Headquarters, the drinks are very free, and the mood can even be half convivial. At the Patterson-Liston Press Headquarters there was a head bartender working for Championship Sports whose name was Archie. He was nice. He was a nice man. It was a pleasure to get a drink from him. You remember these things afterward, it's part of the nostalgia. The joy of the free ride is the lack of worry. It's like being in an Army outfit which everyone's forgotten. You get your food, you get your beer, you get your pay, the work is easy, and leave to town is routine. You never had it so good—you're an infant again: you can grow up a second time and improve the job.

That's the half and half of being a reporter. One half is addiction, adrenalin, anecdote-shopping, deadlines, dread, cigar smoke, lung cancer, vomit, feeding The Goat; the other is Aloha, Tahiti, old friends and the free ride to the eleventh floor of the Sheraton-Chicago, Patterson-Liston Press Headquarters, everything free. Even your news free. If you haven't done your homework, if you drank too late last night and missed the last limousine out to Elgin or Aurora this morning, if there's no poop of your own on Floyd's speed or Sonny's bad mood, you can turn to the handouts given you in the Press Kit, dig, a *Kit*, kiddies, worked up for you by Harold Conrad who's the Public Relations Director. It's not bad stuff, it's interesting material. No need to do your own research. Look at some of this: there's the tale of the tape for each fighter with as many physical measurements as a tailor in Savile Row might take; there's the complete record of each fighter, how he won, how many rounds, who, the date, so forth; there's the record of how much money they made on each fight, how their KO records compare with the All-Time Knockout Artists, Rocky Marciano with 43 out of 49, batting .878, Joe Louis at .761, Floyd at .725 (29 in 40) and Sonny Liston going with 23 for 34, is down at .676, back of Jim Jeffries who comes in at .696. There's a column there, there's another if you want to dig into the biographies of each fighter, six single-spaced pages on Patterson, four on Liston. There's a list of each and every fighter who won and lost the Heavyweight Championship, and the year—remember? Remember Jake Kilrain and Marvin Hart (stopped Jack Root at Reno, Nevada, 12 rounds, July 3, 1905). You can win money with Marvin Hart betting in bars. And Tommy Burns. Jack O'Brien. In what year did Ezzard Charles first take Jersey

Joe Walcott; in what town? You can see the different columns shaping up. If you got five columns to do on the fight, three can be whipped right up out of Graff/Reiner/Smith Enterprises, Inc. Sports News Release. Marvelous stuff. How Sonny Liston does his roadwork on railroad tracks, what Sonny's best weight is (206-212), what kind of poundages Floyd likes to give away—averages 10 pounds a bout— Floyd's style in boxing, Liston's style in boxing. It's part of the free list, an offering of facts with a little love from the Welfare State.

It is so easy, so much is done for you, that you remember these days with nostalgia. When you do get around to paying for yourself, going into a room like the Camelot Room at the Sheraton-Chicago, with its black-blood three-story mahogany paneling and its high, stained Gothic windows looking out no doubt on an air shaft, it is a joy to buy your own food, an odd smacking sensation to pay for a drink. It is the Welfare State which makes the pleasure possible. When one buys all one's own drinks, the sensation of paying cash is without much joy, but to pay for a drink occasionally—that's near bliss.

And because it is a fight, cancer gulch has its few oases. The Press Headquarters livens up with luminaries, the unhealthiest people in America now meet some of the healthiest, complete self-contained healthy bodies which pass modestly through: Ingemar Johansson and Archie Moore, Rocky Marciano, Barney Ross, Cassius Clay, Harold Johnson, Ezzard Charles, Dick Tiger on his way to San Francisco where he is to fight Gene Fullmer and beat him, Jim Braddock—big, heavy, grey, and guarded, looking as tough as steel drilled into granite, as if he were the toughest night watchman in America, and Joe Louis looking like the largest Chinaman in the world, still sleepy, still sad. That's part of the pleasure of Press Headquarters—the salty crystallized memories which are released from the past, the night ten or eleven years ago when Joe Louis, looking just as sleepy and as sad as he does now, went in to fight Rocky Marciano at the Garden, and was knocked out in eight. It was part of a comeback, but Louis was never able to get his fight going at all, he was lethargic that night, and Marciano, fighting a pure Italian street-fighter's style, throwing his punches as if he held a brick in each hand, taking Louis' few good shots with an animal joy, strong enough to eat bricks with his teeth, drove right through Joe Louis and knocked him out hard. Louis went over in a long, very inert fall, as if an old tree or a momentous institution were coming down, perhaps the side of a church wall hovering straight and slow enough in its drop for the onlooker to take a breath in the gulf of the bomb. And it had been a bomb. Louis' leg was draped over the rope. People were crying as they left Madison Square Garden that night. It was a little like the death of Franklin Delano Roosevelt: something generous had just gone out of the world. And now here was Marciano as well, in the couloirs and coffee shop and lobby of the Sheraton-Chicago, a man looking as different from the young contender he had been on his way to the championship as Louis now looked the same. Louis had turned old in the ring. Marciano retired undefeated, and so aged after he stopped. Now he seemed no longer to be carrying bricks but pillows. He had gotten very plump, his face was round and no longer lumpy, he was half bald, a large gentle monk with a bemused, misty, slightly tricky expression.

And there were others, Bill Hartack, Jack Kearns who at eighty-plus still looked to be one of the most intelligent men in America, Sammy Taub, the old radio announcer who used to talk as fast as the cars on the Indianapolis Speedway, "and he hits him another left to the belly, and another, and another, and a right to the head, and a left to the head." Taub made bums sound like champions—it is doubtful if there was ever a fighter who could throw punches fast enough to keep up with Taub, and now he was an old man, a grandfather, a bright, short man with a birdlike face, a little like a tiny older version of Leonard Lyons.

There were many, there were so many, preliminary fighters who got their money together to get to Chicago, and managers, and promoters. There were novelists, Jimmy Baldwin, Budd Schulberg, Gerald Kersh, Ben Hecht. As the fight approached, so did the Mob. That arid atmosphere of reporters alone with reporters and writers with writers gave way to a whiff of the deep. The Mob was like birds and beasts coming into feed. Heavy types, bouncers, plug-uglies, flatteners, one or two speedy, swishing, Negro ex-boxers, for example, now blown up to the size of fat middle-weights, slinky in their walk, eyes fulfilling the operative definition of razor slits, murder coming off them like scent comes off a skunk. You could feel death as they passed. It came wafting off. And the rest of the beasts as well—the strong-arm men, the head-kickers, the limb-breakers, the groin-stompers. If a clam had a muscle as large as a man, and the muscle grew eyes, you would get the mood. Those were the beasts. They were all orderly, they were all trained, they were dead to humor.

They never looked at anyone they did not know, and when they were introduced they stared at the floor while shaking hands as if their own hand did not belong to them, but was merely a stuffed mitten to which their arm was attached.

The orders came from the birds. There were hawks and falcons and crows, Italian dons looking like little old shrunken eagles, gulls, pelicans, condors. The younger birds stood around at modest strategic points in the lobby, came up almost not at all to Press Headquarters, posted themselves out on the street, stood at the head of escalators, near the door of the barbershop, along the elevator strip, by the registration desk. They were all dressed in black gabardine topcoats, black felt hats, and very large dark sunglasses with expensive frames. They wore white scarves or black scarves. A few would carry a black umbrella. They stood there watching everyone who passed. They gave the impression of knowing exactly why they were standing there, what they were waiting to hear, how they were supposed to see, who they were supposed to watch. One had the certainty after a time that they knew the name of every man and woman who walked through the downstairs lobby and went into the Championship Sports office on the ground floor. If a figure said hello to a celebrity he was not supposed to know—at least not in the bird's private handbook—one could sense the new information being filed. Some were tall, some were short, but almost all were thin, their noses were aquiline, their chins were modest, their cheeks were subtly concave. They bore a resemblance to George Scott in *The Hustler*. Their aura was succinct. It said, ''If you spit on my shoes, you're dead.'' It was a shock to realize that the Mob, in the flesh, was even more impressive than in the motion pictures.

There were also some fine old *mafiosos* with faces one had seen on the busts of Venetian doges in the Ducal Palace, subtle faces, insidious with the ingrowth of a curious culture built on treachery, dogma, the evil eye, and blood loyalty to clan. They were *don capos*, and did not wear black any longer, black was for subalterns. They were the leaders of the birds, fine old gentlemen in quiet grey suits, quiet intricate dark ties. Some had eyes which contained the humor of a cardinal; others were not so nice. There was an unhealthy dropsical type with pallor, and pink-tinted bifocal glasses—the kind who looked as if they owned a rich mortuary in a poor Italian neighborhood, and ran the local Republican club.

All the birds and beasts of the Mob seemed to be for Liston, almost without exception they were for Sonny. It was not because his prison record stirred some romantic allegiance in them, nothing of service in India together, sir, or graduates from the same campus; no, nor was it part necessarily and absolutely of some large syndicated plot to capture and run the Heavyweight Championship of the World so that the filaments of prestige which trail from such a crown would wind back into all the pizza parlors and jukeboxes of the continent, the gambling casinos, the afterhours joints, the contracting businesses, and the demolition businesses, the paving businesses, the music of the big bands, the traffic in what is legit and what is illegit—like junk and policy—no, in such a kingdom, the Heavyweight Championship is not worth that much, it's more like the Polish Corridor was to the Nazis, or Cuba to us, it's a broken boil. In their mind Patterson was a freak, some sort of vegetarian. It was sickening to see a post of importance held by a freak, or by the manager of a freak.

II

Before the fight much was made of the battle between good and evil, and the descriptions of the training camps underlined these differences. Patterson trained in a boys' camp up at Elgin which gave the impression of a charitable institution maintained by a religious denomination. The bungalows were small, painted white on their outside, and were of a miserable, dull stained-pine-color within. The atmosphere was humorless and consecrated. Nor was Patterson about. It was two days before the fight, and he had disappeared. Perhaps he was training, conceivably he was sleeping, maybe he was taking a long walk. But the gym up the hill was closed to reporters. So we gathered in one of the cottages, and watched a film which had been made of Patterson's fights. Since it had been put together by a public-relations man who was devoted to Patterson, the film caught most of Floyd's best moments and few of his bad ones.

At his best he was certainly very good. He had been an extraordinary club fighter. As a middleweight and light-heavyweight he had put together the feat of knocking out a good many of the best club fighters in America. Yvon Durelle, Jimmy Slade, Esau Ferdinand, Willie Troy, Archie McBride had been stopped by Patterson, and they were tough men. One reason a club fighter is a club fighter, after all, is because of his ability to take punishment and give a high, durable level of performance. The movies brought back the excitement there used to be watching Patterson on television in 1952 and 1954 when he would fight the main event at Eastern Parkway. I knew nothing about fights then, but the first time I saw Patterson, he knocked out a rugged fighter named Dick Wagner in five rounds, and there had been something about the way he did it which cut into my ignorance. I knew he was good. It was like seeing one's first exciting bullfight: at last one knows what everybody has been talking about. So I had an affection for Patterson which started early. When Patterson was bad he was unbelievably bad, he was Chaplinesque, simple, sheepish, eloquent in his clumsiness, sad like a clown, his knees looked literally to droop. He would seem precisely the sort of shy, stunned, somewhat dreamy Negro kid who never knew the answer in class. But when he was good, he seemed as fast as a jungle cat. He was the fastest heavyweight I had ever seen. Watching these movies, it was evident he could knock a man out with a left hook thrown from the most improbable position, leaping in from eight feet out, or wheeling to the left, his feet in the air, while he threw his hook across his body. He was like a rangy, hungry cat who starts to jump from a tree at some prey, and turns in flight to take an accurate, improvised swipe at a gorilla swinging by on a vine.

But the movies were only half pleasing. Because Patterson's fascination as a fighter was in his complex personality, in his alternations from high style to what—in a champion—could only be called buffoonery. The movies showed none of his bad fights, except for the famous third round with Ingemar Johansson in their first fight—an omission which not even a public-relations man would want to make. In the perspective of boxing history, those seven knockdowns were no longer damaging; Patterson's courage in getting up was underlined in one's memory by the way he came back in the next fight to knock Johansson out in the fifth round. So one was left with the disagreeable impression that this movie was too righteous.

Naturally I got into a debate with Cus D'Amato and a young gentleman named Jacobs, Jim Jacobs as I remember, who was built like a track man and had an expression which was very single-minded. He was the Public Relations Assistant, the man who had cut the movie, and a serious handball player too, as I learned later. In the debate, he ran me all over the court. It was one of those maddening situations where you know you are right, but the other man has the facts, and the religious conviction as well.

What about all the times Patterson has been knocked down, I started.

What times?

What times? Why. . . . I was ready to stammer.

Name them.

Johansson. Rademacher.

Go on.

Roy Harris.

A slip. I could show you the film clips.

Tom McNeeley.

Also a slip, but Floyd's too nice a guy to claim it was, said Jacobs. As a matter of fact. Rademacher hit him when Floyd was tripping over his own foot as he was going backwards. That's why Floyd went down. Floyd's too much of a gentleman to take any of the credit for a knockdown away from a talented amateur like Rademacher.

"As a matter of fact," went on Jacobs, "there's one knockdown you haven't mentioned. Jacques Royer-Crecy knocked Floyd down to one knee with a left hook in the first round back in 1954."

"You better not argue with this guy," said Cus D'Amato with a happy grin. "He's seen so many movies, he knows more about Floyd's fights than I do. He can beat *me* in an argument." With that warning I should have known enough to quit, but it was Sunday and I was full of myself. The night before, at Medinah Temple, before thirty-six-hundred people (we grossed over $8000) I had had a debate with William F. Buckley, Jr. The sportswriters had put up Buckley as a 2-1/2-to-1 favorite before our meet, but I was told they named me the winner. Eight, one, one even; seven rounds to three; six, three, one even; those were the scorecards *I* received. So at the moment, I was annoyed that this kid Jacobs, whom I started to call Mr. Facts, was racking me up.

Therefore, I heeded Cus D'Amato not at all and circled back to the fight. Jacobs was calling Patterson a great champion, I was saying he had yet to prove he was great—it was a dull argument until I said, "Why didn't he fight the kind of man Louis and Dempsey went up against?" A big mistake. Jacobs went through the record of every single fighter Jack Dempsey and Joe Louis fought as champions, and before we were done, by the laws of collected evidence, he had bludgeoned the court into accepting, against its better judgment, that Pete Rademacher was the equal of Buddy Baer, Tom McNeeley of Luis Firpo, Hurricane Jackson of Tony Galento, and that Brian London riding his much underrated bicycle could have taken a decision from Bill Brennan.

Jacobs was much too much for me. I quit. "I'm telling you," said Cus D'Amato, having enjoyed this vastly, "he beats me all the time in arguments."

While this had been going on, two small Negroes looking like starchy divinity students had been glowering at me and my arguments. Every time I said something which was not altogether in praise of Patterson, they looked back as if I were a member of the White Citizens Council. I never did get a chance to find out who they were, or what they represented (Jacobs was keeping me much too busy), but one could lay odds they were working for one of the more dogmatic Negro organizations devoted to the uplift of the race. They had none of the humor of the few Freedom Riders I had met, or the personal attractiveness some of the young Negroes around Martin Luther King seemed to have. No, these were bigots. They could have believed in anything from the Single Tax to the Brotherhood of Sleeping Car Porters for all I knew, but they were dead-eyed to any voice which did not give assent to what they believed already. So it was depressing to find them in Patterson's camp, and thus devoted to him. It fit with the small-trade-union bigotry that hung over this establishment.

Outside, in the air, the view while dull was not so dogmatic. Sammy Taub, the radio announcer of my childhood, had a voice full of an old Jew's love for Patterson. "Oh, Floyd's got the real class," said Mr. Taub, "he's a gentleman. I've seen a lot of fighters, but Floyd's the gentleman of them all. I could tell you things about him, about how nice he is. He's going to take that big loudmouth Liston apart, punch by punch. And I'm going to be there to watch it!" he said with a grin and an old announcer's windup.

Next morning I spent more time with D'Amato on the way to Liston's camp. We went together in the limousine. It was the day before the fight, and D'Amato was going out as Patterson's representative to check on the gloves. There had been trouble with this already: D'Amato had objected to Liston's plan to wear a pair of gloves made by a Chicago manufacturer named Frager. It seems the eight-ounce

Everlast gloves with curled horsehair for padding had not been large enough to fit Liston's hand. So his manager, Jack Nilon, had come up with gloves which had foam-rubber padding. D'Amato objected. His argument was that Liston's knuckles could punch closer to the surface of the glove riding in foam rubber than in horsehair. The unspoken aim must have been to irritate Liston.

But one couldn't encourage D'Amato to talk about the challenger. D'Amato talked only about his own fighters. How he talked! He had stopped drinking years ago and so had enormous pent-up vitality. As a talker, he was one of the world's great weight lifters, not brilliant, but powerful, nonstop, and very solid. Talk was muscle. If you wanted to interrupt, you had to bend his arm off.

Under the force, however, he had a funny simple quality, something of that passionate dogmatism which some men develop when they have been, by their own count, true to their principles. He had the enthusiastic manner of a saint who is all works and no contemplation. His body was short and strong, his head was round, and his silver-white hair was cut in a short brush. He seemed to bounce as he talked. He reminded me of a certain sort of very tough Italian kid one used to find in Brooklyn. They were sweet kids, and rarely mean, and they were fearless, at least by the measure of their actions they were fearless. They would fight anybody. Size, age, reputation did not make them hesitate. Because they were very single-minded, however, they were often the butt of the gang, and proved natural victims for any practical jokes. Afterward everyone would hide. They were the kind of kids who would go berserk if you were their friend or their leader and betrayed them. They would literally rip up a sewer grating or a manhole cover in order to beat their way a little closer to you.

I was certain he had been this kind of kid, and later I heard a story that when D'Amato was little, he started once to walk through a small park at night and saw a huge shape waiting for him in the distance. He said he had the feeling he could not turn back. If he did, he would never be able to go near that park again. So he continued down the path. The huge shape was discovered to be a tree. D'Amato's critics would claim that he spent his entire life being brave with trees.

The likelihood, however, is that for a period D'Amato was one of the bravest men in America. He was a fanatic about boxing, and cared little about money. He hated the Mob. He stood up to them. A prizefight manager running a small gym with broken mirrors on East

Fourteenth Street does not usually stand up to the Mob, any more than a chambermaid would tell the Duchess of Windsor to wipe her shoes before she enters her suite at the Waldorf.

D'Amato was the exception, however. The Mob ended by using two words to describe him: "He's crazy." The term is given to men who must be killed. Nobody killed D'Amato. For years, like a monk, he slept in the back room of his gym with a police dog for a roommate. The legend is that he kept a gun under his pillow. During Patterson's last few weeks of training before fighting Archie Moore for the championship in 1956, a fight he was to win in five rounds, D'Amato bunked on a cot in front of the door to Floyd's room. He was certain that with the championship so close to them the Mob would try to hurt his fighter. What a movie this would have made. It could have ended with a zoom-away shot of the Mob in a burning barn.

The trial of it is that the story goes on. D'Amato was one of the most stubborn men in America. And he was determined that no fighter connected to the Mob in any way would get to fight Floyd. The only trouble was that the good heavyweights in America had managers who were not ready to irritate the men who ran boxing. If they took a match with Patterson, and he defeated their fighter, how could their *ex*-contender ever get a fight on television again? D'Amato may have had the vision of a Lenin—as he said with a grin, "They're always calling me a Communist"—but he never could get enough good managers to begin his new party. Patterson, who was conceivably the best young heavyweight in history at the moment he won the championship, now began to be wasted. He was an artist, and an artist is no greater than his material. The fighters D'Amato got for him now were without luster. So were the fights. After a few years, D'Amato's enemies began to spread the canard best calculated to alienate Patterson. They said D'Amato got him nothing but cripples to fight because Patterson was not good enough to go into the ring with a real heavyweight. To a champion who even now would look for a training camp which might bear resemblance to Wiltwyck, that charity school for near-delinquent adolescents where he first had learned to fight; to someone like Patterson, who as a child would weep when he was unjustly accused; who would get down and walk along the subway tracks on the Eighth Avenue El at High Street in Brooklyn because he had found a cubbyhole for workmen three feet off the rails where he could conceal himself from the world by pulling an iron door close to over him, lying there in darkness while the trains blasted by with apocalyptic noise; to a man who had been so shy as an adolescent that he could not speak to the thirteen-year-old girl who was later to become his wife and so brought a fast-talking friend along to fill the silence; who as a teen-age fighter, just beginning to go to the gym, was so delicate that his older brother Frank once told the reporter Lester Bromberg, "I can't get used to my kid brother being a name fighter. I remember him as the boy who would cry if I hit him too hard when we boxed in the gym"; to a champion who as a young professional had refused to look while his next opponent, Chester Mieszala, was sparring at Chicago's Midtown Gym because he considered it to be taking unfair advantage; to a man who would later sit in shame in a dark room for months after losing his championship to Johansson, the canard that he was a weak heavyweight kept in possession of his kingdom by the determination of his manager never to make a good fight must have been a story to taste like quicklime in his throat. Patterson had put his faith in D'Amato. If D'Amato didn't believe in him. . . . It's the sort of story which belongs on radio at eleven in the morning or three in the afternoon.

The aftermath of the first Johansson fight, however, blew out the set. It was discovered that D'Amato directly or indirectly had gotten money for the promotion through a man named "Fat Tony" Salerno. D'Amato claimed to have been innocent of the connection, and indeed it was a most aesthetic way for the Mob to get him. It's equally possible that after years of fighting every windmill in town, D'Amato had come down to the hard Bolshevistic decision that you don't make an omelet without breaking eggs. Whatever the fact, D'Amato had his license suspended in New York. He was not allowed to work in Floyd's corner the night of the second Johansson fight. And thereafter Patterson kept him away. He gave D'Amato his managerial third of the money, but he didn't let him get too close to training.

If this partnership of Patterson and D'Amato had been made in Heaven, then God or man had failed again. The last sad item was the Liston fight. Patterson had delegated D'Amato to make some of the arrangements. According to the newspapers, Patterson then discovered that D'Amato was trying to delay the negotiations. Now D'Amato was accepted in camp only as a kind of royal jester who could entertain reporters with printable stories. He seemed to be kept in the cabin where I met him at the foot of the hill, forbidden access to the gymnasium the way a drunk is eighty-sixed from his favorite bar. It must have been a particularly Italian humiliation for a man like D'Amato to sit in that cabin and talk to journalists. There were any number of fight reporters who could not go into court and swear they had never had a free meal from the Mob. Some of the food may have been filet mignon. At least so one might judge by the violence of their printed reactions to D'Amato. A reporter can never forgive anyone he has attacked unjustly. Now D'Amato had to receive these cigar butts like a baron demoted to a concierge. He could speak, but he could not act.

Speak he did. If you listened to D'Amato talk, and knew nothing other, you would not get the impression D'Amato was no longer the center of Patterson's camp. He seemed to give off no sense whatever of having lost his liaison to Floyd. When he talked of making the Liston fight, one would never have judged he had tried to prevent it.

"I didn't," he swore to me. "I wanted the fight. Floyd came up to me, and said, 'Cus, you got to make this fight. Liston's going around saying I'm too yellow to fight him. I don't care if a fighter says he can beat me, but no man can say I'm yellow.'" D'Amato bobbed his head. "Then Floyd said, 'Cus, if this fight isn't made, I'll be scared to go out. I'll be afraid to walk into a restaurant and see Liston eating. Because if I see him, I'll have a fight with him right there in the restaurant, and I'll kill him.' I wouldn't try to keep Floyd from having a fight after he says something like that!" said D'Amato.

We were now arriving at Aurora Downs. The limousine took a turn off the highway, went down a blacktop road and then went through a gate onto a dirt road. There was a quick view of a grandstand and part of a small abandoned racetrack. Under the grandstand, the challenger's gym had been installed: it was there Liston had jumped rope to the sound of *Night Train*, performing with such hypnotic, suspended rage that the reporters gave most of their space to describe this talent.

We were meeting now in the clubhouse restaurant, its parimutuel windows boarded up, its floor empty of tables. It was a cold, chilly room, perhaps a hundred feet long, roped off at the rear to give privacy to Liston's quarters, and the surfaces all seemed made of picture-window glass, chromium, linoleum, and pastel plastics like Formica. The most prominent decorations were two cold-drink vending machines, side by side, large as telephone booths. They were getting

small play from the reporters because the day was dank, one of thos
grey September days which seem to seep up from Lake Michigan an
move west. As many as a hundred of us must have come out in ou
various limousines to see the finale of Everlast vs. Frager, and w
gathered in an irritable circle, scrimmaging four and five deep for
view of the scales, an ordinary pair of office scales for small packages
and of two pairs of gloves on a plain wooden table. Disappointed wit
how I came out in the scrimmage, I pulled back far enough to stand o
a chair. The view was now good. A thin man in a green sweater, a ma
with a long, hungry nose and a pocked, angry skin still alive from a
adolescence where one hot boil had doubtless burst upon another, wa
now screaming at everybody in sight, at D'Amato whom he seeme
ready to attack, at Nick Florio, brother of Dan Florio, Patterson'
trainer, and at a man named Joe Triner who belonged to the Illinoi
State Athletic Commission. It developed he was Jack Nilon, Liston'
manager or adviser, a Philadelphia caterer, wealthy in his own right
who had been brought together with Liston by various beneficen
forces in Philadelphia who decided Sonny needed rehabilitation in hi
front window as much as in his heart. So Nilon represented America
business, acting once again as big brother to a former convict wit
talent. How Nilon could scream! It turned out, bang-bang, that th
new gloves for Liston were a fraction over eight ounces. Nilon wa
having none of that. Triner, the Commission man, looked sick
"They weighed eight ounces at the Commission's office today," h
said.

"Don't give me none of that," screamed Nilon. "They got t
weigh in right here. How do I know what kind of scale you use?"

"What do we want to cheat you on a quarter of an ounce for?'
asked Triner.

"Just to get Sonny upset, just to get Sonny upset, that's all,'
screamed Nilon as if he were pouring boiling oil.

Liston now emerged from the depths of the clubhouse and walke
slowly toward us. He was wearing a dark-blue sweat suit, and h
moved with the languid pleasure of somebody who is getting the tast
out of every step. First his heel went down, then his toe. He could no
have enjoyed it more if he had been walking barefoot through a field
One could watch him picking the mood up out of his fingertips an
toes. His handlers separated before him. He was a Presence.

"What the hell's going on?" Liston asked. He had a deep growl o a voice, rich, complex, well-modulated. His expression had the sort of holy disdain one finds most often on a very grand old lady.

They started to explain to him, and he nodded petulantly, half listening to the arguments. His expression seemed to say, "Which one of these bullshit artists is most full of it right now?"

While he was listening he pulled on one of the gloves, worked his fist about in it, and then slapped the glove down on the table. "It still don't fit," he cried out in the angry voice of a child. Everybody moved back a little. He stood there in disgust, but wary, alert, as if some deep enemy were in the room, someone who could damage him with a psychic bullet. His eyes bounced lightly, gracefully, from face to face. Which gave the opportunity to see into them for a moment. From the advance publicity one had expected to look into two cracks of dead glass, halfway between reptile and sleepy leopard, but they had the dark, brimming, eloquent, reproachful look one sees sometimes in the eyes of beautiful colored children, three or four years old. And in fact that was the shock of the second degree which none of the photographs had prepared one for: Liston was near to beautiful. For obvious reasons it is an unhappy word to use. But there is no other to substitute. One cannot think of more than a few men who have beauty. Charles Chaplin has it across a room, Krishna Menon across a table. Stephen Spender used to have it, Burt Lancaster oddly enough used to have it—there was no comparison between the way he looked in a movie and the way he looked in life. They say Orson Welles had it years ago, and President Eisenhower in person, believe it or not. At any rate, Liston had it. You did not feel you were looking at someone attractive, you felt you were looking at a creation. And this creation looked like it was building into a temper which would tear up the clubhouse at Aurora Downs. One knew he was acting, no contender would get violent the day before a championship fight, and yet everyone in the room was afraid of Liston. Even D'Amato did not speak too much. Liston had the stage and was using it. "Let's see that glove, let's weigh it again." They leaped to put it on the scales for him. He squatted and made a huge dumb show of scowling at the numbers as if he were just another blighted cotton picker. "Sheeet, who can read the numbers," he pretended to be saying to himself.

"He's not going in the ring with gloves over regulation weight," shouted another dragon, Pollino, the cut man for Liston, a lean Italian with an angry, chopped-up face.

"Well, this scale isn't the official scale," said D'Amato mildly. "The gloves are eight ounces."

Pollino looked like he'd leap across the table to get his hands on D'Amato's neck. "Wha' do you call official scale?" shouted Pollino. "There is no official scale. I'll bet you a thousand dollars they're more than eight ounces."

Nilon came in like a shrike from the other side of Liston. "Why do you bother my fighter with this? he screamed at the officials. "Why don't you go over to Patterson's camp and bother him the day before the fight? What's he doing? Sleeping? He doesn't have a hundred reporters looking down his throat."

"I don't want to stand much more of this," snapped Liston in the child's voice he used for display of temper. "This is the sort of thing gives reporters a chance to ask stupid questions." Was his dislike of reporters a reminder of the days when four or five policemen would have given him a going-over in a police station while the police reporter, listening to the muffled thuds, would be playing cards in the next room? Liston did not talk to white reporters individually. At Press Headquarters the bitter name for him was Malcolm X. "Just stupid questions, that's all," he repeated, and yet his manner was changing still again. His mood could shift as rapidly as the panoramic scenes in a family film. Suddenly he was mild, now he was mild. He tapped the gloves on the table, and said in a gentle voice, "Oh, they're all right. Let's use them." Then lightly, sadly, he chuckled, and added in his richest voice, "I'm going to hit him so hard that extra quarter of an ounce isn't gonna be any more than just an extra quarter of an ounce he's being hit with." The voice came home to me. I knew which voice it was at last. It was the voice Clark Gable used his last ten years, that genial rum squire's voice, the indulgent "I've been around" voice. Headmasters in prep schools sometimes have it. Liston had it. He must have studied Gable over the years. Perhaps in the movies one sees in prison.

A little more bickering went on between Pollino and Florio. They were like guerrilla troops who have not heard that the armistice has been declared. Then quiet. We were done. But just as the meet was ready to break, Liston held up a hand and said, "I don't want to wear these gloves. I've changed my mind. We've had a special pair made for me. Bring the new gloves over." And he glowered at the officials and dropped his upper lip.

It was a very bad moment for the officials.

Two assistants marched in carrying a white boxing glove. It was half the size of a shark. A toot of relief went up from the press. Liston grinned. As photographers rushed to take his picture once more, he held the great white glove in his hands and studied it with solemnity.

When we got back to the car, D'Amato smiled. "Very unusual fellow," he said. "He's more intelligent than I thought. Good sense of humor."

I made a small speech in which I declared that Liston made me think not so much of a great fighter as of a great actor who was playing the role of the greatest heavyweight fighter who ever lived.

D'Amato listened attentively. We were in a space age, and the opinions of moon men and Martians had also to be considered. "Sonny's a good fighter," he said finally.

Then we talked of other things. I mentioned my four daughters. D'Amato came from a family of seven brothers. "I guess that's why I never got married," he said. "I don't know, I never could figure it out. No dame could ever get me. I wonder why?"

"A lady once told me she'd never marry a man she couldn't change."

"It's just as well I didn't get married," said D'Amato.

On the night of the fight I shared a cab to Comiskey Park with Pete Hamill of the New York *Post*. We caught a cabdriver who was for Patterson, and this worked to spoil the ride. As the fight approached, Hamill and I had been growing nervous in a pleasant way, we were feeling that mixture of apprehension and anticipation which is one of the large pleasures of going to a big fight. Time slows down, the senses become keyed, one's nose for magic is acute.

Such a mood had been building in each of us over the afternoon. About five we had gone to the Playboy Club with Gene Courtney of the Philadelphia *Inquirer*, and it had looked about the way one thought it would look. It was full of corporation executives, and after cancer gulch, the colors were lush, plum colors, velvet reds with the blood removed, a dash of cream, the flesh-orange and strawberry wine of a peach melba, Dutch chocolate colors, champagne colors, the beige of an onion in white wine sauce. The bunnies went by in their costumes, electric-blue silk, Kelly-green, flame-pink, pinups from a magazine, faces painted into sweetmeats, flower tops, tame lynx, piggie, poodle, a queen or two from a beauty contest. They wore a Gay-Nineties rig which exaggerated their hips, bound their waist in a ceinture, and lifted them into a phallic brassiere—each breast looked like the big bullet on the front bumper of a Cadillac. Long black stockings, long long stockings, up almost to the waist on each side, and to the back, on the curve of the can, as if ejected tenderly from the body, was the puff of chastity, a little white ball of a bunny's tail which bobbled as they walked. We were in bossland.

We drank, standing at the bar, talking about fights and fighters, and after a while we came to the fight we were to see that evening. Courtney had picked Liston by a knockout in the fifth, Hamill and I independently had arrived at Patterson in the sixth. So we had a mock fight to pay for a round of drinks. Courtney had bought a cigarette lighter in the Club—it was a slim, inexpensive black lighter with a white rabbit's face painted on the surface. When we put the lighter flat on the table and gave it a twirl, the ears would usually come to rest pointing toward one of us. We agreed that each spin would be a single round, and each time one ear pointed at Courtney or at me, it would count as a knockdown against our fighter. If both ears pointed at one of us, that would be the knockout.

Well, Liston knocked Patterson down in the first round. In the second round the ears pointed at no one. In the third round Patterson knocked Liston down. For the fourth, Liston dropped Patterson. "The fifth is the round," said Courtney, spinning the lighter. It went around and around and ended with one ear pointing at me. Liston had knocked Patterson down again, but had not knocked him out. I took the lighter and gave it a spin. The ears pointed at Courtney. Both ears. Patterson had knocked Liston out in the sixth round.

"Too much," said Hamill.

I had given an interview the day before to Leonard Shecter of the *Post*. I had said: "I think Liston is going to have Patterson down two, three, four times. And Patterson will have Liston down in the first, second, or third and end it with one punch in the sixth." The cigarette lighter had given me a perfect fight.

Well, the Playboy Club was the place for magic, and this mood of expectation, of omen and portent, stayed with us. All of one's small actions became significant. At the hotel, signaling for the cab which was to take us to the ball park, the choice felt wrong. One had the psychology of a ghost choosing the hearse he would ride to a funeral, or of a general, brain livid after days of combat, so identifying himself with his army that he decides to attack first with the corps on his left because it is his left foot which has stepped first into the command car. It is not madness exactly. It is not madness if Montgomery or Rommel thinks that way. If the world is a war between God and the Devil, and Destiny is the line of their battle, then a general may be permitted to think that God or the Devil or the agent of both, which is Magic, has entered his brain before an irrevocable battle. For why should the gods retire when the issue is great? Such a subject is virtually taboo, one must pass by it quickly, or pass for mad, but I had noticed that whenever I was overtired, a sensitivity to the magical would come into me. I now had had little sleep for ten days, and I had been drinking for the last three: when I was very short of sleep, liquor did not make me drunk so much as it gave a thin exaltation, a sensitivity not unlike the touch of drugs in the old days; it was like gasoline burning an orderly flame in the empty chambers of one's reserve. I think one begins to die a little when one has had but three or four hours of sleep each night for a week; some of the cells must die from overexcitement, some from overwork, and their death must bring some of the consciousness of death, some little part of the deep secret of death into the living, weary brain. So I took the cab because it was the second in line at the hotel, and the first cab had not wished to go to the ball park. But a feeling of gloom came over me as if I had committed a serious error.

The driver, as I have said, was for Patterson. He was a big round Negro about thirty with a pleasant face, sly yet not quite dishonest, but he had a pompous manner which seemed to fill the cab with psychic gas as dead as the exhaust from a bus. He was for Patterson, Hamill was for Patterson, I was for Patterson. We were left with nothing but the search for an imaginary conversationalist to argue for Sonny.

How this driver hated Liston! He went on about him at length, most of it not near to printable. "This guy Liston is no good," said the cabdriver. "I tell you the good Lord is going to look down and stop that man because he isn't worth the flesh and blood and muscle that was put into him. Now I don't care," said the cabdriver, going on comfortably, "that Liston was in prison, some of the best men in this country have come out of the can, I nearly did time myself, but I tell you, I don't like Liston, he's a bully and a hustler, and he's no good, he's no good at all, why if you were walking along the street and you saw a beautiful young child, why what would you think. You'd think,

'What a beautiful child.' That's what Patterson would think. He'd go
up to that child and have a pleasant conversation or something, and go
away, but what would Liston do, he'd have the same pleasant conversation, and then he'd get to thinking this is an awful good-looking kid,
and if it's a good-looking kid it must have a good-looking mother.
That man's an opportunist,'' said the driver severely, ''and I tell you
how I know, it's because I've been a hustler, I've hustled everything
you can hustle, and there isn't anything anybody can tell me about
Liston. That hustler is going to get ruined tonight.''

Now the trouble with this speech was that it turned out to be as
oppressive as it was amusing, and one's fine mood of excessive, even
extreme sensitivity began to expire under the dull force of the exposition. It was hopeless to try to explain that Liston, whatever his virtues,
however discovered his faults, could not possibly be as simple as the
driver described him.

It was a fact, however, that Liston did not seem to be loved by the
Negroes one talked to. It was not only the grey-haired Negroes with
the silver-rimmed glasses and the dignity of the grave, the teachers,
the deacons, the welfare workers, the camp directors, the church
organists who were for Patterson, but indeed just about every Negro
one talked to in Chicago. One of the pleasures preceding the fight had
been to conduct a private poll. Of the twenty Negroes polled by our
amateur, all but two or three were unsympathetic to Liston. The word
was out—''You got to stick with the champion.'' I must have heard
that phrase a dozen times. Of course the Negroes spoken to were
employed; they were taxicab drivers, house servants, bellboys,
waiters, college students, young professionals. Some answered cyni-
cally. There were a few with that snaky elegance one finds in colored
people like Sugar Ray Robinson, and had seen at the fringes of
Liston's court out at Aurora, the sort of Negro always seen standing on
a key corner in Harlem, the best-dressed Negro of the intersection. I
had assumed they would instinctively be for Liston, and perhaps they
were, but I was a strange white man asking questions—there is no
need to assume the questions were asked so skillfully or decently that
the truth was obliged to appear. Patterson, was the safe reply. It
demanded nothing, especially if they were not going to see me again
and so would suffer no loss of respect for their judgment. Patterson
was a churchgoer, a Catholic convert (and so of course was Liston, but
the cynical could remark that a Christmas candle in the window looks

nice in a department store), Patterson was up tight with the NAACP, he was the kind of man who would get his picture taken with Jackie Robinson and Ralph Bunche (in fact he looked a little like Ralph Bunche), he would be photographed with Eleanor Roosevelt, and was; with Jack Kennedy, and was; with Adlai Stevenson if he went to the UN; he would campaign with Shelley Winters if she ever ran for Mayor of New York; he was a liberal's liberal. The worst to be said about Patterson is that he spoke with the same cow's cud as other liberals. Think what happens to a man with Patterson's reflexes when his brain starts to depend on the sounds of "introspective," "obligation," "responsibility," "inspiration," "commendation," "frustrated," "seclusion"—one could name a dozen others from his book. They are a part of his pride; he is a boy from the slums of Bedford-Stuyvesant who has acquired these words like stocks and bonds and income-bearing properties. There is no one to tell him it would be better to keep the psychology of the streets than to cultivate the contradictory desire to be a great fighter and a great, healthy, mature, autonomous, related, integrated individual. What a shabby gentility there has been to Patterson's endeavor. The liberals of America had been working for thirty years to create a state of welfare where the deserving could develop themselves. Patterson, as one of the deserving, as one of those who deserve profoundly to be enriched, ends with "introspective." The void in our culture does not know enough to give him "the agen-bite of inwit."

The cynical Negro, talking to a white stranger, would pick Patterson. Yet there was more to it than that. "You got to stick with the champion." They were working, they had jobs, they had something to hold on to; so did Patterson. They would be fierce toward anyone who tried to take what was theirs: family, home, education, property. So too they assumed would Patterson be fierce. They could hardly be expected to consider that the power to keep one's security loses force when it is too secure. Patterson earned $1,825 his first year as a professional fighter, $13,790 his second year, not quite $40,000 his third year when he was fighting main events at Madison Square Garden. By his fourth year, just before he won the title, it was $50,000. Since then he has made more than $3,500,000 in six years. For the Liston fight he would pick up another $2,000,000 from attendance, theatre television, and other rights. The payments would be spread over seventeen years. It was a long way to have come, but the psychic trip was longer. Responsibility, security, and institutional guilt was not necessarily the best tone for the reflexes in his leaping left hook.

But the deepest reason that Negroes in Chicago had for preferring Patterson was that they did not want to enter again the logic of Liston's world. The Negro had lived in violence, had grown in violence, and yet had developed a view of life which gave him life. But its cost was exceptional for the ordinary man. The majority had to live in shame. The demand for courage may have been exorbitant. Now as the Negro was beginning to come into the white man's world, he wanted the logic of the white man's world: annuities, mental hygiene, sociological jargon, committee solutions for the ills of the breast. He was sick of a whore's logic and a pimp's logic, he wanted no more of *mother-wit*, of *smarts*, or *playing the dozens*, of battling for true love into the diamond-hard eyes of every classy prostitute and hustler on the street. The Negro wanted Patterson, because Floyd was the proof a man could be successful and yet be secure. If Liston won, the old torment was open again. A man could be successful *or* he could be secure. He could not have both. If Liston had a saga, the average Negro wanted none of it.

Besides there was always the Mob. Liston had been a strong-arm man for the Mob—they were not so ready to forgive that. He represented the shadow of every bully who had run them off the street when they were children, he was part of the black limousines with four well-dressed men inside, sliding down the dark streets. One did not try to look into the eyes of the men who rode in those limousines.

But there was one reason beyond any other for picking Patterson, and it went deeper than the pretensions of his new dialogue or the professional liberalism of his ideas, his pronouncements or his associates. Patterson was the champion of every lonely adolescent and every man who had been forced to live alone, every protagonist who tried to remain unique in a world whose waters washed apathy and compromise into the pores. He was the hero of all those unsung romantics who walk the street at night seeing the vision of Napoleon while their feet trip over the curb, he was part of the fortitude which could sustain those who lived for principle, those who had gone to war with themselves and ended with discipline. He was the artist. He was the man who could not forgive himself if he gave less than his best chance for perfection. And so he aroused a powerful passion in those lonely people who wanted him to win. He was champion, he was a millionaire, but he was still an archetype of the underdog, an impoverished prince.

And Liston was looking to be king. Liston came from that world where you had no dream but making it, where you trusted no one because your knowledge of evil was too quick to its presence in everyone; Liston came from that world where a man with a dream was a drunk in the gutter, and the best idealism was found in a rabbit's foot blessed by a one-eyed child. Liston was voodoo, Liston was magic, Liston was the pet of the witch doctor; Liston knew that when the gods gathered to watch an event, you kept your mind open to the devils who might work for you. They would come neatly into your eye and paralyze your enemy with their curse. You were their slave, but they were working for you. Yes, Liston was the secret hero of every man who had ever given mouth to a final curse against the dispositions of the Lord and made a pact with Black Magic. Liston was Faust. Liston was the light of every racetrack tout who dug a number on the way to work. He was the hero of every man who would war with destiny for so long as he had his gimmick: the cigarette smoker, the lush, the junkie, the tea-head, the fixer, the bitch, the faggot, the switchblade, the gun, the corporation executive. Anyone who was fixed on power. It was due to Liston's style of fighting as much as anything else. He had no extreme elegance as a boxer, he was a hint slow, indeed he may not have been a natural boxer as was Patterson, but Liston had learned much and attached it to his large physical strength, he had a long and abnormally powerful left jab, a pounding left hook, a heavy right. He had lead in his fists. The only man who had ever defeated him, a club fighter named Marty Marshall, had said, "Every time he hit me, it hurt all over." In his last twenty-five fights Liston had knocked out the other man twenty-one times. So his force appealed to those who had enlisted with an external force. At the Playboy Club, drinking with Courtney and Hamill, I made a bet with a former Harvard man (Business School, no doubt), who told me Liston had it made. He put up fifty against my twenty-eight and we left the money in the bartender's till. I was not to go back.

So it approached. The battle of good and evil, that curious battle where decision is rare and never clear. As we got out of the cab, several blocks from Comiskey Park, two little Negroes, nine or ten years old, danced up to us in the dark, the light of a Halloween candle in their eye. "Give me silver," one of them cried in a Caribbean voice, "give silver, sir," and left us with an orange piece of paper, a throwaway from a nightclub. "Come to Club Jerico after the Fight," said the misspelled legend. "Come to Club Jerico." Je-rico. I—rich.

III

On the afternoon of the night Emile Griffith and Benny Paret were to fight a third time for the welterweight championship, there was murder in both camps. "I hate that kind of guy," Paret had said earlier to Pete Hamill about Griffith. "A fighter's got to look and talk and act like a man." One of the Broadway gossip columnists had run an item about Griffith a few days before. His girl friend saw it and said to Griffith, "Emile, I didn't know about you being that way." So Griffith hit her. So he said. Now at the weigh-in that morning, Paret had insulted Griffith irrevocably, touching him on the buttocks, while making a few more remarks about his manhood. They almost had their fight on the scales.

The accusation of homosexuality arouses a major passion in many men; they spend their lives resisting it with a biological force. There is a kind of man who spends every night of his life getting drunk in a bar, he rants, he brawls, he ends in a small rumble on the street; women say, "For God's sakes, he's homosexual. Why doesn't he just turn queer and get his suffering over with." Yet men protect him. It is because he is choosing not to become homosexual. It was put best by Sartre who said that a homosexual is a man who practices homosexuality. A man who does not, is not homosexual—he is entitled to the dignity of his choice. He is entitled to the fact that he chose not to become homosexual, and is paying presumably his price.

The rage in Emile Griffith was extreme. I was at the fight that night, I had never seen a fight like it. It was scheduled for fifteen rounds, but they fought without stopping from the bell which began the round to the bell which ended it, and then they fought after the bell, sometimes for as much as fifteen seconds before the referee could force them apart.

Paret was a Cuban, a proud club fighter who had become welterweight champion because of his unusual ability to take a punch. His style of fighting was to take three punches to the head in order to give back two. At the end of ten rounds, he would still be bouncing, his opponent would have a headache. But in the last two years, over the fifteen-round fights, he had started to take some bad maulings.

This fight had its turns. Griffith won most of the early rounds, but Paret knocked Griffith down in the sixth. Griffith had trouble getting up, but made it, came alive and was dominating Paret again before the round was over. Then Paret began to wilt. In the middle of the eighth round, after a clubbing punch had turned his back to Griffith, Paret walked three disgusted steps away, showing his hindquarters. For a champion, he took much too long to turn back around. It was the first hint of weakness Paret had ever shown, and it must have inspired a particular shame, because he fought the rest of the fight as if he were seeking to demonstrate that he could take more punishment than any man alive. In the twelfth, Griffith caught him. Paret got trapped in a corner. Trying to duck away, his left arm and his head became tangled on the wrong side of the top rope. Griffith was in like a cat ready to rip the life out of a huge boxed rat. He hit him eighteen right hands in a row, an act which took perhaps three or four seconds, Griffith making a pent-up whimpering sound all the while he attacked, the right hand whipping like a piston rod which has broken through the crankcase, or like a baseball bat demolishing a pumpkin. I was sitting in the second row of that corner—they were not ten feet away from me, and like everybody else, I was hypnotized. I had never seen one man hit another so hard and so many times. Over the referee's face came a look of woe as if some spasm had passed its way through him, and then he leaped on Griffith to pull him away. It was the act of a brave man. Griffith was uncontrollable. His trainer leaped into the ring, his manager, his cut man, there were four people holding Griffith, but he was off on an orgy, he had left the Garden, he was back on a hoodlum's street. If he had been able to break loose from his handlers and the referee, he would have jumped Paret to the floor and whaled on him there.

And Paret? Paret died on his feet. As he took those eighteen punches something happened to everyone who was in psychic range of the event. Some part of his death reached out to us. One felt it hover in the air. He was still standing in the ropes, trapped as he had been before, he gave some little half-smile of regret, as if he were saying, "I didn't know I was going to die just yet," and then, his head leaning back but still erect, his death came to breathe about him. He began to pass away. As he passed, so his limbs descended beneath him, and he sank slowly to the floor. He went down more slowly than any fighter had ever gone down, he went down like a large ship which turns on end and slides second by second into its grave. As he went down, the sound of Griffith's punches echoed in the mind like a heavy ax in the distance chopping into a wet log.

Paret lay on the ground, quivering gently, a small froth on his mouth. The house doctor jumped into the ring. He knelt. He pried Paret's eyelid open. He looked at the eyeball staring out. He let the lid snap shut. He reached into his satchel, took out a needle, jabbed Paret with a stimulant. Paret's back rose in a high arch. He writhed in real agony. They were calling him back from death. One wanted to cry out, "Leave the man alone. Let him die." But they saved Paret long enough to take him to a hospital where he lingered for days. He was in coma. He never came out of it. If he lived, he would have been a vegetable. His brain was smashed. But they held him in life for a week, they fed him chemicals, and made exploratory operations into his skull, and fed details of his condition to The Goat. And The Goat kicked clods of mud all over the place, and spoke harshly of prohibiting boxing. There was shock in the land. Children had seen the fight on television. There were editorials, gloomy forecasts that the Game was dead. The managers and the prizefighters got together. Gently, in thick, depressed hypocrisies, they tried to defend their sport. They did not find it easy to explain that they shared an unstated view of life which was religious.

It was of course not that religion which is called Judeo-Christian. It was an older religion, a more primitive one—a religion of blood, a murderous and sensitive religion which mocks the effort of the understanding to approach it, and scores the lungs of men like D. H. Lawrence, and burns the brain of men like Ernest Hemingway when they explore out into the mystery, searching to discover some part of the secret. It is the view of life which looks upon death as a condition which is more alive than life or unspeakably more deadening. As such it is not a very attractive notion to the Establishment. But then the Establishment has nothing very much of even the Judeo-Christian tradition. It has a respect for legal and administrative aspects of justice, and it is devoted to the idea of compassion for the poor. But the Establishment has no idea of death, no tolerance for Heaven or Hell, o comprehension of bloodshed. It sees no logic in pain. To the Establishment these notions are a detritus from the past.

Like a patient submerged beneath the plastic cover of an oxygen ent, boxing lives on beneath the cool, bored eyes of the doctors in the Establishment. It would not take too much to finish boxing off. Shut own the oxygen, which is to say, turn that switch in the mass media which still gives sanction to organized pugilism, and the fight game would be dead.

But the patient is permitted to linger for fear the private detectives of the Establishment, the psychiatrists and psychoanalysts, might not be ble to neutralize the problem of gang violence. Not so well as the game. Of course, the moment some piece of diseased turnip capable f being synthesized cheaply might prove to have the property of tranquilizing a violent young man for a year, the Establishment would wipe out boxing. Every time a punk was arrested, the police would prescribe a pill, and violence would walk the street sheathed and numb. Of course the Mob would lose revenue, but then the Mob is also part of the Establishment, it, and the labor unions and the colleges and the newspapers and the corporations are all part of the Establishment. The Establishment is never simple. It needs the Mob to grease the chassis on its chariot. Therefore, the Mob would be placated. In a society with strong central government, it is not so difficult to turn up a new source of revenue. What is more difficult is to enter the plea that violence may be an indispensable element of life. This is not the place to have the argument: it is enough to say that if the liberal Establishment is right in its unstated credo that death is a void, and man leads out his life suspended momentarily above that void, why then there is no argument at all. Whatever shortens life is monstrous. We have not the right to shorten life, since life is the only possession of the psyche, and in death we have only nothingness. What then can there be said in defense of sports-car racing, war, or six-ounce gloves?

But if we go from life into a death which is larger than our life has been, or into a death which is small, if death comes to nothing for one man because he swallowed his death in his life, and if for another death is alive with dimension, then the certitudes of the Establishment lose power. A drug which offers peace to a pain may dull the nerve which could have taught the mind how to carry that pain into the death which comes on the next day or on the decades that follow. A tranquilizer gives coma to an anxiety which may later smell of the dungeon, beneath the ground. If we are born into life as some living line of intent from an eternity which may have tortured us or nurtured us in death, then we may be obliged to go back to death with more courage and art than we left it. Or face the dim end of going back with less.

That is the existential venture, the unstated religious view of boxer trying to beat each other into unconsciousness or, ultimately, into death. It is the culture of the killer who sickens the air about him if he does not find some half-human way to kill a little in order to deaden all. It is a defense against the plague, against that plague which comes from violence converted into the nausea of all that nonviolence which is void of peace. Paret's death was with horror, but not all the horror was in the beating, much was in the way his death was cheated. Which is to say that his death was twice a nightmare. I knew that something in boxing was spoiled forever for me, that there would be a fear in watching a fight now which was like the fear one felt for any *novillero* when he was having an unhappy day, the bull was dangerous, and the crowd was ugly. You knew he would get hurt. There is fascination in seeing that the first time, but it is not as enjoyable as one expects. It is like watching a novelist who has written a decent book get run over by a car.

Something in boxing was spoiled. But not the principle, not the right for one man to try to knock another out in the ring. That was perhaps not a civilized activity, but it belonged to the tradition of the humanist, it was a human activity, it showed a part of what man was like, it belonged to his ability to create art and artful movement on the edge of death or pain or danger or attack, and it had much to say about the subtleties of human style. For there are boxers whose bodies move like a fine brain, and there are others who pound the opposition down with the force of a trade-union leader, there are fools and wits and patient craftsmen among boxers, wild men full of a sense of outrage, and steady oppressive peasants, clever spoilers, dogged infantrymen who walk forward all night, hypnotists (like Liston), dancers, lovers, mothers giving a scolding, horsemen high on their legs. There is knowledge to be found about our nature, and the nature of animals, of big cats, lions, tigers, gorillas, bears, walruses (Archie Moore), birds, elephants, jackals, bulls. No, I was not down on boxing, but I loved it with freedom no longer. It was more like somebody in your family was fighting now. And the feeling one had for a big fight was no longer clear of terror in its excitement. There was awe in the suspense.

But then there is nothing else very much like being at a Heavyweight Championship fight. It is to some degree the way a Hollywood premiere once ought to have been; it's a big party with high action—there is the same rich flush of jewelry, bourbon, bare shoulders, cha-cha, silk, the promise that a life or two will be changed by tonight; it is even a bit like a political convention; it is much more like an event none of us will ever see—conceive of sitting in a classic arena waiting for a limited war with real bullets to begin between a platoon of Marines and two mounted squads of Russian Cossacks— you'd have the sensation of what a Heavyweight Championship can promise. A great heavyweight fight could take place in the center of a circus.

Ideally, it should take place in New York. Because Broadway turns out and Hollywood flies in with Las Vegas on the hip, and many of the wings and dovecotes and banlieues of what even a couple of years ago was called Café Society is there, and International Set (always seeing their first fight), and Big Business, and every good-looking call girl in New York, and some not so good-looking, and all the figures from the history pages of prizefighting in America, as well as ghosts there are some to claim—the ghost of Benny Leonard, the ghost of Harry Greb. Plus all the models, loose celebrities, socialites of high and lower rank, hierarchies from the racetrack, politicians, judges, and—one might offer a prayer if one really cared—one sociologist of wit and distinction ought to be there to capture for America the true status of its conflicting aristocracies: does Igor Cassini rate with Mickey Rooney or does Roger Blough get a row in front of Elizabeth Taylor? Is Frank Sinatra honored before Mrs. Woodward? Does Zsa Zsa Gabor come in ahead of Mayor Wagner? The First Sociologists of America are those professionals who sell the hot seats for a big fight in New York.

In Chicago, there was little of this. If there are nine circles to Hell, there were nine clouds over this fight. D'Amato was not licensed to manage in New York. Small matter. Patterson once again would fight in New York without him. But Liston was not cleared to fight by the State Boxing Commission—the shadow of the Establishment lay against him. So the fight was transferred to Chicago which promptly took fire. If Patterson-Liston was not clean enough for New York, i was not cool enough for Chicago. The local newspapers gave the kind of publicity one tastes in cold canned food. The stories on training were buried. Interest was greater outside the city than within. Yet little of Broadway arrived and less of Hollywood. You cannot get producers and movie stars to travel a distance to watch two Negroes fight. A bitch lives to see a white man fight a black man. She's not prejudiced —depending on the merits, she'll root for either, but a Negro against a Negro wets no juice.

And then there was poor weather. The day before the fight was misty, chilly. It rained on and off, and cleared inconclusively on Tuesday, which was cold. Fight night was cold enough to wear a topcoat. Comiskey Park was far from filled. It could hold fifty thousand for a big fight; it ended with less than twenty in paid admissions. Twenty-six thousand people showed. Proportions were poor. Because of theatre television, Patterson would make more money on this fight than any fighter had ever made, and there was much local interest in cities all over America. Parties were got up to go to the theatre, see it on television. The press coverage was larger than average, larger let us say than any of the three Johansson fights or the Marciano-Walcott fights. It was the biggest fight in ten years, it was conceivably the biggest fight since Louis fought Schmeling the second time, and yet nobody in the city where it was fought seemed to care. Radio, with its roaring inside hysteria, had lost to television, that grey eminence which now instructed Americans in the long calm of Ecclesiastes: vanity of vanities, all events are vanity.

So for a celebrity hunter, ringside was nothing formidable at this fight. The good people of Chicago turned out modestly. The very good people—which is to say, the very rich—turned out for ringside, and had a chance to cross the outfield grass, luminous green in the half-light of the baseball towers, and walk to their seats under the great folded wings of the grandstand. Ever since the Romans built the Colosseum, arenas take on a prehistoric breath at night—one could be a black ant walking inside the circle a pterodactyl must have made with its wing as it slept. Or is it hills like dark elephants of which we speak?

I had a seat in the working press five rows from the ring. An empty seat away was Jimmy Baldwin. There had been a chill between us in the last year. Not a feud, but bad feeling. We had been glad, however, to see each other in Chicago. Tacitly, settling no differences, not talking about it, we had thought to be friendly. But the unsettled differences were still there. Two nights ago, at a party, we had had a small fight. We each insulted the other's good intentions and turned away. Now we sat with a hundred-pound cake of ice on the empty seat between us. After ten minutes, I got up and went for a walk around the ring.

The Press section occupied the first six rows. Back of us was an aisle which made a larger square around the square of ringside seats. This was as close as you could come to the fight if you had entered by buying a ticket. So I took a sampling of the house as I walked around the square. If this had been New York, you would expect to find twelve movie stars in the front row. But this was Chicago. Behind us were a muster of local Irish politicians, big men physically in the mold of Jimmy Braddock, not unhappy tonight with their good seats.

The front row to my right and the front row across the ring from me was given over in part to the Mob. They were the most intricate faces one would find this side of Carpaccio or Bellini, chins with hooks and chisels, nostrils which seemed to screw the air up into the head, thin-lipped mouths like thin-nosed pliers:, eyes which behind their dark glasses scrutinized your interior until they could find the tool in you which would work for them, and then would flip away like the turning of a card. Yes, those two rows of seats made up a right angle of *don capos* and a few very special Catholic priests, thin, ascetic, medieval in appearance, as well as a number of field officers dressed in black like subalterns, but older, leaner, with more guilds at their command. They were well-seated. They filled close to every seat around the corner.

It proved to be Patterson's corner.

That was art. They did not have to do much more. Sitting there, they could devote their study to Patterson. He would see them when he came back to his corner, his seconds would be obliged to look at them each time a new round began and they climbed down the steps from the corner. The back of the cornermen's necks would be open to detailed inspection, the calves of Patterson's leg, as he sat resting on the stool, would be a ready target for mental arrows. Like Lilliputians they could shoot thousands of pins into Gulliver.

I completed the tour. The last row, Liston's corner, was routine:

musclemen, mobsters, business-sporting, a random sample. Turning
the angle I came back to my seat, and sat watching a preliminary,
shivering a little in the cold. It was much too cold for a fight. The
sensitivity to magic I had felt earlier in the evening would not come
back. There was just a dull sense of apprehension. Everything was
wrong.

The preliminaries ended. Visiting fighters were called up from the
crowd to take a bow. Archie Moore drew a large hand: he was wearing a black-silk cape with a white lining and he twirled the cape with
éclat. It said: "Go away, all solemn sorcerers, the magic man is
here."

Patterson and Liston arrived within a minute of each other. The
visiting fighters who were gathered in the ring said hello to each man,
shook their gloves, and went back to their seats.

The Star-Spangled Banner was played. Liston stood in his corner
with his handlers, the referee stood in the middle of the ring, and Cus
D'Amato stood alone, eight feet away from Patterson and his seconds.
Since D'Amato was across from me, I could see his face clearly. It
was as pale as his white sweater. His face was lifted to the sky, his eyes
were closed. While the anthem played, D'Amato held his hand to his
heart as if he were in anguish. I had the impression he was praying
with fear.

The anthem ended, the fighters took their instructions from the
referee, and stripped their robes. Their bodies made a contrast. Liston, only an inch taller than Patterson, weighed 214 pounds to Patterson's 189. But the difference was not just in weight. Liston had a sleek
body, fully muscled, but round. It was the body of a strong man, but
the muscles looked to have been shaped by pleasure as much as by
work. He was obviously a man who had had some very good times.

Whereas Patterson still had poverty in his muscles. He was certainly not weak, there was whipcord in the way he was put together,
but it was still the dry, dedicated body of an athlete, a track man, a
disciplinarian: it spoke little of leisure and much of the gym. There
was a lack eating at it, some misery.

The bell rang.

Liston looked scared.

Patterson looked grim.

They came together with no vast impact, trying for small gains.

Each was moving with large respect for the other. Liston had the unhappy sweaty look in his eye of the loudest-talking champion on a city block—he has finally gotten into a fight with one of the Juniors, and he knows this Junior can fight. If he loses he's got much to lose. So Liston was trying to make Junior keep distance.

Patterson was not doing much. He threw a fast left hook which missed, then he circled a bit, fighting from a crouch. He lunged in once very low, trying to get under Liston's long jab and work to the stomach, but his timing was not acute and he drew back quickly. There had been no inspiration, no life, and a hint of clumsiness. But it had been intellectually sound. It caused no harm. Then he tried again, feinting a left hook, and slipping Liston's left jab, but as he came in close, Liston grabbed him with both arms, and they bulled back and forth until the referee separated them. Now, they each had an unhappy look on their faces as if they were big men who had gotten into an altercation in a bar, and didn't like the physical activity of fighting. Each of them looked like it would take three or four rounds to warm up.

All this had used a minute. Liston seemed to have gained the confidence that he was stronger, and he began crowding Patterson to the rope, throwing a good many punches, not left hooks, not left jabs, not uppercuts or straight rights, just thick, slow, clubbing punches. None of them landed on Patterson's body or head, they all banged on his arms, and occasionally Patterson would bang Liston back on the arm. It is a way of fighting. A strong slow fighter will sometimes keep hitting the other man on the shoulder or the biceps until his arms go dead. If the opponent is in condition, it is a long procedure. I was surprised at how slow Liston's punches were. From ringside, they looked easy to block. He had a way of setting himself and going "ahem" before he threw the punch. It is, of course, one thing to block punches from your seat at ringside, and another to block them in a ring, but when a fighter is punching with real speed and snap, you can't block the punches from where you sit. Even from thirty feet away, you are fooled.

All that was fooling me now was Patterson. He seemed sluggish. He was not getting hit with Liston's punches, but he was not hitting back, he seemed to miss one small opportunity after another. He was fighting like a college heavyweight who has gone in to work with a professional and is getting disheartened at the physical load of such sparring. He had the expression on his face of somebody pushing a Cadillac which has run out of gas.

Then occurred what may have been the most extraordinary moment ever seen in a championship fight. It was very spooky. Patterson, abruptly, without having been hurt in any visible way, stood up suddenly out of his crouch, his back a foot from the ropes, and seemed to look half up into the sky as if he had seen something there or had been struck by something from there, by some transcendent bolt, and then he staggered like a man caught in machine-gun fire, and his legs went, and he fell back into the ropes. His left glove became tangled in the top rope, almost as Paret's arm had been tangled, and that murmur of death, that visitation which had passed into Madison Square Garden on the moment Paret began to die, seemed a breath from appearing now, Patterson looked at Liston with one lost look, as if somehow he had been expecting this to happen ever since the night it happened to Paret; it was the look of a man saying, "Don't kill me," and then Liston hit him two or three ill-timed punches, banging a sloppy stake into the ground, and Patterson went down. And he was out. He was not faking. He had started to pass out at the moment he stood straight on his feet and was struck by that psychic bolt which had come from wherever it had come.

Patterson rolled over, he started to make an attempt to get to his feet, and Baldwin and I were each shouting, "Get up, get up!" But one's voice had no force in it, one's will had no life.

Patterson got up somewhere between a quarter and a half second too late. You could see the critical instant pass in the referee's body, and Patterson was still getting his glove off the ground. The fight was over: 2:06 of the First. It must have been the worst fight either fighter had ever had.

Liston looked like he couldn't believe what had happened. He was blank for two or three long seconds, and then he gave a whoop. It was an artificial, tentative whoop, but it seemed to encourage him because he gave another which sounded somewhat better, and then he began to whoop and whoop and laugh and shout because his handlers had come into the ring and were hugging him and telling him he was the greatest fighter that ever lived. And Patterson, covered quickly with his bathrobe, still stunned, turned and buried his head in Cus D'Amato's shoulder.

From the stands behind us came one vast wave of silence. Here and there sounded cheers or applause, but you could hear each individual voice or pair of hands clapping into the silence.

"What happened?" said Baldwin.

IV

What did happen? Everybody was to ask that question later. But in private.

The descriptions of the fight fed next morning to The Goat showed no uncertainty. They spoke of critical uppercuts and powerful left hooks and pulverizing rights. Liston talked of dominating Patterson with left hands, Patterson's people said it was a big right which did the job, some reporters called the punches crunching, others said they were menacing, brutal, demolishing. One did not read a description of the fight which was not authoritative. The only contradiction, a most minor contradiction, is that with one exception, a wire-service photograph used everywhere of a right hand by Liston which has apparently just left Patterson's chin, there were no pictures—and a point was made of looking at a good many—which show Liston putting a winning glove into Patterson's stomach, solar plexus, temple, nose, or jaw. In fact there is not a single picture of Liston's glove striking Patterson at all. It is not highly probable the photographers missed every decent punch. Fight photographers are capable of splitting the strictest part of a second in order to get the instant of impact. The fine possibility is that there was no impact. There was instead an imprecise beating, that is a beating which was not convincing if the men were anywhere near to equal in strength. Something had happened to Patterson, however. He fought as if he were down with jaundice. It was not that he did not do his best; he always did his determined best; he did just that against Liston. It is just that his best this night was off the spectrum of his normal condition. Something had struck at him. From inside himself or from without, in that instant he straightened from his crouch and stared at the sky, he had the surprise of a man struck by treachery.

Now I am forced to give a most improper testimony, because I felt as if I were a small part of that treachery and one despairs of trying to explain how that could be so.

A man turns to boxing because he discovers it is the best experience of his life. If he is a good fighter, his life in the center of the ring is more intense than it can be anywhere else, his mind is more exceptional than at any other time, his body has become a live part of his brain. Some men are geniuses when they are drunk; a good fighter feels a bit of genius when he is having a good fight. This illumination comes not only from the discipline he has put on his body or the concentration of his mind to getting ready for his half hour in the open, but no, it comes as well from his choice to occupy the stage on an adventure whose end is unknown. For the length of his fight, he ceases to be a man and becomes a Being, which is to say he is no longer finite in the usual sense, he is no longer a creature of a given size and dress with a name and some habits which are predictable. Liston-in-the-ring was not just Sonny Liston; much more he was the nucleus of that force at Comiskey Park (and indeed from everywhere in the world from which such desire could reach) which wished him to win or hated him with an impotence that created force, to wit, hated him less than it feared him, and so betrayed its hate since the telepathic logic of the unconscious makes us give our strength to those we think to hate but favor despite ourselves. Just so, Patterson-in-the-ring was not Floyd Patterson sparring in his gym, but was instead a vehicle of all the will and all the particular love which truly wished him to win, as well as a target of all the hatred which was not impotent but determined to strike him down.

When these universes collided, the impact if not clear was total. The world quivered in some rarefied accounting of subtle psychic seismographs, and the stocks of certain ideal archetypes shifted their status in our country's brain. Sex had proved superior to Love still one more time, the Hustler had taken another pool game from the Infantryman, the Syndicate rolled out the Liberal, the Magician hyped the Artist, and, since there were more than a few who insisted on seeing them simply as God and the Devil (whichever much or little of either they might be), then the Devil had shown that the Lord was dramatically weak.

The Goat would demand that this fight be reported in a veritable factology of detail. America could not listen to questions. The professional witnesses to the collision, the pipers of cancer gulch, were obliged to testify to a barrage of detailed punches, and the fighters reexamining their own history in such a mirror of prose would be forced to remake the event in their mind. Yet so long as one kept one's memory, the event was unclear. The result had been turned by betrayal. And it was by one's own person that the guilt was felt. I had been there with half a body from half a night of sleep for too many nights, and half a brain from too many bouts of drinking drinks I did not want that much, and dim in concentration because I was brooding about the loss of a friendship which it was a cruel and stupid waste to lose. And Baldwin too had been brooding. We had sat there like beasts of burden, empty of psychic force to offer our fighter.

Now, too late, in the bout's sudden wake, like angels whose wings are wet, we buried our quarrel; this time it might stay buried for a while. "My Lord," said Jimmy, "I lost seven hundred and fifty dollars tonight."

Well, we laughed. I had lost no more than a paltry twenty-eight.

Later, I went back to the dressing room. But Patterson's door was locked. Over a hundred reporters were jammed into Liston's room, so many that one could not see the new champion, one could only hear his voice. He was resounding very much like Clark Gable now, late Gable with the pit of his mannerism—that somewhat complacent jam of much too much love for the self. Liston had the movie star's way of making the remark which cuts, then balming it with salve. "Did you take your ugly pills?" says the actor to the leading lady, and gives his smile at her flush. "Why honey, dear child, I'm only kidding." So Liston said, "The one time he hurt me was when he got up to a knee at nine. I was afraid he would come all the way up." Which was class. It whipped. A minute later, some banana oil was uncorked. "Yessir," said Liston at large, "Floyd is a heck of a man."

I left that dressing room and tried to get into Patterson's, but the door was still locked. Ingemar Johansson was standing nearby. They were interviewing him over a pay telephone for a radio program. Johansson had a bewildered combative look as if someone had struck him on the back of the head with a loaded jack. He had knocked Patterson down for seven times in one round, there had been wild lightning and "toonder," but he had not been able to keep Patterson down. Now Liston had taken Floyd out with a punch or two or three no witness would agree upon.

"Do you think you can beat Liston," was the interviewer's question.

"I don't know," said Johansson.

"Do you think you have a chance?"

Johansson looked sad and Swedish. "One always has a chance," he said. "I would make my fight and fight it, that's all."

One never did get into Patterson's dressing room. After a while I left and walked around the empty ringside seats. It was cold now. Some of the events of the last few days were coming back to me in the cold air of Comiskey Park. They were not agreeable to contemplate. I had done a few unattractive things. I did not want to count them.

But then in fact I had been doing so much that was wrong the last two days. If one is to talk of betrayal and try to explain what was yet to happen, the account must slip back a bit into what had happened already. On Monday, The New York *Times* had shown a story on the first page of the second section about William F. Buckley and myself and our debate on Saturday night. It had culled some dismembered remarks from the exchange, added a touch of wit from each of us, and called the result a draw. I did not take it well. For I had prepared for the debate, I had honed myself like a club fighter getting ready for the champion. I had been ready, and Buckley, who had been working at other things, was not as ready. He had been speaking in Texas the day before and flew into Chicago only that morning. The afternoon of our debate he was still writing his speech. Saturday night, Medinah Temple had held almost four thousand people. It was built like an opera house with an enormous apron on the stage, and balconies which made a turn around the house through more than half a circle. One spoke with the audience sitting deep to one's left and deep to one's right, close in front and high overhead. Despite its size it was not unlike the theatre in *Les Enfants du Paradis*, and it had been dramatic for our separate styles. Buckley, tall and thin, spoke from high on his toes, his long arm and long finger outstretched in condemnation, a lone shaft of light pointing down on him from above while he excoriated the Left for Cuba, and myself for "swinishness." In my turn I led an intellectual foray into the center of his positions, arguing that if conservatism was a philosophy which saw each person in his appointed place so that men were equal only before God and in Eternity, that the radical in his turn conceived the form of the world as a record of the war between God and the Devil where man served as God's agent and sought to shift the wealth of our universe in such a way that the talent which was dying now by dim dull deaths in every poor man alive would take its first breath and show what a mighty renaissance was locked in the unconscious of the dumb.

Afterward, the people I met on the street and in restaurants or at a party would congratulate me and say I had won. And I had felt exactly like a club fighter who has won a very big fight. But the test of a poor man is profit, and I squandered mine. Something pent up for years, dictatorial and harsh, began to slip through my good humor after I read the verdict in the *Times*. There might be other debates with Buckley in the spring. He would be ready next time. It was raw to lose a victory. I did not take it well. Actors speak of a motor inside themselves. I could not stop mine, one did not want to now, and I drank because the drink was fuel.

Yes, I had done everything wrong since then, I had even had the fool's taste to be pleased with the magic of the cigarette lighter. If I had been a part of the psychic cadre guarding Patterson, I had certainly done everything to make myself useless to him. I could even wonder at that moment, my mind quick with bitterness toward the *Times*, whether the entire liberal persuasion of America had rooted for Floyd in the same idle, detached fashion as myself, wanting him to win but finding Liston secretly more interesting, in fact, and, indeed, demanding of Patterson that he win only because he was good for liberal ideology. I had a moment of vast hatred then for that bleak gluttonous void of the Establishment, that liberal power at the center of our lives which gave jargon with charity, substituted the intolerance of mental health for the intolerance of passion, alienated emotion from its roots, and man from his past, cut the giant of our half-wakened arts to fit a bed of Procrustes, Leonard Bernstein on the podium, John Cage in silence, offered a National Art Center which would be to art as canned butter is to butter, and existed in a terror of eternity which built a new religion of the psyche on a God who died, old doctor Freud, of cancer. Yes, it was this Establishment which defeated Patterson precisely because it supported him, because it was able to give reward but not love, because it was ruled by a Goat who radiated depression like fallout searches for milk.

A long night was to follow, of curious pockets and creepy encounters. Too much magic had been put into one place, and now it was as if a bomb had exploded prematurely, imperfectly. The turbulence of the air had eyes of calm, and gave telepathic intensity to the dark. One would think of an event with rising concentration and around the turn of one's thought would appear, quite real, smacking of the flesh, some man or woman who belonged to the event. Walk-through the Park, a person shouted my name. Then another cry. It was the voice of each of the men who had promoted the debate with Buckley, John Golden and Aaron Berlin. We took off extempore together to have a drink and go on to my party, and on the way, walking through the streets of the South Side near Comiskey Park, two gloomy Negro adolescents fell in and walked along with us. They were eighteen or nineteen, shabby. They wore flat leather caps. One had turned the short peak around to the back of his head. They had been blasted tonight by Floyd's defeat. Everything would be more difficult now. They did not want to hate Patterson, but they could hardly speak.

Poor Patterson. He was alienated from his own, from his own streets, his own vocabulary, his own manager, he was even alienated from his own nightmare. What could the Establishment tell him of that odyssey which set him once walking on subway tracks to discover a hole not too many inches away from where the trains went by. "Oh," said the Establishment, "he wanted to go back to the womb. How interesting!" But they could not tell one why he had this wish, nor why it was interesting. The womb was part of their void, of the liberal void, they would not begin to guess that a champion who could find a way to go to sleep minutes before a big fight must have learned early to live on the edge of his death. The psychic roar of a prizefight crowd was like the sound of the subway. Yes, Patterson had gone out early to explore because he had known, living in terror down in Bedford-Stuyvesant part of town, down in a world of curse, evil eye, blasted intent, that the forces of the past which had forced their way into the seed which made him now wanted no less than that he be extraordinary, that he be great, that he be a champion of his people. But he had succeeded too quickly. He had come too early upon the scene. The Establishment had made him a Negroid white. His skin was black, his psychology had turned white, poor blasted man, twice cursed. He could have the consolation that his championship had gone on to another black.

But it was unfair. He deserved more than this, more than this gutted performance. One would now never know if he lost before he reached the ring, whipped by the oatmeal of the liberal line, or if the Devil had struck him down with vastly greater ease than the Devil had intended.

No matter how, the result had been awful. That this brave, decent, sensitive, haunted man should have been defeated with such humiliation. It was awful.

The party was very big, and it was a good party. The music went all the way down into the hour or two before breakfast, but no one saw the dawn come in because the party was at Hugh Hefner's house which is one of the most extraordinary houses in America and the living room where much of the party was going was sixty feet long and more than thirty wide, and almost twenty high, yet there were no windows, at least I never saw the sky from that room, and so there was a timeless spaceless sensation. Staying as a houseguest in his home, there had been servants ready all twenty-four hours these last few days, one had been able to get the equivalent of any drink made at any bar at any hour of the world, one could have chili at four a.m. or ice cream at ten, the servants had been perfect, the peace when empty of the house was profound, one never saw one's host except for once or twice in some odd hour of the night. He had a quality not unlike Jay Gatsby, he looked and talked like a lean, rather modest cowboy of middle size; there was something of a mustang about Hefner. He was not the kind of man one would have expected to see as the publisher of his magazine, nor the owner of the Playboy Club, nor certainly as the undemanding host of his exceptional establishment. Timeless, spaceless, it was outward bound. One was in an ocean liner which traveled at the bottom of the sea, or on a spaceship wandering down the galaxy along a night whose duration was a year. The party went on, and I drank and I drank some more. The swimming pool was beneath the dance floor, and there were bathing suits for those who wanted them, and some did, and people went to look through the trapdoor in the living room which pried open over a fall of fifteen feet into a grotto of the pool below. Above was the orchestra and the dancers in a Twist. The Twist was not dead in Chicago, not hardly. If there were such a thing as sexual totalitarianism, then the Twist was its Horst Wessel, and all the girls with boy's bodies were twisting out their allegiance. I hated the Twist. Not because I had become a moralist on the stroke of twelve, not because I felt sex without love was determined to be bad, but because I hated too much life for sex without any possibility of love. The Twist spoke of some onanism which had gone on forever, some effort which had lost its beginning and labored to find no end, of an art which burned itself for fuel.

Now, after the knockout, in some fatigue-ridden, feverish whole vision of one's guilt and of Patterson's defeat—for of course the fighters spoke as well from the countered halves of my nature; what more had I to tell myself of sex versus love, magic against art, or the hustler and the infantryman?—out of a desire to end some war in myself, as if victory by Patterson might have given me discipline, and the triumph of Liston could now distract me only further, out of a fury to excise defeat, I began in the plot-ridden, romantic dungeons of my mind, all subterranean rhythms stirred by the beat of this party, to see myself as some sort of center about which all that had been lost must now rally. It was not simple egomania nor simple drunkenness, it was not even simple insanity: it was a kind of metaphorical leap across a gap. To believe the impossible may be won creates a strength from which the impossible may indeed be attacked. Fidel Castro alone in the jungle, with a dozen men left, seven-eighths of his landing party dead, lost, or captured, turned to his followers in the sugar-cane and said, "The days of the dictatorship are numbered." If he had been killed that moment they would have said he died as a madman. He was not mad, he was merely all but impossible. But in his mind, he saw a set of psychic steps which led to victory. And in my mind, half-gorged from juice, the beginning of a resolution was forming. I did not know it, but I was getting ready to tell myself that I must have a press conference next morning in which I would explain why Floyd Patterson still had an excellent chance to defeat Sonny Liston in their next fight, and why in fact—this would be indigestible for The Goat—why the fight which had taken place had been a mysterious dumb show substituted by inexplicable intervention for the real event. Opportunity came. This was a party like a pinball machine; there were bonuses on the turn of the lights, and a little later I was having a drink with a man from Championship Sports, I had drinks with several of them that night, but on the conversational ride we took together with the liquor, I dunned this man into some half-muttered acceptance of an idea which did not seem at all impractical at two in the morning. I would do publicity for the second Patterson-Liston fight, I was the only man in America who could save the second fight because I believed that Patterson had a true chance to beat Liston the next time they met. And it made sense: at that hour, in the blasted remains of the promotion, with no thought of a return of all promising, the confidence I offered was enough to trap the promise of a conference for the press. Liston was seeing reporters at eleven-thirty; I could have mine at eleven, a semifinal on the eleventh floor.

"And what will you say?" asked the reporters, a little later.

"I'll say it tomorrow."

But the party did not end until seven in the morning. I had the choice of sleeping for a few hours or not sleeping at all, and decided it would be easier not to fall asleep. So I talked for an hour or two with the housekeeper while the drinks began to fade, and then shaved very slowly and dressed and went out to walk the twelve or fifteen blocks from Hefner's house to the hotel. I was tired now, I felt something of the exhilaration a fighter must know in the twelfth or thirteenth round of a fifteen-round fight when he has fought his way into some terrain of the body which is beyond fatigue and is riding now like a roller coaster on the beating of his heart, while the flashbulbs ricochet their red-and-green echoes of light into his skull. The awe of his venture has fined down now into the joy that whether he wins or loses, he has finally lifted into flight, something in himself has come up free of the muck.

At the hotel, I went first to fight headquarters downstairs. In the eyes of the man from Championship Sports who had agreed last night to let me meet the press, I could now see a critical lack of delight.

"It's been changed," he said. "Sonny Liston is having his conference at eleven. You had better have yours afterward."

That would not work. After Liston talked to the reporters they would want to file their stories.

"What floor will it be on?"

"The ninth."

I thought to go to the ninth floor. It was a large mistake. Later I learned reporters were waiting for me on the eleventh. But an amateur's nose for the trap is pointed to the wrong place. I was afraid to go to the eleventh floor for fear the conference would begin two floors below. Naturally, Liston was late. On the ninth floor, in the banquet room, there were but a few reporters. I went up to the dais, sat down on a chair at one end. For several minutes nobody paid attention. Then one or two men became curious. What are you doing up there, they wanted to know. Well, I was going to sit up there, I told them, while the champion was having his press conference. Afterward I wanted to say a few things. To what effect? To the effect that I still thought Patterson was the better fighter.

A few of the movie cameramen here for TV newsreel began to take their interest. They came up with light meters, set cameras, measured distance. A flashbulb went off, another. The room was filling.

Now officials began to ask me to leave. They asked pleasantly, they asked with bewilderment, they asked in simple menace. I kept saying that I had been invited to speak at this conference, and so would not leave. Who had invited me? Reporters wanted to know. I had the sense to say I would not give the name until it was my turn to speak. I had some sense it would be bad for the man who invited me—I did not want to offer his name for nothing.

"If you don't leave," said the last official, "we'll have to remove you by force."

"Remove me by force."

"Would you give a statement, Mr. Mailer," said a reporter for the *Times*.

"Yes." The answer was formal Chinese. "I came here prepared to make a case that I am the only man in this country who can build the second Patterson-Liston fight into a $2,000,000 gate instead of a $200,000 dog in Miami. I wish to handle the press relations for this second fight. For various and private reasons I need to make a great deal of money in the next two months." Two or three journalists were now taking careful notes.

Then I felt a hand on my shoulder. Its touch was final—the end of a sequence. "Would you come with us?" On one side was a house detective. On the other side was another house detective.

"No."

"We'll have to carry you out."

"Carry me out."

They lifted the chair in which I was sitting. I had not expected this to happen. It was too simple. And there was no way to resist. The publicity from a scuffle would feed a circus. Nonetheless, if you are not a pacifist, to be transported in a chair is no happy work. Once we were quits of the dais, there was nothing to do but slip off. I walked to the elevator. Fifteen minutes of cool, reasonable debate went on downstairs before one of the detectives agreed to telephone up for permission. I would be allowed at least to see Sonny's conference with the press.

When we got back, Liston was much in command. He sat in the center of the long table, on the dais, flanked by four or five men on either side. Questions were admiring, routine. "What did you think of Patterson's punch?" someone asked, a reporter.

"He hits harder than I thought he would," said Liston.

"He never landed a punch."

"That's true," said Liston, "but he banged me on the arm. I could feel it there."

Someone asked a new question. Liston answered in a reasonable voice. Then he said something grim. About reporters.

"Well, I'm not a reporter," I shouted from the back of the room, "but I'd like to say . . ."

"You're worse than a reporter," said Liston.

"Shut the bum up," shouted some reporters.

"No," said Liston. "Let the bum speak."

"I picked Floyd Patterson to win by a one-punch knockout in the sixth round, and I still think I was right," I shouted to Liston.

"You're still drunk."

"Shut the bum up," shouted several reporters.

A reporter asked another question. Nilon was quick to answer it. I had had my moment, lost it. The conference went on. There were questions and answers about the finances of the fight. I was weary. After a while, I sat down. The faces of the people who looked at me were not friendly. When the conference ended, I went up to a reporter who was a friend. "Next time ask your question," he said. "Don't stand there posing."

An ego made of molybdenum could not have concealed from itself that one had better not quit now. The losses would be too great.

So I went back to the dais and tried to approach Liston. Two very large Negroes stood in the way. "I want to talk to the champion," I said.

"Well, go up front. Don't try to approach him from behind," snapped one of the Negroes.

"Fair enough," I said, and went down the length of the table, turned around, and came up again to Sonny Liston from the front. A man was talking, and I waited ten or fifteen seconds till he was done, and then took a step forward.

"What did you do," said Liston, "go out and get another drink?"

He was sitting down, and I was standing. Since he sat there with his forearms parallel, laid out flat on the table in front of him, it gave to his body the magisterial composure of a huge cat with a man's face.

"Liston," I said, "I still say Floyd Patterson can beat you."

A smile came from the Sphinx. "Aw, why don't you stop being a sore loser?"

"You called me a bum."

Each of us was by now aware that there were reporters gathering around us.

Something unexpected and gentle came into Liston's voice. "Well, you *are* a bum," he said. "Everybody is a bum. I'm a bum, too. It's just that I'm a bigger bum than you are." He stood up and stuck out his hand. "Shake, bum," he said.

Now it came over me that I had not begun to have the strength this morning to be so very good as I had wanted to be. Once more I had tried to become a hero, and had ended as an eccentric. There would be argument later whether I was a monster or a clown. Could it be, was I indeed a bum? I shook his hand.

A few flashbulbs went off, and Liston's face looked red to me and then green and then red and green again before the flare of the light left my retina. His hand was large and very relaxed. It told little about him. But a devil came into my head. I pulled his hand toward me, and his weight was so balanced on his toes that his head and body came forward with his hand and we were not a foot apart. "Listen," said I, leaning my head closer, speaking from the corner of my mouth, as if I were whispering in a clinch, "I'm pulling this caper for a reason. I know a way to build the next fight from a $200,000 dog in Miami to a $2,000,000 gate in New York."

Out of Liston's eyes stared back the profound intelligence of a profound animal. Now we understood each other, now we could work as a team. "Say," said Liston, "that last drink really set you up. Why don't you go and get *me* a drink, you bum."

"I'm not your flunky," I said.

It was the first jab I'd slipped, it was the first punch I'd sent home. He loved me for it. The hint of a chuckle of corny old darky laughter, cottonfield giggles, peeped out a moment from his throat. "Oh, sheeet, man!" said the wit in his eyes. And for the crowd who was watching, he turned and announced at large, "I like this guy."

So I left that conference a modest man. Because now I knew that when it came to debate I had met our Zen master. I took a cab and rode the mile to Hefner's place, feeling the glow of fatigue which is finally not too unclean, and back at the mansion lunch was chili so hot it scorched the throat. I had a glass of milk, and Baldwin dropped by and we spoke in tired voices of the fight and after a while he inquired about the health of my sister and I replied that she was fine, she was looking beautiful, why didn't he consider marrying her, quick as that, which put me one up on old Jim again, and we shook our writer's hands and said good-by, each of us to go back to New York by separate flight, he to write his account, I to mine. Next day, and the following day, and even on the days of the next week, some favorite pets of The Goat kept taking little bites at me. First it was a red jaybird named Mr. Smith and then it was A. J. Liebling, a loverly owl. (One couldn't mind what an owl didn't see, but it was supposed to hear.) Then a wily old hamster named Winchell gobbled some of the remaining rump, and Dorothy Kilgallen, looking never in the least like a chinless lemur, took the largest bite of all. She wrote that I had tried to pick a fight with Archie Moore. Well, I had never tried to pick a fight with Archie Moore because Mr. Moore had indicated already that he could manage to handle a pugilist like Mr. George Plimpton of *The Paris Review*, and Mr. Plimpton and I were much in the same league. Indeed, Mr. Moore had said, "I almost broke my back not hitting Mr. Plimpton."

It could have been very nice. Nobody minds if they read in the papers that they were thrown in a swimming pool when in fact they did not go near a glass of water. The lies of The Goat were not onerous and his pets were sweet: it was just that later one was called in to see a high probation official and was told that probation, about to end, would now be extended further. One would have to pay this bit for the caper. I did not mind so much. I had learned a lot and educations were paid for best in cash. But what I lost was also nice, I was sorry to see it gone. Some ghost of Don Quixote was laid to rest in me and now I could never be as certain as that morning on the walk whether Patterson indeed could ever bring in his return. To shake the hand of the Devil must quiver the hole: who knew any longer where Right was Left or who was Good and how Evil had hid? For if Liston was the agent of the Devil, what a raid had been made on God, what a royal black man had arisen. Sonny, the King of Hip, was Ace of Spades, and Patterson, ah, Patterson was now an archetype of all which was underdog. He would be a giant if he won. If he could rally from his flight and shave the beard he glued on his mouth; if he could taste those ashes, and swallow to the end, and never choke; if he could sleep through the aisles and enormities of each long night, pondering if the

Devil had struck him down (and so might strike again—what fear could be worse than that!) or, even worse, be forced to wonder if the Lord had passed him by for Sonny, if Sonny were now the choice, having carried the blood of his Negritude through prison walls; if Floyd could sleep through those long dreams, and be cool to the power of the dead in Liston's fists (and the rents in his own psyche); if Patterson could keep from pulling apart and could put himself together; if he could shed the philosophy which drained him and learn to create for himself till he was once again the heavyweight with the fastest, hardest hands of our modern time; if he could go out into the ring with the sullen apathy of his followers now staring him in the eye; if he could move in and take that next fight away from Liston and knock Sonny out, then a great man would be with us, and a genius our champion rather than a king. So one would hope for Patterson one more time. Genius was more rare than royalty and so its light must reach a little further into our darkness down the deep waters of sleep, down one's long inner space. The first fight had been won by the man who knew the most about Evil; would the second reveal who had studied more of the Good? would they meet in the clangor of battle or the fiasco of a doomed dead cause? would we witness a dog in Miami or the lion of New York?

THE TWELFTH PRESIDENTIAL PAPER
—On Waste

- **Truth and Being; Nothing and Time**
- **The Metaphysics of the Belly**

A LAST OPEN LETTER TO JOHN FITZGERALD KENNEDY

Mr. President:
In these pages, I have talked about existential politics, the need for a hero, the meaning of politics as the art of the possible. I have made perhaps a hundred small expeditions up the possible tributaries of this theme, and have dilated on the danger of our time—totalitarianism. Now if you would ask for me to put the meaning of this book in a sentence or two, I am ready. Existential politics would say: Political rights like human rights are best won by a face-to-face confrontation.
That is what is good about revolution.
It would be convenient if one could end here, but the two most curious, difficult, and doubtless most offensive passages of writing are still to come. Classical politics begins with the notion that a great many facts and a few phenomena are hard, measurable, and concrete, and thus may be manipulated to produce corrective results. Existential politics, however, derives not from politics as a prime phenomenon, but from existentialism. So it begins with the separate notion that we live out our lives wandering among mysteries, and can construct the few hypotheses by which we guide ourselves only by drawing into ourselves the instinctive logic our inner voice tells us is true to the relations between mysteries. The separate mysteries we may never seize, but to appropriate a meaning from their relationship is possible. The first preoccupation of the existentialist is not then the fact

293

itself (for the fact is invariably a compression of nuances which alienate the reality—see Appendix A), but rather is the root from which the fact may have evolved.

So for example in a period of local economic crisis with rising unemployment, the existential politician might be forced to act in much the way of the average politician—he might have to tinker with lowering the interest rate on corporate loans in order to stimulate new investment. But since this method does not go to the root, he would know that the real solution is more likely to be found over the years in the concealed nature of the waste within the industry, the poor workmanship, the deterioration of materials, the inflated value, and the literal cancers (such as institutional advertising) which are to be found in the industry's mode of production.

There have been political leaders who kept themselves functioning on medical drugs—Adolf Hitler is one who comes to mind—and our economy has been allowed to deteriorate in its very expansions by the fiduciary drug of the war economy. If the cold war were magically to cease next year, we would face an economic crisis whose proportions are beyond measure, even as a drug addict suffers paroxysms, apathy, and collapse when his drug is withdrawn. Some large part of such an economic crisis would derive from the huge proliferations of waste in the economy.

Well, one is hardly equipped for economic analysis, but the principle that growth cannot be understood without going into the nature of waste is true—if it is true at all—for society as well as for the individual. Waste is a proper obsession for existential politics, and growth cannot be anticipated without an expedition into the meanings of waste. Since our first intellection of the process comes from an understanding of ourselves, our own growth and our own literal waste, our ability to create, and our intimate processes of destruction—our literal scatology—this paper descends to a primitive theme, the root of the matter—man's private elimination of his private waste. From here (if one is to speak Germanically) may a path be found to the root of economics.

It is perhaps an exceptional request to make of a President—that he be ready to go along on an existential journey into the deeper meaning of scatology—but then a President is a master-politician, an artist of politicians, and like other artists must be ready to contemplate everything human and inhuman in the psychic life of his Republic, including *those ideas—as I wrote once in another context for the First Lady—including precisely those ideas which encounter the rude, the obscene, and the unsayable.*

Let me offer in recompense a poem from Deaths for the Ladies.

> *Superhighways*
> *cut through*
> *profit and*
> *passion*
> *and so*
> *inhabit*
> *the moon*
> *before we've*
> *learned*
> *its mountain*
> > *road*
> > *which*
> > *winds*
> > *in*
> > *slow*
> > *curves*
> > *of the*
> > *root*
> > *toward*
> > *the ore*
> *and her nugget*

Yours not insincerely,
Norman Mailer

Truth and Being; Nothing and Time

A Broken Fragment from a Long Novel

Now that there is no doubt I am going to die, and my death will be by that worst of diseases (for it is other than disease), I think the time may be here to tell the story of the revolution which came to New York in the second half of the Twentieth Century, of its outrageous internal history, of my part in it, and the style of my mind. If I do not offer my name, it is because I am one of the actors in the mystery, a principal of the revolution, and I would not like to detract from any excitement attached to my actions by linking all of my person in this first breath with the four consonants and two vowels of cancer. For it is indeed just that rebellion of the cells from which I am dying . . . at the rate . . . it is curious that I do not know the rate. Might it not tell us something of the impulse within the disease if we were to measure this rate of growth from day to day of the malignancy of the cells? I am certain the formula would belong to one of those exquisite curves of increase or deterioration which lit my adolescent comprehension of mathematics, as for example some equation to determine an exponential expansion, or the curve of the logarithm. (Even the terms are no longer secure to my memory; but as meaning dissipates, sound presents its attractions.) Since I mention these curves, however, best it is for me to admit that there is only one curve I expect to be found in the graph of the rate of growth of my mutinous cells—it would have, I suspect, some relation to the formula for the rate of increase in the decomposition of radium to lead. For this is not merely a scientific image to me, but the precise metaphor to describe the possessions and dissipations of my Self over these years, it is exactly the measure—this transit from radium to lead—of certain beauties of love, sex, flesh, and other sweetmeats of Being, which were transmuted by the intensity of my ambition into purposeful and more or less lost radiations of consciousness. Radium emits that which it will radiate and in giving of itself to whatever matter surrounds it, or is brought before it, radium diminishes to lead. One can feel little pity for it: radium has never learned to receive. So its history among the elements must present an irony or two: among themselves (that is to say, among the elements) do they speak of radium as the royal fool, the King Lear of the atoms? They do not dare, I think. Radium is too dangerous. It alters wherever it reaches. But in fact I am close to indulging an unwise vice because metaphors live for me with the power of mechanical laws. It is an evil philosopher who cannot mourn his own passing, and if that art work— a tear of pure compassion for oneself—were to emerge in my eye, it would be for the loss of my sensitivity to the dialectic, a sensitivity which was perhaps as exquisite in me at my best as any mind in this century. There were others who possessed the dialectic with greater power; the Frenchman Jean Paul . . . Sartre I remember now was his last name had a dialectical mind good as a machine for cybernetics, immense in its way, he could peel a nuance like an onion, but he had no sense of evil, the anguish of God, and the possible existence of Satan. That was left for me, to return the rootless disordered mind of our Twentieth Century to the kiss *sub cauda* and the Weltanschauung of the Medieval witch. The kiss *sub cauda*: if I had not come to recognize over the years of my career that nobility of form and aristocracy of manner are the last hope of man, I would not explain that *sub cauda* means beneath the tail, the hole in the highness of the cat, the place the witch would kiss when out she voyaged to visit the Demon (or is it in?), cats being classified by Medieval logic as the trinity of the Devil shaped into One. Naturally. But to give a taste of what I offer, to prove that there are dreams, essays, baths of flesh I never found behind each word and curious phrase, let me hold for a moment all disquisition on the character of my compassion for myself and offer instead a nugget of new ore. The hole, the royal hole (forgive my gentility, but I do not wish to jar the ghosts of the Time whose style I inhabit for this writing), the hole, the brown one, rich as purple in some, withered to dun-green for others, flower, weed, perfume, ill-fumed, cathedral and shanty, pleasure, pustule, muscle, orifice, avatar, pile and grave, is the final executor of that will within us to assign value to all which passes through. Do we bite into an apple? It is not perfect, not often. Good cells and poor, tastes, monotonies, and taints mill in the vaults of our digestion; the needs, desires, snobberies, and fashions of our will devil one's sense of selection, twist our taste: good cells of the apple, tart let us say, brave in the way the cell of an apple can be brave—I think such a bravery might exist, might it not? (the tart cell could maintain its taste against a bland environment for the years of its life) and yet brave or bland could be ignored, could be flushed away, good mistaken for bad, nourishment lost, because the form of *our* character was too insensitive to absorb the most particular character of my brave cell in the apple. So out it goes, pushed into the Styx by the body, buried with the foulest hoodlums and lowest slime, the dullest scum and deadest skin of those fecal molecules, ejected already into the journey to the end of the hole. What rich possibilities and poor wastes are shit into the vast bare lands of sanitation by the middle-class mind. So it is that some of the best and some of the worst of us are drawn to worship at the congregation of the lost cells. (Why is their color brown?—I have pondered this question for years.)

Yes, there are those of us who worship our own, there are all too many who prostrate themselves before another, and there were even a few like our revolutionary leader who was drawn toward his own and rarely repelled by others. It is characteristic of revolutionaries, passionate lovers, the very ambitious, the greedy, the stingy, and dogs, to fix on what is excreted by others; it is typical of Narcissists, children, nuns, spinsters, misers, bankers, conservative statesmen, dictators, compulsive talkers, bores, and World War I generals accomplished at trench warfare, to be forever sniffing their own. But the intelligent and conservative among you are annoyed already for there is a tendency to my remarks which you detect with unease, you fear I lead the argument into the alp of the high immoral. I do; but perhaps my aim is to rescue morality. To be conservative does not mean to be cowardly: follow my argument, for you quit it at a loss—I am not necessarily archbishop of the New Royal Scatological in our society.

Good. We are drawn to shit because we are imperfect in our uses of the good. If all we eliminated was noxious, hopeless, used up or never-intended, it would be a pervert or a maniac who found the subject attractive. But not all of what we give away is useless. There is a spirit to nourishment, an elan to food, a dash of the existence of an Other—who among you would presume to argue that the flesh of a brave animal is the same in flavor, substance, or final effect upon us as the meat of a contented cow? Each cell in each existence labors like all of life to make the most of what it is or can be, each cell is different, perhaps even so different as one of us from another. So perhaps we do not digest all that is good for us. Indeed, some is lost because it is too good for us, we do not deserve it, the guilt in the enzymes of our stomach prevents the process. (Who among you? scientists? chemists? doctors of organism? can prove that guilt is *in*capable of entering an enzyme?) Yet other riches elude the peristalsis—the best of us cannot absorb a nutrient which is beyond the possibility of our style: particles of food which urge us to be generous are disagreeable to the stingy; spices which gratify our sense of the precise are lost and refused by thicket-witted minds. The dung of the brave is filled with riches for the fearful: precisely those subtleties, reservations, and cautions the courageous dislike are grace and wit for the coward; the offal of the fool has sweets to accelerate a genius—a dull mind must reject those goods for fear the head would hemorrhage from unexpected and indisposable enthusiasms. All the mineral riches of stone, the essences of earth, the spirits of the Wind, creativities of the Sun, omens and intimations of the moon, scalding and compassionate courses of rain, pass upward into the aristocracies of nature, into the nutrient offered us by plant and animal. The wealth of our ground enters us—we digest a million insinuations a day, and fail to digest perhaps a million more, for all of us are too narrow for the wealth we devour, and expel the exquisite in time with the despised.

But if excrement is the enforced marriage of Tragic Beauty and Filth, why then did God desert it, and leave our hole to the Devil, unless it is because God has hegemony over us only as we create each other. God owns the creation, but the Devil has power over all we waste—how natural for him to lay siege where the body ends and weak tragic air begins. Out of the asshole pour the riches of Satan—these souls of nutrient, these lost cells spurned by the universe of the body they traversed, their being about to be cast into the lower existence of Chance. For you see, and do not be altogether nervous (since the explanation, if given in haste, will be amplified at leisure), there are three possibilities of Being. There is Culture when one exists in a milieu, when one's life is obedient to a style—the peasant in his village lives in Culture like bacteria in a petri dish. There is History, the highest form of life; it has the turns and starts, the surprises, the speed of change and the fires of courage an animal knows on a long trip to search for food. And there is Chance. That is the life of an organism which has been deprived of the possibility to organize itself—it is the lowest form of active life, it is entropy. (A word to remember.) With Chance we can depend no longer upon ourselves (which is the grace that History offers) nor can we even depend on growth in obedience to the shape of the culture which conceived us, no, we are cast loose, we are blown, we are transported, we are shifted, pushed, we are carried by forces larger than ourselves toward fates of elimination which inspire terror. Those freight trains dense with the bodies of victims moving from a camp of concentration to a camp of extermination (small intestine and colon of German Idealism), those souls so soon to die by gas in a room as bleak as the lavatory of a men's penitentiary, they were souls ripped from Culture or defeated in History, and so linked into the purposeful streamings of

Chance as she went toward the abyss. Yes, it was I who first demonstrated to the world by the rigor of philosophical argument (a Herculean labor) that the state of Being in the Twentieth Century was close to the extinction of itself because of the diseases and disasters of soul over the centuries, the victories of the Devil. Being was now warped. History, Culture, and Chance—that choice offered to Being from the beginning of our existence was turning into the contrary of itself. History was now made by cowards who gave no shape to History even as they blurred the shape of what we saw (those modern buildings without faces) Culture was untimely ripped—the foods of Being and the maintenance of Being grown thick, anomalous, and bland with hybrid growths from the field, antibiotics, and a technological jargon for the cure of the body. Only Chance prospered in the Twentieth Century. The circuits of the circuitless turned to purpose. One had only to rip one's roots free from Culture, relinquish one's dreams of authority, one's sense of self, one's love of adventure, one's desire to make a History, relinquish oneself to Chance, and all was planned. One's life, emptied of novelty, organized, cleansed, plotted, secure, unpursued, could then proceed in the monotonies of welfare from the cradle to the tomb. Chance was a purposeful stream moving the bodies of all millions of us away from roots, below history, out of grace. The progression was from man to merde, the Twentieth Century was the rush of all souls to search out shit, to kiss the Devil, to rescue a molecule of the brown from its extinction. For think: we began all this (and disturb yourself not unduly if you have comprehended but little, for we return again and again) but we began with the kiss *sub cauda*, the kiss to the hole of the cat. The cat—that marriage of grace and cruelty, self-centered, alien, alone, what can the cat use in its food of tender cells, compassionate meats, philosophical greens? It cannot— the drop of the cat is rich in royal and generous affections; one has only to absorb, and one will love with grace. Yes, such waste has all the darting odors of fish-meat and love. The witches knew it; they were burned for no less than the addition of this dung to their cakes-for-the- encouragement-of-love and more than one saint was present, the rack of hagflesh burning in his nose, his legs twisted with the ache of a witch's soul being returned finally to her separate masters. St. Exquisita of Odometamo, that unpredictable and much despised saint of the Twelfth Century, almost excommunicated three times for heresy (that rare and only saint admired to my knowledge by the Marquis de Sade), was the first I know to suggest that the witch was the finest jewel of the Devil because she was a woman originally of noble soul much beloved by God, who had been rifled by Satan in the womb, which is to say that witches generally are born of evil mothers, God investing the cruel placenta with the spirit of a rare soul, as if God wished to steal—if one may speak this way (for St. Exquisitas of course could not)—one human of evil back from the Devil. What the Devil owns, he generally cares for, although he is not perfect as a custodian any more than God is all foreseeing as a lover, but as a rule of thumb (since one is hardly so divine oneself as to speak with authority of the Divine Economy) God must raid upon evil to recover it, even as the Devil lusts to capture love. So St. Exquisitas gave his formula for the creation of a witch: God anoints the womb of an evil creature in the moment of her conception and in turn is tricked of his effort by the Devil who is so alert that this particular one of his creatures might be lost (for God being wealthy and a snob never chooses any ordinary lady of evil) that Satan follows behind God and poisons the anointment with his tongue.

Thus, at last, a hint of my style and the character of my mind.

The Metaphysics of the Belly

Interviewer: I feel anxious today. I can't seem to get serious. A year ago we had an interview. "The First Days Interview," you called it. You said at the time it was the beginning of a book. You were going to call it* The Psychology of the Orgy. *Then I don't hear from you again. Months go by. All these months. The piece gets printed. I become a bit of a figure. Suddenly you call me up. Let's go on with the interview,*

*Printed in *Paris Review* #26.

you say. I arrive tape recorder in hand. Now you say you want to do a book on Picasso. I'm confused. I don't know anything about Picasso.

Mailer: That's one reason you were chosen.

Interviewer: I feel like the old lady in Death in the Afternoon. *Tell me, what happened to* The Psychology of the Orgy? *That pricks the ears much more than Picasso.* Psychology of the Orgy—*it's not like you to throw away a good title.*

Mailer: What I have to say about Picasso may not be so dull.

Interviewer: I think he'll be the pretext for you to express yourself on a thousand subjects. I wonder if you have any real personal attachment to Picasso's work?

Mailer: Picasso is good for my eyesight.

Interviewer: Look, I have a confession to make. Our last interview was a vast success in certain limited circles. Marvelous, people kept saying to me, the way you weren't afraid to talk back to Mailer. Oh, he's not so hard to talk to, I would tell them, he's really rather reasonable.

Mailer: So you have a vested interest in continuing to talk back to me.

Interviewer: Let's say I was innocent in the first interview, and didn't realize I was being that effective. Now I look at you professionally. I can't afford to have you drop my standards by making facetious remarks that Picasso is good for your eyesight.

Mailer: I was telling the simple truth. My eyes have been bad lately. I read a book for an hour and suffer eye-strain the rest of the day. Eye specialists have been useless. So have all sorts of eyeglasses. Even Mr. Huxley was no use. I tried the exercises in *The Art of Seeing*. They only strained my eyes somewhat further. But looking at Picassos does not tire them. In fact I've started work for the day with severe eye-strain, having awakened from a sleep which has been more or less satisfactory for every part of my body but my eyes, and after a morning of studying twenty, fifty, or a hundred reproductions of Picassos, my eyes have felt a bit relaxed for the first time in months.

Interviewer: Do you have any idea why this is so?

Mailer: The idea is too complex to be introduced so quickly. I would be obliged to compress it, and so seem facetious all over again.

Interviewer: Give me a hint.

Mailer: We see with the mind as well as the eye. Since the eye leads through the retina back to the mind, we can say that we see objects with two halves of the mind, with a physiological apparatus, and with a part of the psyche. If these two halves of the mind are critically different, one is seeing in two ways at once. Strain develops.

Interviewer: Sounds like schizophrenia.

Mailer: Nothing so royal. Look. If I read a line of prose, its immediate meaning is clear to my physical vision, to that part of my mind which is literal and therefore moves quickly. "Now is the time for all good men to come to the aid of the party" I read. "Perfectly clear" says the muscle of my eye, and moves on to the next sentence. But my conceptual faculty holds on to the sentence. It makes associations with the words. "Now" signifies the present, which is an enormous word to me. I write often of the enormous present, of psychopathy, of how mass man has no sense of past or future, just Now. So that word halts me conceptually. I cannot afford to ignore the way it is used in a sentence. And then there's "time" which is the most remarkable and mysterious of words. It's even more mysterious than "God." We can have an idea of God, most of us do sooner or later, but who has any concept of what time might be? And the construction, "Now is the time," which makes a subject and noun of "Now" is particularly interesting if one believes, as I sometimes do, that the secrets of existence, or some of them anyway, are to be found in the constructions of language which have come down to us. "Now is the time" is an odd way of putting things, as if "Now" is palpable and "time" is some sort of appurtenance which is attached to one place or to another, to Before, or to Now. I won't go into discussing "good men" or "party" but they are obviously capable of stirring a number of unconscious thoughts and dim associations which must be ignored if I'm to keep on reading at a reasonable rate. The result is that one part of my mind works against the other. My eyes begin to feel like an automobile driven by a man who has one foot on the accelerator, and the other on the brake.

Interviewer: Shouldn't this be true for all of us?

Mailer: No. Most people keep concepts firmly in category. "Now" is the flat quiet moment of the present, "time" is a few simple numbers one reads from a watch.

Interviewer: But not in their unconscious, I presume.

Mailer: Their unconscious doesn't erupt into the conscious routine acts of their daily life, as does mine. They save all larger thoughts for sleep, which is the tidy way to do it.

Interviewer: Whereas your ambition drove your unconscious out of the water, so to speak, and into the light.

Mailer: So to speak.

Interviewer: One of the ground rules is not to mock each other's metaphors.

Mailer: Certain artists, those who see associations and connections everywhere, tend to live in a psychic medium which is heavier, more dense, than the average man's. It is harder for them to move because there is more conscious mind for them to move. Joyce is the first example. And he went blind. Which does no harm to my thesis. If the mind reacts too powerfully to the stimuli before it, then the eye must see less in order to keep one's inner pressure at a bearable level. One goes blind not from seeing too little but from the overladen possibilities of seeing too much.

Interviewer: Almost as if there's a biological law.

Mailer: But I'm sure there is. Beauty, as the Greeks kept nagging, was harmony. Well, it has other qualities as well I hope, danger, ecstasy, promise, the transcendence of terror—all the emotions which give life to us in the West—but harmony, I fear, is what beauty is first. It means that separate parts function in a lively set of rhythms with one another. No organ is too fast or too slow vis-à-vis another organ. The pleasant relation inspires proportions in the outer forms which are healthy, harmonious, and beautiful.

Interviewer: This is not insignificant, you know.

Mailer: I know.

Interviewer: Hold on. You're saying that aesthetics is not abstract, that our concepts of beauty are not arbitrary but a function of nature.

Mailer: It's obviously more complicated than that. Upon occasion we can see beauty in disease, or beauty in the sinister, beauty even in the ugly. But that is because we have traveled a private road whose events have reinforced a few of our faculties. Compassion for example, illumines the ugly, makes it beautiful. As we look upon an ugly face—provided it is *our* kind of ugly face—we see how it could have been beautiful, we see the loss implicit in it, we feel tender toward the disproportionate or even anomalous development of features in it. Their inversion of beauty stimulates some inner sense in us of a beauty which failed to be, at least until that moment when we conceived that this ugly sight could have been beautiful. So at that instant, looking at a plain face we can feel intimations of beauty. Beauty—so runs this argument—has its root in any being which is harmonious, imaginative, adaptable, brave, artful, daring, good for life, good for the continuation of life.

Interviewer: Fantastic!

Mailer: Why?

Interviewer: Do you realize the enormity of what you're saying? It turns a good many ideas on their head.

Mailer: That is the function of fashion: to turn modest ideas on their head.

Interviewer: How about art for art's sake?

Mailer: Art for art's sake. My notion reinvigorates that notion, doesn't it?

Interviewer: Yes, because aesthetes are not going into an ivory tower any longer, not by your logic. If they devote themselves to a search for beauty, they are engaged in a most valuable act—at least, according to you—to discover those secrets of life which give life.

Mailer: Well, I don't know. Only noble artists discover noble secrets and manage to give them back as art. Most of the artists who believe in art for art's sake are over-elegant greedy sorts. The debate still continues, you see. One can argue which kind of life is harmonious and what is not. The leaves and vines Aubrey Beardsley adored so completely grew only in a hot-house, a conservatory, or a tropical garden. There was no toughness in such beauty.

Interviewer: But if a great artist believed in art for art's sake . . .

Mailer: He would be closer to life, I think, than a great politician who believed in politics for politics' sake.

Interviewer: I understand what you're saying about beauty, and I don't even know that I disagree with it, I mean I can see its relation to your sexual theories.

Mailer: Please don't anticipate the argument.

Interviewer: But in any case I don't see how you can apply your yardstick to the present. Look at the particular aesthetic experiences which give beauty to people today. In music, John Cage's One Minute and Thirty-six Seconds of Silence or whatever the title is; on the stage, The Connection, or Albee's work, or Tennessee Williams and his deep mahogany scatology; the novel, well leave it with William Burroughs whom you admire and his violent jangled shattering sense of obscenity; and then the Abstract Expressionists and their messes—

talk of scatology. I still don't understand their painting—and the Surrealists, full of abortions, Picasso and his mistresses whom he chooses to make look like monstrosities. Well, I could fulminate, I could say, "Call me Square and give me Velasquez," but to tell the truth I do get a sense of beauty from all these artists, or at least a sense of very private excitement like meeting a woman at a dinner party and knowing you were meant to go off with each other if you each had enough courage . . . Whereas Greek sculpture, natural function, that leaves me gasping up the Muse on a dead dead beach.

Mailer: It bores me as well. But it was the beginning of beauty. It stated the basic condition. Perhaps Greek sculpture is no longer so beautiful to us because it lacks the sense of danger with which we live.

Interviewer: Modern art has that sense of danger?

Mailer: It has a sense of doom.

Interviewer: Doom of what?

Mailer: The species. Take the artists you mentioned. Suppose the condition of our existence is now so plague-ridden that we have sunk beneath the level of scatology.

Interviewer: I don't follow. You mean we've sunk so low that scatological thoughts give life?

Mailer: For a good many people they do.

Interviewer: Life may not be so bad as that.

Mailer: There are horrors beneath the surface, cannibals in all of us, mad animals. And for a reason. It's as if we're stifling, as if the air we breathe is no longer air but some inert gas. (*Holds up a hand.*) Look, I've gotten into serious matters much too soon. I think a discussion of beauty is premature, I think it would need all of this book to explain anything at all. Let me say just that the modern condition may be psychically so bleak, so overextended, so artificial, so plastic—plastic like styrene—that studies of loneliness, silence, corruption, scatology, abortion, monstrosity, decadence, orgy, and death can give life, can give a sentiment of beauty.

Interviewer: You cannot desert the argument until you give some indication of how this is possible.

Mailer: May I use the word soul instead of psyche?

Interviewer: If it encourages the expression of ideas, yes.

Mailer: Postulate a modern soul marooned in constipation, emptiness, boredom and a flat dull terror of death. A soul which takes antibiotics when ill, smokes filter cigarettes, drinks proteins, minerals, and vitamins in a liquid diet, takes seconal to go to sleep, benzedrine to awake, and tranquilizers for poise. It is a deadened existence, afraid precisely of violence, cannibalism, loneliness, insanity, libidinousness, hell. perversion, and mess, because these are the states which must in some way be passed through, digested, transcended, if one is to make one's way back to life.

Interviewer: Why must they be passed through, transcended?

Mailer: Because the scatology is within and not without. The urge to eat another does not exist in some cannibal we watch in the jungle, but in the hinge of our own jaws. The love of death is not a mass phenomenon; it exists for each of us alone, our own private love of death. Just as our fear of death is also ours all alone. These states, these morbid states, as the old-fashioned psychologists used to say, can obtain relief only by coming to life in the psyche. But they can come to life only if they are ignited by an experience outside themselves. If I am secretly in love with death and terrified of it, then the effort to restrain and domesticate these emotions and impulses (which are no less than the cross-impulses of suicidal bravery and shame-ridden cowardice) exhaust so much of my will that my existence turns bleak. A dramatic encounter with death, an automobile accident from which I escape, a violent fight I win or lose decently, these all call forth my crossed impulses which love death and fear it. They give air to it. So these internal and deadly emotions are given life. In some cases, satisfied by the experience, they will subside a bit, give room to easier and more sensuous desires.

Interviewer: Not always?

Mailer: Not always. Hemingway, it seems, was never able to tame his dirty ape.

Interviewer: Dirty ape?

Mailer: It's a better word than id or anti-social impulse.

Interviewer: I think it is.

Mailer: Once we may have had a fine clean brave upstanding ape inside ourselves. It's just gotten dirty over the years.

Interviewer: Why couldn't Hemingway tame his ape?

Mailer: Because he may have had too wild a one inside him. The grandeur of one's work is a measure of how outrageous is the ape. People were always criticizing Hemingway for being self-destructive, obsessed with death, immersed too deeply in a cult of violence, perpetually trying his manhood, and so forth. Well, as I'll try to argue a little later, the first art work in an artist is the shaping of his own personality. An artist is usually such an incredible balance of opposites and incompatibles that the wonder is he can even remain alive. Hemingway was on the one hand a man of magnificent senses. There was a quick lithe animal in him. He was also shackled to a stunted ape, a cripple, a particularly wild dirty little dwarf within himself who wanted only to kill Hemingway. Life as a compromise was impossible. So long as Hemingway did not test himself, push himself beyond his own dares, flirt with, engage, and finally embrace death, in other words so long as he did not propitiate the dwarf, give the dwarf its chance to live and feel emotion, an emotion which could come to life only when one was close to death, Hemingway and the dwarf were doomed to dull and deaden one another in the dungeons of the psyche. Everyday life in such circumstances is a plague. The proper comment on Hemingway's style of life may be not that he dared death too much, but too little, that brave as he was, he was not brave enough, and the dwarf finally won. One does not judge Hemingway, but one can say that the sickness in him was not his love of violence but his inability to live as close to it as he had to. His proportions were tragic, he was all-but-doomed, it is possible he would have had to have been the bravest man who ever lived in order to propitiate the dwarf.

Interviewer: But at any rate, if I follow you, encounters with danger were not self-destructive but healthy for Hemingway.

Mailer: He could feel good next day. His psyche was out of the dungeon. He could work. His insides were not tense and empty.

Interviewer: Because—I'm trying to think in your way now—the death within him had met a death without, and so a temporary peace was found?

Mailer: Let's say he was going out to shoot a lion and felt marvelous. Well, there is a kind of mind which would say, "He's self-destructive. He feels good because he's going to kill himself." What I'm trying to argue is that he felt good because encountering death would give him more chance to live. From a very early age he must have felt his ordinary death within him (his routine sickbed death that is) as a kind of slow oncoming plague of washed-out memories and burned-up talents. So he was brave enough, as not many of us are, to go looking for death (since if he survived, his life would be better) but he was finally not brave enough to triumph at this kind of life. It was a desperate imbalance. What made him great as a writer was that he could ride it so long.

Interviewer: Talk of death always makes me contemplate loneliness. You've stimulated me. I think I could guess now what you might say about John Cage and his silent musical compositions.

Mailer: What would I say?

Interviewer: Well, roughly, that there is a frightening detachment in each of us, an inner silence, neither divine nor doomed, just lost in endless orbit. Nothing seems able to reach it. It is as if our souls are stricken. An arbitrary period of silence in a concert hall might encounter that anguish. There, could you have said it better?

Mailer: I would have tried to find one turn of wit.

Interviewer: Well I'm new at this.

Mailer: You're doing all right.

Interviewer: I must say your ideas are not unathletic. I feel more or less vigorous now.

Mailer: Still, you were leading up to a point. And you seem to have lost it.

Interviewer: Oh! Wait! What was I talking about?

Mailer: Many things. Were you leading up to the mess?

Interviewer: Scatology. Of course. Death may be noble, and loneliness also, but how does a scatological art work raise the reader or the audience to catharsis? Why is such an aesthetic experience good for life?

Mailer: I don't want to discuss scatology now. It's too complex. It may be more complex than death. So I'm going to stay away from this now. I prefer to steal back to it from time to time.

Interviewer: You have to give a hint, however.

Mailer: Why must I?

Interviewer: I hoped I could avoid having to say this, but your name does not inspire the sort of confidence which keeps people waiting. You are not Lord Russell after all, or Wittgenstein, or Heidegger, or Sartre.

Mailer: Not yet.

Interviewer: Perhaps not ever.

Mailer: No doubt never.

Interviewer: A hint.

Mailer: Feces are seen as the most distasteful and despised condition of being. They are precisely that part of the alimentation in the universe which we have rejected, and, mind you, rejected not morally, not emotionally, not passionately . . .

Interviewer: In the sense that vomit is passionate?

Mailer: In the sense that vomit is passionate. No, feces have been rejected viscerally. It is our being, our organism, which rejects them. They are a total statement of our nature. This cannot be used, says our nature, this is not to be absorbed but to be cast away, this is to be not chosen. From deep within ourselves, our cells have chosen what can be used and what can not. Nothing is more despised than what we have chosen not to want.

Interviewer: I've heard the Arabs feel so strongly about this, that they institutionalize their hands. With their right hand they eat and wash their faces. With their left hand they wipe themselves. The left hand is never allowed to touch food.

Mailer: Yes.

Interviewer: One hand for life, the other for death.

Mailer: You set up your opposites much too neatly. An attractive opposite, tersely worded, can bury more thought than it uncovers. One hand for life, the other for death.

Interviewer: What does that bury?

Mailer: Why, it buries one's understanding that feces are not equivalent to death, and that all of us have a very bad conscience about shit which is exactly why it is so obsessive to us.

Interviewer: Would a healthy man have a bad conscience?

Mailer: No. But few of us qualify for the word. Our characters are usually not as rich as the food we eat.

Interviewer: So we excrete not only what we despise but what is too good for us as well?

Mailer: Or too special. The act of elimination is excruciating to some part of the psyche. I expect it is the part which governs the digestive processes of the body. Because we eat, I imagine, not what our cells need, so much as what our habits demand.

Interviewer: Suddenly, you're too abstract for me.

Mailer: I'm saying that a cell is like a little animal. It knows exactly what it wants to eat, what is good for it. But a cell is not a psychic structure. It may be a part of the machine which makes up a habit, it may work for a habit, but it has no powers of command. It cannot choose what it wants, it can only receive it.

Interviewer: Please carry this further.

Mailer: A habit is a psychic structure. What it's composed of literally need not concern us, but since it is a construction of mind which sits in authority upon the body, we can think of it as a law which is intangible but more or less absolute in its effect upon citizens.

Interviewer: Make this concrete. You're still too metaphorical.

Mailer: A man goes into a store to choose some food. His cells, a good many of them, let us say, need calves' liver that evening, but his habit is to please his dinner guests and liver seems insufficiently festive, so frogs' legs are ordered. Later that night, the cells make do with frogs' legs, but liver was their need.

Interviewer: You're speaking of a decision; of a choice, not a habit.

Mailer: The habit is at several removes from the cells. The habit is to please one's guests. If liver is out of fashion, it will not please the guests. The habit which dominates the cells is that they must conform to fashion. What is significant here is that the part in a civilized man which makes the decision to choose his food has little to do with his need.

Interviewer: You would argue that he can't feel his need as clearly as a savage would.

Mailer: Of course not. Habits usually are anti-neurological structures. They are built up and they are maintained precisely by insulating our senses from most stimuli.

Interviewer: I don't see how you have anchored this thesis. Your man wanted liver, he got frogs' legs, but what's there to keep him from making the best of it, from extracting the good juices out of the meat in old Froggie's thigh, and getting rid of the gristle? Where does bad conscience come in?

Mailer: You have the instinctive vice of American thought.

Interviewer: You're just annoyed because I blew a hole in your thesis.

Mailer: But you didn't. You took my example, assumed it was all of the reality, and proceeded to draw a moral to your own satisfaction. But I gave you just a few of the facts, not all of them. Reality is always more complex than the example. That's why I hate to get into explanation too soon.

Interviewer: Defend your thesis.

Mailer: My man ordered frogs' legs. But the urgency of his cells, their cry for liver, registered as a dull lust in his mind. So as he stared about the Gourmet shop, he bought a little tin of foie gras.

Interviewer: You didn't mention this before.

Mailer: An example is not a logical universe. I can do with an example whatever I wish, because its purpose is to explain, not to prove.

Interviewer: I concede, but I still think it's unfair.

Mailer: He eats the foie gras with his drinks, eats it with relish. Ceremoniously it enters his stomach which receives it like a High Church serves a rich wedding. But there is so little foie gras! And he cannot gorge. He must serve his guests first. Which involves other habits. Habit-life precedes cell-life in civilized man. Just a little foie gras and his cells need a lot of liver. Upon this cruel disproportion follows another—the frogs' legs. The part of the psyche which over-sees digestion, let us call it The Eater, has to make a new decision, because its powers of digestion cannot do an equally good job on liver and frogs' legs both.

Interviewer: Why not?

Mailer: Because the chemicals necessary for each would adulter-ate one another.

Interviewer: Is there scientific proof of this?

Mailer: I'm sure there's not. I invoke a simpler principle. One can't do two good and difficult things at once and do them both very well. I can't write a book with my right hand and paint a picture with my left. At the same instant, I can't make love and sing high opera. Nor can I digest foie gras and frogs' legs equally well. One or the other must suffer.

Interviewer: Your stomach may not work the way you do.

Mailer: It's bound to. There would be very few problems in life if our organs could perform two or more complex highly differentiated functions equally well at once.

Interviewer: For the sake of the argument I concede again. I want to know where you're heading. I think I see it.

Mailer: If you do, take over yourself.

Interviewer: Go one more step.

Mailer: The Eater chooses the frogs' legs. Reluctantly. He would prefer the foie gras, but there is simply not enough and the intestines would have too much work evacuating half-digested frog flesh—I exaggerate the imperfection of the process, of course. Therefore, the arts of digestion are applied to the frogs' legs. The best sweets in the foie gras, digested as formal second choice, are lost. The inner savory of their wealth is not reached.

Interviewer: Why not?

Mailer: Because life in its need to protect itself tends to make what is best in itself most inaccessible.

Interviewer: Whereas civilization tries to make the best in itself most available.

Mailer: Well, it would claim to.

Interviewer: I think that's the first ideal of democracy. To make the best most available. What a logical impasse! In your terms democracy is then opposed to life.

Mailer: It endangers life in the name of a noble ideal.

Interviewer: We'll never get to Picasso, thank God.

Mailer: We're getting there. Once we look at the pictures I won't want to stop in order to discuss these matters. But now I must ask you: I know where we are, but where *were* we?

Interviewer: Yes. I know. The foie gras. The best of it was lost. The richest parts.

Mailer: The Eater took a middle course. What was useless, despicable, or uninteresting in the frogs' legs and in the foie gras was eliminated. But what was superior in the foie gras was also lost.

Interviewer: So in despising his waste, the man is partially dishonest.

Mailer: Since his cells cannot inform him of the small tragedy they underwent last night, he has only an imperfect sense that there was something wrong with the foie gras. "It disagrees with me," he says, "I won't order it any more." Three days later he buys three cans, gorges on it at lunch, and then upbraids himself for lacking discipline and eating the things which are bad for him. Except for this sense of guilt at his poor character, it would have been a marvelous lunch.

Interviewer: You're saying that civilization hurts the inner communication of mind to body and body to mind.

Mailer: Go further. Say the obsession of many of us for scatology is attached to the disrupted communication within us, within our bodies.

Interviewer: I had the impression for just an instant that there's a theory of disease possible in this somewhere.

Mailer: There is the possibility of illness every time opposites do not meet or meet poorly, just as there is the air to gain life every time opposites meet each other nicely.

Interviewer: Dilate a bit on this.

Mailer: They can be opposites within us—the part of my eye which sees physiologically as opposed to that part which views conceptually. But one can speak of opposites between man and nature, or man and man: the water I drink, the block of marble worked by the sculptor, the audience and the play, a mood and its occasion, the good rider and his good horse, the blocking back and the line-backer, the skier on the snow, the style of sex, a sail into the wind. I become conventionally rhapsodic, the point is that life seems to come out of the meeting of opposites. Communication is a poor word, because life does not come from communication but from meetings, from opposites coming together.

Interviewer: Communications has a technological connotation to me.

Mailer: It involves machines and electronic apparatus and services of distribution. It invariably implies the injection of information into a passive being. But one can use it in speaking of the body, one can say that a particular part of the body communicates poorly with another part because we are by now not only biological but mechanical. There are habits in all of us which function with the precision of a machine. And when certain functions in our body are unable to meet other functions at the necessary instant, one can speak of a failure of communication. One may even well suspect that the basis of chronic disease and the excessive virulence of much infectious disease, particularly the viruses, comes precisely from an inner field of communications which is poorly designed or badly abused. The message which did not get from Ghent to Aix is the metaphor for a drama which goes on constantly within us. My man who wanted liver and got frogs' legs would, if his stomach had been able to speak to him with the clear simple chords of an animal's belly, have escaped bad conscience and a touch of indigestion.

Interviewer: But if bad communication is virtually the sole basis of disease—a fascinating concept, by the way—why do you equate it to scatology or at least make the connection there?

Mailer: Because feces are the material evidence of the processes of communication within us. Life comes from the meeting of opposites.

Conceive of man as a tube, mouth at one end, anus at the other. In that sense man is like a worm, a pipe, a tunnel, a drill which bores through a bed of nutrition, disgorging it behind. We cannot see the air we exhale, not normally, not unless we have tobacco smoke with which to shape it, but we can study our urine and feces. In one way or another, most of us do. They are the expression of what we have done well and what we have done badly to that medium of food through which we passed. When we have communicated nicely within ourselves, the stool reflects a simple reasonable operation (cowflop is for example, modest in its odor) but where we have failed, as with the foie gras, the odors and shapes are tortured, corrupt, rich, fascinating (that is attractive and repulsive at the same time), theatrical, even tragic. There are odors not alien to beauty in the dung. The sense of life they give has tragic beauty which tells us something rare and very good for us has been lost again, something fine is just beginning to rot. The history of the life we never see within us, its triumphs, tragedies, states of calm and states of inanition are returned to us in the color, the shape, the odor and the movement of our stool. For those qualities are the curious stricken record of our near past. We despise what we had once and now can possess no longer, especially if we fear having used it badly. Yet we cannot forsake it altogether. Obsessively we return to the study because hope for how to turn our life into more life is contained in that history.

Interviewer: Eloquent. I must observe that it is rash for you to be too eloquent on this subject.

Mailer: I wished to avoid it earlier.

Interviewer: True enough. But since we now find ourselves here, let me say I still don't understand, not really, the intense virulence of people's reactions to scatology.

Mailer: Perhaps the prophetic aspects create the rage.

Interviewer: I don't follow you.

Mailer: The food you ate yesterday was too rich for you, says the odor in the water closet. Eat as improperly today and you will be ill. But this is much too simple. Say rather that the senses bring deep messages to the unconscious, quick deep messages. And they are measured carefully by the scale of past experience. A carpenter makes a hundred measurements a day. If you ask him to mark off five inches without a tape, he is bound to be able to do it within an eighth of an inch. So it is with our stool. Our senses know what it says to us. But so often the messages are intolerable. You are sickening slowly, remarks the wad, your life as you lead it now is hopeless. You must engage death, perversion, promiscuity, and the fear of hell before you will be better. Your health is to eat the body of your mate, your secret desire is to be trampled in an orgy. This is what the oracle of the unconscious may divine from the feces. No wonder shit is despised. Its message is too terrible.

Interviewer: Isn't this a little too much to discover from the inner history of a meal?

Mailer: Food possesses character. We consume character when we eat.

Interviewer: I'm not so certain. Food may be no more than food. How do we know it isn't?

Mailer: I don't. I guess. It seems more reasonable to me that food possess character than that it doesn't. One man leads a sedentary life, and another works hard, wouldn't the bicep of one be different in character from the other? Why, if we were to eat both biceps . . .

Interviewer: You take the plunge into cannibalism?

Mailer: Only for the sake of the argument that one bicep would communicate qualities of strength, fortitude, and discipline, whereas the other would tend to make one lazy, slack, and unregenerate.

Interviewer: But which is which?

Mailer: I assume the worker's bicep communicates fortitude and power.

Interviewer: It might be just the reverse. The worker's arm might be disgusted, used up. All that's left in his cells which can feed you is the desire to be lazy. Whereas the lazy arm is bursting with unused energy.

Mailer: Three cheers for overtaking me. But will you now agree that food may possess character?

Interviewer: We don't know what character it possesses.

Mailer: I suspect our unconscious does.

Interviewer: How convenient is this unconscious.

Mailer: The hand is plucked instinctively from the flame before the mind realizes the finger is in the fire. Let's save time. Of course the unconscious is close to the senses, it is the animal part of oneself. And it studies what it eats, it knows the inner life of the body's organs, it hears what has happened to the food, what qualities it possessed, what reactions it aroused. Take steak, assume it provides strength for the muscles. Or if not steak there must be obvously one or another particular food to provide such strength. Whatever the food may be which offers strength, we can be sure it is good for a man doing heavy work, and that it is probably poor for a lady whose strength may depend upon the excellent demands of her weakness. For an intellectual beginning a program of conditioning exercises, steak may be just a little too full of strength, it may fire his muscles into doing too much too soon. So The Eater might decide to digest the steak cursorily, might decide to pass by the molecules containing the kernel of the strength. The stool, bursting next day with the most vital elements of the steak might give back in its form and odor the dispiriting news that The Eater in the intellectual had indeed decided he was not yet strong enough for steak.

Interviewer: But if The Eater knows this already and so makes a decision to eschew the qualities of finest strength in the steak, why does the unconscious have to discover it in the stool? I thought The Eater was part of the unconscious.

Mailer: Not all parts of the unconscious communicate perfectly well with one another. That is part of the theory of disease we postulated. There are ways for the unconscious to speak from one part of itself to another, but we are not always able to use them.

Interviewer: Being receptive to the message of the bowels is one way?

Mailer: Children are always asking you to look at their stool, and are disappointed when we say, "That's nice, dear," and turn away.

Interviewer: You're saying that our prevailing social habit is to lay a foundation in the child for a future failure of communication?

Mailer: In certain people this particular tension is sufficient to find not only the sight but the subject of feces quite sickening. It is for example particularly abhorrent to the English. Their intellectual categories offer no course in the archaeology of the Self. The French on the other hand know that *merde* has a purchase on fortune.

Interviewer: I don't want to be grisly, but if old scata has so much to do with fortune and telling the future, why aren't there cults? Why isn't divination from the stool some small but worthy competitor of the horoscope or numerology?

Mailer: People who go to hear their fortune are not existentialists, but essentialists. Full of self-pity, they wish to believe that their fortune is already written, and to their advantage of course. They do not want to discover that they are still responsible for what they do with themselves. So what kind of interest could they have in any testament of the bowels which might speak of the history within themselves? Such study reveals character—informs them of their moral fortune.

Interviewer: What is moral fortune? I never heard that expression before.

Mailer: If there is Heaven and if Hell exists, one's moral fortune indicates where one is likely to go. I suppose it is not unlikely that a man bound for Hell could sniff out the fact this was his destination. Such a man might detest all thought of shit.

Interviewer: Herr Doktor, you've been talking about the bowels much too long, and it's getting on my nerves.

Mailer: The trouble is that I have to present one more large annoying idea before we can go on.

Interviewer: Certain large ideas can be expressed briefly.

Mailer: You'll agree that a society is best judged by the way it treats the citizens, the slaves, the subjects, the masses who compose it.

Interviewer: What do you want to say?

Mailer: That food be considered capable of possessing a soul.

Interviewer: You mean that as we eat we are like a society acting upon its citizens, that food clanks from its cradle to the tomb as through us it moves, that noble souls in the food are not sufficiently appreciated by us and so die tragically, just as societies sometimes lose the gifts of some of their best men? Presenting this enormous metaphor merely to say that food has a soul! Why should it, why indeed should food have a soul?

Mailer: Because it is a being.

Interviewer: A being. It's a good existential word, I know, but you've got to do something for it. What is a being? Please don't tell me a being is something which is alive.

Mailer: I won't. Especially since certain organisms which are alive cannot be called beings.

Interviewer: Then a being is not all of life?

Mailer: A being is anything which lives and still has the potentiality to change, to change physically and to change morally. A person who has lost all capacity for fundamental change is no longer a being.

Interviewer: Being is used then as synonymous to soul?

Mailer: Soul is eternal. At least that is the general agreement on its meaning. Soul is what continues to live after we are dead. It is possible, I should think, that if the soul does exist, that if there is such an entity, that if there is indeed a part of us which is eternal, or which can under certain conditions remain eternal, that the soul could well have the property of being able to migrate from body to body, from existence to existence, sometimes rising, sometimes falling, sometimes getting lost forever.

Interviewer: Whereas being is corporeal, is there before the eyes?

Mailer: I think so. I would assume that when the soul enters a particular tangible existence, it weds itself to that existence. So long as the soul is part of a creature it is not free of it, not free to leave when it chooses, not unless sudden death is chosen. So long as the soul resides in a body or is trapped in a body or at war in a body or indeed even enamored of the body in which it finds itself, the soul must exist in a relation with that body which is not unlike marriage. The soul affects the body, the body is able to affect the soul, they grow together or apart, they are good for one another or merely cool and efficient, tolerating one another because they would be savage and wasteful if apart. A panoply of possibilities exists in every being, because a being is a creature which lives in the world, which has shape, color, form, which has life and a soul within it, a soul which will be changed by its existence in the world. Or at least that is how I would postulate a being.

Interviewer: Being is the existence of soul in the world?

Mailer: Being is first the body we see before us. That body we see before us is that moment of the present for a soul, a soul which must inevitably be altered for better, for worse, or for better and worse by its presence in a body.

Interviewer: And individual cells have souls, individual souls?

Mailer: I think they do. I think everything which lives had a soul at its birth, or it could not otherwise have been born.

Interviewer: Fresh food has a soul?

Mailer: Yes, usually.

Interviewer: But canned food. What about that?

Mailer: Less soul.

Interviewer: It's dead.

Mailer: Not altogether. Let's say for the present it's in a kind of limbo. What characterizes food, I would speculate, is that the soul tries to cling to it as long as it can. A tin of sardines is still a being of sorts, a being of a lesser category. It may not be alive as an organism, but its flesh retains life, the cells have not rotted, the protein molecules are intact, if you will, and the oils and the carbohydrates still retain in their structure the character of the sardine.

Interviewer: Let me recapitulate. Character in this case is the still-standing structure of the carbon molecule given the cells by the previous history within one little sardine of its soul at war with and/or loving its body?

Mailer: Let's say the soul left a taste. Some sardines taste better than others.

Interviewer: It's one thing to have a taste. It's another to have a soul.

Mailer: Why does one sardine taste better than another?

Interviewer: Because its meat is better.

Mailer: What does that mean?

Interviewer: The meat is healthier, that's all.

Mailer: And health? What is that?

Interviewer: A harmonious condition of body.

Mailer: How does that come about?

Interviewer: In the case of the sardine?

Mailer: Yes.

Interviewer: From being a better swimmer than the average sardine. Naturally good constitution inherited from its mother.

Mailer: Who was also a superior swimmer?

Interviewer: Yes.

Mailer: Why was she so good?

Interviewer: You're tireless.

Mailer: Humorless.

Interviewer: You're going to insist the mother's soul was superior to the soul of other sardines and so left a superior taste?

Mailer: I think I will.

Interviewer: Why this passion to put the soul into the sardine?

Mailer: Because the act of eating is always a small execution.

Interviewer: And you find it less hideous if a soul is released, as a cell is devoured?

Mailer: If I believed a calf had one single chance to live, no more, I could not in good conscience eat it. I might eat it anyway but logic would say I should be a vegetarian.

Interviewer: Whereas now, the soul of the calf passes into you, becomes a part of your being.

Mailer: Yes.

Interviewer: I see now why Mexicans eat bull's balls.

Mailer: A delicacy.

Interviewer: Why don't all men eat bull's balls? Why aren't they worth twice their weight in platinum?

Mailer: Because very few people are ready to receive them.

Interviewer: You mean your soul has to be the equal of the souls you ingest?

Mailer: There has to be a meeting of opposites.

Interviewer: A feminine man would enjoy bull's balls?

Mailer: Or a masculine man. You mustn't puzzle too hard at these celestial mechanics.

Interviewer: Oh, I think they're first rate, I just don't navigate among them too well as yet.

Mailer: Your approach lacks existential ease.

Interviewer: Teach me the new grace.

Mailer: Allow me then to signify the bull's balls as equal to virility. For the sake of my demonstration let it be that whoever eats them gains virility. The meeting of opposites takes place therefore between a male principle, the bull's balls, and something female in the soul of the man who eats.

Interviewer: Or the woman.

Mailer: Or the woman. It doesn't matter, you see, whether you have a masculine man, a feminine man, a masculine woman, or a feminine woman. What characterizes all of them is that in partaking of the bull's balls each of them wishes to gain virility.

Interviewer: To simplify it, let's speak just of men. Why, in the first place, wouldn't all men wish to gain virility?

Mailer: Virility implies more than the stamina of a stud. It offers power, strength, the ability to command, the desire to alter life. So its consequences in life are often to increase responsibility or danger. A virile man can be afraid of more virility. If he's driving his car too fast already, he may look for cream of chicken or malted milk. So with the feminine man. He may not want more virility because he has no habits for it. What's the use of commanding women he could not command before, if he does not know how to fight off other men, and is not ready to learn. What freezes the homosexual in his homosexuality is not fear of women so much as fear of the masculine world with which he must war if he wishes to keep the woman.

Interviewer: What you're saying then might be put this way: in choosing bull's balls, the man whether strong or weak must be ready to offer up something feminine in himself. So as to leave himself less feminine afterward?

Mailer: Perfect.

Interviewer: Which is to say that we cannot select effectively unless the action we choose exists in a real and close correspondence to the new proportions our soul desires for itself.

Mailer: Yes.

Interviewer: If we wish to be more masculine we must first satisfy something feminine in ourselves.

Mailer: The reverse is also true. If we eat a bland food, a food we can dominate completely, that is to say a food whose character, whose—permit me—whose echo of the soul, is compliant, tender, passive to our seizure of it, we satisfy something masculine in ourselves. A man with ulcers is burning with the masculine need to dominate details in his life he simply cannot dominate. So in drinking milk, a bland food, a food more feminine than himself, he can discharge this backed-up masculinity. But of course he uses up masculinity in eating bland food, he alters his proportions.

Interviewer: You imply he has no choice?

Mailer: Not if he's sick with an ulcer. Bull's balls and tequila would have him run amok or fall into a hospital bed.

Interviewer: Since the proportion of masculinity and femininity in oneself would tend I think to remain more or less stable, what it comes down to is that people choose bull's balls only when they want to change.

Mailer: Yes. Only a few people want bull's balls at any one time. The existential gamble is too fine, it leads to greater seriousness, greater commitment in one's life, or to greater danger. One might think one wanted such change, but at the moment of digesting it, at the moment of choosing to open those reservoirs of enzymes, those ductless glands which are able to reach the finest molecules, The Eater might to his surprise feel panic, might be too cowardly to take on the consequences implicit in the essence of true bull's balls. So an imperfect cowardly digestion would take place. And its odor, the odor of fear, would be revealed next day in the stool, revealed to that part of the unconscious we may just as well begin to call The Critic. The Critic having a fine edge for form would also detect that the shape of the stool was slack.

Interviewer: If The Eater accepted the challenge, the stool would be different?

Mailer: The smell of a decent death would be present, the soul in the balls of the bull would have entered the body of the man who ate it. That particular soul would have risen to a higher existence. So the stool would have an aroma of content. As indeed it often does. What is so particularly hideous in a really bad smell is that one breathes the odor of a partial death, a soul has been torn on a rack. Part of it was seized by The Eater, part was refused, and so is dying in the stool.

Interviewer: Is it always the fault of The Eater? What if the food is bad?

Mailer: Then the choice is more complex, as for fact it always is in life. For no food is altogether perfect, and if it is almost perfect, it is still bound to have a most particular character which may not correspond too closely to the specific need of The Eater. Sometimes good food cannot be digested well because the requirements of The Eater were too narrow. So the partial death of the food might smell bitter, it would know the bitterness of being rejected by a larger being which was too stingy. Or conversely it might be digested too greedily, too avariciously, by The Eater, and so suggest it was bruised. Such a death might smell of wine. The corruption of The Eater would be present within it.

Interviewer: And bad food. What of bad food?

Mailer: Its death would almost always be partial I should think, and it would be drowned in bile, the body of The Eater would express his contempt at how bad the life had been, at how little the death had to offer. But if the best were extracted from the bad food, its odor might also prove decent or half-decent. It might have died well.

Interviewer: How could that be?

Mailer: Something good in the bad food might have taken a brave leap and met The Eater. So there might be some trace of dignity in the death of those souls. They might be complete, not partial. There might be the decent smell of a hay field. Grass and weeds are mediocre after all, but their death is complete when they're reaped, and if the weather is good they die well. There are arts to digesting bad food. The poor know them better than the rich. Most of the people on earth would get indigestion from good food.

Interviewer: What about the man with ulcers?

Mailer: The greater part of milk becomes urine and urine is another discussion.

Interviewer: No soul in it?

Mailer: Just spirit.

Interviewer: To think I asked a simple question about a man with an ulcer who takes a glass of milk.

Mailer: I wish you hadn't.

Interviewer: Do you feel ready to discuss the meaning of urine and its link to the Spirit?

Mailer: I don't. I fear I don't. It is a day's journey.

Interviewer: Later perhaps.

Mailer: Later. We must discuss it later.

Interviewer: Let's go back to where we were.

Mailer (*gloomily*): I distrust all talk of Soul and Spirit. I dislike styles which use such words.

Interviewer: I want to know what happens with food which is the reverse of bull's balls, with food which is weaker than The Eater, calming, sedative, gentle, feminine, creamed chicken and so on.

Mailer: A brave man who wishes to become less brave is eating it?

Interviewer: If you wish.

Mailer: At the critical moment, at the meeting of the opposites, he might give up his courage with grace, he might absorb the gentler qualities his being requested for that meal with good spirit and deep relaxation. His stool would have a happy smell. A gentle soul would have been received completely. But if, at the critical moment, The Eater rebelled, was horrified at the amount of manliness which must be devoted to the chicken, if The Eater felt shame at deserting danger and looking for calm, then indeed the chicken would be poorly used, the death of its souls would be most incomplete, and the odor would be sour. Gentleness refused turns sour. It curdles.

Interviewer: You're saying that the secret emotions of one's being, the basic emotions, courage and cowardice, betray their presence in the odor.

Mailer: And greed as well, or cupidity, ambition, compassion, love, trust, tenderness, savagery. The way in which we take souls from the food is the mirror of the dirty ape inside. If most of us abhor shit, it is because most of us are a little hideous inside.

Interviewer: Tyrants to the weak?

Mailer: Tyrants to the souls in the food who at that moment are more helpless than ourselves. Beyond a doubt.

Interviewer: Of course there's always ptomaine.

Mailer (*ignoring this*): Ambitious people pass bad shit. Because they use people around them. They certainly use people who are under them. I once met a very wealthy man whose mistress could talk about nothing but food. She was obsessed with what everyone around her had had to eat that day. It's taken me until now to realize that she saw herself as food for the tycoon, his family, and friends. Everyone at her dinner table was a potential cannibal to her person. So she had to know what you ate the night before because that to her was a clue which showed whether you had designs on her precise flesh.

Interviewer: You mean she saw herself as a certain kind of food?

Mailer: Rock hen, no doubt.

Interviewer: You're beginning to enjoy yourself too much. I think it's time we closed for the day.

Mailer: What a long day.

Interviewer: Would you round off our inquiry with a remark?

Mailer: A commercial remark?

Interviewer: Let us say a capsule.

Mailer: Ambitious societies loathe scatological themes and are obsessed with them.

Interviewer: Disappointing.

Mailer: Not at all. One could study the past with such a thesis as the tool. If indications in Mayan culture show much scatology, one can assume that civilization died from an excess of ambition which throttled the Being of too many.

Interviewer: And if there is no trace of scatology?

Mailer: If by the internal logic of the findings, the art, the fecal or non-fecal forms of the pottery, the wall painting, the architecture, there seems little scatology, one may assume there was not enough ambition, that the culture was calm, well-regulated, and was probably destroyed by a catastrophe which left it too passive to find the power to rise again.

Interviewer: You're enjoying yourself much too much. Tomorrow you must speak more of form.

Mailer: I will not enjoy myself much tomorrow.

Interviewer: You know you never came back to Picasso and why he is good for your eyes.

Mailer: Now I fear we will never get back.

Interviewer: Of course we will. Why not?

Mailer: Beyond form, is soul, spirit, madness, eternity, and the void.

Interviewer: I will try to sleep on that.

APPENDIX A—Professional Mendacity

From a review of *The Fine Art of Literary Mayhem*, by Myrick Land, in *Time* Magazine, January 18, 1963:

> Why did they feud? Says Novelists Vance Bourjaily, *characterized* by his friend Norman Mailer as *"insignificant"*: "Literary feuding is one of a number of fairly silly things which writers do when they're not writing well . . . a sort of athletic metaphor for our real situation, and a very inaccurate one." (Italics mine.)

This is the passage in Land's book from which the *Time* reviewer took his first quotation:

> In *Advertisements for Myself*, Mailer had decided that the first two novels of his off-and-on friend, Vance Bourjaily, were "insignificant." He had also said that Bourjaily was a writer who had survived because of his "really nice gifts as a politician."

". . . I kept expecting him [Bourjaily] to go Madison Avenue," he had written. "I was certain he would sell out sooner or later. Instead he did the opposite, wrote a novel called *The Violated*, which is a good long honest novel . . . He is the first of my crowd to have taken a major step forward, and if his next novel is as superior to *The Violated* as was *The Violated* to his early work, he could end up being champion for a while . . ."

He had then added:

"But I doubt if he could hold the title in a strong field, for his taint is to be cute."

Bourjaily's words on literary feuding appear in a four-page letter he wrote to Myrick Land. This letter was printed in the book the reviewer had read. Let me quote from another part of that letter:

I wrote to Norman (after reading *Advertisements*), thanked him for what he'd said about me that was favorable [and] added an obscenity for the rest . . .

Then, referring to a letter I wrote back to him, Bourjaily went on:

[Mailer's letter] was pretty much like mine in tone, or like I think mine was in tone—candid enough about points of difference, *but with none of the dramatic reproaches which inaugurate feuding*. (Italics mine.)

If Henry Luce learned the art of proper quotation at Yale, one is satisfied, Mr. President, to come from Harvard.

APPENDIX B—Projects and Places

I've always felt professional curiosity for the chronological details of other writers' work. Here in this appendix (like the data appended by photographers to their pictures) are some details about the pieces included in this book. Unless specifically mentioned, the work was done in New York, and the piece is uncut. Generally the period an article was worked on is given as well as the place and month of publication, but for the columns taken from *Esquire* and *Commentary*, this has not been done since all of these columns were written from a month to two months before publication.

"A Program for the Nation" was written at two or three in the morning some time in February, 1959. It was printed in *Dissent*, Winter, 1960. Trimmed slightly for publication here: some of its ideas are repeated in other pieces.

" 'She Thought the Russians Was Coming' " was written in February, 1960. It was printed in *Esquire*, June, 1960, and reprinted in *Dissent*, Summer, 1961.

"Superman Comes to the Supermarket" was written in late July and August of 1960 at Provincetown. It was printed in *Esquire*, November, 1960. The title of the piece was changed by the editors without my knowledge from "Superman Comes to the Supermarket" to "Superman Comes to the Supermart." Here, I've changed the title back. The intercalations (the advertisements in italics between each section) were done by an editor at *Esquire*. I've trimmed them for publication here.

The "Open Letter to John Fitzgerald Kennedy and Fidel Castro" was obviously written at two separate periods. The letter to Castro was finished in November, 1960; the letter to JFK was done in April, 1961, the week after the Bay of Pigs. It was printed in the April 27, 1961, issue of the *Village Voice*. Earlier that week I had submitted the Castro letter to the New York *Times*, the New York *Herald Tribune*, and the New York *Post*. None of them would print it, not in full nor in excerpt.

"An Evening with Jackie Kennedy" was begun in Villefranche in March, 1962, continued in Paris, and finished in New York in May, 1962. Since one had stopped smoking in January, the writing went slowly. Published in *Esquire* in July, 1962.

The Miscellany begins with cuttings from my column, "The Big Bite," in the November and December, 1962, and January and March, 1963, issues of *Esquire*. They are printed in sequence here.

The second "Open Letter to JFK" was written in the middle of December, 1962, and was printed in the *Voice*, December 20, 1962.

The poems were written at odd periods in 1961 and 1962. Unless otherwise mentioned they were published in *Deaths for the Ladies*, G. P. Putnam's Sons, March, 1962. "Open Poem to JFK" was written in Bucks County in October, 1961, and published in the *Voice*, November 23, 1961. "A Glass of Milk" was published in the *Voice*, February 1, 1962. "Poem to the Book Review at *Time*" was written in answer to a review of *Deaths for the Ladies* in *Time* Magazine, March 30, 1962, and was published in their Letters column, April 6, 1962. One of the poems, "Interplanetary," from *Deaths for the Ladies*, was cut.

The "Impolite Interview" was recorded in October, 1962, with

Paul Krassner, over several hours. The transcript was returned to me in December and worked over during odd periods in the next few weeks. It was published in *The Realist*, Issue #40. It was printed with the following preface:

> This interview is not a verbatim record of the tape. Paul Krassner gave me the option to go through the transcript, edit it for repetitions, and add material where I chose. I did this. I did not try too much to round off my remarks or write little essays but did my best to keep the additions in the rough style of the original. While it would give a false impression to pretend that the interview as printed here is faithful to the original, I would like to think it is true to the mood of what was said, to the sound of our voices, and to three-quarters of our literal speech.
>
> N.M.

It has been cut again for publication here to four-fifths of its original printed length.

"Responses and Reactions II" was in *Commentary*, February, 1963.

The *Esquire* column on the week when New York waited for nuclear war was printed in *Esquire*, April, 1963. Several paragraphs were cut.

"The Real Meaning of the Right Wing in America" was written during September, 1962. It was published in *Playboy* in January, 1963, and to my great pain was retitled: "The Role of the Right Wing in America Today" and subtitled: "A Liberal's View." I wrote a letter to *Playboy* which was printed in February begging the editors to call me anything but a Liberal.

The two short pieces about totalitarianism come from *Esquire* columns in the May and August, 1963, issues.

"Responses and Reactions I, III, IV," were written for *Commentary* and appeared in the December, 1962, issue, and the April and June, 1963, issues. To the first column (which was here cut) was prefaced the following note:

> Martin Buber's two-volume collection, *Tales of the Hasidim*, has probably had a greater impact on non-Jewish writers—whether theologically inclined or theologically indifferent—than any other Jewish book of recent times. But the *Tales* have perhaps worked an even more powerful fascination on Jewish writers and intellectuals, and particularly on those who

stand outside the organized Jewish community. Prominent among the latter group is Norman Mailer, whose informal bimonthly column on the *Tales* appears for the first time in this issue.

The review of *The Blacks* was written over a two-week period in May, 1961, and was printed in two parts in the May 11 and May 18 editions of the *Voice*. It was cut for publication here. In the June 1 edition of the *Voice* Lorraine Hansberry published an attack to which I answered on June 8.

"Ten Thousand Words a Minute" was begun the first of October, 1962, and was not finished until November 20, 1962. Altogether, it took seven weeks, but this final version was done in the last three weeks. The first four weeks were lost on a false start. I would like to thank Harold Hayes of *Esquire* for some excellent editorial advice, and Arnold Gingrich for seeing the possibilities in a very long piece about a championship fight which had been a fiasco.

"Truth and Being: Nothing and Time" was written in December, 1960. It was published in *Evergreen Review*, Issue #26, Sept./Oct., 1962.

"The Metaphysics of the Belly" is part of a longer manuscript on Picasso which was worked on in June and early July, 1962, in Provincetown. It was never submitted for publication.

Appendix C—A wandering in prose: For Hemingway

Summer, 1956

Why do you still put on that face
powder which smells like Paris when
I was kicking seconal and used to
get up at four in the morning and
walk the streets into the long wait
for dawn (like an exhausted husband
pacing the room where you wait for
the hospital to inform you of wife
and birth) visions of my death seated
already in the nauseas of my tense
frightened liver—such a poor death,
wet with timidity, ordure and the
muck of a Paris dawn, the city more

beautiful than it had ever been, warm
in June and me at five in an Algerian
bar watching the workers take a
swallow of wine for breakfast, the
city tender in its light even to me
and I sicker than I've ever been,
weak with loathing at all I had not done,
and all I was learning of all I would
now never do, and I would come back
after combing the vistas of the Seine
for glints of light to bank in the
corroded vaults of my ambitious and
yellow jaundiced soul and there back
in bed, nada, you lying in bed in hate
of me, the waves of unspoken flesh
radiating detestation into me because
I have been brave a little but not nearly
brave enough for you, greedy bitch,
Spanish lady, with your murderous
Indian blood and your crazy purity
hung on courage in men as if it were
your queen's own royal balls, and I
would lie down next to you, that smell
of unguent and face powder bleak and
chic as if the life of your skin depended
now not on the life my hands could give
in a pass upon your cheek, but upon the
arts of the corporation mixing your
elixirs in hundred gallon vats by
temperatures calibrated to the thermostat,
bleak and chic like the Hotel Palais
Royale ("my home away from home" we had
seen written by Capote in his cuneiform
script when the guest book was passed
to me for the equivocal cachet of my
signature so dim in its fashion that
year) and I took up the pen thinking
of the buff-colored damp of our indifferent room where we slept in misery

wondering if we had lost the loots of
anticipation we had commanded once so
fierce in one another—or was it only
me? for that is the thought of a lover
when his death comes over him in that
scent of the creams you rubbed on your
face while I slept the half-sleep of
the addict kicking the authority of
his poison—how bitter and clean was
the taste of the seconal. And now in
March of sixty-one the scent of that
cream came over me again as you kissed
me here at this instant, wearing it
again, knowing I detest it because again
it drives the secret of my poor augur
for eternity into those caverns of my
nose which lead back among the stalactites
of the nostril to the dream and one's
nightly dialogue with the fine verdicts
of the city asleep, and all souls on the
prowl talking to one another in the
dark markets of heaven about the future
of what we are to be if one obeys the
shape we gamblers have given to that
tool of destiny—our character. And the
smell of the corporation is still on
your skin mocking what I have done to
mine.